LT Henderso
Henderson, Dee.
Undetected

P9-CLD-591

Seneca Falls Library
47 Cayuga Street
Seneca Falls, NY 13148

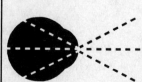

This Large Print Book carries the
Seal of Approval of N.A.V.H.

UNDETECTED

UNDETECTED

DEE HENDERSON

THORNDIKE PRESS
A part of Gale, Cengage Learning

GALE
CENGAGE Learning·

Farmington Hills, Mich • San Francisco • New York • Waterville, Maine
Meriden, Conn • Mason, Ohio • Chicago

Copyright © 2014 by Dee Henderson.
Scripture quotations are taken from the *Holy Bible*, New Living Translation, copyright © 1996, 2004, 2007 by Tyndale House Foundation. Used by permission of Tyndale House Publishers, Inc. Carol Stream, Illinois 60188. All rights reserved.
Thorndike Press, a part of Gale, Cengage Learning.

ALL RIGHTS RESERVED
This is a work of fiction. Names, characters, places, incidents, and dialogues are the product of the author's imagination and are not to be construed as real. Any resemblance to actual events or locales or persons, living or dead, is entirely coincidental.
Thorndike Press® Large Print Christian Fiction.
The text of this Large Print edition is unabridged.
Other aspects of the book may vary from the original edition.
Set in 16 pt. Plantin.

LIBRARY OF CONGRESS CATALOGING-IN-PUBLICATION DATA

Henderson, Dee.
    Undetected / by Dee Henderson. — Large print edition.
        pages ; cm. — (Thorndike Press large print Christian fiction)
    ISBN 978-1-4104-6815-4 (hardcover) — ISBN 1-4104-6815-1 (hardcover)
    1. Women—Research—Fiction. 2. Sonar—Research—Fiction. 3. Military surveillance—Equipment and supplies—Fiction. 4. Command and control systems—Equipment and supplies—Fiction. 5. Sonar—Equipment and supplies—Fiction. 6. Radar—Military applications—Fiction. 7. Large type books. I. Title.
    PS3558.E4829U43 2014b
    813'.54—dc23   2014005885

Published in 2014 by arrangement with Bethany House Publishers, a division of Baker Publishing Group

LT

Seneca Falls Library
47 Cayuga Street
Seneca Falls, N.Y. 13148

Printed in the United States of America
1 2 3 4 5 6 7 18 17 16 15 14

The Son radiates God's own glory and expresses the very character of God, and he sustains everything by the mighty power of his command. When he had cleansed us from our sins, he sat down in the place of honor at the right hand of the majestic God in heaven.

Hebrews 1:3

1

Far below the surface of the Pacific Ocean, the USS *Nevada* glided silently through the waters. The storm 450 feet above the ballistic missile submarine barely disturbed their smooth, quiet ride.

Commander Mark Bishop stood off to the side in the command-and-control center, alert to what was happening but letting his crew do their jobs. The executive officer, his second-in-command, was serving as officer of the deck while the various stations were manned by the third watch. After 79 days at sea, they were at the top of their game, running drills and practice exercises with precision, handling busy nights like this one with a professional focus.

The storm above was hiding a full moon. For the crew of the *Nevada* it didn't matter if the moon or the sun was out — they ran their own 18-hour version of a day aboard the sub with three watches lasting 6 hours

— but they tracked the phase of the moon and the topside weather so they would know conditions should they need to make an emergency ascent and surface.

They were eight days away from the end of this patrol. Handwritten signs counting down the hours were becoming artistic contests between divisions — engineering was holding the top spot in Bishop's opinion — and the chief of the boat reported crew morale was good. Mark had already made the rounds through the four levels of the *Nevada* on the prior watch, and he tended to concur. Problems were remarkably few for this late in a deterrent patrol.

They had four days of relative calm before they would be moving into the busy waters off the western coast of the United States, where they would be dealing with the surge in surface traffic along the shipping lanes. But that didn't mean no one else was out here in the ocean with them. Bishop left the command-and-control center and walked forward to the sonar room.

A submarine crew was blind when underwater; the only way to tell what was around them was to listen. The sonar guys were listening tonight with some of the most sophisticated acoustical devices ever created. A dome full of hydrophones stretched across the front of the submarine, and a towed array — a long cable set with more hydrophones — was now deployed and trailing behind them. Sophisticated software took the data, created a three-dimensional picture of all the noise around the boat, then worked to identify the direction and source of the sounds.

Bishop stepped into the narrow room. His sonar chief, Larry Penn, standing behind his seated men, slipped off his headphones and offered a quiet, "The whales are moving east."

"Got a count?"

"Four, plus two young."

Penn handed the headphones over, and Bishop listened for a minute to the haunting whale song. At least one male in the group, Bishop thought, given the sophistication of the melody. Bishop handed back the headphones. "Have you marked this audio for the marine biologist?"

"I'm having it dubbed," Penn confirmed.

Bishop was sure he had encountered more whales in his years on the job than most marine biologists would in their entire careers. The oceans were more active than most people realized, and whales traveled for thousands of miles just as submariners did.

"Anything more on the faint surface contact?"

"The acoustical signature identifies it as the fishing trawler *Meeker III* out of Perth, Australia."

"He's far from home tonight." The Navy maintained files of acoustical signatures for every military ship and submarine in service around the world, as well as most commercial vessels. Given enough time, they were able to identify nearly every ship they heard above them.

"Got time for a question, Captain?" The sonar technician at the broadband console stack turned to ask.

His rank was that of commander. It would be another two years before he might be promoted to the rank of captain, but Navy tradition designated that the man in command of a boat be addressed as Captain regardless of his rank.

"Give me the question, Sonarman Tulley."

"Do whales drink water?"

He'd been caught by that question two patrols ago. "No. They extract water from the food they digest. They don't drink salt water."

"Good answer, sir," Tulley replied.

Trying to stump the captain was considered a time-honored custom on the *Nevada*.

Those who succeeded were noted on the captain's board for the day and got a good-natured pat on the back from fellow crewmen. Sometimes even from the captain himself.

At the sonar terminals tonight were two experienced operators along with an ensign on his first patrol. The waterfall displays were filled with small blips in all directions. The ocean was noisy tonight, both above them and below. They were crossing over the moonless mountains — a range of seamount formations deep in the ocean — that were staggering in their size and height, but none of them reached the ocean surface. Numerous volcanic vents below them were releasing magma, creating hot, flowing spirals of ocean water that climbed to the surface like chimneys. Fish congregated to feast on the plankton that bloomed in the mineral-rich water.

Nevada's sonar operators were listening for obstacles that the ship could hit — seafloor features not on the navigational maps — as well as surface ships and other submarines. In an emergency ascent to the surface, Bishop would like to reach open waters rather than turn an unlucky fishing vessel into tinder. Other submarines might have hostile intent or might simply run into him by accident. Even a friend was a potential danger to the submerged *Nevada.*

The sonarman monitoring the narrowband console stack leaned forward. "Sir, possible new contact. Bearing 082." He worked to bring the sound into sharper focus. "Surface contact, two screws." The software searched for a match to the sound. "Possibly the transport vessel *Merrybell,* sir."

The sonar chief reported the new contact to the command-and-control center. "Officer of the deck, sonar. New contact. Bearing 082. Surface ship transport vessel *Merrybell.*"

It was a routine night. Bishop felt a sense of contentment. The men were eager to be home, but while on watch they were giving the *Nevada* their A-game. The boat was in good hands. They wouldn't miss whatever could be heard out there. It took an enormous amount of trust in the sonar guys for the rest of the crew to be able to sleep well while underwater. They all knew if the sonar crew made a mistake, a collision risked the safety of the boat and the lives of all aboard.

Bishop had come forward to the sonar room to more than just observe operations. He turned the conversation to his concern for the next few days. "A Russian sub, an Akula II, was hiding at 135 fathoms, 87

12

miles off Washington State, when the *Ala-bama* came home from patrol," he said. "The Akula was using the noise of the shipping channel and the current along the continental shelf to stay hidden. We need to assume he's around, and I doubt he's going to tuck himself into the same spot again. I want a good, solid look at the continental shelf before we approach."

"If he's there, we'll find him, sir," Penn assured him.

"I'm counting on it."

They would be able to hear the Akula before it heard them, all things being equal. But Bishop would like to tip the odds even more in his favor. "Any sign of the *Sea-wolf*?"

"Not yet, sir."

Their job was to hide, and the USS *Ne-vada* crew took it as a point of honor that no one — friend or foe — had ever located them while on a deterrent patrol. But in this situation it would be prudent to seek out some help to ensure they had a clear route home. The USS *Seawolf* would be in the waters to the east where they were heading, guarding the front door to the Naval Submarine Base Bangor. Cross-sonar with the *Seawolf,* and the picture about the possible Russian Akula would get a lot clearer.

"As soon as you get a glimmer of a contact that might be the *Seawolf,* we'll go all-quiet and see if we can't slip in beside him unnoticed before we say hello."

Penn grinned. "I like it, sir."

Commander Mark Bishop headed back to the command-and-control center. If asked what he did for a living, he tended to offer the deliberately low-key reply, "I'm in the Navy," and leave it at that. He was the commander of the ballistic missile submarine USS *Nevada* gold crew. He was one of 28 men entrusted with half the U.S. deployed nuclear arsenal.

His job was to keep this nuclear submarine operationally safe, its crew of 155 trained and focused during their 90-day submerged patrol, and be prepared to launch a missile carrying a nuclear weapon on valid presidential orders. A civilian conversation about his work couldn't go very far when nearly everything he did was classified.

They were off hard-alert, the USS *Maine* had taken over for them, but they could be back to that highest readiness level within three to five hours.

There were always two ballistic missile submarines on hard-alert — in their watch area ready to fire — patrolling in the Pacific,

another two on hard-alert in the Atlantic, with two more in each ocean ready to come to hard-alert within a few hours. The remaining six boomers in the U.S. fleet of 14 were in port undergoing maintenance and resupply, preparing to return to sea. The number of subs made possible a rotation home every 90 days while maintaining a constant strategic deterrent for the nation.

Each ballistic missile submarine was assigned two crews, a gold crew and a blue crew, who would alternate taking the submarine out on patrol. Three days after he arrived back in port, Bishop would hand over the *Nevada* to his counterpart on the blue crew, and the submarine would undergo 25 days of refit — maintenance and resupply — and then the blue crew would take her out to sea to patrol for the next 90 days. Bishop and the gold crew would get the *Nevada* back in four months' time.

His crew considered having to share the *Nevada* with the blue crew to be a painful time-share. The men loved having four months onshore, but they hated to give up *their* boat to others' hands. The grumbling would begin soon after they set foot back on the *Nevada.* If an item could be moved, blue crew left it somewhere gold crew wasn't expecting. The first few days would be spent returning the coffeepot, training materials, onboard movies, wrenches, maintenance logs, *Nevada* photos, and the boat mascot to the proper gold-crew-designated spots. Repairs and maintenance not up to gold-crew standards would get fussed over and typically redone. The rivalry between the two crews over who best handled and cared for the USS *Nevada* was intense. Bishop considered it a healthy attachment to the boat on which they depended for their lives and for their country's safety.

The *Nevada* was 560 feet long, the center third housing 24 Trident II D-5 missiles standing four stories high. Each missile carried eight nuclear warheads. The USS *Nevada* was one of the most lethal weapons ever built and, paradoxically, also one of the safest.

The training never stopped. The drills never stopped. Safety was life, and submariners lived it like no other profession on earth. They knew their boat inside and out and focused intensely on what could go wrong, how to prevent it, and if it couldn't be prevented, how to immediately fix it. There had never been a ballistic-missile submarine lost at sea since this class of submarines began to patrol the oceans over 30 years ago. Bishop considered it a sacred trust to maintain that record.

He was in the second of his three years in command of the USS *Nevada*. After three years, the Navy would congratulate him on a job well done, send him back to shore duty, and in due course promote him to captain. He was in no hurry to get that promotion. This was the sweet spot of his career. The best job in the service was the one he now had. He was taking full enjoyment in every day of this command.

His next job might be to oversee a squadron of six missile subs, or serve at the Pentagon, or teach at the Naval War College. A challenging job would emerge, he knew, but shore duty meant his not being at sea. He was going to miss this job when it came his turn to relinquish command, and that day would inevitably come. But it wouldn't be tonight.

Bishop paused beside the navigation officer and studied their position on the horizontal digital display table. The boat's location and all known contacts were electronically identified and constantly updated. The navigational map for this stretch of the Pacific had been updated just before the patrol began, and this new map had exquisitely detailed topology. The continental shelf and the canyons leading away from it stood in perfect relief. If the Akula was out there, the territory he could be hiding in was vast, and the terrain gave him numerous places to select. There was no need to risk a contact. But where to position the boat for the next few days was the question.

"XO, I have the deck and the conn," he informed his second-in-command.

"The captain has the deck and the conn," Lieutenant Commander Kingman confirmed, passing authority back to Bishop.

"Helm, come to heading 040."

"Come to heading 040, aye, Captain."

Let the *Seawolf* do the hunting. Bishop's job was to stay silent and never be seen. He'd follow the whales for a while. They were heading the direction he wanted to end up, and they were traveling with their young. The enormous mammals would stay well clear of any submarine they heard ahead of them. Trailing miles behind the whales and watching their movements would tell him a lot of useful information. He wished to hide. The whales would help him do so.

The world seemed like a quiet place when submerged on patrol, but Bishop was aware it was more illusion than fact. Strategic Command sent out a daily naval update, highlighting ships that might be in their area, passing on general news about military deployments around the world, often mentioning diplomatic missions and trade tensions and political concerns from all points of the globe. The military sat at the crossroads of so many dynamics going on between nations. Some nations were rising in stature, in wealth and influence, while others were declining, whose leaders strained to stay in power by any means necessary rather than fall.

It had been a quiet patrol, but sometimes the quiet wasn't the whole story. Bishop wondered if North Korea had come close to blowing something up, if Russia was arguing about natural gas shipments to Europe again, if Japan and China had more fishing boat skirmishes along the chain of islands whose ownership they disputed in the East China Sea. The daily briefings were useful, yet they were never quite enough to satisfy his curiosity about the dynamics of what had *almost* happened.

From the military history he had studied and the classified briefings he had for this job, Bishop was more aware than most of how close the world often was to war. A boomer didn't patrol the ocean at hard-alert status because the world had turned peaceful. It remained a deterrent against the fact the world was inherently the opposite — unstable and prone to warfare.

And if he had to pick a subject to lose sleep over at night, he would choose North Korea. When nuclear weapons were considered the reason the nation continued to exist, when warheads were stockpiled in dangerous numbers, North Korea remained an immediate threat to South Korea and a serious threat to Japan. Bishop would prefer rational actors when it came to military matters, and he wasn't convinced the new North Korean leader had a rational view of the world around the isolated country. Bishop knew some of the classified captain's-eyes-only tasking orders were launch package codes for North Korean targets.

The world might be quiet tonight, but he didn't make the assumption it was calm. Following the whales for a while sounded like a smart way to stay undetected.

She needed to get out of Boulder, Colorado. Gina Gray peeled an orange and studied the night sky through the window above the kitchen sink. The conviction had been growing over the course of the last few weeks. She needed to make a major change.

Breaking up with a guy was always difficult, but this hadn't been her choice, and she hadn't seen it coming. It put her in an uncertain mood. And continuing to cross paths with Kevin Taggert at work was too high a price to pay for her peace of mind. It was time to leave.

She'd put off the decision for weeks, for she enjoyed working at NOAA's Marine Geology and Geophysics Division. But her task of mapping the seabed of the world's oceans using satellite data was essentially finished. She'd solved the last technical problem, incorporating the earth's gravity map with the radar data. The algorithms were finished, and now it was just processing time. A set of detailed seabed maps for the Pacific were complete, and they were beautiful in their exquisite detail. They were already in use by the Navy. The rest of the world's five oceans would follow as computer-processing time was available, and her colleague Ashley had that task well in hand.

The maps were a major step forward in knowledge about the oceans. The satellite data significantly improved both accuracy and coverage, so much so that in two years of work she'd managed to render obsolete the accumulated knowledge of decades of previous maps of the ocean floors created by surface ships using side-scan sonar. Her maps were practically works of art. But not many would get to appreciate the full impact of what she'd accomplished. The military was exercising its right to classify the resolution of her maps and would only release a version to the public with a lower level of detail.

She understood the reason the data would be classified. Telling an enemy — or for that matter, even a curious ally — the depths and locations of the underwater trenches and seamount formations along the Pacific Northwest would give them the ability to hide their own submarines more easily, to watch who entered and exited the Strait of Juan de Fuca, headed for the Naval Base Kitsap at Bremerton or the Naval Submarine Base Bangor. Other naval bases around the world would similarly become more vulnerable. Keeping the higher resolution maps classified would give the U.S. an advantage at sea that was worth protecting.

Gina accepted the military decision, even though it complicated matters for her personally. Her résumé wouldn't be able to show the true extent of her work, but those who appreciated what she could do with large data sets would see the notation on the page and know the actual work product was classified. At least this project wasn't being classified at a level where she couldn't even reference the work in her résumé — something that had happened with her sonar work.

But she hadn't taken this project on for the scientific credit it would give her. She'd taken on the seafloor mapping project to keep submariners — Jeff Gray, her brother, chief among them — safer. An accident like the USS *San Francisco,* which had hit an underwater formation, killing a crewman and nearly sinking it, wouldn't happen again. Seamounts everywhere in the world's five oceans would now be clearly marked on the new navigational charts incorporating her seabed data.

Her brother was out on the USS *Seawolf* somewhere in the Pacific tonight and wasn't due back in Bangor for a few weeks. She couldn't use him as an excuse to head to the West Coast, though that was where she most wished she could be — at Jeff's place, tucked in safe with the last member of her family.

Her dream of being married by the time she was 30 looked further away than ever before. Her options were fading. As painful as it was to absorb the breakup with Kevin, she couldn't afford to pull back from dating again if she was going to keep her dream alive. She'd have to shake it off, patch together her self-confidence, and move on. Kevin hadn't meant to cause her so much turmoil. He'd broken things off as gently as he could, done it with kindness by saying it wasn't her; it was simply that it wasn't going to work out for the long term and it would be better to conclude that now and keep their relationship a friendship.

It *was* her. This was the third serious relationship to end in essentially the same way. And she was at a loss for the reasons and what to do about it. She didn't understand what had gone wrong, so she didn't know what to fix. She was adaptable, willing to change, willing to make adjustments. She just needed a guy to like her enough to stick with her while they figured out how to make a relationship work for the long term.

She wanted to get married. She was 29, reasonably pretty, she had a good smile, her weight was under control, she could converse on most subjects with some knowledge, she went to church, she was nice to people, and the fact she wasn't married when she wanted to be just didn't make sense. It was the kind of failure that fit into the bucket of things she simply couldn't understand.

"Just one guy, God. Surely somewhere there is one guy for me," she mentioned quietly as she gathered up the orange peels and dropped them into the trash. She even kept a fairly neat house. She wasn't the best cook in the world, but she was decent enough with a cookbook.

Her speech could lock up on rare occasions, but it had happened only twice in the last two years with Kevin, and it was more an embarrassment for her than a concern. The doctors compared the phenomena she experienced to a stutterer who had difficulty getting the words out. She couldn't believe that was the problem. The speech freeze would clear itself on its own in a minute or two. She mentally pushed away the concern. If she wanted to find reasons for Kevin's decision, she could talk herself in circles. He hadn't given her one.

Jeff would help her out. It's what big brothers did. She could ask him to introduce her to Navy guys he liked. Surely on a base where more than ten thousand people worked, there would be a few eligible, nice, single guys whom Jeff thought might like her. She wouldn't mind being a military wife.

She had worked on sonar projects in the

past — her idea for cross-sonar now kept Jeff materially safer than he had been before. If she married a military man, there would always be ocean work she could do for the Navy, regardless of where they were based. If she got lucky enough to marry a submariner, she already knew she liked the Bangor area, in the northwest part of Washington State. The other home port for submarines stateside was at Kings Bay, Georgia. While she hadn't visited it, Jeff had thought it a nice enough place for the year he had been stationed there.

Gina finished the orange.

She had a couple of new sonar ideas worth exploring. A phone call would put in motion the security clearances necessary to let her pursue them. She could be on the West Coast tomorrow, tucked into a lab at Bangor, have some time to herself to work. She could stay at Jeff's place. It would give her physical distance from Kevin. It would keep her occupied until Jeff got back from his sea patrol.

If she retreated to Chicago, her other option, she ran the risk of giving up on her dream of marriage. She had held on to the family house there as her home base. She loved the science projects she could tap into at the university she had attended for so many years, and she felt at home at the church she had attended since her teens. But the five years working in Chicago were marked by two relationships that had not worked out, and she didn't know who else in her circle of acquaintances there would think to ask her out on a date if they hadn't done so in prior years. With the move to Boulder she'd had two years dating Kevin and a chance for what she dreamed of to come true. She'd just have to try again.

Go west, she decided. Work on her sonar ideas. Ask for Jeff's help. It was at least a plan. Better than staying in Boulder and trying to find polite things to say when those encounters with Kevin brought back the sadness of a dream that was dying.

Have Jeff introduce her to Navy guys he liked, keep an open mind. She would make a concerted effort not to dismiss any guy who showed an interest, regardless of how unlikely she thought he might be from their initial introduction. She wasn't dreaming about a perfect match anymore. A good guy would be fine. Someone willing to commit to building a good marriage. She just had to figure out where he was, put herself in his path, say hello, and hope for the best.

Bishop thanked the petty officer who

brought him more coffee, put his fork through a stack of pancakes, and reviewed the drill plan for the next watch. Fresh eggs, milk, and fruit ran out three weeks into a patrol, and the sub didn't resurface for more supplies unless there was a major equipment failure aboard and provisions could be picked up as an incidental extra. Bishop chose to stick with pancakes and bacon, occasionally cinnamon rolls, rather than adapt to powdered milk and an egg substitute.

He wanted two more fire drills focused on the command-and-control center before this patrol was finished. They were complex drills, and he didn't want to run them too close to reaching the continental shelf or when they were sailing under a shipping channel. He penciled in the drills for 6 and 18 hours out, added a note for the drill coordinator that he wanted to also have the sonar room face an equipment failure during the first of the fire drills.

Back on base they would run the fire drills at the Trident Training Facility with real flames, heat, and suffocating smoke. But at sea they would simply use waving red flags. The alarm would sound, the rush of the fire crew from all locations in the boat would jam ladders, fire suits would be donned, equipment would be hauled in, and tight

28

places to work in would get even tighter as others in the crew raced to get the boat to the surface to vent the invisible smoke.

As the fire took out communications and navigation controls, the crew would find conditions rapidly deteriorating. With actions they needed to take no longer available by turning a knob or setting a switch on a panel, they would have to revert to coordinating manual overrides with crewmen elsewhere in the boat to conduct operations — all while the drill was running against the clock. Men would be sweating and adrenaline would be running high before it was over. In the after-action assessment, Bishop and the drill coordinator would declare the submarine lost or saved based on the speed and sequence of the crew's actions.

The drills were intense for a reason. Bishop worried as much about fire as he did flooding. A fire became very hot, very fast, inside the confined circular construction of a submarine, the heat and smoke forced into a swirling, expanding inferno that would make it impossible to breathe in a matter of minutes. Fire was one of the nightmare scenarios, and when it hit the control room, the switch you needed to save your life could be on the panel that had just lit up in flames. Submarines were basically computer hardware, electrical equipment, audio equipment, power plants, missiles, rocket fuel, batteries — with a few people fit in around them. Unlike a pipe, where age and corrosion could be inspected and repaired, not much that was a fire hazard on a sub was visible before it failed.

The phone on the wall to his left buzzed. Bishop reached over to answer it.

"Captain, sonar. New contact, sound signature USS *Seawolf.*"

"Very well."

He headed up to the command-and-control center. They were four days out from Bangor. The tempo of this day and the next three was destined to get progressively faster, even without the drills.

The officer of the deck gave him a summary of the current situation on the boat, and the chief engineer added details to the nuclear-plant update. Bishop paused by the navigation table to check the chart overview. "The captain has the deck," he announced.

"The captain has the deck," the weapons chief confirmed, passing back authority.

"Sonar, control. Where's the *Seawolf?*"

"Control, sonar. *Seawolf* is bearing 076 degrees, range 41 miles, depth 520 feet."

"Sonar, report all other contacts."

30

"Eight surface ships, all distant. A tanker and four cargo ships to the north, three fishing vessels to the west."

Bishop wanted to pass near the *Seawolf* — under the command of his friend Jeff Gray — coming in on her port side and below her. But he didn't want to sail directly toward her. They would both be trailing towed sonar arrays that water currents would be pushing around, and if the Russian or some other sub was out there, they would need maneuvering room.

"Conn, come to heading 095 degrees, make your depth 825 feet."

"Come to heading 095 degrees, depth 825 feet, aye, Captain," the conn officer confirmed. He then handed the same order on to the helmsman and planesman.

"Passing 280 to the right, sir," the helmsman called out, marking the turn. "Passing 045 . . . steady on course 095, sir."

The planesman called out the increasing depths, "650 feet . . . 750 feet . . . leveling out at 825 feet, sir."

Bishop looked over at his executive officer. "XO, give me all-quiet on the boat. I'd like the *Seawolf* to appreciate just how difficult we are to hear coming."

Kingman smiled his appreciation. "All-quiet, aye, Captain." He reached for the intercom and set it to 1MC to broadcast throughout the boat. "*Nevada,* this is the XO. Rig for all-quiet. We're going to snuggle with the *Seawolf.* Let's remind them who's the better boat."

Discretionary sources of noise like the trash compactor would be shut off, routine maintenance which might cause a pipe to be struck or a tool to be dropped would be postponed, men not needed on station would slip into their bunks to minimize movement, and all casual conversations would cease. The already quiet boat would turn into a silent ghost in the water.

Bishop walked forward to the sonar room.

Sonar Chief Larry Penn said quietly, "Our noise profile is dropping, Captain."

The boat's sonar was powerful enough to pick up the sound of snapping shrimp when they were in Dabob Bay, and in the ocean they used that same power to listen for changes aboard their own boat. It wasn't uncommon for sonar to report a valve problem in the torpedo room moments before Weps called forward to report the same issue. Noise was a diagnostic tool in a sub designed for quiet.

With the *Seawolf* and the *Nevada* coming together on similar tracks, the distance between them closed quickly. When the two vessels had come to within 15 nautical miles, Bishop said quietly, "Let them know we are here."

Penn typed in a command at the right console and turned on cross-sonar.

On the *Seawolf* a sonar technician likely hit his knee on the terminal rack and said a few words he would be glad his mother could not hear. He was, however, quick to report the new contact to his command-and-control center, for the *Seawolf*'s forward speed dropped abruptly.

"Link us," Bishop directed.

Penn entered the command.

Bishop saw the cross-sonar link establish and watched as the radar screen display mapped out parts of the ocean the *Seawolf* had passed through recently, giving them a first look at the waters around the Strait of Juan de Fuca. All looked calm over the last 24 hours.

Cross-sonar was a set of elegantly simple ideas that, when put together, allowed two subs to share sonar data with each other while not being overheard. Their conversation couldn't be distinguished from the ocean noise because it was based on and built into the ocean noise.

"Start the cross-sonar search."

"Start the cross-sonar search, aye, Cap-

33

tain." Penn entered the command.

The sonar dome and the towed sonar array on the *Nevada* paired up with the sonar dome and towed sonar array on the *Seawolf*. The effective range expanded as four hydrophone sets listened in concert to the ocean. Contacts began to appear at distances substantially greater than either sub could hear on its own. Most were surface ships.

"New contact, bearing 276 degrees, looks deep," the spectrum sonarman in the far left seat said, excitement in his voice. He typed fast, running the search to match the sound and pin down the exact name. "Identified as Akula, class II, K-335. It's the *Cheetah,* sir."

"Go get him, Jeff," Bishop murmured to himself.

The *Seawolf* had seen the Akula too. Cross-sonar dropped. The screen showed the *Seawolf*'s abrupt acceleration in speed on a direct vector for an intercept. The *Seawolf* was a fast-attack submarine designed for combat with just such an opposing submarine. The *Cheetah*'s captain was about to have a very bad day.

Bishop breathed easier. The obstacle he'd worried about for the return home was now a known quantity — and the *Seawolf*'s

34

focus. Jeff would be on the Russian sub until he was driven well out to sea.

"Bring up the data replay."

Bishop watched cross-sonar paint in the Akula again. It was out at the edge of the range of what even cross-sonar could find. The Akula had never heard either the *Nevada* or the *Seawolf,* of that Bishop was certain. All the Russian captain would know was that he had a U.S. fast-attack submarine coming into firing position in his baffles. No shots would be exchanged, as both sides during peacetime used these skirmishes as interesting training exercises, but the Russian captain would still be smarting. He would have been slowly and carefully maneuvering for days to work his way into that trench off the continental shelf as a place to hide.

Allies and enemies alike were trying to figure out what the U.S. was doing that had increased the sonar range to such a degree. The assumption would be that new, more sensitive hardware had been deployed. Bishop thought cross-sonar might survive a decade unmatched before someone decoded what they were doing. Cross-sonar was just software and some very elegant reasoning. Espionage was the real threat. Someone on the U.S. side giving away the secret, someone stealing it by hacking into a server or physically making a copy of the algorithms were the more likely ways it would become known by other nations.

Bishop had been stunned when he got his first detailed, classified briefing on how cross-sonar functioned. It gave them a priceless advantage at sea and seemed so obvious once he saw the individual pieces and how they fit together. But it had taken a 20-year-old college student working on a Ph.D. sonar thesis — her brother in the submarine force having sparked her interest — to come up with the ideas and put them together into a powerful and operationally useful combination.

Bishop walked back to the command-and-control center. He'd take full advantage of the tactical advantage cross-sonar gave him, and be very grateful the U.S. had the capability before anyone else. "Conn, bring us to heading 010. Make our depth 400 feet." He would turn the boat north of the shipping channel into water that would have less surface-noise clutter.

As the order was acknowledged and implemented, Bishop picked up the intercom and switched it to 1MC. "*Nevada,* this is the captain. We just nudged an Akula away from the coast, and the *Seawolf* is giving chase.

We're turning toward home. Secure from all-quiet."

Crewmen began discussing the sequence of events of the watch, in good spirits and laughing occasionally. Bishop pulled the notepad from his left shirt pocket, scanned the original plan for this day. Engineering wanted to run a test on the batteries, he'd penciled in a fire drill, and a second watch meeting with his senior chiefs would review the repair and maintenance situation on the boat in preparation for homecoming. A missile drill prompted by a flash EAM — Emergency Action Message — was scheduled during third watch to pull together the entire crew on their primary time-critical mission. A rather routine day had started with an unexpectedly nice opening move, compliments of the Akula.

Bishop put the list back into his pocket. "XO, would you like the deck?"

"Yes, sir."

The executive officer checked with every chief in the control room, conferred with the weapons officer the longest, studied the navigational chart, scanned every status board, then looked to Bishop. "I am ready to relieve you, sir," Kingman stated.

The XO was going to be ready to command a boat as his next duty station if

Bishop had anything to do with it. Hours in control mattered. And toward the end of this watch, the boat was going to get hit with a fire drill, a good experience for his second-in-command.

"I am ready to be relieved," Bishop said.

"I relieve you, sir."

Bishop picked up the intercom. "This is the captain. The XO has the deck."

Bishop stepped back from the captain's chair as the ship log was updated to show the change in command. Rather than leave the command-and-control center, he settled in next to the weapons officer and out of habit checked the pressure status in every missile tube. Bishop would offer quiet counsel, suggestions, watch for trouble, step in if needed — he had his XO's back. He doubted it would be needed. Kingman was learning fast. As his experience in the job grew, the list of events he'd already handled successfully was getting longer.

When the XO's first order of business was to contact sonar, ask for an update, then contact the chief engineer, Bishop relaxed even more and changed his plan. "Officer of the deck, a visual confirmation of the weapons board status seems prudent."

The boat was a lot more than what could be seen from this room. It was also conversations with those who had their hands on the parts that made up the whole. Over-reliance on what was visible from here could leave a captain vulnerable to a stuck gauge or a misreading indicator light.

His XO took the suggestion immediately. "I concur. Petty Officer Hill, please join the commander for a visual inspection of the missile firing system."

Petty Officer Hill, who had managed to avoid one-on-one time with Bishop so far during the patrol, paled as he stood. "Yes, sir."

Bishop only smiled, sympathizing with the young man's obvious nerves but not giving much allowance for them — or for the fact that the petty officer would turn 22 a few days after this patrol ended. This crew was young, but well trained. The pop quiz was going to last until they returned. Once Hill got a few answers right, his confidence would find its footing.

Bishop headed with Hill down one level, his plan to stop first at the missile control center, where two security officers armed with Beretta M9s would be standing guard, then go down another two levels and aft to the missile bay where they could read the gauges monitoring the condition of each of the 24 Trident missiles.

It was practically impossible for a nuclear weapon to misfire. The solid rocket fuel in the launch missile, however, was a combustible type A substance, and it was unforgiving if mishandled or if its environment suddenly changed in temperature or pressure. A three-stage rocket deciding it was time to spin up and fire was the kind of short circuit in the system that would make life very unpleasant for the crew when the missile hatch was closed.

"Petty Officer Hill, why is armed security stationed at the missile control center during a deterrent patrol?"

"Directive 781, sir."

"Do you believe the shoot-to-kill order is necessary?"

"SecNav believes it is necessary. And I believe him."

"What is the firing depth for a Trident II D-5 missile?"

A short pause, then, "I don't know the exact depth, sir. I do know it's a shallow launch."

"What pressure is required in the missile tube before the outer hatch may be safely opened?"

"Equalized pressure to the ocean, sir. The fiberglass inner dome cover would otherwise crack, and water would damage the missile."

"Does seawater ever touch a missile during launch?"

"No, sir."

"Why not?"

"The missile rises to the surface surrounded by the pressured nitrogen gas used to launch the D-5 out of the tube."

"You're learning, Petty Officer Hill. Good answers." Bishop nodded to the security officer and stepped into the missile control center to speak with the weapons duty officer for this watch.

2

Gina stopped along a bluff on Amberjack Avenue and stepped out of the car just as the rising sunlight filtered through the trees to the east. She watched as a submarine being maneuvered by tugboats pulled away from Marginal Wharf out to deeper Hood Canal waters, then watched the sub turn south. The USS *Pennsylvania,* she thought, given the pier from which it had departed. Probably traveling to Dabob Bay for a day of shakedown tests, as it wasn't due to leave on patrol for another six days. Dabob Bay was a 35-minute sub ride from here and a deep enough inlet at 100 fathoms to allow for a sub to dive, for most systems to be tested, and for dummy torpedoes to be fired. Any problems discovered could then be fixed back at the pier before the boat left for the Pacific.

Gina was glad she had come west to wait on her brother's return rather than stay in

Colorado. Naval Submarine Base Bangor had the feel of a national park. It was 11 square miles of forest preserve surrounding an assortment of base buildings, including four piers on the Hood Canal waterway where submarines docked. At the center of the base, on a bluff encircled by more barbed wire with posted warnings that guards were authorized to use deadly force, was the Strategic Weapons Facility — 85 bunkers holding nuclear warheads, launch missiles, and solid rocket fuel. Lightning rods around those bunkers towered 50 feet in the air.

The base had some of the highest security clearances she had ever encountered, but once her credentials had been issued and inspected at every checkpoint, she was free to move around the area. With two-thirds of the base made up of untamed forest, she could take walks along quiet roads surrounded by towering trees. She could head up to Cattail Lake and watch ducks and great blue herons, beavers and river otter, look for great horned owls, and find numerous raccoons. Sightings of coyotes and red foxes were a regular occurrence, and she'd heard that both a bobcat and a cougar had been spotted in the last month, attracted to the area by the various animals that were their prey. Early yesterday morning she'd had to wait for deer to clear the parking lot so she could walk to Jeff's car. The base had so much wildlife that a fish and game warden worked on the property full time.

Gina was growing accustomed to seeing submarines at the piers and often gliding through the water. The USS *Ohio* had reported back to port two days ago. The boat's black hull now gleamed off Delta Pier A, its massive length dwarfed by the sheer size of the triangle docking port that could accommodate four submarines with ease — five in a pinch — and fully dry-dock one needing propulsion repairs. The USS *Jimmy Carter* was departing tomorrow, with the USS *Nevada* due back in this week. Something was always happening. It was a beautiful place to be stationed, peaceful, even though it was a very active military base.

She thought about driving across to the Toandos Peninsula to watch the action in Dabob Bay but talked herself out of it. When Jeff got back he'd likely offer her front-row seats for sub watching if she was interested, take her down to the piers, show her around. Occasionally VIPs were given a ride on a sub through the Admiralty Inlet and Hood Canal, and it had been offered to her in the past. She'd always declined. The

Trident Training Facility was as close to being inside a sub as she cared to be.

It would be claustrophobic to be in such a tight space with so many people. Closing the hatch and going several hundred feet below the water's surface didn't strike her as a smart thing to do. It was safe; it just wasn't smart. Jeff would laugh at her conclusion, though he would not try to change her mind. He'd agreed with her observation that it wasn't smart being hundreds of feet below the surface of the ocean — it was simply an adventure, and he was wired to seek out the best adventure he could find.

Gina did find sonar to be an interesting science. She had spent a decade studying the largest data sets she could find, and sonar data was a unique kind of very large, very complex audio data. A high percentage of the noise a submarine heard with sonar was the ocean itself: rockslides, small earthquakes, underwater volcano eruptions, waves crashing on the shore. Or living things such as snapping shrimp, schools of fish, seals, whales and dolphins vocalizing to one another. Some of those sounds traveled halfway across the ocean. And all those sounds, for purposes of a submarine's mission, were a form of white-noise static that had to be weeded out in order to find useful audio information about another submerged submarine or a vessel on the surface.

Gina had arrived in Bangor with a couple of new sonar ideas that might make it easier to locate another submerged submarine in all that ocean noise. Her ideas might not go anywhere, but it was interesting work just to find out.

Vernon Toombs was the lieutenant commander who ran the Naval Undersea Warfare Center's new acoustical research lab. He had arranged for her to borrow his office from eight p.m. until six a.m. each day and have sole access to audio lab three from eleven p.m. to five a.m. She could spool up any audio file she wished to study. It was a comfortable place to work with SCIF security throughout the building. No electronic monitoring could be done of a conversation or computer data runs from outside the building. The night hours she'd requested were ideal for the large-scale data studies she needed to run, as she could absorb all the computing power to crunch on one specific problem.

Vernon had already told her if she wanted to stay around and work on sonar for the long term, the door was wide open. The office she was borrowing could be her own.

The pay was good, there would be freedom to follow her interests wherever they led, and the lab resources were some of the best in the world. It was a persuasive pitch. She might consider it, depending on how the next few weeks worked out.

There were drawbacks. She had her own security team that now kept tabs on her 24/7. The military assumed the base was an espionage target, and what she knew about cross-sonar put her and highly classified information at risk if it became known she was the original source of its design. Security was there to make sure she didn't have a problem while she was in the Kitsap area, and it would likely be tasked to stay with her for the first few weeks after she left to make sure she hadn't been identified and targeted. As the price for working on the sonar data, she reluctantly accepted the arrangement. She knew should she ever be designated a national security asset, the secure detail wouldn't end when she left Bangor.

Gina watched the sub depart, the morning sun glistening on the wet, black hull, then returned to her car. She pulled back onto the road, the security car behind her. She liked the three guys who had been assigned to her; one was always with her in rotating shifts of 12 hours. They were also there to help her secure the notebooks she used and the server-data rack she pulled at the end of a night's work session. What she did with sonar was not particularly hard to figure out, she thought, but she did understand that the military viewed her as a resource to protect, just as they protected the officers who had detailed knowledge of the strategic weapons deployments.

Kevin had been no more than a fleeting memory since she got here. She was functioning, the sadness was lifting at the margins, and she was looking forward to Jeff's arrival back on land. Life went on.

Breakfast at the Inside Out Café located in the Bangor Plaza was her usual stop after work, but she decided she could tolerate one more oatmeal raisin bar her brother stocked at his condo. It had been a long work night, and she was ready to get some sleep. She would like to get at least the first of the two sonar ideas sorted out before Jeff got back on land, but she didn't know if that arrival was days or weeks away. A fast-attack submarine stayed out to sea while it was operationally useful for it to remain in an area. The USS *Seawolf* was due back sometime this month, and she'd probably learn it was in port the moment Jeff walked in his front door and stumbled over her shoes.

Commander Mark Bishop entered his stateroom two floors below the command-and-control center of the USS *Nevada,* 14 hours after he had last left it. The officer of the deck would wake him if anything needed his attention, on the boat or in the ocean around them. Unfortunately he was one of two people aboard who knew another fire alarm was going to sound in a few hours. It would make his needed sleep a bit on the short side, as 18-hour days aboard a submarine — rather than the usual 24-hour days — made for a patrol that was lived on shorter, more frequent periods of sleep. Every hour he could get at this point in a patrol was welcome.

Mark nudged off his tennis shoes, unzipped and removed his poopie suit, the solid-blue coveralls worn by every submariner at sea. Polyester with only a touch of cotton to keep lint from being an issue for the air filters, the garment zipped in the front and had six pockets — two in front, two slash pockets on the front of each leg, and two back pockets. Sewn above the right pocket was M. BISHOP, with a gold star inside a gold circle above his name signifying he presently had Command at Sea. A seven-point silver oak leaf on each collar showed his rank of commander.

Onshore, the working uniform had changed yet again to the Navy's version of camouflage — a blue and gray aquaflage that he personally thought was uncomfortably warm but otherwise serviceable. For official events, correct attire, thankfully, was still either the white or blue dress uniform, depending on the season.

He had something tucked in most of the pockets, so he fished items out to drop on his desk before putting the blue coveralls in the laundry bag. The crew did their own laundry, sharing one washer and dryer, but it was considered bad luck for the commander to wash his. One of the cooks had volunteered, and Bishop had given in gracefully rather than upset tradition, though he was glad he had packed six of the suits for this patrol rather than the normal five. That way he would have one fresh in reserve should they get a visit from a rear admiral or other dignitary at disembarking. They were not supposed to shrink in the laundry, but either he was putting on more weight than normal during the patrol or they were getting overheated in the dryer.

Bishop stretched out on his bunk with a

sigh, his body finally acknowledging the aches that had settled into his bones over the last 86 days.

The rotation of three watches gave the patrol a constant set of fresh eyes and minds monitoring operations. A third of the crew was asleep at any point in time. As the commander, he fit in sleep when he could while maintaining a rotating presence across all three watches.

The enlisted men bunked nine to a room, their berths nestled between massive missile tubes in the center third of the boat. The 15 officers aboard shared 5 staterooms. As commander he had a stateroom of his own, including a desk and chair, and a bed tucked into a narrow room slightly bigger than a closet. Small, and yet it was precious privacy, something every man aboard craved after the first week.

Eye level above his bunk, Mark had taped four photos, and he studied them for a moment before he closed his eyes. They were there to tug him back to the outside world and life outside this boomer for a few moments at the beginning and end of his day. They were carefully chosen, selected specifically for this patrol.

His wife, Melinda, icing a cake she'd made for her mom's birthday — one of his favorite photos of her snapped during their nine years of marriage, and one of the last photos taken in the month before she died. His parents and two sisters, along with assorted nieces and nephews. His brother Bryce, with his new wife, Charlotte, both looking very content, seated together in the stands at Wrigley Field enjoying a baseball game. An older photo of his astronaut brother Jim, decked out in full space-suit gear as he headed across the walkway for a rocket ride on one of the last space-shuttle flights.

When the day finally came for him to relinquish command, Mark was going to need his family to fall back on. He had spent his career working to qualify for the job he now held. Once these three years were over, he was going to have to come up with a new dream, a new goal in life. What it would be was still taking form. Late at night, he had begun to think about his future.

He would be turning 41 this year. He could retire from the Navy when he'd put in his 20 years, pursue a civilian career. Or he could see about staying in until mandatory retirement at age 62. He thought a promotion to captain was likely, given his service record. Beyond that, a promotion to rear admiral and appointment as a flag officer would be a challenge, given the stiff competition and limited openings.

He would stay in the Navy if given his preference and keep his work life in order. It was his personal life that needed attention. He missed his wife, missed being a husband. He wanted someone to come home to after sea patrols. He wanted someone there to share those shore duties with him. Melinda would have encouraged him years ago to move on, but he hadn't been ready. It had felt disloyal to think about replacing her. And the idea of dating again, starting over with someone else, made him sigh just thinking about it.

But, he told himself with hands locked behind his head as he gazed at his photos, it was time. The reluctance was still there, but he'd force himself to do what needed to be done when he got back to land. He wasn't going to have a different future unless he revived his social life and got out there again, started seeing someone, started putting serious time into developing a relationship with a woman.

The question of who always bubbled up right behind any decision to finally take the step. Maybe Linda Masters. He liked her, had known her and her family for years. She taught history at the local high school and had the ability to spark interest in a subject most students found boring. In her late 30s, she had an interest in Western art and Old West artifacts, and time spent at an auction with her was an entertaining afternoon. They were comfortable friends, and it could possibly be something more if he wanted to pursue the idea. He'd start with dinner and a movie. If the first date went well, he could invite Linda to the gold crew's backyard barbecue he always hosted after they had been back in port a couple of weeks. It would give him a chance to see what his broader group of friends thought of her.

Meeting Melinda for the first time had been a bit like getting hit with a two-by-four. He'd thought *wow* and spent the next year convincing her she should think the same about him. Linda fit into the more thoughtful category, a woman friend who might become more. He was realistic about the idea of being married again. He'd already had a very good marriage. He would be fortunate to find that again. It wasn't likely a second marriage would have that same intensity of passion that he'd had in his youth. But it could be a good one just the same, if he could find someone equally committed to building a good, strong marriage.

Mark hadn't yet met his brother's wife, Charlotte. The schedule hadn't permitted a flight back to Chicago, but he planned to take a leave and go see them during the next few months ashore. The photo above him and their marriage was what had gotten him thinking again about the possibility for himself. Bryce sounded happy. Mark was relieved and grateful to hear it — he'd have Charlotte to thank for that when he met her, he was sure.

He reached for his *When in Port* list and added a few more items: find a welcome-to-the-family gift for Charlotte, go fishing with Jeff, take Linda to dinner and a movie, find a good home for Melinda's dollhouse collection — maybe Melinda's mom had changed her mind? He tucked the list back under the rubber band.

Odd, of all the things he had around the house that were Melinda's, it was the dollhouse he had held on to the longest. Its Southern-belle-mansion style was filled with nearly 40 rooms of tiny furniture, wallpaper, little pictures, rugs, lamps. He used to buy Melinda something for it as a gift to mark the beginning and end of patrols. She had loved that miniature house. Looking at it was a way to remember a shared history and good memories. But it wouldn't do to have it displayed in the living room the first time he invited a woman in for coffee and a conversation.

I wish life was simpler, Jesus, than it is. The thought crossed his mind as a prayer, and it instantly summed up what he was feeling. Life was growing more complex, not less. The day Melinda had been killed in a car accident had been by far the worst day of his life. Now he was lying here planning the future, but truthfully he had no idea what the future held. God did. There was comfort in the simple fact that nothing occurring in his life would be a surprise to God.

His belief in and passion for God was one of the things he and Melinda had shared. He found stability and purpose in the fact God loved him. Key to whom he chose as a wife would be someone who shared his faith. *Someone with a nice smile, Jesus,* he added to his prayer. He'd just spent 86 days surrounded by guys — a few women were deploying on boomers now, but none had been assigned to gold crew for this particular patrol — and he missed seeing a woman's smile. He wanted a future with a wife who had a nice smile, and a personality that had her smiling often.

A few handwritten verses were tucked beside the photos. Mark carefully slid a three-by-five card from the band holding it in place, his printing still clear despite the multiple times he'd handled it.

The Son radiates God's own glory and expresses the very character of God, and he sustains everything by the mighty power of his command. When he had cleansed us from our sins, he sat down in the place of honor at the right hand of the majestic God in heaven.

There were few things in Scripture that touched him more deeply than this verse from the first chapter of Hebrews. He'd copied it over so he could memorize the words describing the person of Jesus, His character, His conduct, and His purpose. He'd started public ministry when he was 30, was crucified at age 33, resurrected three days later, and now He sat at the right hand of God in heaven. Every time Mark read the passage, he came back to the same conclusion. Jesus had hit the sweet spot of a life well lived.

I wish that for myself, God. Mark returned the card to its place. He wanted to have a good next chapter in his life — something that had purpose and value. He closed his eyes on the thought, wondering if what was coming was going to include a new wife, and let himself slide into sleep.

■ ■ ■ ■

Bishop settled into the captain's chair in the *Nevada*'s command-and-control center. The surface above was busy with activity: cargo ships, fishing vessels, even the faint hull noise of sailboats. Both sonar and navigation had their hands full keeping track of everybody. Bishop studied the men around the room. Three months' worth of conversations and curiosity on his part had filled in large sections of their professional history, personal interests, and situations onshore. They were his crew, his second family, and he knew them well.

He smiled. It was time to get them home. "Navigation, distance to the Strait of Juan de Fuca."

"Five miles, sir, to the outer buoy."

"Very well." The waiting of the last few days was finally over. Bishop reached for the intercom. "Sonar, control. Report all near contacts."

"Control, sonar. Surface ships, fore and after, the closest 520 feet to our starboard."

Bishop looked to his right. "XO, bring us to periscope depth."

The XO confirmed the command, then set it in motion. "Helm, set our depth to 85 feet." The boat began to rise.

"Leveling at 85 feet, sir," the planesman confirmed.

"Raise the periscope," Bishop ordered.

The navigation officer raised it, and the XO moved to the periscope and began a circle turn, searching the waters above and around the boomer. "All clear above and ahead, Captain."

Bishop went and looked for himself to confirm the finding. "Surface the boat."

"Surface the boat, aye, Captain," his XO replied. "Dive Officer, surface the *Nevada.*"

The dive officer flipped switches on the ballast control board, forcing air into, and water out of, the compartments surrounding the hull, making the submarine more buoyant and taking it to the surface.

The USS *Nevada* broke the surface with a burst of cascading water. Their normally smooth ride began to feel choppy as the boat responded to waves for the first time, its controlling planes on the sail now out of the water, the boat rocking side to side ever so slightly as it moved forward.

"Petty Officer Hill, please pass me that red case," Bishop said.

The XO picked up the intercom and flipped the switch to 1MC. "Crew of the *Nevada,* this is the XO. The captain is breaking out his sunglasses."

A cheer echoed throughout the boat.

"Open the boat."

The first lookout headed up the ladder, opening hatches as he went. A rush of air smelling of salt water, pine, and fish swirled inside. After 90 days of filtered air, it was a strong smell, almost tasty it was so sharp.

A communications specialist headed up the ladder, carrying equipment to activate comm lines from the bridge and lookouts above to the command-and-control room below. Behind him, two seamen carried segments of a curved, stiff Plexiglas windshield to outfit the bridge for some protection from the spray kicking up over the bow.

"XO, the captain is transferring to the bridge." Bishop headed up the ladder after the second lookout man.

The first bright rays of sun to strike his face, the first breeze of ocean air — Bishop cleared the last rung of the ladder and gave himself half a minute to simply stand and appreciate it. The day was nearly perfect. For once they weren't under a blanket of rain and light fog, which so often accompanied early mornings along the western coastal waters. Within the near distance, sailboats were skimming in among commercial vessels, and beyond them two ferries transported people and cars. Looking down from the height of the bridge sail, the USS *Nevada* stretched nearly two football fields before and behind him, the wet, black, curved hull gleaming in the sunlight. He spent 90 days of a patrol in small rooms packed with people, and it was easy to forget just how massive the submarine was until he saw it once again from this perspective. Bishop moved behind the protection provided by the Plexiglas and picked up the phone after it had synced into the system. "Control, bridge. Steady at two-third speed."

"Bridge, control. Steady at two-third speed, aye, Captain."

Bishop watched their arrival committee maneuver to match their speed and join up with them. The Coast Guard cutter *Vincent* settled in off the bow, the *Sparks* falling in behind. The two vessels were part of the Maritime Force Protection Unit that served the submarine fleet during surface transit. The *Nevada* had reported their arrival into the area an hour before to give the Coast Guard a bit of warning. It wasn't often a boomer surfaced. Civilians would inevitably approach, hoping for a better look, and would need to be directed away.

Traversing the 155 miles from the Pacific

through the Strait of Juan de Fuca, the Admiralty Inlet, Puget Sound, and then into Hood Canal was a graduate course in navigation and communication. The floating section of the Hood Canal Bridge would be moved aside for them to pass through. They were scheduled to dock at Naval Submarine Base Bangor, Delta Pier B, just after sunset. The next 16 hours were going to be intensely focused activity but also routine. They were now essentially pulling into their own driveway.

The varying depths in the channel during the transit made traveling on the surface the wise course of action. But Bishop never liked the visibility it gave to others. He glanced over at the security officer now standing at the back of the sail, binoculars scanning ships in the area. These were the most dangerous 16 hours of the voyage, since they were fully configured with missiles and their location was now known to anyone watching. Sinking a submarine from land or surface wasn't nearly as easy as hitting it with a torpedo into its belly. But the lookouts would be scanning for anything that might be hostile, and the Coast Guard cutters were specifically watching for any vessel that might try to ram the submarine. Given the history of the few collisions between a sub and a ship in the past decades, the *Nevada* would take a collision with a shudder and a few dents in the hull, while the other vessel would be turned into shredded salvage scrap. The bulk of the *Nevada* was underwater even when they traveled on the surface.

Bishop picked up the phone again. "Control, bridge. XO, would you like the deck?" he asked.

"Yes, sir."

Kingman jumped at the opportunity, and Bishop smiled, having expected that. "I stand ready to be relieved."

Moments later the phone rang back. "Bridge, control. The XO is transferring to the bridge. The weapons officer now has the control-center watch."

"Very well."

The XO climbed the ladder and joined Bishop in the sail. Kingman checked in with both lookouts, placed a call to the chief engineer, spoke with navigation, then turned to Bishop. "I am ready to relieve you, sir."

"I am ready to be relieved."

"I relieve you, sir." Protocol completed, Kingman picked up the phone. "Control, bridge. Officer of the deck has passed to the XO. Come to heading 050."

Bishop watched the buoy markers and the

subtle signs of the water current. He had long ago memorized depths and buoy markers throughout this transit. The channel was wide for the first 60 miles, but then narrowed considerably so that every movement became tight point-to-point piloting. He'd keep an eye on things, and keep Kingman from getting himself in trouble.

It took time to turn a submarine. Unlike a vehicle, where a turn of the steering wheel to the right turned the car instantly, a submarine turning to the right might travel another 600 feet forward as it made that turn. When the channel was only 70 feet wide in places, turns had to be begun early and smartly. Running over a buoy marking the channel edge was considered more than bad form. It could risk beaching a two-billion-dollar submarine on a shallow stretch of bottom silt and rock, and cost a commander his job.

"Navigation, bridge. Time to the next turn?" Kingman asked.

"Bridge, navigation. Seven minutes, twenty seconds."

Hours later the USS *Nevada* passed through the now-open Hood Canal Bridge, people scrambling out of their cars to watch the massive submarine slip through the opening. Bluffs on either side of the waterway held dense forests coming down to the water, along with a sprinkling of expensive homes glimpsed through the trees overlooking Puget Sound.

The *Nevada* made the final turn toward home. No matter how many times Bishop made this journey, the impact was still the same — pride in the crew, appreciation of the beauty around him, and a deep sense of relief that another patrol had ended without incident. Their home port appeared ahead on the east shore of Hood Canal.

"Engineering, bridge. All stop," the XO ordered.

The sub's forward speed began to slow, and only momentum now carried the boat forward. They came to a peaceful pause, just north of the fourth pier. Two tugboats joined up and nudged the boat in concert toward Delta Pier B. Crewmen turned cleats on the boat's smooth hull upward to allow mooring ropes to be secured. The *Nevada* snuggled into its berth.

"Good job, XO," Bishop said.

Kingman grinned. "Thank you, sir." Sweat had turned the edges of his hair wet, and his face showed exhaustion to go along with the pleasure. The man had completed an extended workout getting the *Nevada* in

without a scratch on her hull. It was Kingman's first time navigating the entire 155-
mile transit — 16 hours in command, figuring out what to do when. Bishop had
provided occasional summaries of what
came next, just as a good caddy would
provide a pro golfer, but Bishop had never
needed to step in with stronger advice or
direction. Bishop remembered well his first
time piloting unassisted through the transit.
It was a sweet relief and well-earned success.

People were waiting for them on the pier
— contractors and Navy personnel who ran
the maintenance and supply operations for
Bangor — several of the faces familiar, as
many had worked on the base 20 years or
more. Security concerns now prevented
civilians from being on the pier, so families
would be waiting for the crew at the Squadron 17 ready room. Bishop watched as
marines from the Weapons Storage Facility
took up their station, each of them fully
armed. They would remain in place around
the clock while missiles were aboard.

The walkway swung over from the pier to
Nevada's exposed surface deck. Bishop
pushed up his sunglasses and headed from
the sail down the ladder into the command-
and-control center. Men were securing the

boat, shutting down equipment, and preparing to connect for power to the shore.

Bishop picked up the intercom and set it to 1MC. "This is the captain. Welcome home, crew of the USS *Nevada*. A good patrol, and a solid chance at the battle E this year. You did the *Nevada* proud. Families are gathering at the Squadron 17 ready room. Enlisted not assigned duty stations for the overnight watch are dismissed after the boat is secured. Report back to the boat at 0900 for hand-over preparation. All officers report in to the commander. Captain out."

A good patrol, and he felt the relief of having gotten his men safely home to their families. But as he secured the mic in its place, he knew he would not have anybody waiting for him in the ready room. It was time to change that.

3

After 90 days without sunlight, Commander Mark Bishop preferred running errands at night for his first few days back onshore. Even with dark sunglasses, the sun's rays seemed overly bright. Life onshore — traffic, dogs barking, advertising everywhere he looked, crowds passing by — seemed loud and chaotic. At night, at least this assault of sights and sounds was tempered. He was a man in good shape, but being in command of a deterrent patrol left him physically beat, tired to the bone. When he stepped onshore the toll made itself felt. For the next couple of weeks he planned on 12 hours of sleep a night to get himself feeling less like an old man, good food, and as much time *not* being in charge of anything as he could arrange.

The *Nevada* was still claiming most of his time, yet that was soon coming to a conclusion. Hand-over of the boat to the blue-crew commander was just 10 hours away, at which time this patrol would officially be over. What he wanted tonight was ice cream, and at two a.m. on Bangor base — with his home and a 24/7 supermarket nearly a half hour away — the choices were between what the Squadron 17 ready room had left in the freezer or what the newly opened 7-Eleven across from Bangor Plaza had available.

So, ice cream from the convenience store, then back to the USS *Nevada* for another three hours of paper work, clear his personal belongings from the captain's stateroom, and prepare for final walk-through. A skeleton crew was aboard tonight, monitoring the reactor shutdown and off-loading sonar recordings. The full contingent of gold crew would be back at the sub at 0800 for the final crew call and hand-over to the blue crew, with the ceremonial awarding of dolphins appropriately scheduled for the Bangor Plaza Conference Center's *Nevada* ballroom at noon.

He would have the privilege of pinning 14 of his crew this afternoon. Getting approved to wear the dolphins — proof you were qualified to call yourself a submariner — required demonstrating the knowledge and function of 70 distinct systems on board, from navigation to missile control. The 70 signatures collected on your qual card came from senior crewmen evaluating your competency. Then you had to survive two verbal exams by the chief of the boat and the captain. Getting pinned with dolphins was a key milestone during the first two years of a submariner's life. Those being awarded today had earned it.

Once dismissed from the ceremony, the gold crew's 30 days of R and R would start in earnest. A month from now, training and class assignments would post, and for the two months after that, men would be busy with two-day to three-week refresher courses at the Trident Training Facility or at the Submarine School, Groton, Connecticut. Half was cross-training for other jobs aboard the sub; the rest focused on the equipment the crewman was responsible for repairing, maintaining, and operating on the boat. The final month before blue crew returned with the *Nevada,* gold crew would begin preparations for their next patrol. It was four months of life onshore with a cadence that worked. When it ended, most of the crew would be looking forward to going back to sea. Mark would be one of them.

He planned to spend part of his month of R and R rehabbing the deck behind his house, then expected to spend two months attending classes and working on special projects for the Submarine Group 9 commander. It would be a very pleasant summer. He hoped to fit in as many fishing trips as he could arrange. He'd never bought a boat, figuring enough friends owned one that buying gas and helping swab the decks would get him a fishing partner or a set of keys when he wanted to go out. Catch some fish, get some sun, enjoy the water from above rather than below, see how a first date with Linda went — he had his core plan for his summer in mind.

He pulled into the parking lot of the 7-Eleven on Ohio Street. Ice cream. Then finish preparations for the hand-over of the *Nevada.* When this day ended he'd be on R and R. It already had the feel of being a very good day.

Mark noticed the security before he noticed her. A security officer was at the door of the 7-Eleven, standing by the spin rack of potato-chip selections, unobtrusively checking out those who came and went. Mark recognized him, was acknowledged in return with a brief nod, and with that recognition Mark came to sharp alert. He scanned the store, expecting to see the rear admiral who

71

ran Bangor getting himself a sandwich, but saw no one in uniform among the four individuals in the store. Mark headed toward the back of the store, paused to see what bakery goods were left, considered a day-old donut, then talked himself out of it.

She was standing at the glass doors of the freezer display, studying ice-cream choices. She finally reached in and selected a pint, the dark ribbing around the side of the container one he recognized as dark chocolate with brownie chunks. She wore an oversized Navy jacket in blue and gold, faded jeans, beat-up tennis shoes, her long brown hair pulled back in a ponytail.

He glanced over a second time as she turned toward the checkout counter. "Gina?"

She stopped and looked back at him.

Gina Gray. It had been two years since he last saw her. She was working in Colorado, her brother Jeff was still at sea. There was no reason for her to be on the West Coast, and yet here she was, at Bangor, wearing one of Jeff's jackets. She smiled when she recognized him.

He had his reason for the security.

He stepped in her direction. She looked good. Thinner than he remembered, but otherwise she hadn't changed. She looked

72

as young as some of his crew, and just about disappeared in the jacket — like a high school cheerleader wearing a football player's letter jacket. She was . . . what? — he tried to remember — a decade or so younger than her brother? So 26 now? Or 28? He'd known her for four years before he realized there was a Navy department that existed because of her ideas. She'd created cross-sonar.

"What brings you to Bangor?" he asked.

She started to answer him, and her words froze. Her eyes closed as she fought the embarrassment of it.

He relaxed, waited. He knew about her occasional difficulty with words. It was a kind of stage fright that people experienced before a speech with a large audience or when performing in front of a crowd. But for her it came and went in an unpredictable fashion. Much like a stutterer had moments when the words wouldn't come, Gina had moments when her speech didn't cooperate. Mark had his ideas for why it happened so often with him over the years, but he'd kept those thoughts to himself. She got embarrassed enough as it was.

A minute passed. The words weren't returning.

He chose a pint of cherry chocolate chip

ice cream for himself, picked up two plastic spoons from the basket beside the hot-dog relish, reached over and took her ice cream pint. He gently tugged her hand. "Come with me, Gina."

He paid for her purchase and his. He gave a nod to the security man as he directed her outside.

Jeff had introduced them at a backyard barbecue seven years ago. A good man and protective of his sister. *"Gina, the genius,"* Jeff liked to whisper with affection, his arms draped across her shoulders. He'd give her cover from the crowd when her words wouldn't come and shyness overwhelmed her. She was interesting, Mark thought, for her unusual life and abilities. She had never met his late wife, but he knew Melinda would have liked her.

With a nearly full moon and a gentle southwesterly wind, enjoyable Bangor views of the night sky welcomed them outdoors, and he nodded north so they could walk a bit and be away from those who might overhear a conversation. Security fell in a ways behind them.

He opened his ice cream; she opened hers.

"It's good to see you, Mark," she finally said softly.

"The same." He took a bite of ice cream,

glanced her way. "I saw Jeff in passing four days ago, off the coast. He was having a good time. I left him chasing an Akula."

She smiled. "He'll enjoy that."

"Your cross-sonar works like a charm. Fast-attacks use it all the time to sync up when they're protecting a battle group. But it's been handy even for us boomers, especially when we're at our most vulnerable, coming into home port."

"I'm glad to hear it."

"What brings you out to Bangor?" he asked again.

"I had some sonar ideas I wanted to explore, and I needed to get away from Boulder for a while."

"Something happen?"

She shrugged. "A guy I met there . . . well, we broke up. It's been hard seeing Kevin at work every day. And the satellite mapping work I've been doing of the oceans' seabed is done but for the processing time."

"I've seen a couple of the new navigation maps. Those yours?"

She nodded.

"The detail is superb."

"Thanks."

"I'm sorry to hear about Kevin. Jeff's mentioned him a few times."

Mark knew Gina had been dating Kevin

Taggert for the last two years. Her brother thought he was okay, but Mark could hear in the way Jeff talked about it that he was kind of cool on the guy. Kevin was a government academic who also worked at NOAA, maybe a good fit for her on paper, but not so much in reality. The fact the relationship had broken apart wouldn't surprise Jeff.

"Kevin was kind about it, but I didn't see it coming. Not sure why I didn't." She shook her head. "You had a good patrol?" she asked.

"All-quiet," he said. "The best kind."

"Got a chance for the battle E this year?"

He smiled. "Working on it. *Nebraska* is going to be stiff competition." He wanted to win Best Boat of the Year, and his crew was giving him their all to make it happen. They were a competitive bunch of guys.

He liked Gina. Always had. She was younger than his sisters. She had started college at 14, taken an interest in sonar because her brother was pursuing a career as a submariner. The Navy had gotten a fortunate break there. She could have turned her interest to medicine or biochemistry. Cross-sonar was so classified, the Navy department that deployed what she'd developed had been given the name Sonar Maintenance and Acoustical Hardware Longevity Program. The name alone suggested it was too boring a department to be curious about, which was effective at keeping interest low as to what was being done.

"Gina, the genius," Jeff would say with affection, while privately Mark knew he worried about what his sister was going to do to keep from being bored. It was one thing to be a gifted child, another to be a gifted adult. She was ahead of where knowledge was at in her own fields of study, and finding something to keep her absorbed required breaking new terrain. Jeff was concerned about the pressure she felt from expectations on her to produce new science. She had the skills to go where she would like and work on what was appealing. Finding a job would never be an issue. But that led to a nomadic life. The crosscurrents of boredom, others' expectations, and whether she could settle down someplace long term all added to her brother's concerns for her future.

Jeff had hoped Boulder would be a good place where she'd be able to stay for more than a few years. Jeff's big-brother worries were shared by Mark too, now that he realized she was again in transition. He remembered similar worries with his own sisters before they'd married and settled down, starting families of their own.

Gina had come to Bangor to see her brother. Mark got that priority without her having to say it. The fact she was here weeks before Jeff was due back in port told Mark more than she had said about Boulder and how badly the breakup had hit her. Gina was keeping herself busy while she waited by working on her sonar ideas. Probably true enough.

"Some sonar ideas, is it? Care to talk about what you're working on?"

She gave him a long look, as if considering whether she wanted to answer him. "What if you could actively ping," she finally said, "and the other guy couldn't hear you?"

He stopped, stunned. "That's possible?"

"It's one idea I'm here to explore."

It felt like a punch. She was a national-security nightmare.

One advantage the U.S. had over every other submarine force in the world was its ability to be quieter than the other guys, to hear them coming by passively listening. The only way another country's submarines could find a U.S. sub was by a mistake on the part of the U.S. crew, or by an active ping — sending out a sound through the water and listening for the returning echo. But the fact they generated the sound gave away their own position. It was a basic tenet of submarine warfare that to ping was to get yourself a torpedo in reply. But if it was possible *to ping without being heard* — it turned on its head basic submarine warfare tactics.

Mark started walking again. He wanted to wince, but his job had trained him to accept the unthinkable and deal with it — fast, logically, and with a steady, cool calm. The implications of her idea were reverberating through his mind. This was more than just dangerous territory; it was destabilizing.

If an enemy nation — or, for that matter, their allies — would ever find out what was in this woman's head, billions of dollars of military hardware would be at risk, and decades of underwater dominance would disappear. The oceans would become a level playing field, even if the numbers were still vastly superior on the U.S. side. No wonder security was hovering over her.

He looked over at her. "Who have you told?"

She offered a slight smile. "You." She ate another bite of her ice cream. "I asked Lieutenant Commander Toombs if I could use the lab here to run down my ideas, since moving around terabytes of classified data is a bureaucratic nightmare. He arranged for me to use his office at night and opened up an audio lab for me so I could work without interruption. I'm running the idea against the data from the USS *Ohio* encounter with the British sub *Triumph*. The *Ohio* was cross-linking sonar with the USS *Michigan* when it happened. It's a big data set. So I snuck out for ice cream while it runs."

Gina had moved on from working for the Navy six or seven years ago, and this was the idea she had nudging around in the back of her mind? Mark couldn't help wondering about the ideas she hadn't taken the time to explore.

"The concept isn't without its limitations," she added. "It requires cross-sonar to be running. The active ping is faint, which theoretically means it will work better with one sub above and one below a thermal line. The amount of cross-sonar conversation necessary is exponentially higher than a cross-sonar search, a fact that risks someone being able to gather enough data to crack the algorithm behind cross-sonar itself.

"And operationally it will only be helpful at the margins. The odds that two U.S. subs, with towed arrays deployed, running cross-sonar, miss hearing an enemy sub are very small. Their noise profile is too high. But an active ping should give you added range so you can pick them up at a farther distance than what cross-sonar on its own can give you."

Bishop appreciated the limitations, but he already saw one key use. "An active ping would solve the problem of a sub lying in wait, with its engines and propulsion powered down, drifting and waiting for someone to come across his path. Right now we have to trust luck — someone on board drops a wrench, or closes a hatch too loudly, or the natural drift requires them to engage the drive shaft every few hours to keep from settling too deep. But the new electric-diesel combination subs can rest on the ocean bottom on the continental shelf, down around 400 to 500 feet, and are difficult to locate until they lift off the ocean floor. An active ping that couldn't be traced to its originating location would be a significant help in finding them."

She nodded and slid the lid back onto her ice cream. "There isn't enough data in this British sub encounter to give me more than a probability that this works. It looks promising, but I don't know if it's more than that."

"What do you need?"

"A couple more weeks and I'm going to

be at the end of what I can do with the existing data. I need a sea trial to test the idea. And that's going to be a problem. It can't be run at Dabob Bay. It's going to take ocean time. I need two fast-attacks and a boomer, although I might be able to give an answer with three fast-attacks. I need the right mix of sea conditions, with a choreographed set of maneuvers to create the permutations in data I need to see. There will be a massive amount of data to record. And if I'm wrong, that sea trial risks giving away cross-sonar to anyone within listening range."

"You lay out the probability it works, you'll get your sea trial to gather data," he predicted.

"I hope so." She started to say something, stopped, appeared to change her mind, and simply said, "I don't expect this idea to hold up, Mark. But it's probably going to take that sea trial to put my finger on where it falls apart. I think it may prove fragile, only working a portion of the time based on the sea conditions. It seems extra sensitive to white noise, which is what I'm trying to test for now with the existing data. Nothing would be worse than running a test that tells you all is clear, only to find it didn't see an enemy sub sitting nearby."

"All of a submariner's life is probabilities, Gina. If this could find a quiet sub that other techniques miss — even if it could do it in only one out of five times it was tried — it would still save lives. Whether the risk to cross-sonar being reverse-engineered is worth it depends on the variations where this proves helpful and the time it takes to execute the ping."

She nodded. "Anyway, that's what I'm working on."

"I appreciate you telling me, trusting me." They had started walking again, and he closed up his own ice cream. "Earlier, you said ideas, plural. What else are you exploring?"

"I'd rather not say until I know if it is even feasible. I'm still looking for a data set that will let me explore the idea. It's . . . well, it's kind of out there, even for me," she admitted.

"This idea was kind of out there too," he remarked. "Let me know if you need some help finding that second data set. I'll see if I can get you what you need."

"Thanks." She glanced at the time. "I need to get back to the lab. My data run should be finishing up."

"I'll stay in touch, Gina, see if I can find out for you when Jeff is due back in port."

"I'd appreciate it."

"Can I tell anyone what you told me tonight?"

She bit her bottom lip, then nodded. "Use your discretion."

"One person, I'm thinking. Rear Admiral Hardman."

"I'll trust your decision on it."

Mark saw her safely back to the 7-Eleven parking lot. Security would drive her back. He held the passenger side door for her, said a quiet good night.

If he had wondered what else he was going to be doing during his R and R, a chunk of it had just filled in. He'd keep an eye on Gina until her brother got back to port and discreetly alert the Navy to what was coming.

Operational security meant closing down knowledge of this to a very few people who absolutely had to know. She'd elected to tell him. She, without a doubt, was going to tell her brother. They needed someone with rank involved, which led him to Rear Admiral Hardman. Keep it at that, hopefully, and keep her buffered from people bothering her. She didn't yet need help for the work — she needed time, data, and the freedom to work uninterrupted.

He had a headache. *An active ping that*

could not be heard. What he hadn't told her was the fact she had raised the risk to her brother's life by over half, depending on if this worked, and if and when other countries acquired the capability. Espionage inevitably acquired everything significant. Jeff commanded a fast-attack, and shooting them, sinking them early in a confrontation was the only way to take on a battle group and survive.

Mark got into his car, sat behind the wheel thinking, sighed, and hoped Gina's second idea wasn't also going to turn on its head established submarine tactics. His job was changing because of this woman, and he wasn't entirely sure it was a good thing. Her cross-sonar discovery was a significant help. This new idea . . . this active ping that couldn't be heard . . . was going to be a great addition right up until the day an enemy could also do it — and then it was going to really hurt. He'd spend the 90 days out on patrol, bracing himself to hear a torpedo in the water with the *Nevada* as its destination.

The number of subs the U.S. had operationally deployed, the tactical advantages they had, were formidable. But science could shake what was a solid wall and open new cracks. They needed her ideas. He didn't believe in a one-person-only kind of discovery. Gina's having the idea guaranteed others would eventually have the same idea. It was better to know the science and what was possible than to hide from it and simply hope no one else would figure it out.

Other countries might pursue the idea for a while and set it aside as too far out there, as not viable. But the U.S. wouldn't make that mistake. They would understand its capability and its limitations, they would classify it above code-word clearance, and then they would figure out how to defend against the day someone else figured out the same thing.

The military was a proactive branch of government. Sticking their heads in the sand was just plain dumb. He was one of 28 men entrusted with half the deployed strategic nuclear deterrent, and *dumb* wasn't in his vocabulary. He had a solid grounding in nuclear engineering and military history, well-learned tactical smarts and operational skills. The Navy would need to get ahead of this possibility as quickly as it could.

Mark parked in the Delta Pier lot. The USS *Nevada* needed his focus for the next few hours. Hand-over was a thousand details being coordinated at all levels of the boat, and he was the one who backed up his crew. Some of the classified materials regarding missile codes and launch packages were for his eyes only. His attention had to be on the hand-over, and he'd put it there for the next few hours. But he intended to get back to Gina before the day was over. They needed an agreement on how she'd proceed, whom she'd speak with, and he needed a word with the security personnel watching out for her. That security now wasn't a courtesy but a national-security priority.

His job had taught him how to understand the important, urgent, and necessary, and cope when they collided. Get the *Nevada* safely turned over to the blue crew. Then see how he could help Gina. It was going to be a busier day than he had originally planned. He should have bought something with caffeine to go with that ice cream. He was tired down to his bones, and for a fleeting moment he wished she had told someone else. He sighed. *Jeff's sister.*

She'd told the right guy.

4

Just before six a.m., the duty officer showed Commander Bishop into Rear Admiral Henry Hardman's office. The head of Submarine Group 9, Hardman was the man responsible for every squadron, submarine, and submarine crew at Bangor.

"A good patrol, Bishop."

"Thank you, sir."

The rear admiral poured coffee, handed him a mug, and waved him to a chair. "I'm speaking at noon to *Nevada* gold. Something urgent enough you need to jump that schedule by six hours — you've got my attention. What do you need, Commander?" He returned to his desk and sat down.

Bishop was relieved to have this conversation sitting down. "You're aware Gina Gray is in town?"

"I am. She asked for access to the acoustical lab to explore some sonar ideas. Toombs didn't have details on what those ideas were.

She's not one to share details until she can put her hands around the substance of an idea was my perspective on it."

"I've known her for a few years through her brother, Jeff Gray. I had a conversation with her last night."

"You look . . ." Rear Admiral Hardman set down his coffee. "Why don't you just tell me the bad news?"

"What if you could actively ping, and they couldn't hear you?"

Hardman thought for a moment, then winced.

"I'm the first person she's told. It made sense you should be the second to hear."

"Appreciate that," Hardman replied.

Bishop waited as Admiral Hardman thought it through. This was the man he trusted most in the Navy, the one who'd been his mentor and advisor as he worked toward becoming a ballistic missile submarine commander. The admiral had fought in combat when submarines were firing torpedoes at each other. He'd been at sea watching the USSR split back into individual countries. He'd seen underwater warfare tactics evolve. If there was one man able to capture the implications of Gina's statement quickly and to its full effect, it was this man.

Hardman looked over at him. "She works alone?"

"Always has."

"I was around when cross-sonar appeared as her Ph.D. thesis: *What if two subs could cross-link sonar data and not be overheard?* She hadn't said a word to anyone. I think I was the fourth person to read the foundation documents for it. Jeff was selectively alerting people to what she'd figured out. She had it all in her mind — the algorithms, the data cherry-picking formula, the speeds that might be possible. We gave her the lab access she needed, and she built a functional scale model of it in the deep-water tank and had cross-sonar running in under a month. It worked without modification at sea trials two months after that. We put it operational in the field within a year and have been frustrating enemies and allies alike ever since.

"I've known for years she was going to drop another earth-shattering idea on us one day. *What if you could actively ping, and they couldn't hear you?* Of everything I thought I might hear, I didn't see that one coming." He picked up his coffee mug, spun the liquid, finally looked over. "Until her brother is back onshore, you've got another job to do."

"Figured as much, unless you want Toombs to take it from here."

"She chose you to tell. She got into town less than two weeks ago. I gather she had the idea in mind, she just needed the data to test it against?"

"Appears that way. She didn't offer details on how it works, just that it requires cross-sonar to be running. She was running a data set last night — the USS *Ohio* encounter with the Brit's *Triumph*. *Ohio* was cross-linking sonar with the *Michigan* when it happened."

"Okay."

"She's going to need a sea trial test to get the full data she needs to study. Two fast-attacks and a boomer, different sea conditions. At a guess probably the Molokai Ridge, the continental shelf, and maybe an arctic ice. Nothing is noisier than glacier ice cracking and crashing into the sea."

"A month out, the USS *Connecticut* is wrapping up tests on an upgrade package for the MK48 torpedo," Hardman said. "The *Ohio* will need a shakedown after refit. If the *Nebraska* flows out of the dry dock smoothly, it could be pushed a week on the deployment window. Sit down with the schedulers and look at the next few months, see what's possible." Hardman set aside the coffee.

"If this were anyone other than Gina Gray," the man continued, "I'd say hand it off to the Undersea Warfare Center to schedule and plan a trial. But this is an idea we're going to want to keep close to the vest — nothing written down that describes it, no whispered conversations, no allusions to the fact it's out there. For now, just you and me, and when he's back, Jeff. Ask her not to speak to anyone else. The word is you're looking at testing an upgrade to cross-sonar, which will improve its speed. That will be sufficient for what you need to do."

"Yes, sir."

"Does she realize the danger in this idea?"

"She does, although I don't think she fully appreciates all the implications yet."

"As long as we can do it, and no one else can."

"I hear you, sir," Bishop said. He glanced at the time. He had to get back to the *Nevada,* and the admiral had someone waiting for him in the outer office. Bishop rose to his feet. "Security is around her, but it's temporary. You might want to quietly see if it can be raised to national security asset without having to tell anyone why."

"Done." Hardman leaned back in his

chair. "She hit us with cross-sonar when she was 20, and now this when she's 30. I think I may want to retire before she hits 40."

Bishop smiled, understanding the sentiment.

"Put me on a close update loop, Commander."

"Yes, sir." He returned the coffee mug to the used side of the service tray and headed toward the door.

"Bishop?"

He turned.

"Every military career has the odd kind of eddies and currents that can turn an officer into a flag officer — you're in one now," the admiral said. "SecNav will have this on his desk within hours of confirmation that it works."

"I'm aware of that, sir," Bishop replied. "I'm more concerned with how to buffer her, as the weight of the Navy is going to come hard after that point, wanting to dissect her work."

"For now, four people know. Let's leave it at that and let her work."

Bishop nodded his agreement. "Gold crew would like to present you with the Seaweed Trophy at noon," he said.

Hardman laughed. "I've earned it. See you

in six hours, Bishop."

"Permission to come aboard?"

In the command-and-control center, Bishop leaned over to look up the ladder, recognizing the voice. "Permission granted."

The *Nevada*'s blue crew commander, Nathan Irish, descended the ladder. "Good to have you back, Mark."

"Thanks, Nathan. It was a busy deployment. Brits, Aussies, Chinese, and Russians were all showing their colors in the Pacific. We were dodging everybody on this patrol."

Bishop's XO entered the center from deeper in the sub. Bishop turned to hear Kingman's update.

"Captain, weapons, operations, and admin have completed their hand-over. Engineering is in the process of taking the final reactor readings. Lieutenant Commander Mann and I are ready to do the walkthrough and send gold crew topside."

"Granted." Bishop held out his hand. "Take yourself topside when you're done and find your wife. I'll see you at the pinning. Excellent patrol, XO." There was a wealth of pride in those final words, and the handshake reflected it.

"Thank you, sir."

Bishop glanced at Irish. "Come down to

the stateroom, Nathan. I've got the update on the missiles for you."

Men cleared ladders and moved to the side in the passageways to let them through as Mark Bishop and Nathan Irish headed down to the captain's stateroom.

Bishop closed the door behind them. He motioned Nathan to take the desk chair. He spun the lock on the personal wall safe — there were three safes in the room — and pulled out his classified notes to give to Nathan. "Missile updates."

While Nathan read, Bishop tugged up the bunk to get access to the storage below and confirm he had left behind no personal gear. He verbally gave Nathan the highlights of the report. "Tridents 9 and 11 need recertified, 21 has to be replaced because it has aged out, and there's still a problem with tube 4. We cooked through an extra two canisters of nitrogen holding the pressure constant. They want to pull out the Trident, blast the missile tube with a shot of their special 'creamy red' to check the seals, then repressurize it empty. I'm thinking there is a hairline crack in the first locking seal. Tube 4 took that dropped ladder four patrols ago, which put a dent in the base casing, and I think this will flow back to that event."

"We're going to be at the Explosives

Handling Wharf for days," Nathan guessed. "Any problems with the repairs on the dome?"

"None, but I put on the schedule new photos of the hull to confirm the patch took the pressure without forming a cavity. We were never below 1,500 feet, so it wasn't severely stressed."

Bishop stretched himself out on the bunk and reached to carefully peel back the tape and take down his pictures and note card. "I moved the second deck power relay module up in priority on the TRIPER list, but odds are good there's not going to be time to deal with it on this refit. It's bound to fail at the most inopportune time. Once it goes, anything you need to divert forward of the missile bay has to be done manually. It's got to be in the master board — everything else has been swapped or tested out."

"That one's a headache rather than a crisis."

"Medical still needs new refrigeration. They've promised it will make this refit, but you'll want to stay on top of that one. The cooks hate sharing their refrigeration with the blood supply."

"Noted."

"Those are the big items; the paper runs five pages for the small ones." Bishop glanced over. "How's blue crew?"

"Short by two. I lost my Jack of the Dust provision master to the USS *Maine* and my best radioman broke his leg last week. I'm backfilling with guys from the USS *Kentucky*. Blue crew is dreading the 18-hour days of refit more than they are the time away on patrol."

"I hear you." Bishop got up from the bunk, pulled out his wallet, and tucked the photos and note card inside it. The missile keys and the authentication cards would be checked by the commander of the Strategic Weapons Facility in — he looked at his watch — 18 minutes, when the *Nevada* officially went off patrol. "Rear Admiral Bowen should be here soon. Anything I can answer before he arrives?"

"Start at the back of the boat and work your way forward. What's the story behind the maintenance notes?"

Bishop talked through the maintenance they had done at sea. The boomers were aging, and everything had to eventually be swapped out for refurbished parts as a portion of the TRIPER program or else fixed in real time when it broke.

Knuckles rapped on the door at 10 minutes to the hour. "Permission to enter, Commander."

97

"Granted."

Rear Admiral Scott Bowen, Commander of the Strategic Weapons Facility Pacific, stepped into the stateroom carrying a briefcase. Bishop and Irish both came to attention. "At ease, gentlemen." He set the briefcase on the desk and unlocked it. "Gold crew, your authentication cards, please."

Bishop entered the access numbers on the red wall safe, opened the outer safe door, then spun a dial to enter the combination for the inner safe door. He removed a two-inch-high gray square box and used the commander's key from around his neck to unlock the box. Inside were six rows of authentication cards, each card sealed inside a thin piece of shiny metal foil.

A machine at the National Security Agency generated a string of randomly arranged numbers and letters, printed the identical code on two cards, then foil-wrapped each card while it was still inside the machine — the generated sequence was never seen by a person. A number, stamped in white on each foil surface, indicated the two packets held the same contents.

One set of the authentication cards was placed in the captain's safe the day before a boomer left for patrol. A matching set of the authentication cards would arrive at Strategic Command, with a subset beginning with the number one taken directly to the White House for the President's Nuclear Briefcase — often called "the football" — carried by an Air Force officer everywhere the president went. A genuine Emergency Action Message from Strategic Command or directly from the president would begin with the number stamped in white on the foil, and the message would end with the string of numbers and letters found on the card inside that foil packet.

The *Nevada* blue crew commander, Nathan Irish, took an envelope from his pocket, slit the seal, and removed a sheet of paper that Bishop had signed three months before departure.

"The authentication keys not used during the patrol," Bishop said. He read off numbers on the packets as Nathan checked the list. "The four keys that were used during the patrol," Bishop added, taking out the opened foil packets, showing them to Nathan, and reading off the numbers.

"Verified, Commander," Nathan confirmed.

Rear Admiral Bowen signed the sheet confirming the numbers and placed the gray case into his briefcase. "*Nevada* gold, your commander's key." Bishop handed over the key. "Now the missile keys."

Bishop removed the ring of 24 missile keys from the safe. Rear Admiral Bowen took the keys, inserted them one at a time into a series of locks along the edge of a long narrow white case, turning each one. "Keys are verified."

"Blue concurs," Nathan said.

Rear Admiral Bowen placed the missile keys in the briefcase. The day before blue crew left on patrol, the missile keys, new authentication cards, a new commander's key for a re-keyed gray box, and new safe combinations would all be given to Nathan Irish.

The foil-wrapped card used to authenticate a genuine presidential message and the 24 missile keys were two parts of the arming mechanism aboard the *Nevada.* In the missile control room safe — the combination known only to the chief weapons officer on board — was an enabling key that turned on the system. The final piece of the puzzle — the master firing trigger — was locked in another safe, and the only two people who knew that safe combination were the head of Strategic Command and the President of the United States.

Rear Admiral Bowen locked the briefcase

and cuffed it to his wrist. "Thank you, gentlemen. USS *Nevada* is now off duty. May all her patrols be so quiet." He left the stateroom, his job finished.

Bishop took a deep breath, let it out, and accepted that the job was done. He looked at Nathan. "I stand ready to be relieved of command," Bishop said simply.

"I relieve you of command," Nathan replied in kind.

They shook hands. "The boat is yours. Take good care of her, Nathan," Bishop said.

"I'll do my best, Mark."

Irish picked up the phone's receiver on the wall. "This is the captain. Sound Blue."

The topside speaker gave the four whistles of blue crew assuming command.

Bishop shouldered his duffel bag and headed back through narrow corridors and up the ladders until he stepped out on the slopping deck of the USS *Nevada* just aft of the sail. More than 50 men could comfortably walk on the deck surface. Bishop glanced up at the sail rising a story above him, felt again how small he was compared to this submarine on which he served. Topside security had already changed over to blue crew personnel. Bishop walked across the ramp and off the boat that was no longer his to command.

"Lieutenant Junior Grade Greg Olson," the master of ceremonies announced.

Bishop pinned the dolphins on Olson's aquaflage uniform. "Congratulations, Lieutenant. You've earned the right to be called a submariner."

"Thank you, sir."

"Ensign Richard Quail," the master of ceremonies next announced.

Bishop accepted another set of dolphins from the Chief of the Boat and pinned them on Quail. "Congratulations, Ensign. You've earned the right to be called a submariner."

"Thank you, sir."

Bishop didn't immediately move away. "Good job stumping your captain with the last question of the patrol," he said in a low voice. "You had that one saved up for the final day?"

Ensign Quail smiled slightly. "Yes, sir."

Bishop smiled back. "You do the *Nevada* proud."

He walked the stage pinning 14 of his men with dolphins as their families and crewmates looked on.

Rear Admiral Hardman took the podium to congratulate the men and welcome the crew home.

Before the rear admiral could return to his seat, the chief engineer for *Nevada* gold came forward. He presented Hardman with the Seaweed Trophy — in commemoration of all the clinging tangles work related to the sea always caused — the award received in good humor by the rear admiral and the crew.

Bishop let his Chief of the Boat conduct the final business of the day. "Crew of the *Nevada,* you are dismissed," the man announced.

Cheers erupted across the ballroom.

Bishop moved through the crowd, speaking with gold crew family members, stood for pictures with crewmen, made a point to greet the four mothers of infants born while the fathers were at sea.

The ombudsman for the gold crew joined him. Amy Delheart, his chief engineer's wife, was a volunteer and the only civilian on his small staff. He depended on her for an in-depth knowledge of the crew's families and what happened onshore while they were out on patrol. "A very nice ceremony, Mrs. Delheart. Thanks for your help getting it organized."

"My pleasure, Commander."

The 104 wives of gold crew personnel looked to her as their lifeline while their husbands were away. Mark had read her shore summary as soon as they docked. Four births, three car accidents, one burglary. The events weren't as serious as they sometimes were. He would talk more with her about the marriages that were shaky, the ones having financial difficulties, and similar topics, when she sat down with him later for a full debrief.

"Have a date for me?" she asked.

"Announce the commander's backyard barbecue for Saturday, April 29th," he confirmed. "Gold crew and families, significant others are all welcome. We'll go nine a.m. to nine p.m. again this year."

"It's a wonderful tradition. Families are looking forward to it."

"So am I." Bishop signaled his chief engineering officer. "Your husband is now on R and R. Take him home," he ordered with a laugh. "I'm going to go find civilian clothes and somewhere with a pizza. I'll call you in a couple of days to set up a time for a full debrief."

Bishop made a decision as he drove away from the Pizza Hut. He turned not toward his home but toward Jeff's condo. Gina Gray was now a concern on both a professional and personal level. Jeff wasn't here yet to watch out for her. Bishop nodded to security as he made his way up the walk, carrying the remainder of an order in a pizza box. Jeff's car was in the driveway. Mark assumed she was driving it while Jeff was at sea. He rang the doorbell.

It was three minutes before the door opened and Gina appeared. "I woke you up," Mark said, apologizing. It was just after three. He'd figured she would have slept and been up by now. She was in jeans, T-shirt, bare feet, her eyes still looking sleepy as she brushed her hair back with her hands.

"One of the hazards of working nights. It's no problem. I would have been up soon anyway." She lifted a hand to cover a yawn, contradicting her words.

"I stopped by to offer a quarter of a leftover pizza, ask if you needed anything, and to pass on some news."

"The pizza's welcome." She lifted the lid, nodded her thanks. "I'll have a good meal to take along tonight. I'm good, Mark. It's comfortable here."

"I've confirmed Jeff will tentatively be home on April 25th."

"Thanks for that good news."

"I also spoke with Rear Admiral Hardman. We'd like you to keep news of what you're working on to the small group who already knows, plus Jeff. There will be a sea trial as soon as you're ready for one. I can plan it for you or you can have Jeff plan it after he gets back — whatever you're comfortable with. Just let us know what data you need collected, and we'll map out the maneuvers."

"Seriously?" Her surprise sounded genuine.

"Whatever you need, Gina, the admiral wants you to have. I'll make sure you get it."

"He doesn't want to see data, probabilities, and risk assessments first?"

Bishop smiled. "He wants to know if it works. It will be my job to design a sea trial that minimizes the risks."

The phone rang behind her. She glanced over her shoulder. "Come in a minute, Mark. I've been taking messages since Jeff's machine long ago filled up."

She disappeared into the kitchen with the pizza box. Mark stepped into the entryway, closed the door behind him, and stayed put rather than trail after her.

Gina rejoined him a few moments later. "Sorry."

"You need to shut off the ringer if you hope to get some decent sleep."

"True." She pushed a hand through her hair again. "You went out on a limb with Rear Admiral Hardman for an idea that might not work."

"Not much of a limb. If it does work, the cost of putting the boats to sea and the time spent for the sea trial will look in hindsight like the obvious decision. If it fails, you'll be able to tell us why, and we'll know what to watch for if someone else tries to develop the technique. But the more I think about it, I believe it's going to work, Gina."

She looked at him, uncertain. "Why would you think that?"

"Cross-sonar is a brilliant combination of simple ideas elegantly put together. You've got the ability to make the leaps of imagination necessary to create ways of doing something out of whole new cloth. If I had to guess, I'd say what you're working on right now is probably deceptively simple."

She didn't answer him for a long moment. She sat down on the carpeted steps to the second floor and wrapped her arms around her knees. She finally nodded, more to herself than him, and glanced up. "Define a ping for me."

He tilted his head, realized he was about to get schooled, and leaned back against the doorjamb with a smile. "A ping is a sound

107

generated by a submarine, which will echo off of other objects. By listening to those echoes, software can identify where another sub is located."

She nodded. "The concept was developed decades ago and has been done essentially the same way ever since."

"It works well at finding objects in the water, in particular other submarines," Bishop agreed. "But it gets the guy who pinged killed. It's a basic tenant of submarine warfare that to ping is to get yourself a torpedo in reply since the sound gives away your own position."

He pushed his hands into his pockets. She looked so young sitting there, and yet this was the lady who had come up with cross-sonar. "What's your idea, Gina?" he asked softly.

"Acoustical hardware today can hear very faint echoes. I don't need to use a loud sound for the ping. I can use something just above a whisper and still hear the echoes. My idea is so simple, Mark, I've hesitated to say it." She bit her lip. "I simply removed generating a man-made sound for the ping. I'm recording ocean noise and replaying a brief clip of it, whatever was the loudest moment in the last couple of minutes."

He blinked at her comment, felt himself

miss a breath.

She went on, "I record ocean noise, replay a fraction of it as my active ping, create an echo template based on the precise sound I'm sending out, listen for that echo, and declare if another submarine is out there. It's the traditional active ping that's always been done, just a different sound source.

"The algorithm requires a very precise echo template, six digits less than a minute of a degree, and that template has to be generated in real time for the sound being sent out. It requires cross-sonar running and four hydrophone sets in sync. It takes massive computing power and exquisite acoustical hardware — both of which the U.S. submarine fleet now has deployed on its fast-attacks and boomers."

She spread her hands. "To someone listening, the ping sounds like ocean noise because that's what it is. Oh, and the idea has built-in security. That realization was an added surprise — a pleasant one — for me. Every ping I generate is different. Even if you suspect one faint sound might have been something odd, you never hear it again. I don't know how you'd tell you're being actively pinged by this algorithm. I have a difficult time picking out an audio file with pings from one without pings, even when I know what I should be trying to find."

She looked up at him. "It's not that I'm brilliant, Mark. It's that technology lets me do more than was possible a decade ago. I've got very good acoustical hardware and massive computing power at my disposal. A trick, really — using the ocean noise, doing a ping that's just above a whisper. I removed the man-made ping. That's the idea. That's all it is."

" 'Gina, the genius,' " he said softly, seeing something quite different. "How many have worked on sonar for decades yet never bothered to see what you just explained? It's a gift, Gina. I appreciate that you see it all as simple. The idea may be simple, but the fact you brought it to light is not."

She offered a small smile. "It may not work. I don't know if the computations can be run fast enough when the sub is also running normal sonar operations. I don't know if the algorithms searching for the echo template will be overwhelmed in a noisy sea. And it's possible I have entirely missed a crucial variable."

"What's your biggest concern?"

"The echo that comes back from the sub running cross-sonar with you may be so loud you essentially go deaf to the other echoes. You're going to whisper a ping, and it's going to be an echo back that sounds like a gong being struck — the companion sub is close to you and the hydrophones are in sync with each other. That first echo is going to be intense."

Bishop smiled. "I can't wait to find out, Gina, what this is like at sea. The idea makes sense. When you're ready for that sea trial, we'll find out those answers. Just tell me the type of data you'd like collected. I'll put a plan together that will give you what you need."

She got up from the step. "I appreciate the help. I'll get you some notes — it's likely going to be a few more weeks."

Mark moved away from the door. "When you tell Jeff, have him sit down first. Operationally, it's going to be a fascinating set of tactical decisions for us to work out."

He pulled a card from his pocket. "Phone numbers for where to find me — office, home, and cell — and my XO, Seth Kingman, is on there as well. If you've left a message for me and haven't heard back within the hour, Kingman will track me down for you. He knows you might call, so use the resource. Cell reception can be tricky around here, given the terrain, or if I'm down a couple of levels in a sub."

"Thanks." She tucked it in her pocket. "Enjoy your R and R, Mark."

"I always do. Lock the door behind me, Gina." He stepped outside and waited until he heard the dead bolt thrown before he walked down the steps.

He got in his car, keys in his hand, but just sat and for a brief moment closed his eyes. *"I removed the man-made ping."* It was like hearing Michelangelo say, "I removed the marble that wasn't David." Her idea would work. It was so conceptually simple, even first-year sonar students would grasp the concept and its implications.

Espionage, though, was a real problem that could not be ignored. It took cross-sonar running and four sets of hydrophones listening to capture that echo template. This wouldn't be easy for other countries to emulate. Knowing what was happening and being able to reproduce it were not the same thing. The U.S. protected cross-sonar, and until that fell, this new approach to detection would be somewhat safe. But this idea was so versatile it could be done with a network of sonar lines deployed on the sea-floor or it could be run from surface ships.

U.S. submarines would have to assume they'd been located from the moment they identified an enemy vessel within their threat radius. It would mean living with torpedoes hot, setting up shooting solutions against every submarine and boat within sonar range. If they couldn't hear someone pinging them, they would have to operate as if they'd been seen.

Mark glanced back at the condo. Gina Gray was coming up with ideas with far-reaching implications. He wished Jeff was home so she had someone to talk with. She was smart enough to make the discovery and also to understand many of its implications, and those would provide their own unique burdens.

Mark headed home, ready for the sustained R and R and not being in charge for a few weeks. He'd done what could be done today and would occasionally check in on Gina while she was in Bangor, until Jeff got back.

He wondered idly what her breakup in Boulder had really been about. Dating for two years suggested something serious, and Gina didn't strike him as flighty. Something had happened. The Navy was reaping the benefit with her focus on sonar ideas. If there was one thing he did understand, it was burying strong emotions in work. It would help her to a point, but eventually she'd need to talk with someone about what happened if she was going to put it behind her and get on with her life. He hoped she would have those conversations with her brother as soon as Jeff returned.

Mark Bishop pulled on rain gear before walking out onto the Marginal Wharf, maneuvering around forklifts with pallets of supplies and guys hauling personal gear. The USS *Seawolf,* now tight against the north side of the wharf, didn't even rock as waves on Hood Canal splashed against the sides of the boat and washed over her deck.

He had seen the *Seawolf* captain come topside. Mark moved to the end of the walkway to meet him. "Good to have you back, Jeff." He took the duffel bag from his friend, offered a coffee to take its place.

Jeff Gray ignored the fact he was standing in the rain — he'd been on the bridge for the 16 hours of the transit and was already soaked. "A nice patrol, if rather hopping," he said, sipping the coffee. "The shipping channel was as busy as the August rush of arriving Christmas orders. My sonar guys are still smarting at not seeing you coming."

Mark grinned. "*Nevada* runs nice and quiet when I ask it of her."

"So I found out — again."

"Need to stay?"

"My XO has it handled for now. I'm taking the night watch. Want to run me over to Bremerton Hospital? I've got a crewman who needed a medevac who I need to check on."

"Sure. What happened?"

"Gallbladder was our guess."

At the parking lot, Mark tossed Jeff's duffel into the back of the truck. Inside the truck, doors slammed, Mark turned on the heat and handed over a towel. "Gina is here."

Jeff took that news with a pause of the towel. "I'll love to see her, but since she hadn't planned this visit months ago, I'm guessing it isn't going to be good news."

"She broke up with Kevin. Made another breakthrough in sonar. She's staying at your place and working nights at the new Undersea Warfare Center's acoustical research lab."

Jeff closed his eyes and half laughed. "I hope she quits breaking up with guys. She has her best ideas when she's trying not to think about her personal life." Jeff sighed and dropped the towel around his shoulders. "It's not funny, but it's a pattern. Thanks for the heads-up. She was in love with the guy, or thought she was. You would think she would get a break at least occasionally with the guys she chooses. They keep turning out to be wrong for her."

"I'm sorry for her sake to hear that. She knows you're coming in today. I was looking for her on the pier, figuring she would be here to greet you. She's got clearance."

"She's been in Bangor on arrival days in the past. She knows I need the first six hours or so to settle the boat. She'll likely have a meal waiting for me at the condo." Jeff finished the coffee. "So, she's made another breakthrough in sonar?"

"What if you could actively ping, and the other guy couldn't hear you?"

Jeff pulled in a long breath, then groaned. "I don't know whether to be proud of her or annoyed at her for making my job more difficult. That is one dangerous proposition."

"I'd rather know it's possible than have it used on us before we knew it could be done," Mark replied.

"Very true," Jeff agreed. He glanced over. "She told you."

"I think she wanted someone to tell, and you weren't around."

"Appreciate you stepping in."

"You'd do the same if a sister of mine showed up while I was at sea." Mark took Trident Avenue to the Bangor main gate

116

and headed south on Highway 3 toward Bremerton. "I told Rear Admiral Hardman what she's working on. It stays at four of us — Gina, you, me, and Hardman — while he figures out how to contain this. She'll need a sea trial to put together the data, and you're going to help me plan it."

"Fine by me. Shore time just makes me fidgety. I could use something to focus on. Never let it be said my sister made my life boring. I will be glad to see her. So what's going on with you?"

Mark wasn't one to talk much about personal matters, but there were some issues where it helped to have Jeff's reaction. "I figured I would ask Linda Masters out to dinner and a movie. Right now we're playing phone tag — she's at a teaching seminar in Colorado Springs, but it's going on the calendar when she gets back."

"That's bigger news than Gina. I'm proud of you, Mark. You're showing a heartbeat again."

"I don't remember dating being this intense."

"It's not the dating. It's the fact you don't do casual, never have. I like the idea. Linda's got . . . well, *class* if you want one word. She's got a life, a good one, and would fit in nicely with you. I already know you enjoy her company — why else would you be showing up wearing an authentic cowboy hat and boots after going to auctions with her? She makes you laugh. It's a good thing. Besides, Melinda would have liked Linda."

"You always were good at speeches."

Jeff grinned. "Gina says I like to deconstruct her just for the fun of annoying her. I know you, Mark. You've been in a holding pattern, waiting for the day you decide to think about a lady again. It's time."

"It's time," Mark echoed, oddly comforted by Jeff's words. He didn't need the reassurance, but it felt good just the same. "So what are you going to do about Gina's breakup?"

Jeff shook his head. "Don't know. She'll talk about what happened eventually. She'll clam up for a good while first, though. Without even knowing what Kevin said or did, I'd like to give him a piece of my mind for dating her two years before breaking it off. If he had done it at a year, at least the damage wouldn't go so deep.

"She gets hurt easily, Mark," Jeff continued, his tone serious. "It's something I never really understood until she hit about 18. I realized then how much being so far ahead of her peers in school left her hurting from the unthinking comments people make. Being an adult no doubt has made it easier now, but it's still there, when people realize how smart she is. I'll lay good money Kevin finally decided he didn't want a wife smarter than himself. She'll win more grants, more fellowships, more awards, and he'd always be in the shadow of her spotlight. Or more likely —" Jeff stopped abruptly and winced — "I'll bet Gina being Gina and loving the guy asked questions about his work, thought about the problem he was working to solve, and made a suggestion that turned out to be right. In love with him, she wouldn't have been able to help herself; she would have wanted to help him out. She probably solved in a few weeks what he'd been working on for months or years."

"He's an idiot if that's what happened and he let it bother him."

"It will be that, or a variation of that. She asked me when she was 14 who was going to want a smart wife. I should have ignored her age and realized she was right to be worried."

Mark glanced over at Jeff. "Fourteen?"

"She likes to think ahead."

Mark laughed. "I don't envy you the problem you've got, but you did get an interesting sister. My sisters were more conventional. They just dated way too much for my comfort before they settled down with the guys they married."

"At least Gina is smart enough to come find me. Even with the age gap, we've always been pretty close," Jeff said. He folded up the towel and tossed it in the back. "Rain's going to make the fishing good along Hood Canal. Want to head out Thursday morning for a couple of hours?"

"Sure. I've already been testing out the coves. Triton gave up some nice bass."

5

The commander's backyard barbecue looked like a success. Mark Bishop picked his way upward through the people sitting on the deck steps, crossed it, and nodded his thanks to a crewman sliding the patio door open for him.

Gina Gray was standing at the kitchen sink washing celery stalks and humming softly to herself along with the music pounding outside. A plastic cup beside her looked like it held fruit punch and sherbet. She was busy, being helpful, and yet she also seemed content. He slid the armload of shucked ears of corn onto the counter beside her. "Glad you came, Gina."

She glanced over, eyed the corn on the cob. "You throw an interesting barbecue."

He grinned. "Thank you. The crowd eats everything that comes out of this kitchen before the day is done. The rule on sink duty is 15 minutes, then you plop that sticker on someone you want to give it to for the next 15 minutes."

"So I was told. Jeff's already said Penn is next. What do I do with the corn?"

"Wash them, send them back outside. Someone will wrap them in foil and toss them on a free spot on one of the grills."

"I can handle that."

He pulled another bottle of barbecue sauce from the cupboard. Chicken was ready to grill, and he retrieved six packages of brats and four of hot dogs from the refrigerator, then paused beside her. "Can I get you anything?"

"I'm good."

"Glad to have Jeff home?"

Her face lit up with her smile. "Very much so."

He lingered for a brief moment, captured by the smile. "You love him a lot."

"Yeah. He's all that's left of family now that our parents have passed away."

"I didn't know that."

"Technically there are a couple of distant cousins, but Jeff doesn't like them much."

Mark remembered a past conversation. "Kelly and Kyle?"

"Jeff's been talking."

"He does that when we hit R and R together and we're out fishing somewhere.

He talks about you, his crew on the *Sea-wolf,* what you're working on, who he's dating."

"And what do you talk about?"

"Whatever topic he's brought up."

She grinned. "Okay."

"I go to fish. The conversation is like an interesting radio station with long silent pauses for the commercials."

She laughed softly. "You like my brother."

"One of the best friends I've got in Bangor. Somewhere in the back of the refrigerator you'll find a blue Tupperware with a piece of cake in it. I hid it for you when Jeff mentioned you might stop by today."

"All right . . ."

"I missed your birthday."

Her face turned a touch pink. "Thank you."

"My sisters prefer chocolate icing over white cake and insist on a corner piece. Since I didn't know your preferences, I went with theirs."

"I'll enjoy it."

Petty Officer Peter York entered the kitchen. "There you are, Gina. Hey, Commander." He slid the second plate he held onto an open spot on the counter, lightly touched a hand to the small of her back.

123

"The hamburger is cooked to overdone, as requested, and I got you the last of the coleslaw."

"Thanks, Peter." Gina held Mark's gaze for a last brief moment, then looked at Peter. "Let me finish up the corn on the cob and then I'll turn over the sink duty to Penn. I'd like to see the clam pit after we eat."

"I'm game."

Mark nodded to York and headed out with the items for the grills, pleased to see Peter had chosen to spend part of his day with Gina. He'd make sure she had a good afternoon.

Two-thirds of gold crew would make this barbecue, bringing their families along, before the day was over. As announced, the gathering began at nine in the morning and ran until nine at night, with food the one constant.

He had a house on an inlet so his backyard ran down to a river shoreline, though it wasn't deep enough for a boat to dock. But it offered a good view. His neighbor to the east was part of gold crew, and the neighbor to the west was a friend who helped throw this party. The spillover populated their backyards too, and the crowd of guests were able to spread out enough to make it a relaxed and fun social event.

More than half of his crew was married, with most of them starting families. Mark scooped up a toddler who had gotten away from his mom, got two sticky hands and a pat on the face to go with a smile as he returned the boy to his mother. Children's shrieks of laughter at the water games, ball toss, Twister, and hopscotch competed with the live music by the guys forming an impromptu band on the side driveway. Someone had hauled over a drum set and a few electric guitars, and keyboards had appeared midmorning with power cords now snaking out from his garage.

It was a party, but also a kind of commander's triage. Mark kept the food flowing, offering a smile and quick word with his guests, while his attention never stopped roving and observing. A lot was happening today at a deeper level than a backyard barbecue.

Gold crew guys needed to be on good terms with one another. Annoyances could build if somebody was getting on your nerves during a 90-day patrol. This was a chance for the guys to recalibrate, share a laugh, work a grill together. They needed to ease off that stress with each other.

Gold crew wives needed a day to relax

with the other wives, no longer having to wonder if their husbands were safe, or when they were coming home, and talk about homecoming stories. There were friendships here among the women that were strong, that were being forced to grow stronger the more times gold crew headed out. Eight couples were pregnant. Five of the women were likely to give birth during the next patrol. The husband wouldn't be there for her, but other gold crew wives would. That support made Navy life for families possible.

Mark would make a point to talk with every wife and girlfriend at this gathering. Though their husbands and boyfriends had volunteered, the women hadn't but were making similar sacrifices. The least he could do was let them know that sacrifice hadn't gone unnoticed. And occasionally during those brief one-on-one conversations, a wife gave him a comment that would change his approach in how he mentored a particular crewman.

All wasn't well in this extended work family. Five couples were close to divorce, seventeen were having financial problems serious enough for him to know about it, six were dealing with teenagers having a particularly rough few years. The patrols and the separations were especially hard on the kids.

The older enlisted guys helped keep tabs on what was happening. Most families did adapt to military life and the regular separations, and they created a routine that worked for them. Others made the wise decision not to reenlist and moved on to civilian life.

Mark knew he had been very blessed in his marriage to Melinda. She had never felt a conflict between his love for her and the fact he'd had to leave her. The boat would ship out on a predetermined date, and he would be gone for three months, regardless of the circumstances going on in their personal lives. He'd had to go on patrol when she was desperately sick with the flu, another time five days after she had found out she'd been laid off from her job, and even worse, two days after her father had a heart attack and it wasn't known if he would pull through.

Mark had done everything he could to arrange help for her while he was gone, but he hadn't been there at times when she had every right to expect it. She'd never once asked him to leave the Navy. She'd let him stay with the job he loved even though it cost her. She had loved him, been proud of him. That was the one constant he had in his memories of life with her. He'd had a wife who loved him deeply, and it had turned out to be a very good marriage.

Mark picked up sodas from the ice chest and went to join the guys pitching horseshoes. The one thing this group would never be was dull or fully settled. It would always be in flux, and part of his job was to be aware of what was happening, channel matters to a good outcome when he could influence what occurred, be prepared for the fallout when family matters went south. The Navy had a divorce rate that alarmed him. Some cash out of his own pocket for a day of food and conversation, a chance for him to assess what was going on had always seemed like a wise use of his time and funds. Besides, it was the one day he got to be off duty with his crew. The barbecue was for his own benefit too.

The barbecue was finally winding down. Mark Bishop felt the fatigue of a long, satisfying day. Jeff turned a folding table on its side, pushed back the lock bar, and kicked the legs to fold up into the table base. Mark added more plastic chairs to the stack he would return to the rental shop. Jeff might not be gold crew, but Mark had roped him into coming over for the day just the same.

"Did I hear Linda Masters is engaged?" Jeff asked as he carried the table over to lean against the chairs.

"She is," Mark replied. His plan to ask her out to dinner had turned into a call congratulating her. He hadn't been that surprised when she told him her fiancé was a fellow teacher she'd known for many years. Three months away could change a lot of things onshore. It wasn't the first time he'd bumped into an unexpected turn of events after he got back from patrol, and it wouldn't be the last.

"You can't let this be some kind of sign, a reason to stop and rethink restarting your social life."

Mark sent Jeff a glance. He'd talked more than he intended about his future plans while they were fishing. "I'm not taking it that way. Jessica stopped by this afternoon. I hadn't realized she was back in town. I was thinking I'd give her a call."

Jeff looked around the driveway to see who was nearby. "You like Gina. Ask her to dinner."

The comment caught Mark off guard, especially coming from her brother. The image of Gina in his kitchen a few hours ago flitted across his mind. She'd looked good.

The thought was quickly followed by reality. Mark shook his head. "I'm too old for her, Jeff. She's too young for me. She was in kindergarten when I was learning to drive."

"She might be young in years, but she's got a mind that is ancient, it's got so much knowledge crammed into it."

"She's 12 years younger than me."

"Eleven and a half to be precise. That isn't 20 years younger, you know. Give her the benefit of the doubt and at least see what you think after a date."

The idea didn't sit well. She was on the rebound from one breakup, and she didn't need someone treating her as a trial run. "No. Jessica is the right next call for me," Mark said, comfortable with the decision.

Jeff frowned briefly, then sighed and turned another table on its side to fold up the legs. "Gina's asked me to introduce her to Navy guys I like."

Mark swung his head around. "She what?"

"She finally started talking, and as usual she had her layers packed. The breakup with Kevin shook her up pretty bad. She's willing to admit that. She's also trying to move on. She wants my help."

"What are you going to do?"

"A kid sister asks you to do something,

it's not much of a decision. I'm going to do what she asked."

"She spent most of the afternoon with Peter York."

"He's okay. He was at her side 10 minutes after we arrived, doing his own introductions. Kind of nicely rolled over her, I think, and wrapped her up as his for the day."

"Smart man," Mark commented. "If not York, then who are you thinking about?"

"A sonar guy from the *Nebraska,* Daniel Field."

Mark considered that and nodded. "Field is a good man. A Southern gentleman."

"You'd be better."

"Not in the cards, Jeff. She's too young, she's your sister, not to mention Rear Admiral Hardman considers her my work assignment until this sonar idea she's sorting out is clarified." He needed to change the subject. "Have you decided where you're heading on leave?"

"Gina wants to pack up her Boulder apartment and ship her stuff back to Chicago. I'm going to handle that for her. She's ambivalent about returning to Colorado anytime soon, and I talked her into staying here. I'll spend a few days skiing in the area while I'm there. Probably take George Tinn along with me to help haul the boxes down

131

two flights of stairs. I'll be back here in about 10 days. You'll watch out for Gina while I'm gone?"

"Sure, that I can do." Mark picked up the last chair. "So she's moving back to Chicago?"

"I don't think she knows where she's heading next. She's got preliminary interviews at several universities and a few NASA research locations lined up. Something big in science she can sink her teeth into — having nothing to do with the oceans this time — would be my guess."

Mark carried the first of the folded tables to the pickup truck. Jeff hauled over another one.

"Jessica, huh?" Jeff asked.

"Have a problem with that?"

"She'll put you to sleep, Mark. She's a nice woman, but when you've met her, spent a few days in her company, you've discovered all there is to know about her. Melinda had layers on layers, and you loved that. Find someone with history, someone with a packed calendar, a busy woman going lots of directions. Tiffany, if you want a name."

Mark laughed. "Your description of Melinda is right on, but Tiffany as a wife for me? We're on different planets on that one.

She's got fitness clubs and gyms popping up all over the area, she's got energy leaking out of her, she's the definition of a bubbly personality — and she would drive me nuts inside of a week. She's also . . . what, a decade younger than me?"

"Eight years. You're going to have to accept going younger if you want to find a woman who's flexible enough to adapt to being a Navy wife. It's not an easy transition, Mark."

"Why don't *you* ask Tiffany out?" Mark countered.

Jeff grinned. "Already have on occasion." He pushed another folded table into the truck bed. "But can you imagine Gina and Tiffany in the same room?"

Mark thought about it. Both women collected information — Gina's tended to be facts and thoughtful, while Tiffany's leaned toward social and conjecture. But both were never boring to talk with. "They might do better together than you think."

"Whoever she turns out to be, my wife's got to get along with my sister or my life would not be worth living."

"You're thinking about getting married?"

Jeff shrugged. "You're not the only one getting older."

"Good for you."

"Didn't say I was going to do something about it."

Mark smiled. "You will. The idea spreads until it's the only good idea you've got left, and you have to do something about it. Ask Gina about Tiffany before you make an assumption. She might surprise you."

"Why don't you do the same?" Jeff replied. "Ask Gina out before you assume she's too young for you."

Mark glanced around as the screen door bounced shut, and the conversation was abandoned before he answered. Gina and Peter York were coming down the front steps, Peter carrying the box of leftover cupcakes that Mark had asked him to take to the family center on base.

"Anything else you want me to drop off, Commander?" Peter asked.

"That's it. Thanks for the help."

"No problem. Gina and I are going to go see the moon fog that rises over the Hood Canal on cool nights like this. I'll bring her home in a few hours, Jeff."

"Sure thing."

Peter put the box in the back seat, then held the passenger door for Gina.

Mark sent Jeff a glance as the car pulled out. "Looks like you won't have as much to do as you thought. I'd say she just got claimed."

Jeff frowned after the car. "You'd better give me the details you know on him."

"I know York is good at his job, and he has a clean personnel jacket. Home is Idaho, I think. This was his first patrol with *Nevada* gold. I thought he was dating a girl from his high school days, but I'm nowhere current on that. Kingman knows him better. You should give him a call."

"I'll do that," Jeff said. "I think he's younger than she is by a couple of years."

"That a problem?"

Jeff shook his head. "According to Gina, women live longer than men so she should look for a guy younger than herself."

Mark smiled. "Another remark back from when she was a teenager?"

Jeff nodded, then turned serious. "It was a conversation I'm not likely to forget." He lifted the last table into the truck bed. "I want her married, Mark, happily, so my life can go back to being calm again."

"Just wait until you turn on the porch light to find her kissing a guy good-night."

Jeff scowled at the thought.

"Don't worry, you'll survive," Mark laughed.

Jeff was at the kitchen table finishing a bowl

of ice cream when he heard Gina return home. He smiled as he heard the shoes land by the doormat. She followed the light and came to join him. "Have a good evening?" he asked, trying to sound low-key.

She rested a hand against the back of the chair opposite him. "A very nice evening. Peter showed me around more of the Bangor base, and then we drove over to the Toandos Peninsula so we could see water in three directions as the fog rose." Gina got another spoon from a drawer, then turned back to the table. "Share a bite or two?"

He slid the bowl over. "Leave me the cherry."

She settled into the chair. "He was a perfect gentleman. He's hoping to get engaged to a lady who's currently in London with a college exchange program."

"Really? I didn't see that coming."

"I did, early on. He mentioned his girl wasn't able to come to the barbecue, he was at loose ends, and asked if he could show me around. He was a safe date, so I took it." She looked across the table at him, smiled. "I didn't want you hovering, keeping an eye on me all afternoon."

Jeff studied her. "Did you change your mind about me introducing you to some guys I like? Because the barbecue was crowded with possibilities."

"I didn't change my mind. I just didn't want a speech freeze in a crowd when you started making introductions. It's easier one-on-one." She gestured with her spoon. "Who did you have in mind? I might have met him."

"Near the top of my list, I'd like to introduce you to Daniel Field. He's a sonar guy on the *Nebraska.*"

"Because of the sonar work I've done?"

"It's purely incidental that he's well versed in sonar. He's a gentleman, from the South, and he'll treat you right. He's got a solid reputation and is well liked around Bangor. Bishop agrees he's a good man."

She went still. "You told Bishop what I asked you to do."

"I wanted to find out if he had an interest himself. You two would be good together."

She looked shocked, took a breath, then another before she asked, "What did he say?"

"A case of mistiming on my part. Someone named Jessica had already crossed his path," Jeff replied. He wanted his sister with someone he trusted. Bishop had been a long shot, but one he would have been very comfortable with for his sister. Bishop had sounded certain about the no, so Jeff was going to his next best idea. "You'll like Daniel. I was thinking we could do an informal foursome so I could introduce you. I'll invite Tiffany and Daniel to join us for an evening out. That way it's a date, but a casual one. I won't let us get split apart into couples unless you decide you're comfortable with him. Tiffany can carry the conversation if you don't feel like saying much. She's got that cheerful, outgoing kind of personality that naturally fills in pauses in a conversation."

"I like that plan," Gina said with a nod.

"I'll set it up for before I go to Boulder."

Gina finished a quarter of the ice cream and slid the bowl back. Jeff scooped up the cherry she'd left for him.

"What would you think about Bishop if he did ask you out?" he asked, curious.

She hesitated. "I don't know. He's your friend, Jeff. That could make it awkward."

"No protest that he's too old for you?"

"I promised myself I would keep an open mind on the details."

"Wise move."

"He's been married before. He's probably got expectations for someone vastly different from me."

"I didn't even think of that when I was talking with him," Jeff admitted. "You would have liked Melinda, and she would have liked you. I'm glad Bishop is thinking about getting married again, but I don't think Jessica's the right fit. He was thinking about a woman named Linda Masters, but she got engaged while he was on the last patrol."

"Tell me about Tiffany. Have I met her before?"

Jeff found her abrupt switch in the conversation telling, but accepted it. "Tiffany is the lady who owns and runs the gym over on Beach Street."

Gina grinned. "The one you go to impress with your workout routine for an hour every day when you're home?"

Jeff chose to ignore the embarrassment her comment caused since she was partially right. "That's her."

"Have you been dating her?"

"We've been out a few times," Jeff said. "You can tell me what you think of her after the dinner."

"I'll do that and be nice in my comments," Gina offered. "So tell me more about Daniel Field. What do you know about him?"

Jeff had made several phone calls and filled in more of the blanks about the man. "He's a Georgia native, has three sisters, all of them older than he is. He's third-generation Navy. Daniel spent six years at

Kings Bay before transferring to Bangor. He's considered the best sonarman on the *Nebraska.*" Jeff tried to remember what else he'd learned. "He's on the Bangor baseball team, plays second base. He's known for his ability on the guitar."

"How old is he?"

"I'd say around 27 or 28."

"He sounds like an interesting man," Gina decided.

"If it doesn't work out, I'll come up with someone else," Jeff assured her. "I remember my promise."

"So do I, which is one reason I came to see you." She smiled as she got up from the table. "I'm glad you're my brother."

"Remember that when you're fussing over the fact I ask what time you'll be home."

She laughed. "Good night, Jeff."

He listened as she headed upstairs, then finished the ice cream. She was going to be married by this time next year, he could just about count on it. He'd find the right husband for her, someone who would love her well and a man he could tolerate. They'd be having holidays together for the next 50 years.

For the first time in his memory, he felt kind of old. He sighed, got up and put the bowl in the dishwasher, set it to run. Gina had alphabetized his spice rack again. He smiled when he saw it and deliberately moved the cinnamon next to the garlic. He'd give her a day or two to realize something didn't look right. His sister was restless. She didn't have to say it for him to see it. She puttered around here, moved his furniture, organized the cupboards, and then worked too many hours. The sooner she got settled with a good man, the better off she was going to be, and the less he would worry about her.

6

Large-scale posters of abstract artwork adorned the walls of the Squadron 5 ready room. Mark noted the change and wondered who had been decorating. The place looked nice. He needed to give his ombudsman a budget so Mrs. Delheart could work on theirs. "How's your sister doing?"

Jeff pushed a page across the desk for him to sign. "Working too hard at night, coming home and sleeping during the day, getting that distracted look on her face as we're talking when she has a random thought about something she's trying to figure out. Leaving sticky notes on my mirror about things she forgot to tell me. Cleaning my place to the edge of spotless and insisting I quit hanging out with her and go do something like fish or have a date or see a game with the guys. Driving me nuts with her protests everything is fine."

"Ever think there — ?"

Jeff held up a hand and gave a small nod toward the open door. Mark looked around.

Gina hesitated, her hand raised to tap on the doorjamb.

"Come on in, sis. We're just coordinating training class schedules."

She looked tired, Mark thought. She wasn't fooling anyone who knew her with those assurances she was fine. Her smile aimed at him was brief, a bit polite but also a touch uncertain.

She had a flash drive in her hand. "I made a model of what I need for the sea trial. It's basic — just three stick submarines moving around in a three-dimensional cube."

"Close the door. Let's see it," Jeff said, holding out his hand.

He plugged in the flash drive and loaded the computer-generated video. Stick submarines appeared, moving around in an ocean box with various marker lines tagging the distances she would like to check.

"I need two subs to basically sit there with cross-sonar running," Gina said, "while another sub travels directly away from them at good speed for six hours, moving above and below a thermal line. Then he turns, comes back on any vector he chooses to rejoin them, and stops within a thousand feet."

Jeff nodded. "Sounds simple enough."

"I have three basic questions," Gina continued. "Does a cross-sonar ping find the moving sub? How far away does it find the sub? And can the sub hear that it's being pinged?"

"What's the kicker?" Mark asked.

"I need the test run in four different parts of the sea," Gina replied. "The quiet of Tufts Plain where ocean noise is minimal. Near the vents at the Schoope Ridge where the ocean is full of geological noise. Near the continental shelf where the ocean is filled with rushing currents and ravines with their echoing sound. And finally in the coastal waters near the shipping lanes where it's filled with man-made noise."

"Add a fifth area — arctic ice," Mark offered. "Glacier ice cracking and falling into the ocean is the most complex background noise out there."

"Perfect, thanks. I need the raw audio for what all three subs hear during the tests. It's going to be a massive amount of data to record."

"Not so bad," Jeff calculated. "Six hours outbound, six inbound, five locations, we'll take high-density drives along to swap out between locations." He reran the video movements. "A simple enough trial design.

We can get all but the sea ice in . . . what"
— he glanced at Mark — "five days, counting transit time?"

"I'd prefer to test ice in the Atlantic, up
around Greenland in January. But for now,
Glacier Bay off the Alaska coast might be
noisy enough to give us a sense of what we
need."

"Glacier Bay would be fine," Gina said.

Jeff shut down the video. "Gina, even if
this works, the Navy may turn the concept
into a studied-forever black hole, trying to
figure out how vulnerable it makes cross-
sonar before they consider putting it into
operational use. Or they will likely get
bogged down running more extensive trials
to satisfy the skeptics that it really works."

"I expect both," she said with a shrug. "I'd
like to hand off the algorithms and the
concept and let someone else take over the
concerns about the fact this can be done. I
know it's dangerous whenever a new capability makes it easier to find and see a
submarine. It's a potential risk to the U.S.
fleet as much as it is a help."

"Don't worry about that part," Mark assured her. "Concentrate on the science. The
Navy is good at adapting to changing reali-
ties. How far away are you from having the
algorithms in place to generate your soft

ping and the echo template?"

"Everything looks ready on the software side. I've been generating pings on demand, checking by hand the echo template created, watching the software search for a match. I don't have it pretty-packaged yet — the code annotated with comments and a software installation program built. I'd suggest for the trial simply swapping in a drive with the updated cross-sonar software, then reverting back to the prior drive with the certified version of cross-sonar once the trial is done. I'll probably need about six hours of time to train the sonar operators on what they need to do."

"I'll talk to Rear Admiral Hardman," Mark said. "Jeff and I can get the trial plan put together. Boat schedules have a window opening up on May 22nd for us to go to sea with the *Nebraska, Ohio,* and *Connecticut.*"

"You're going to sea with us, Gina," Jeff mentioned.

She looked over, startled. "No, Jeff, I'm not."

"You should be there to make sure you're getting the data you need and to diagnose any problems."

"Two subs will be running the new software," she replied quickly. "I can't be on both, so there's no need for me to be on either one. I can explain to the sonar guys what to watch for, and the software's very simple to use — a couple of commands, some data files to save. I'll have all the details written down."

"We'll talk more about that later." Mark stepped in to sideline the subject before it could become an issue. The intensity in her voice had Mark trying to remember an occasion where she'd been down in a sub. He could tell Jeff wasn't clicking into the fact there was actual fear behind Gina's protest. Was she claustrophobic? And wouldn't that be a honey of a problem, for they really did need her out at sea with them on this trial. Otherwise they would have to risk surfacing to send message traffic and try to troubleshoot problems with her onshore, which would seriously complicate getting the accurate trial results they needed.

"How strong a thermal do we need to find, Gina?" Mark asked, hoping to change the subject. "And how often do you need the target sub above and below it?"

His diversion got her to shift her attention from Jeff back to him. Mark jotted notes on the water temperature spread she was looking to get. "There's always a strong thermal around the Gilbert Seamounts. Jeff, touch base with Anderson, see if he can direct us to a likely spot on the Tufts Plain."

"I'll give him a call. And we can probably find an offshoot of the deep-sea current with a thermal near the continental shelf."

"I'll pull the Aquarius satellite data and take a look," Mark agreed. He accepted the flash drive Jeff handed him. "A week, Gina. We'll have the trial plan together."

Jeff tossed the training schedule into the out-box to send over to the Trident Training Facility. "You want to join us for an early lunch, Gina?"

"Thanks for the offer, but I'm heading home."

"You need some sleep," Mark said quietly.

She glanced over at him, accepted his comment with a nod. "I'm done with the long nights of data runs, and the software is solid. I'll catch up on my sleep now, lighten the work hours." She got to her feet. "Call if there's anything you need."

Mark watched her leave. "Have you introduced her to Daniel Field yet?"

"We're having dinner this Friday so I can make a casual introduction. I made it a foursome, Tiffany along with Gina and Daniel, so the conversation shouldn't be a problem even if they don't hit it off."

"He's a nice guy. She'll like him," Mark

predicted.

"I'm hoping she does," Jeff said.

Gina's first impression of Daniel Field was *cute.* Southern charm with the added appeal of California-surfer blond hair and a sleek muscle build. She saw the good humor in his face within moments of sitting down across the table from him. A man for whom laughter and a smile seemed to be the norm of his day. How he had stayed single for so long was a mystery. She could see she had his interest — that was clear when he soon was paying far more attention to her than the sparkling blonde seated beside him. Tiffany, an athlete who owned fitness clubs and gyms, shared Daniel's good looks. But tonight it was Tiffany and Jeff hitting it off. With a deftness that charmed Gina, Daniel rearranged the seating after the salad was delivered for easier conversation with her.

She felt like she always did on a first date: nervous, a touch flustered. She could tell Daniel was trying to impress her. It was in the small things, the fact he rose when she first joined them, held her chair. He asked questions and then kept the conversation casual and on subjects she brought up. She offered as topics Bangor and Chicago, movies and books, then got him talking about boating and surfing — and heard in his voice that she'd uncovered a passion of his. The man loved the water. For him the water was a place to unwind, spend his free time, entertain. He had her laughing as he described trying to teach his nephew to waterski.

The main-course dinner plates were being picked up an hour after they sat down. "Do we want to consider dessert?" Jeff asked around the table.

Tiffany laughed. "Absolutely. I want something rich and chocolate. One benefit of my active job is the freedom to enjoy desserts."

"Gina?"

"Daniel mentioned the Ice Cream Shack is near here. I thought we might go for a walk, share some ice cream. We'll rejoin you and Tiffany in, say, an hour?"

Daniel looked surprised, but he tagged on to the suggestion with pleasure. "A very good idea," he said, already rising to his feet. "I'll cover the dinner tab on the way out, Jeff."

"Thanks — we'll argue about that later."

Gina met her brother's confused look with a slight smile. She realized Jeff could get serious about Tiffany, who probably knew it too. Jeff was the one who didn't seem to have clued in yet. "See you two in an hour." She smiled at both of them and slid her hand into Daniel's to follow him out of the restaurant.

She was determined to use the next hour to break some further ground and find out more about this very attractive man. Was he as good as he looked? First dates were awkward, but second ones were easier. The *Nebraska* wasn't due to leave on patrol for several months. If he asked for a second date, she was going to say yes. She wasn't making an early decision about what she thought of him, but Jeff had been right in one respect. She did like him.

"Nicely done, splitting us off. I appreciate it," Daniel mentioned after paying the table's dinner bill and holding the restaurant door for her.

"My pleasure," Gina replied. "My brother is attempting to avoid the fact that he's falling for Tiffany. I'd like to encourage that relationship along while I'm in Bangor."

"You'll be doing Jeff a very good deed. And I like your suggestion too, may I add. Ice cream is this way." He turned her eastward.

"Can I ask a very personal question, now that we're on our own?" She glanced up at him, then away, feeling shy.

151

He turned her way with a smile. "Sure, if only because I'm curious what matter you consider very personal."

"How come you're not already . . . well, taken?"

"Ah, the 'what's wrong with the not-half-bad-looking guy' question." He laughed. "It's not for lack of trying. I've been engaged three times. The first time her parents objected because we were both only 19, I was heading to the Navy, and she still had a future as a gymnast. They convinced her to break it off.

"The second time was with a fellow Naval Academy graduate. She was heading to a job as a helicopter mechanic, and I was off to Kings Bay for my first submarine patrol. She asked me to call it off after we were engaged eight months. Our schedules kept conflicting, and the wedding date had to be moved twice. The work of a long-distance relationship cooled whatever she thought of me. That one literally broke my heart." He glanced at her, then continued.

"The third time I fell hard for a woman who went to my church back home. She moved out here to get a job, we got engaged, found the house we'd buy after the wedding. But she had a previous boyfriend who tracked her down to Bangor, talked her into changing her mind and giving him another chance. She told him no the first half-dozen times he asked, said she'd moved on and was getting married. But the truth was she was in love with the guy, even I could tell that. I told her we'd put things on hold for six months, that I wasn't going anywhere. But she needed to sort out if she was marrying me because she was over him, or she was marrying me because it hadn't worked out with him, or she was marrying me because she loved me. Within those six months she gave me back the ring, they got married, and it appears to be a happy match. No doubt best for all of us.

"I've got relatives that number close to a hundred when you count second cousins, all wondering at the string of bad luck I'm having getting to the altar. So you are looking at a guy who's still hopeful but also realistic." He shrugged, then concluded, "Life probably is going to throw an additional curve or two at my plans to settle down and raise a family in the best Southern tradition."

"I admit," Gina cautiously offered, "that I've heard stories about guys like you, and I thought they were more legend than fact." She looked over at him briefly. "I've got a more negative track record. I've now had three serious breakups. Kevin was the latest. We'd been seeing each other for two years, and I'm still not sure why he called it off."

Daniel reached over to take her hand. "I'm sorry for it, Gina, but for my sake, I'm glad he did. I'd like very much to get to know you better. There's not a sonarman in the Navy who hasn't heard the rumor that it was a college student who created cross-sonar. Jeff told me it was you when he asked if I'd like to come to dinner and meet you. I would have been thrilled at the introduction even if you were recently engaged. The fact he set up the evening as something of a double date — I feel like that phone call was a gift, and I'm still wondering at my good luck that Jeff called me."

She found it interesting to hear how a sonar guy saw things. "I know cross-sonar is a big deal — I began to realize how big after the Navy classified everything I'd written and created a department just to handle it — but at the time I was working on it, I didn't understand that part of it. To me it was a Ph.D. thesis and a practical attempt at helping my brother to be safer in a sub."

"It's been a very useful tool in the fast-attacks and boomers' tool kit over the last several years. Are you back in Bangor to work on more sonar ideas?"

"A couple of them I'm mulling over. Mainly I'm back to see Jeff and take some time to decide what I want to focus on next." She spotted the ice cream shop ahead. "How about we not discuss work any longer? I love it, I know you do too, but it's . . . well, work."

Daniel chuckled. "Agreed," he said as he swung open the ice cream shop door for her.

Gina finally chose two scoops of ice cream in a bowl — pralines and cream, chocolate marshmallow. Daniel chose a waffle cone with a scoop of raspberry swirl, another of caramel vanilla with pecan clusters.

They walked back toward the restaurant where they'd had their dinner, but at a slow pace to enjoy the evening and their dessert. "This beats a piece of pie," she said around a bite.

"An excellent idea you had," Daniel concurred.

"Jeff told me a few things about you," Gina said. "You were born in Georgia, have three older sisters. I know you play the guitar and are on the Bangor baseball team."

"Jeff told me you're his little sister," Daniel said, "that you're smart, kind, good-looking, and good company. I was amused

155

that he led the list with a reminder you were his little sister — probably a not-so-small warning he's watching out for you. But first impressions, I think he was spot-on with his list."

"Thanks."

"You're welcome. I do like music a great deal and I'm not bad on the guitar. There's a concert next Thursday, opening night at the Seattle's Best Festival. I happen to know two of the guys in the band featured that night. I play backup for them at church when they're leading worship. Would you be interested in getting a bite to eat, taking in some music, and then meeting a few musicians?"

She didn't know much about music but thought it all sounded interesting, experiencing a concert with someone who was so passionate about it. "Sure, that sounds fun."

"Pick you up at five at Jeff's place?"

She smiled. "It's a date. Thank you, Daniel."

"I'll enjoy sharing the evening with you. You can think about the food you like best, and I'll make us reservations somewhere that would be considered upscale casual. Jeans are fine; we'll be walking a bit."

"I'll plan for comfortable shoes." She finished her ice cream. "Would you mind if we did seafood? I know you have it often, living here, but I'm still on Boulder's version of restaurants where seafood is more expensive than steak."

"There's an offbeat restaurant called Burrie Bark — a neighborhood place, not too noisy, with a good variety of fresh-caught seafood. And with a hat-tip to the chef with origins in Louisiana, they have a great Cajun chicken on the menu that I like occasionally."

"Perfect." Gina tossed her empty bowl and spoon into a trash can, wondering at the ease of this evening and how smoothly it had become planning a second date. Life was looking up. He was a guy near her age with a history of hoping to get married. With merely the evening to go on, she liked him a great deal. She glanced over at him. *Could he possibly be the one?* The idea percolated through the back of her mind as he turned the conversation toward family and asked about hers.

Her parents had died in an accident seven years ago. Family for her now meant Jeff, which wasn't much of a conversation point. "Let me see the pictures you have in your wallet," she suggested, knowing there would likely be more than a few. From comments throughout the evening, Daniel was all about family.

Daniel dug his wallet out and simply handed it to her. The first photo under plastic was an older couple. "My parents," Daniel confirmed. She turned the sleeve. "My three sisters." He smiled, then flipped the sleeve to the next. "Half a dozen of various cousins. I'm the designated water-ski instructor. When they hit age 16, they come see me for lessons when I'm home."

"You enjoy the water."

"I like living near an ocean. I love to watch a sunset while out on the boat. Like most guys at Bangor, we trade around our boats. Whoever is just arriving, getting transferred, or retiring will be looking to get rid of a boat or buy one. I keep changing the one I'm using. I like to buy a beat-up one, fix it up, and resell it — gives me something to do that keeps my free days busy, and I like tinkering with a motor. I'm decent with a sail but prefer a motorboat." He glanced over at her. "Could I put a placeholder down for a day on the water with me?"

Gina couldn't think of a reason to decline more substantial than the fact she didn't much like being out on the water. Yet maybe she'd like the water more on a boat with Daniel. "I wouldn't mind a day where you could show me the docks, your current boat, and we could take a brief outing so I could tell how the water and I do together. To be honest, I haven't had much experience on the water."

"A calm day, a few hours out there, and you'll have your answer," he put in reassuringly. "I'm not going to get crushed if you're one who doesn't take to the sea. My mother won't step foot on a boat, even mine, and I rather love her anyway."

Gina felt herself blush and dodged the charming smile directed her way. She motioned toward the restaurant up ahead and glanced at her watch. "We've been an hour?"

"Right at that."

She paused as he laid a hand on her arm. "It's been a pleasure, Gina. And I promise to tell your brother as little as you would like me to say about the evening."

She laughed. "Whatever you like, Daniel, as Jeff and I eventually do talk about most things. Although if he asks me about you, he'll know I have an equal opening to ask about his interest in Tiffany, so I don't expect many questions."

Mark Bishop finished a call with his brother Jim and set the phone aside. He'd established a routine for the days he didn't need to go over to the base. Make coffee, eat breakfast with the newspaper at hand, then work on the home project of the day, which at the moment was in rehabbing the deck. He'd spent the morning buying the new wood he needed, then began tearing up the old planking. He paused for lunch around noon, flipping through a dog-eared cookbook his wife had nearly worn out. A dessert in the oven was a good reminder this was a home, not just a house. He'd get something baking before he fixed himself a sandwich.

It was a beautiful, sunny Tuesday, and he was in no hurry to get back to pulling up old planks. Mark stirred up a batch of brownies, following his wife's notes to improve on it with extra chips and sweetened condensed milk. He had just swiped a finger along the edge of the spatula to taste the chocolate when the doorbell rang. He laid the spatula across the measuring cup, then walked through the house to the front door to see who had stopped by. A good percentage of gold crew eventually found their way to the commander's house to chat, ask a favor, or check out a *Nevada* rumor.

He opened the door. Surprise caused him to still. He shook it off and smiled. "Hello there, Gina. Come on in," he said, pushing open the screen door and stepping out of her way. "I'm just finishing up some brownies. Give me a minute to get them in the oven and I'll be right with you." He walked back to the kitchen, letting her decide if she wanted to follow or not.

He knew she got embarrassed when her speech froze, and it happened too often around him for his comfort, most often in the first few minutes they were together. Delaying the start of a conversation had always seemed like a smart way to finesse the problem. He reminded her of someone, he thought, somebody who'd teased her in the past. He'd ask her, but if he was right, he wasn't sure he was ready to hear that story. And if it wasn't that, then it was because he personally made her nervous, and that would be even more painful to accept.

She joined him in the kitchen.

"Can I get you something? Water? Tea? A soda?" he offered while he scraped the batter into a pan.

"I'm fine."

She walked over to the colored glass bottles displayed on the shelf by the kitchen window. "Your wife collected beautiful things."

"She did," he replied easily. "Melinda liked to hunt garage sales and flea markets

161

for colored bottles. She insisted I not buy them for her at antique stores — too expensive, she thought — but to let her find them by chance. Do you collect anything?"

"Models." She looked faintly embarrassed. "My Chicago home is full of them. Engine cutaways so you can watch various parts move, anatomy teaching models, papier-mâché creations of whatever I'm trying to understand. Models force you to simplify things. I use a lot of food dyes, along with a child's plastic toys when I'm modeling water dynamics."

He smiled at the image. "That sounds like fun."

"A holdover from childhood. The majority of the models I've collected are now badly out of date. These days you can get working models of nearly any system, from blood vessels in the body to the skeleton of a trout — if you visit the websites of various universities. . . ." She drifted to a stop.

Puzzled, Mark glanced over at her, saw the color in her cheeks and watched her push her hands into her back pockets. *Worried she's talking too much.* He really was making her nervous. "Don't knock what works," he reassured her. "Models are hands-on. I'm going to guess Jeff added a good model of the *Seawolf* to your collection?"

"I've got my own submarine fleet," she replied with an embarrassed smile.

"What brings you by, Gina?" he asked matter-of-factly as he set the temperature for the oven to preheat.

She picked up her bag, pulled out a folded page. "Would you be able to add this configuration into your sea trial planning?"

He took the page, looked at it, then back at her.

"I can't explain why," she said, "but I need to see that data."

He assessed that statement, nodded. "Okay. Not a problem." He set aside the page, then waved her to a seat at the kitchen table. "Join me for lunch. I hate to eat alone. I'm having a ham sandwich and chips. Do you want yours heated or cold?"

He really didn't give her an option to say no, and she didn't try to decline. She pulled out a chair. "Cold, please."

He opened the refrigerator and got out deli slices, cheese, Miracle Whip, lettuce, and opened a drawer for a package of hamburger buns. "Your page looks clear enough, but give me the color of it — tell me about the data you want gathered."

"In the various ocean noise profiles, I need

163

the boomer to go silent, provide as minimal a noise signature as possible."

"All-quiet," Mark mentioned. "The command is called 'all-quiet' when we become a silent ghost in the water."

"That's a perfect description of it. I need the other two subs to start cross-sonar and look for the boomer. It's fine if they begin right next to it and can easily see it — I just need them to go out to a distance of about 100 miles running cross-sonar. I need them moving away from the boomer, toward it, below it, and above it. I especially need some solid data with the boomer silently above them. Whether they can see the sub or not isn't important. What I need is the raw acoustical data from the two subs running cross-sonar."

"Your second idea, you're working on a new search algorithm?"

She hesitated. "Something like that," she finally replied. "A very quiet sub, cross-sonar trying to find it, different ocean noise conditions — I'll have what I need to check out something that's been nagging at me."

"I'll add the configuration to the sea trial plan." Mark handed her a plate and a sandwich, found a bag of potato chips. "Jeff mentioned you're considering heading somewhere new after the sonar work is finished here, that you're not going back to Boulder."

She picked up the sandwich, turned the bun to better hold the lettuce and cheese. "I've been working on the oceans for several years. It's time to find a big new territory to explore. The sun interests me. Solar flares, coronal mass ejections — there's some fascinating behavior going on in the sun, and it's a complex, dynamic system, a big data set. That's the common thread in what I enjoy working on most. They are doing some interesting work at the NASA Goddard Space Flight Center out in Maryland, and down at the NASA Jet Propulsion Laboratory in Pasadena. I think I might enjoy working in California."

"It's got nice weather." The oven chimed. Mark got up to put in the brownies and set the timer. "I'm hoping to get you to say yes about coming to sea with us for the trial," he said as he retook his seat.

She licked Miracle Whip off her finger and shook her head. "I can't do it, Mark."

"May I ask why?"

She gave him a rueful glance. "I don't like water that much. I definitely don't like the idea of being underwater in a sub. It's not a few hours we're talking here; it's a few days. I'd be a danger to the boat if I freaked out.

Or I'd get so stressed my speech would freeze, and that would nullify any reason I was there."

"Your nerves would be fine. Really. Being in a submarine is not the sensation you might expect. It's like being in a basement. It's cool, well lit, and busy with people. Would you consider at least trying it before you said no? Ride with us on the *Nebraska* from the pier to the ocean, about a 16-hour journey. If you decide to say no at that point, we'll set you off with the Coast Guard cutter *Vincent* just outside Cape Flattery. I'll personally walk you across to the cutter, and they'll take you back to the Bangor dock."

She was quiet for a good minute before she looked over at him. "I'll think about it, Mark. That's the best I can offer."

"I'll mention one more thing. The boomer you and I would be on will be missile-free for the sea trial. It's coming out of dry dock for maintenance on the missile tubes, and the boomer won't reload new Tridents until it's ready to go back on patrol. Daniel Field is one of the sonar guys on the *Nebraska,* so you'll know someone on board besides me. And there will be four women in the crew, so you'd share a stateroom with them for the days we're at sea."

She nodded. "I heard women were starting to deploy. How has that worked out?"

"Women serving in the submarine fleet is working just fine. The Navy adapts, it always has." He reached for the potato chips. "So did you and Daniel have a good dinner?"

"You heard about that." She glanced over at him, then quickly back at her plate.

Interesting, he thought, that he'd embarrassed her. "I know Jeff was going to introduce you," he offered in explanation.

"He's a very nice man. We're going to a concert at the Seattle's Best Festival Thursday night."

"I've heard it's a great event for music. You'll find someone, Gina. If not Daniel, a guy like him. Don't give up on the dream. Being married is nice."

"You had a good marriage."

"I had a very good marriage," he confirmed. He'd already embarrassed her; he might as well ask the question he'd wondered about. "Want to talk about what happened with Kevin?"

She shook her head. "No. Three in a row end up in a breakup, the particulars don't matter so much anymore, just the pattern." She pushed back her plate. "There are days being smart feels more like a curse than a blessing."

"I can sympathize, even if I don't fully understand what it's been like." He heard old hurts in her statement, ones she obviously wasn't interested in talking about, and he chose to move them to a new topic. "Jeff's arrived safely in Boulder?"

She smiled. "He's been there two days, and he already nearly broke his ankle skiing new snow. He's having a good time. He was packing my apartment this morning. Jeff admits to one close call with a lamp and a cracked picture frame. I'm just relieved he's taking care of the apartment for me so I don't have to go back. My belongings will soon be in boxes headed to Chicago."

"You were wise to decide to move on," Mark said. As it looked now, Jeff would be back five days before the sea trial got under way — enough time to review the trial plan, pack, and convince Gina she should come with them. Jeff would coordinate the sea trial on the *Connecticut,* and Mark would take Gina with him on the *Nebraska* if they could get her to say yes. "Anything else I can do for you while he's gone?"

"I'm fine, Mark, but thanks for asking." She pushed back her chair. "I need to get going. I didn't mean to interrupt your day."

"You should stay for dessert. Brownies will be done in a few minutes."

"Which is why I'm leaving before that happens. I won't be able to resist."

He walked with her through the house. "I hope you think seriously about coming along for the sea trial, Gina. I think Jeff would like you to experience what he does for a living, at least once."

She bit her lip, and he wanted to reach over and stop the gesture — he'd seen it a couple of times now. She was nervous, uncertain . . . both.

"I'm not one for trying new adventures, Mark. I find they often end up badly for me."

"Trust me and say yes anyway," he recommended. He glanced at the street. "Security is with you?"

She nodded. "Connolly drove. He's been insisting lately that I let them chauffeur me around."

"Good. Let them. At least while this sonar work is under way. Jeff and I will worry less about you then."

"It makes me feel strange, the security."

"It's for both your sake and the Navy's."

"I know. I just wish it wasn't necessary. It's another reminder of how un-normal my life is."

Mark understood that was the real distress she felt, the difference between her life and what she thought of as a "normal" one. She'd spent a lifetime being different from her peers. "There's a difference between what's normal for others and what's normal for you," he told her. "Life gets easier when you can accept that," he added, trying to offer some advice without being pushy.

"Is yours different from normal?"

"How many people do you know who answer the phone in the middle of the night, wondering if it might be the President of the United States on the other end? He has the phone number of every ballistic missile commander. If things are beginning to get hot somewhere in the world, we hear directly from the commander in chief before we leave on patrol."

She looked away, then glanced back. "North Korea?"

Mark didn't confirm or deny it. The North Korean regime was unstable, had nuclear weapons, was making progress on mobile missile launchers, and had ripped up the armistice agreement that had kept peace, such as it was, on the peninsula. One of the real fears was a North Korea opening move of a nuclear bomb dropped on the South Korean capital of Seoul. "Think of normal as being what God intends for your life," Mark said. "Un-normal is everything that's something other than His plans for you. Life gets easier that way, Gina. Go ahead and stress about what you should care about, but ignore the rest."

She half smiled. "That's experience speaking?"

"Some. When you can't simplify your life, you can simplify what you choose to care about. You'll never be able to control where your science takes you. You won't be able to control things like security decided by others. You can decide what you're going to be responsible for, and let the rest flow off as just what is."

"When Daniel and I went for a walk and ice cream on Friday night, he never mentioned the security that was following me."

"He noticed it, Gina. And I am confident in saying it's not going to be on his list of concerns about going out with you. The fact you come with unusual factors just makes you one of a kind. It doesn't make you odd."

"You really think so?"

"Not all guys are idiots like Kevin. Ask Daniel next Thursday what he thinks about the security. I'll predict it's not going to be an issue."

"At least it's temporary," Gina replied.

Mark didn't correct her, even though he knew it was likely she would be designated a national security asset and that security would become permanent. It would be better to first get her to accept the idea of temporary security, then when it became necessary, help her through the fact it wasn't going to end. "I hope you and Daniel have a good time at the concert."

Gina nodded. "Thanks for the lunch, Mark," she said, giving him a full smile, then heading down the walk to the waiting car. For the second time in as many weeks, Mark felt the impact of one of Gina's full smiles. His "You're welcome" was a beat late. After she slipped into the passenger seat of the car, he closed the front door of the house and heard the oven timer go off. He headed back to the kitchen. Gina would be fine. And Daniel Field was a lucky man.

7

The USS *Ohio* and the USS *Connecticut* were already away from the pier, heading out to the Pacific. USS *Nebraska* was in final preparations to push away, the tugboats coming into position. Bishop pulled down on the *Nevada* ball cap the wind was trying to carry off his head. Rain had swept through overnight, leaving the morning clear and crisp with a typical southwesterly wind coming across the Hood Canal.

Jeff had boarded the *Connecticut* with a last-minute warning that Gina might change her mind. Bishop was determined not to let that happen. He stood on the pier and watched her walk toward him. He could tell she was still gathering her courage to do this. He stepped forward and took the duffel bag she carried.

She was dressed in jeans and tennis shoes along with two layers of shirts as he had recommended. He handed off the duffel bag to a seaman, who hustled across the walk-way with it. *Get her things below, before she changes her mind.* Bishop smiled when her gaze met his. He didn't have any problem guessing her thoughts at the moment.

"We'll walk across to the deck, go down the aft ladder," he told her calmly. "I'll take you through the boat to the command-and-control center, where I'll introduce you to the *Nebraska*'s commander, John Neece, our host for this sea trial. Then I'll take you forward to the sonar room where you'll be working and get you situated. Daniel Field will already be there. If you want to bypass a conversation for any reason, just bump my arm or squeeze my hand, and I'll step in."

She nodded.

"You'll have 15 hours before you have to make a yes or no decision, so just relax and enjoy this, Gina. You haven't committed yet. You can step off to the Coast Guard cutter *Vincent,* and they'll bring you back to this very pier if you decide not to go on the sea trial. The sea is relatively calm today, so the transition from sub to cutter won't be a hard one to make. We're good?"

"Yes. We're good."

"You got some sun," he mentioned, stall-ing for another moment in hopes she'd relax a bit more.

"Daniel took me out on his boat."

"Enjoy it?"

"The time with him, the dock and the lunch and the 'I did that' experience of it — yes. The water, not so much."

Bishop chuckled. "He didn't try to talk you into learning to water-ski?"

She shook her head. "He's a smart man, Daniel Field. He said I looked cute in the life vest he insisted I wear, and partway through the day on the water he pulled out the navigation maps and put me to work plotting our course, then taught me to use the radio properly. That was fun. He promised to teach me how to use the depth finder next time so I can find where the fish are congregating."

"You'll enjoy that." Bishop reached for her hand. "Jeff and I, Daniel, we spend a lot of our lives on submarines. There are a hundred guys just like us on the *Nebraska*. So you're going to trust us for the next few hours and not worry about where you are. You're just going to keep busy thinking about the task at hand and learning something new. Okay?"

She solemnly nodded once more.

"Here we go." He headed across the walkway, her hand in his. "When we're on a catwalk in the missile bay, just look at the person in front of you rather than down."

"You had to mention that."

"We could use the ladder in the forward sail and go down directly into the command-and-control center, but I think it will help you to see just how big this submarine is if we use the aft ladder and traverse through the boat." The sailor on the deck getting ready to throw the mooring line off one of the cleats gave her an encouraging smile. Word was around the boat that this sea trial was hosting a VIP, and it hadn't taken the crew long to figure out it was a woman coming aboard to work with the sonar group.

Mark stepped off the walkway onto the black curved hull of the boat, walked with her across the surface toward the back of the sub. "You can't close your eyes when you go down a ladder. Just move slowly. I'll go first. I won't let you fall." He stepped down the ladder, kept a hand on her ankle to make sure she had her footing on the step before she moved down.

She was cautious on the first steps until she descended far enough to get a handhold on a rung, and then she got a bit more comfortable. There were a lot of rungs. She took the final step off the ladder, glanced around, then looked at him.

She still seemed tentative, he thought. "It's quite a hike from here," he said. "A boomer is nearly two football fields long." He got a small smile from her. "Watch the door hatches so you clear your footing," he cautioned. He took her hand again and led her through the boomer, along narrow passageways. Curiosity had her looking around at everything. She was quiet, and he'd been expecting that — just not this quiet. She'd asked not a single question during the journey. He would have explained what they were passing, but he wanted to leave it for another tour, and make satisfying her curiosity a reason for her to decide to stay on board.

"Welcome to the command-and-control center," Bishop said, easing her into the room just ahead of him so she could have an unobstructed look around the busy room. It was fully staffed with nine men and one woman now at stations.

The commander of the USS *Nebraska,* John Neece, came over to meet them. "Welcome to the *Nebraska,* Miss Gray."

"Thank you, Captain."

"Bishop." John offered his hand. "It's good to have you aboard."

"Thanks for the use of your boat, John."

"It's going to be a pleasure trip, Bishop, compared to some. We're ready to sail. Come join us topside if you like, Gina, once we're in transit. There's no place like the bridge of a sub for enjoying how beautiful this stretch of Washington State really is."

"Thank you, sir."

Bishop pointed. "Head through that passageway, Gina. The sonar room is just forward."

Daniel Field got to his feet as they appeared in the doorway, smiled at Gina. "Welcome to my office, Gina. You can sit here beside me, and I'll walk you through the operations. But first let me introduce you to the other sonar guys on this watch. I'd like you to meet Kerns, Waller, and Dugin."

She nodded at the introductions and took the seat he had indicated.

Bishop squeezed her shoulder, leaned over to whisper, "Relax." She glanced up to give him a brief smile.

Bishop stepped out of the sonar room, caught the attention of Lieutenant Junior Grade Sharon Walters waiting to join them. "Thanks for volunteering for this, Sharon."

"My pleasure, sir."

"It's a coin flip whether she's staying, so for now just explain what's happening on the boat as we make the transit and answer any questions she might ask. Don't be surprised if she's pretty quiet. You know how to handle it if she can't get the next word out?"

"Jeff explained. I'm good, sir. I'll send someone to find you."

Bishop stepped back into the sonar room. "Gina, I would like you to meet one more person. This is Lieutenant Sharon Walters. She'll be your sea buddy for this trip. Anywhere you go in the boat, if Daniel or I are not with you, she will be. She's a fountain of knowledge about how everything works, so ask anything you like."

Gina nodded. "It's nice to meet you, Sharon."

"This is going to be fun," Sharon replied with a smile.

Bishop briefly rested a hand on Gina's shoulder again. "I'm going to be topside with the captain."

Gina glanced up. "Better you than me."

Bishop grinned. "Enjoy your first sail. Take good care of her, Daniel."

"Will do, sir."

Bishop paused at the sonar room door, saw Gina's seat was empty, though Daniel was still there.

"Gina's doing fine, Commander. Sharon took her on a tour to show her the stateroom where she'd be bunking, then they were going to the officers' wardroom to see what's for dinner."

The sea trial notebook was open in front of Daniel, and Bishop could see he had been reading ahead, looking at the upcoming locations. The men he had requested for the first sonar watch were all here. They had high enough security clearance levels to read them in on the true purpose of the sea trial, and they had been individually approved by Rear Admiral Hardman to know the details. Bishop closed the door. "Questions?" He knew Gina wouldn't have been discussing the specifics.

"The test references a cross-sonar ping — that's obviously new," Daniel said.

"She may have designed an active ping that can't be heard. We're going to check its range and see if our target sub can figure out he's being pinged."

Silence met his simple summary. The other men glanced between each other. "You're not kidding, are you?" Dugin finally asked.

Bishop smiled, shook his head. "No."

"The *Ohio* is our target?"

"Yes."

"And he won't hear us looking for him?"

"I doubt he has even a hint that something is happening. The active ping isn't just buried in the ocean noise, it *is* ocean noise."

"She's using ocean noise as the ping? Gina got that to work?" Daniel blinked as that settled in. "How very cool. Who else knows about this?"

"Rear Admiral Hardman signed off on you four as the sea trial team. So it's the four of you, your captain, Jeff on the *Connecticut* to swap the data drives from their vantage point, the sonar chief on the *Ohio* to capture what they are hearing — if anything — Gina, Rear Admiral Hardman, and me. That's it for who you can discuss this with. We're clear on that?"

"Yes, sir," Waller replied for the group.

"If this sea trial proves a cross-sonar ping works, and the effective range looks interesting, then this software and the capability will be handed off to the Undersea Warfare Center to figure out how to deal with the fact it can be done and to think about deploying it as a capability across the fleet."

"You've *got* to convince Gina to stay aboard, sir," Daniel said. "She's got to be here to see this work."

"I'm hoping she will stay," Bishop agreed. "But she's trained Jeff and me on how her new software works in case she decides to leave, and she's convinced me we could handle the sea trial without her if necessary. We'll focus during the next five days on answering two questions. What's the effective range of a cross-sonar ping? And does the target hear the ping? We get those questions answered across various sea conditions, and this is going to be a good trip."

"A fascinating five days," Daniel concurred.

"You said the ladies were eventually heading to the officers' wardroom?" Bishop asked.

"Yes."

Bishop left the men to talk among themselves about the trial plan, and he went to find Sharon and Gina.

Gina was working on a dish of chocolate ripple ice cream. Sharon was finishing a cheeseburger and fries. Gina had found a friend, Bishop thought, listening in on their conversation as he poured himself a cup of coffee. He settled into a seat beside Gina. "We're coming up on the decision point, Gina. Would you like to stay, or do you wish to go?"

She gave it a moment of thought before she nodded. "I'm good to stay. I can't say knowing we're diving is going to be pleasant, but I'll cope. The *Nebraska* is a huge place, Bishop, and crowded."

"Boomers are the nicest subs in the fleet. A fast-attack is a bit tighter."

"What can I get you, Commander?" the petty officer serving the wardroom asked.

"A cheeseburger and fries look fine, thanks."

Bishop picked up the phone on the wall. "Captain, Bishop. Take us under at your discretion. A shallow angle, for our guest's comfort, please."

Within a minute the order "Dive, dive, dive" came over the *Nebraska* intercom, the dive alarm sounded, and the order to dive repeated. The ballast tanks filled with water with an encompassing *whoosh*. Bishop watched Gina, saw her look up.

"You don't give a girl time for second thoughts."

He just smiled. "If you have to know where we're at, the station boxes throughout the ship will give you the keel depth and our location. If we were carrying missiles, the boxes would be dark, as it's then classified information even for the crew aboard the boat."

"I can avoid looking at that for a while."

"We've met up with the *Ohio* and the *Con-*

necticut. They're cruising about 20 miles to our west, confirming the area is clear with cross-sonar. We're going to travel in a pack for the next eight hours. The plan is to get some sleep, then begin the sea trial at the start of the next watch. We'll be approaching the Schoope Ridge by then, making the first test an ocean filled with geological sea noise. Then we'll turn southwest and conduct a test over the Tufts Plain."

"I don't know if I'll be able to sleep."

"You'll sleep, and probably deeply," Bishop predicted. The petty officer brought him in his meal, and Bishop reached for the ketchup. "After the first 10 to 20 hours aboard the boat, the newness wears off, and this is going to start to feel monotonous — a lot of traveling, running the sonar tests, and traveling some more. Once the first sea trial test is finished and we've been through the process, your constant presence in the sonar room won't be necessary. Plan to sleep whenever you feel tired. We'll wake you if we need you."

Bishop felt the boat's slight tilt ease off and glanced at the station box. They were 380 feet underwater. "We're level now, will likely stay at this depth for the next several hours."

"It's smooth. I thought there would be a

sensation of rocking like a boat has."

He shook his head. "The transit on the surface from Bangor out to the Pacific was the roughest part of the ride. Once submerged, a submarine will stay smooth like this."

Bishop ate a French fry, picked up the cheeseburger, and watched as Gina kept glancing over to the display showing their depth. "Feeling nerves about being underwater?"

"My stomach is queasy," she admitted.

"If it helps, remember that we can be on the surface from this depth in under a minute in an emergency ascent. All a guy in the control room has to do is throw the chicken switches — the two heavy metal levers above the ballast tank status board — and we go up fast. It will feel like a very quick elevator ride."

"I'll remember. Sharon told me about angles and dangles."

Bishop shot the lieutenant a look, not thrilled to hear it. Angles and dangles were designed to shake loose anything on the sub not attached and stored properly, which might make noise later in a patrol and cause problems. The sub would go through 20-plus-degree ascents and descents, angled turns and fast stops, over a period of 30 or more minutes. It was a roller-coaster ride and not for the faint of heart.

"She asked," Sharon shrugged, amused at his look. "She also asked where you were bunking, but I wasn't sure of that answer."

Bishop glanced over at Gina. "The captain and XO both offered to share their bunks, depending on the watch." He saw Daniel Field in the doorway and waved him in. The watch had changed. "If you're good here, Gina, I'm going to go make a call on the chief engineer. He's a friend from academy days."

"I'm good. Thanks for talking me into this, Bishop," Gina said.

"I'll do my best not to steer you wrong," he promised. "Daniel, get her to laugh. She's nervous about the depth."

Daniel grinned. "Glad to, sir."

"Couldn't sleep?" Bishop asked quietly. Gina had a game of solitaire laid out on the officers' wardroom table.

"Wide awake," she admitted. "The chief of the boat just left. We had a fascinating discussion about his career as a submariner. I'm glad you got me here, Mark. There's so much to learn."

"I'm relieved you're enjoying it. Still nervous about being underwater?"

"Intensely, but not thinking about it. Until you asked me," she added with a slight smile.

"Yours is a good solution," Bishop replied with an answering smile, "and I won't ask any more about that unless you want to tell me." He filled a cup with coffee and sat down to keep her company. He'd spent the last three hours in engineering reminiscing with the man who'd been the best man at his wedding. He didn't feel like turning in yet himself. He watched her scanning the cards looking for a move, reached over and tapped the red six to show her the last remaining play. She made the move, turned the card faceup, and it led to no further moves. The game couldn't be won. Gina gathered up the cards and slid them back into the box.

"They are serving midrats — the midnight meal — if you would care for something to eat," he suggested.

She shook her head. "I've eaten more in the last few hours than I do in a typical day."

"It's one of three primary things to do on a submarine. Work, eat, sleep."

She looked over at him. "How does it feel to be out here at sea and not be in command?"

"Very odd," Bishop replied, surprised

she'd thought to ask the question. "The instinct to be in charge runs deep. Hence my own restlessness. I am impressed, though, by what I've seen. John Neece and his *Nebraska* blue crew do this job very well. They may win the battle E this year, and it would be well deserved."

Gina got up and put the cards away, poured herself a cup of coffee. It was one of the few Bishop had seen her drink. When she sat down across from him, sipping at it, he thought it was more about having something in her hands than actually wanting the beverage.

Her expression turned serious, and she pushed the mug in a small circle on the table, then looked at him. "Would you mind talking to me about why you do the job you do, Mark? It's been an underlying thread in a lot of conversations I've had on this sub, but no one discusses it directly. You would fire one of those missiles on a presidential order."

"Yes," he replied simply, leaving it at that.

"I don't understand military life, how you can adjust to the knowledge you would be killing so many people when you do your job." She glanced at him again, motioned with her hand in an apology. "I didn't mean that as a criticism or an insult. It's just . . .

this is unlike any other job I've ever talked about with someone."

He could tell she wanted to understand, and this was one of the rare cases where he would like to pursue the conversation so she did understand. "I'm a realist, Gina, with a deep appreciation of good and evil," he replied. "You can't simply hope that wars never happen again. The presence of a strong military is a deterrent to war. A functioning military is designed as much to keep the peace as it is to win a war when it becomes necessary to fight."

"You don't think a fleet of boomers carrying a bunch of nuclear weapons is a bit of overkill in today's world?" she wondered.

"No. There is great hope my job will be a lifetime of peaceful patrols without a missile ever being fired. I pray for that. But the boomers' presence at sea is a strong statement to anybody toying with the idea of unleashing their own nuclear or chemical weapons." Bishop had these philosophical conversations occasionally while fishing with fellow submariners, but he avoided them as a rule with civilians. Gina was listening carefully, wanting to know the *why* of it, and he decided to condense a lifetime of thinking about the matter into a few points that might help her.

"First principles, Gina? The building blocks?"

She nodded.

"God made a world that was all good, but because He also gave people free will, the potential for evil was there from the beginning. God didn't make evil, but He allowed for the possibility of it in order for His gift of free will to have substance and be real. It took men using that free will to sin to make evil actually happen. Ever since that first conflict between what God wanted and what man wanted, evil has taken different forms. Murder has been in our history since the beginning. Nations going to war are simply a larger expression of that conflict between individual men."

Gina pushed aside the coffee mug. "Having the most lethal weapons means you win the war if and when it comes."

"Something like that," Bishop agreed. "Gina, I'm neutral in answering the underlying question you pose — was it a good thing or bad that nuclear weapons were created? I've thought about it a lot over the years.

"Look at history before and after the development of nuclear weapons. World War I involved massive-scale chemical warfare. Ten million people in the military and another six million civilians died in that war. World War II killed sixty million people, twenty-five million in the military, and another thirty-five million civilians. We've had a very bloody history before there were nuclear weapons.

"Then nuclear weapons appeared at the end of that war. The atomic bombings of Hiroshima and Nagasaki killed two hundred fifty thousand people, as the radiation of the blasts continued to kill its victims over the next few years. There is no question that nuclear weapons are incredibly destructive. But those nuclear bombs also brought to an end World War II, stopped the horrendous losses of life on the battlefields and in the camps."

He looked across the table at her, still listening intently. "A credible argument can be made that nuclear weapons have stopped World War III from ever beginning. The weapons are sufficiently powerful to halt two large armies from colliding again directly. Thus the Cold War began, and proxy wars were fought in places like Vietnam. Deaths in wars have continued in the hundreds of thousands across the years, but not on the scale as in the first two world wars.

"I would launch a nuclear weapon on valid orders from the president because I understand there are circumstances where a nuclear weapon may be the lesser of two evils. No rational leader is going to use a nuclear weapon in times of peace. In times of war —" he paused a moment — "the use of a nuclear weapon to end a conflict might actually be the right thing to do. The deaths that would result are on one side of the ledger, seen against the deaths that would result from the war continuing on.

"The U.S. maintains a credible nuclear deterrent against other countries that might attack us with nuclear or chemical weapons. Our weapons stay aimed and ready to launch in order to keep that deterrent a viable and real-time truth. No one challenges that deterrent because it is sufficient and real. True power is the power to keep the peace."

Gina carefully thought through his words. "Hence the term *superpower.* With such an overwhelming strength, our adversaries avoid direct confrontations with us."

"Yes. You know, Gina, I think a lot about David, a man who fought a lot of wars but who also had a heart after God. I would prefer the world to be at peace. I pray for that. But I also know I am one of the final cards in the deck. There are 28 men this nation trusts with half the deployed nuclear arsenal. I'm one of them. The president can count on me to follow his orders if they ever come."

"Does it feel like a burden?"

"It feels like the weight of the world on some days," Bishop admitted. He breathed in deeply. "I treat the job with the utmost of care. The *Nevada* gold crew works hard to run the boat with excellence. From what I've seen of *Nebraska* blue, this crew is also exceptional. The boomers are manned by some of the most hardworking Navy men and women in the service. It's an honor to serve with them. We all carry that burden to one degree or another, and none more so than the captain."

She propped her elbow on the table and rested her chin on her hand. "Why did you choose the sea? Of all the places you could have chosen to serve, why the Navy?"

He smiled. "I settled on being a submariner when I was 15. I grew up in Chicago, like you. Family vacations were a chance to visit the coasts. My parents like to explore historical sites, and my brothers and I, along with my sisters, loved to find a good beach.

"Oceans are huge. I'd look at the surface of the sea and wonder what was lurking beneath. The fact there was a job that would let me spend most of my days sailing around deep in the oceans seemed like an ideal adventure. And I guess I'm wired to protect people. A military life was a common mission with a group of like-minded men where I would easily find my place.

"I was smart enough that there would be scholarships to pay for college, but joining the Navy and heading straight through with them opened doors to some of the nuclear-engineering hands-on training, letting me pursue degrees at the Naval Postgraduate School and the Naval War College. I've never regretted that decision."

He paused to finish his coffee, then said, "I'm like Jeff in many ways. Submarines are an open door to the exploration of new territories. I love being underwater in the middle of an ocean."

"Jeff really loves the sea too. Every time I visit I can tell — he's a man doing his dream job."

"We both are." Bishop set aside his mug. "What you are doing with sonar really matters, Gina. We are blind out here, dependent on what we can hear. No one values more what you've been able to contribute in sonar breakthroughs than we do."

"It's good science," she agreed, then stopped. "Up until it starts to be used by others against the United States, making it possible for enemies to find you when before they could not." She shook her head. "I've got security around me, Mark, around the clock. It's pretty obvious how concerned the Navy is about the espionage threat."

"There will come a day when what you've figured out is known by other countries, ones we wish would not have the knowledge," Bishop agreed. "Don't worry about it. We'll be prepared with new tactics long before that day arrives. Others would still have to have the technology to exploit it, would have to see us before we see them, and be close enough to do something with the knowledge. The key is the fact we know the science first. Don't underestimate how valuable that timing is. It won't come as a surprise to us. First knowledge gives us a significant advantage."

He reached over and gently tapped a finger on her hand. "We need to know those ideas of yours, Gina. All of them. Don't hold back. We need to know what you can discover, even if the truth comes with complex implications and new Navy departments to manage it. Cross-sonar changed this profession. Cross-sonar with an active ping may be on the verge of doing so again. And that's a good thing, not bad. We'll adapt and manage to the new reality. It's what the Navy does."

She looked away, then back at him, her expression troubled. "Do you understand how much pressure I feel when you say that? Ideas are dangerous, Mark. You can understand that better than most."

He knew she needed to adapt to that pressure, needed to cope with what would inevitably be part of her work life. He changed the conversation slightly, curious about something. "Why are you afraid about where science might take you? Do you feel if you find something that has both good and bad implications, it's something you should not have discovered?"

She took a deep breath and let it out. "What I do has consequences. I would rather work on something that has better odds of helping than causing problems."

"An admirable goal. How many ideas do you dismiss because you aren't sure what the good or bad implications might be?"

"Lots — that's a normal course of events."

"You apply a moral filter to what ideas you work on."

"Of course."

Bishop understood it, but found her perspective interesting. "Science is the study of what God created. Your discovery of something doesn't change its existence. It's already there. If you figure it out, or some-one else does, does that change things?"

"It does for me. I don't want to find out things that are dangerous, Mark. It makes me feel queasy when I do."

"That's a lot of self-prescribed guilt to be carrying around, Gina, and not reflective of how things are. You can't see the future, where something might go, or what one discovery might lead to that might improve the outcome of another one."

"But I can be careful."

"As long as careful doesn't mean you are denying who God designed you to be — curious, smart, and figuring things out. I think you may be carrying the wrong bur-den, one I know you were never meant to carry. You don't know where science will lead, but that's the whole point of being as smart as you are. You're on the edge of what is known, and there's lots of new territory out there. Being afraid to step out and explore, to see what's there, isn't what God had in mind for you. I'm certain of that."

"If I find something that will put Jeff in more danger, I should just accept that?"

"You're assuming you're the only one who will find it, Gina. Maybe you are the *first,* but you will not be the *only.* Answer me this. If today China could actively ping and we couldn't hear them, the correct response on your part to protect your brother would be to figure out what they were doing so this nation — so Jeff — wouldn't be vulnerable. You would be racing to solve this science as quickly as you could, right?"

"Yes."

"So it's good science if someone else finds it first, and you're hurrying to catch up to what they are doing? But it's bad science if you're the first one to see it?"

She bit her lip. Bishop reached over and covered her hand with his. "Gina, the world can survive just fine with whatever you find. You're smart, and that wasn't a death sentence. It's a tool God gave you to become who you were created to be."

"So whatever the results are with this sea trial, it's a good thing?"

Bishop smiled. "Yes. Absolutely."

"Your view of the world is so amazingly simple."

Bishop laughed. And she realized what she had said. She blinked. "I probably shouldn't have implied a guy who commands a ballistic missile submarine has a simple world view."

"I don't know," Bishop replied, still chuckling. "It was a first."

She looked embarrassed, and he eased her

away from it. "It's hard on you being smart — I do understand that, Gina. I'll never have to wrestle with the questions you do. But I've known you a few years. You carry too much worry, not enough curiosity and joy. Relax."

Bishop searched to find the right words. "Please understand something. God didn't create evil in the world, but He did create free will, which allowed for the possibility of evil. Science isn't like that. What you explore and find, God did create. It already exists. When you find it, you are discovering something God made. And everything God created is good. God said so in Genesis. He looked around at everything He had made and said, 'It is very good.' "

She stared down at her hands as his point registered with her.

"How men use science can be evil, I'm with you a hundred percent on that," Bishop added. "People can misuse items God created. But that has everything to do with man's free will and tendency to evil, not science. What God created is good. So do what you were created to do. Break new scientific ground. Help us understand the dynamics of what God created.

"You can't protect the world from itself, Gina. You can only give good men the tools necessary to do their jobs. We need to know what is possible. Quit fighting a battle with yourself over who you are. You're an explorer, and a very gifted one. I'm personally going to enjoy watching what you figure out over the next decade." He leaned forward, shocked to see her blinking back tears. "Hey, there."

She wiped her eyes with the palms of her hands. "I've heard the opposite of that so many times." She sniffed and tried to smile. "I think I'm tired."

"No, I think I somehow just stepped on your personal gremlin. I'm sorry, Gina. I come on way too strong at times."

"Don't be, please. An intentional conversation of substance is something I crave and hardly ever get. You just somehow managed to run right over what Kevin said, but in the opposite direction."

"Well, in that case, ditto, and repeat everything I just said."

She laughed shakily. "I'm going to go get a couple hours' sleep before we find out the answer to the current sixty-four-thousand-dollar question — does a cross-sonar ping work or not?"

Bishop nodded. "Do that. And enjoy this discovery, whatever the outcome. It's a good thing."

"I'm coming to believe that." She pushed away from the table. "Good night, Mark."

"You know the way to the stateroom?"

"I do."

"Then sleep well, Gina."

He watched her head out. He got up and got himself another cup of coffee. Somewhere in that conversation had been several profound points, and he tried to put them into a coherent memory, knowing he wanted to bring Gina back to this topic again. She didn't say much most of the time, and yet this level of analysis sat just below that silence. He'd give her one thing, she wasn't boring. She might struggle with her words occasionally, may not have found her footing with a serious relationship, but it was not because there wasn't substance there to unpack.

"Jesus, I know you understand her. I wish I did," Mark prayed quietly as he found a spoon to stir sugar into his coffee. "Your insights would be welcome. I need them."

She worried about finding out something new, because of what someone might one day do with the information, Bishop thought. It was his best answer to what was going on. She tied herself in mental knots. She wasn't timid. She was simply afraid of how smart she was, what she might figure out. He knew that was the core problem.

He had no idea how to help ease that stress she felt. She was approaching 30 and was far ahead of current knowledge in her own fields of study. For the next 30 or 40 years, she would be stepping out onto new terrain. Either she was mentally ready for the pressure of that, or she was going to choke and pull back from who she was just to find some peace. And if she did so, the Navy and the country were going to lose a talent the world couldn't replace. *Gina, the genius.* God had made her unique, one of a kind.

Bishop didn't understand why she had crossed his path rather than someone else's, someone better suited for this. But he wasn't one to ignore what was in front of him. She needed a better footing for who she was and what she was doing with her life. He could at least relate and help her wrestle that one to an answer. He just wished she had more years of experience to help with her perspective.

She was too young. He knew that was a key part of the problem. Too young to figure this out on her own. Jeff could help her, but maybe he was simply too close, too much her only family, to give Gina the clear mirror she needed. Daniel would be able to help her if she let him, but Bishop thought Gina would use the new relationship more as a distraction from the science than as a way to help resolve the matters she wrestled with.

She wasn't going to have an easy future until she got this settled in her own mind. Was science good and to be explored, or was it to be cautiously weighed for its good and evil potential before she pursued it? The truth was somewhere in the middle of that Gordian knot.

He had to live with the fact he could follow orders and by doing so kill upwards of a million people. Bishop rubbed the back of his neck and accepted that God probably *had* dropped her across the right person's path. He had spent more days inside his own Gordian knot than he would care to admit. He'd found his peace. Gina would too, with enough time and help sorting out the questions.

8

Bishop stood at the back of the sonar room, monitoring events as the first of the sea trial tests got under way. Daniel Field was thumbing through the setup pages, pausing occasionally to consult with Gina beside him. Bishop was content to watch them work, knowing it would give Gina more confidence to be in the middle of things. He was responsible for the sea trial, but part of leadership was in knowing how to trust others to do their jobs, to monitor what was happening and step in only if necessary.

"Recorders are capturing all audio data?" Daniel asked.

"Affirmative," Waller replied.

"The area is clear of other subs listening in on us?"

"All clear," Kerns confirmed.

Daniel picked up the phone. "Control, sonar. We are ready to begin the sea trial, Captain." He nodded, put down the phone, and turned the page in the trial plan. "Let's get started. Gina, would you like to start cross-sonar? Link us with the *Connecticut.*"

She hesitated briefly, then leaned over to use his keyboard and typed the command to turn on cross-sonar. Bishop watched as the link came active and the screens filled in with the additional *Connecticut* sonar data.

"Cross-sonar is running. We've got a good link," Daniel confirmed. "Running a cross-sonar search." He sent the command. "Do we see the USS *Ohio*?"

"Yes, faintly," Kerns replied. "He's on bearing 260, moving directly away from us. Range is . . . 46 miles."

"We wait for him to disappear outside the range of cross-sonar," Daniel instructed.

Minutes passed with Daniel occasionally triggering a cross-sonar search.

"We've lost contact with the USS *Ohio,*" Kerns finally announced. "I've got a quiet screen."

"Set a clock for five minutes," Daniel told Dugin, who reached to set a timer on his console.

Bishop gave Gina a smile when she glanced back at him. This was the norm of submarine operations, the waiting between events. But when he was in charge of the boat, there was always something going on to occupy the captain. This time it was simply waiting.

Daniel picked up his headphones, moved a cursor over a line of noise patterns on the waterfall screen before him, listened, then tapped his screen as he smiled. "There may not be any submarines or surface ships around to hear your idea tried out for the first time, Gina, but you do have an audience of dolphins. Going by the sounds, I'd say 40 or more of them are fishing as a group, circling a school of mackerel, then darting through the mass to grab and catch a fish to eat." He handed her the headphones to listen for herself.

Her smile widened. "All these clicks — they're using their echo sonar to confuse the fish?"

"Yes. A school of fish gets spooked, they tighten the cluster they're in, which makes for better fishing for the dolphins."

Daniel took the headphones when she handed them back and cued the audio into a side file for the marine biologist.

The timer chimed. "That's five minutes, Daniel."

Bishop straightened. It was now or never for Gina's idea. Daniel looked back at him, then at Gina. "You should do the honors,"

Daniel offered.

"I'm too nervous. You do it. Send a cross-sonar ping," Gina replied, leaning forward in the chair, her hands gripped between her knees.

Daniel typed the command.

Bishop scanned the numerous displays, watching for a change.

"He's lit up like a Christmas tree!" Dugin exclaimed, jazzed. The broadband console stack showed the *Ohio* in bold brightness across the waterfall display. Even the narrowband console stack had a good picture of it in the trace.

Gina closed her eyes and laughed. Daniel reached over and patted her back. She used both hands to rub at her face, then push back her hair. "It's still a surprise when that happens, when an idea works outside of the lab."

"This one works beautifully," Daniel said with a grin.

"Send a cross-sonar ping every 15 minutes. Let's see how far away the *Ohio* can get and we can still find him," Bishop told Daniel. He was watching for any change in the *Ohio*'s course and wasn't seeing one. The *Ohio* hadn't heard the ping, wasn't changing course.

"Every 15 minutes, aye, sir."

Gina swung around to look at him. Bishop stepped forward to gently squeeze her shoulder, share a smile, and then stepped out to have a word with Commander Neece. The world had just shifted. Let her enjoy the moment. Life was going to get more interesting in the months ahead as the Navy adapted to this science, and as the rest of the world came to realize the U.S. was finding their subs with ease.

Bishop spoke briefly to Commander Neece, then moved to the radio room and sent a one-word message to Rear Admiral Hardman. When he returned to the sonar room, he hunkered down near Gina. "Everything looks good on the recordings being made?"

"I just checked the files. I'm getting the data I need," she confirmed.

The timer chimed.

"The 15 minutes have expired. Sending another ping," Daniel announced as he typed the command.

"Got the *Ohio* again, bright and clear," Dugin said.

"Here as well," Waller said, studying the narrowband console stack.

"You were right, Gina, to come West to explore this sonar idea," Bishop said softly. "Don't ever think otherwise."

She solemnly nodded. "Thanks for that, Mark."

They found the USS *Ohio* every 15 minutes for the next five hours. A celebratory mood built inside the sonar room.

"This is an incredible sonar application," Daniel said, tapping the screen.

Gina simply nodded, her eyes watching the *Ohio*. "Geological ocean noise doesn't seem to bother the echo template. It's still able to find a lock. The big question waits for the shore debrief: does *he* hear *us*?"

Bishop rested his hand on her shoulder. "Before departure I told the *Ohio*'s captain if he heard a ping, to break from the trial plan and give me a 45-degree turn starboard, followed by a 45-degree turn to port. The sub has been running straight away from us since the trial began. He hasn't heard us."

Gina swung around to look up at him. "That's a really useful bit of news."

He smiled. "I didn't put it in the trial plan as I knew that would be the only thing you would remember after reading the document. How's the thermal look? Is it a steep enough temperature contrast for what you need?"

"It looks good. He's randomly moving

above and below that thermal line, and the ping is still finding him."

The timer expired again. Daniel sent another cross-sonar ping.

Silence followed.

"Anything, Dugin?"

"No."

"Try again," Gina said to Daniel.

He sent another ping.

"Nothing on the broadband, Daniel," Dugin said.

"Nothing on the narrowband either," Waller added.

"We've just found the effective range of a cross-sonar ping," Gina guessed. "What's the range on the last successful ping?"

Dugin ran back the data file and made the calculations. "Range is 62 miles beyond what could be done before."

Daniel laughed. "Gina, that's like turning on the lights at the front door of a dark house and seeing the burglar in the basement. It's fabulous. And it's an active ping. Even if the sub was sitting on the ocean floor and silent, this would be coming back as an echo."

Gina looked faintly embarrassed by the praise, but she smiled. "The *Ohio* will keep moving away until he's been traveling for six hours, then turn and come back to us.

Increase the pings to every 10 minutes. He'll come back toward us on a different heading of his choosing. Let's see if we pick him up again around that additional 60-mile mark."

Dugin nodded and set the timer for 10 minutes.

Bishop stepped out to have cold drinks sent up from the galley, then settled in to listen as Gina and Daniel resumed their casual conversation about boating during the winter months. One of the things Bishop had noted over the last few hours was how good Gina was at asking questions without saying much about herself. It was interesting that even in a casual setting she was trying not to be the focus of attention.

Bishop offered her one of the peanut-butter bars the chief cook had sent up along with the sodas. Food was frowned on in the sonar room, but snack bars fit into the gray area that most captains overlooked. He was personally partial to the blueberry bars the *Nevada* cooks had perfected, but the recipe was still a closely guarded secret and hadn't filtered out to the other boats yet.

"New contact, bearing 020." Dugin interrupted the conversation, sliding on the headphones to listen while he typed quickly, focusing in on the contact. "It's the *Ohio.*

We've got him back, Daniel."

"Keep pinging every 15 minutes until he is beside us," Gina suggested. "I want to know for certain he can't hear us even when he's close in."

"Will do," Daniel confirmed, reaching for the phone. "Control, sonar. New contact bearing 020, the *Ohio* on a return course." He hung up the phone.

Bishop caught Gina's attention. "Ready to get a proper dinner, Gina?"

"You should go," Daniel agreed. "We've got this covered. We'll run a cross-sonar ping every 15 minutes for the next few hours, and rotate people so everyone gets a break. We know the cross-sonar works and its range; now it's just seeing if the *Ohio* ever realizes she's being pinged. It's a simple test from here."

"Thanks, Daniel." Gina looked over at Bishop. "Lead the way? I still get lost."

Bishop motioned with his hand. "It's a common problem on a boat this big. I'll bring her back here, Daniel, before the test concludes. She'll want to check the files to make sure the trial plan is complete and confirm what gets archived."

"I'll save that step until Gina can review it," Daniel agreed.

■ ■ ■ ■

Bishop waited until Gina was seated in the officers' wardroom and had chosen her dinner preference — she selected the lasagna — before he brought out the box the chief cook had handed him.

"Congratulations, Gina, on another brilliant sonar idea," he said as he handed the box to her. "I suggested to the cook a reward was in order."

She tugged open the lid, grinned, and lifted out a richly iced cupcake from its holder. "Thanks, Mark. And to the cook." She unwrapped the cupcake, and her smile relaxed. "I'm having dessert before dinner."

"I'd say it's earned. Tired?"

"Long-term tired, like a rung-out dishrag. All the nerves of 'will it work?' have popped. It feels great, but also like I've just finished a marathon since I landed at Bangor."

"Another four days at sea to try out the various ocean noise conditions," he said, "then back to port, a couple weeks of lab time to review the data, present your findings, and then insert the word *vacation* somewhere."

Gina nodded. "Sounds about right for the near term."

Their dinner arrived — he had echoed Gina's choice — the plates of lasagna hot from the galley, served by a petty officer who also brought along hot breadsticks, salads, and cold soft drinks.

"Where do you like to go to relax?" Bishop asked Gina as they began the meal. "I can recommend a beach in Hawaii."

"I'm more likely to curl up with a pile of novels and a TV remote, turn the phone off, and vegetate at home."

"Have you ever been much of a traveler?" he asked, curious.

"I enjoyed tagging along with my parents, or joining Jeff somewhere, but I'm not one to announce a place, pack, and go. Travel for me is more a matter of who I'm going with — *where* is almost an incidental."

"Interesting. Do you like snow?"

She shook her head. "Hate it. You?"

Mark grinned at her emphatic answer. "I've been known to pack a decent snowball. Why do you stay in Chicago if the weather doesn't appeal, now that your parents have passed away?"

"Habit. It's familiar territory, and a nice home with good memories I'm reluctant to sell. The years at the university led to open doors for me there, and the college's connections with other institutes around the world means I can work on satellite data with an Australian researcher, or link into the NASA data feeds, and do both comfortably from their campus or from a high-speed connection at home." She studied him as she broke a breadstick. "Your family is still in Chicago?"

Bishop nodded. "Most of them. I'm planning to head back there to see my brother Bryce and meet his wife, Charlotte — he recently married — at some point during this shore rotation." He picked up another breadstick. "Talk to me about growing up in the city."

"Why?"

"I'm curious." Before these five days were over, he'd like to fill in a lot of the holes about what he knew of Gina Gray. This particular trip had the one thing he rarely got: hours of time to talk between segments of the sea trial without the pressure of command resting on him. He planned to take advantage of that fact. Gina interested him.

"I liked the tall buildings," she said thoughtfully, "being downtown and looking up, wondering how someone had figured out how to build them so they wouldn't fall down. And I liked the libraries. There were always books to read that interested me. The crowds I could have done without. I always felt like I got lost in a mass of people."

"Were you a popular kid?"

Gina shrugged. "Lots of people were always in my life. I can't say that was the same thing as being popular. I had friends from the chess club and from the Bible trivia team, and in the Young Explorers group — that was before I was 10. After that it started to be mostly tutors and high school students and academic camps where I could get 'challenged.' "

She paused, fork in hand. "What I mostly remember is I wasn't sure what people wanted from me. If they wanted me to get an A on a test, I'd study for it and get an A. If they wanted me to discuss a subject, I'd learn enough to converse about it. People kept waiting for me to do something or choose something, I guess, and I had no idea what they really wanted from me. I was simply curious about things. I liked it when someone who knew what they were talking about would dive into a discussion of whatever was their passion. What I didn't understand from what they said, I'd go find books and figure out later. That part was fun."

"You weren't particular about the subject matter when you were young?"

"Not really. I liked everything — music

216

and math, astronomy and physics. I liked to understand how things worked. If they arranged for me to talk to someone with a passion for rocks, I'd dive into geology and have a good time. Or if someone wanted to take an engine apart and show me its parts, I'd enjoy being an auto mechanic. I was content to go with the flow, and the adults around me kept wanting me to select and focus on something. It was kind of frustrating, to tell the truth."

Bishop heard the remembered annoyance in her soft words and thought about her at age 10, waking up to a new day simply inquisitive about the world and everything in it. Jeff must have some interesting stories to tell about having breakfast with Gina when she was a child. "Tell me the first thing that really fascinated you."

"A caterpillar," Gina replied promptly. "I was five. I was stunned at the realization God made this fabulous creature with all these little legs and fuzzy body, and it would transform into a butterfly and fly. I still haven't seen anything as cool in all my years as an adult."

"You collected them?"

She shook her head. "Just watched them. I'd go out into the yard and figure out where they created their cocoons, and Jeff

217

would rig up video for me so I could watch them as they came out as butterflies."

"An awareness of God at age five. Did your parents raise you in the church?"

"They did, but faith and church were more my thing and Jeff's than theirs, I'm sad to say. I don't think they ever connected personally with God. Whereas I connected on a personal level from the very first. I loved the fact there was a God who had made me, who had created everything around me. Jesus made sense to me. He's real. He's personal."

"He likes you," Bishop remarked gently.

She pointed her fork at him. "Exactly." Gina gave a smile that seemed to come from a rich memory. "I wasn't smarter than He was. I adored Jesus for that fact. Every question I had, Jesus knew how to answer. That was such a relief. Not that He would always answer, but I knew I could search for an answer and find one, and it often felt like God was helping me go the right direction with my search." She pushed back her half-eaten plate of lasagna.

"Jeff was always good at letting me talk about whatever topic or details were on my mind, but with everyone else I always was trying to calibrate what I would say to who my audience was. It got tiring. I didn't have to do that with Jesus. I'd bump into something cool God had made, and I'd promptly tell Him all about what I'd found and bombard Him with questions about it." Gina paused and smiled. "I still do." She glanced over. "It must sound pretty childish, but I guess I haven't outgrown that habit."

"I find it interesting that you're self-conscious about it. God likes your enthusiasm. You must feel that at times."

"I do. You like church?"

"Sure. God, faith — it's the part of life that helps make sense of everything else. I don't have to wonder at my foothold there. I mess up, God's going to forgive me and help me pick up the pieces, get my life back on track. If I'm willing to listen, He'll steer me away from trouble before I get into the mess in the first place. It's one of the reasons Melinda and I had such a good marriage. I could apologize to her when I blew it, and she'd show me that same forgiveness even if I didn't deserve it." Bishop smiled. "Of course she'd nag God for a few weeks afterwards about what He asked her to put up with, and how she wanted to be a good wife, but not a saint, so would He please not let me do that again."

He glanced over, caught Gina's gaze, realized he'd managed to shift onto very personal terrain and had left her uncertain what to say. She offered a soft smile. He relaxed. "You'll have something similar, Gina, when you're married and you're working on how two people meld together to one. Faith in God, church — share those things with your husband. It helps makes the rest of living together work out okay."

"Did the two of you ever fight?"

Bishop thought back on it, shook his head. "Not antagonism, butting heads, angry at each other. Melinda and I often wanted different things and couldn't both have what we wanted — someone was going to have to give ground — and those situations could be very painful when it was something important to each of us. But we accepted the fact that we wanted different things and didn't try to change what the other person wanted. We would simply figure out some kind of compromise together. There's no such thing as not having to sacrifice in a marriage. We both made a lot of them. And marriage was a lot about learning to extend courtesy to the other — sharing schedules, calling when plans changed, not making commitments without first touching base with each other — adapting to being a couple."

"You liked being married."

Bishop nodded. "Ever have a moment when you were growing up where something had happened and your first thought was 'I can't wait to tell Jeff'?"

"Sure."

"It was like that a lot during the years I was married. Sharing life with Melinda. It didn't have to be profound or big; it was simply the fact I could share the details of what happened with her. Not that I was the one talking most of the time — Melinda was something of a chatterbox, and I'd get in a sentence every once in a while. But she listened well to what I did say." He got lost in a memory for a moment, then glanced over at Gina. "What I miss most . . . she always used to say good-night just before she'd drift off to sleep. I miss those words, the *good-night.*"

"Someone was there, someone to share the end of the day," Gina said softly.

She understood. Bishop nodded. "Someone was there. That's why you get married, Gina. Beyond all the other details of why, it's having someone there when the day begins and when the day ends. It's being together and sharing life."

Gina leaned back in her chair, reached for

the soft drink, studied the ice as she spun the glass, then sighed and glanced up. "I bet Melinda said yes when you first asked her out, and you got married within a year and had a wonderful marriage without ever having had a breakup along the way or had the 'maybe you're not the one for me' conversation."

"I got lucky, or better yet, blessed," Bishop agreed, understanding her shift in the conversation to her situation.

"I'm glad for you, Mark, I really am. You got the ideal at least once. It must hurt an extra amount to have lost something that was so good."

"It has."

"I'm tired of waiting for that to be my story." She put down the glass. "What do you think of Daniel Field?"

Bishop rapidly shifted mental gears to absorb the fact that she wanted to know his opinion, surprised by the question. He didn't rush to answer and was careful to try and give her an honest one. "I think the right question is, what do *you* think of him? I'm not aware of any red flags — I'd tell you if I was. I think he's a good man with a solid reputation, well liked around Bangor. Jeff chose well when he made that introduction for you. The two of you seem like a good match."

"I keep waiting for the crash into the wall."

Bishop laughed. "You debate and analyze too much, Gina. Nothing says this time is going to end in disaster." She picked up her glass again, her expression staying on the edge of pensive, and Bishop wondered what she was thinking about so seriously. He wished he hadn't attempted the light comment, which had managed to kill the conversation, and backpedaled. "What can I help with?"

She shook her head. "We should get back."

Bishop glanced at the time and nodded. She was going to leave him in the dark as to what was on her mind regarding Daniel, and it was going to nag at him for the next several hours.

"There's the last ping. The *Ohio* is coming to a stop off our port side," Daniel said.

Gina leaned forward to see the image on the waterfall screen. The ability Daniel had to decipher subtle changes was impressive to watch. She glanced around the sonar room. "An excellent job, guys. Thank you."

"It was fun," Waller replied with a smile. "The rest of the trial plan — we do this test again in different ocean conditions over the next few days?"

"Yes. The ping probably won't work as well. It might even fail in a more noisy sea," Gina cautioned.

Daniel patted her shoulder and grinned. "O ye of little faith. It will keep working." He tagged the audio files to off-load to the high-density drive. "You want the cross-sonar log too?"

"Please."

He dumped the log file out to the drive as well. "One set of cross-sonar ping data, now archived for review." Daniel reached for the phone. "Control, sonar. The first leg of the sea trial is complete." He hung up. "I'm glad you decided to stay and see this trial in person, Gina. It's an incredible piece of software."

"It was a good first test," she agreed.

"You're for understatements, right?"

The door opened, and Gina looked over and straightened as Commander John Neece stepped into the sonar room. "Congratulations, Miss Gray, for a brilliant idea and implementation."

She felt her face grow warm. "Thank you, Captain."

"Your second data request — we're going to rig for all-quiet and let the *Connecticut* and the *Ohio* start a cross-sonar search to find us."

"That's perfect, sir."

She hoped no one in the room asked why she wanted that all-quiet data, but as the captain left, the guys returned to discussing crew assignments for the next watch.

"You should get some sleep, Gina," Bishop suggested, closing the manual he was flipping through. "We're the sitting target, so the boat isn't going to be doing anything but drift here during this test."

Gina considered that and nodded. "Probably a good idea. I can tell I need it."

"Sharon can take you down to the stateroom. Plan to sleep as long as you can."

She nodded, glanced over at Bishop, reached over and rested her hand lightly on his. "Thanks for today," she offered, her voice low. "I enjoyed it, both the sonar test and the conversation."

"It was my pleasure," Daniel replied, rising to his feet to see her off. "Sleep well, Gina."

Gina did sleep very well. She headed to the officers' wardroom seven hours after she had gone to stretch out. Bishop was reading a thick report. He looked up as she entered, smiled, and nodded to the seat opposite his. "Ready for breakfast?"

"I've got time before the next test?"

"Plenty of time. We'll be over the Tufts Plain in about 40 minutes. If no other subs or surface ships are around to be concerned about, we'll get started with the next test shortly thereafter. I'd like it if you were there at the start just to be sure the files you need collected are properly recording, but after that feel free to use the time as you like. I'll find you if there's a concern I need you to address."

"I was thinking I might have Sharon give me a more complete tour of the boat."

"You'll enjoy it, Gina. A boomer grows on you the longer you're aboard. You fall in love with the boat."

"I'm beginning to pick out all the things that make this submarine function. Blue pipes and valves are fresh water. Orange pipes are hydraulic fluid. What are the red arrows?"

"Air outlets so crewmen can plug in masks and be able to breathe during a fire," Bishop replied.

The petty officer stepped in to get her breakfast order. She chose an omelet and hash browns. "I'd like to hear about your first command," she said.

Bishop simply smiled. "How about we talk about something not sub-related? What was the last book you read for pleasure, not work?"

"Jerry McKowen's biography — he's a nuclear physicist — titled *Fireball.*"

"You enjoy biographies?"

"When it's as much about the career someone has as it is the person. What about you, Mark? The last book you read for pleasure."

"I'm partial to a good mystery. The last one, John Sandford's *Dead Watch.* Before that, Dean Koontz's *The Husband.*"

She shuddered. "Too vivid for my tastes. I don't like to be scared, even when it's make-believe."

He absorbed that answer, nodded. "Most recent movie?"

That was more difficult to remember. "I watched *Moneyball* several times, as I enjoyed the math behind sabermetrics. You?"

"I'll go with a DVD, an old Hallmark movie called *Duke.* I'm a goner for a good dog flick."

Gina laughed at the admission.

"Are you a baseball fan?" Bishop asked her.

"I understand it, but I don't follow a particular team. It takes too many hours to keep up with all the games played during a season." Her breakfast arrived. "What should I ask Sharon to show me first?"

"The laundry. When you mention to people you were able to spend a few days at sea on a submarine, the three questions you're going to get asked the most are about the restrooms, showers, and food. The two questions after that are the sleeping berths and the laundry. No one ever asks to see the laundry and doesn't know how to answer that one — it's one washer and one dryer, for a 155-person crew."

Gina smiled. "I was thinking I would start with the torpedo room. Jeff mentioned the *Nebraska* carries a few MK48s."

Bishop nodded. "Boomers have four torpedo tubes, enough for defense and a limited offense while we try to disengage and disappear from the fight. A fast-attack submarine like the *Seawolf* has eight torpedo tubes and can hold its own and re-engage in battle easily. If you want to start with the torpedo room, you'll be heading down to the fourth level."

"I'm slowly getting the hang of the ladders. Will they mind a visit?"

"No. Sharon will give a call ahead if she thinks a department needs to know to expect visitors. She'll likely give a call to engineering so they have a radiation badge available for you."

"A lovely thought. The idea of being at sea is tough enough. Knowing I'm at sea with a nuclear reactor . . . I may skip visiting the back of the boat."

Bishop chuckled. "You can have Sharon stick to places like the radio room and kitchen."

Gina nodded. "She was heading up to the radio room to get a look at the Navy daily brief."

"It's worth the read," Bishop mentioned, glancing at the document he'd turned over when she joined him.

She didn't ask to see it. She'd seen the classified stamp on the cover. Her security clearance was high enough to cover it and about any other document on this boat, but there were times she would rather not know something. Her mind was already on overload with what she was learning about the sub operations. "You'll be in the sonar room most of the day?"

"Plan to be," Bishop said.

"After I confirm the sea trial files are recording properly, I'll take that boat tour with Sharon, then come find you in the sonar room this afternoon."

9

Gina was becoming used to the USS *Nebraska*. The sound was a constant hum of conversations that echoed through the sub's corridors. The air was so clean of all bacteria it was odorless . . . until she passed close to a guy who'd been sweating on one of the treadmills. The various small rooms were packed with people no matter where she turned — submariners ready to offer her stories, laughter, and tall tales, men focused on monitoring screens, maintaining equipment, and tackling repairs.

The stateroom Gina shared with Sharon and the other three women in the crew reminded her of a very small, very crowded dorm room. After three days aboard the *Nebraska,* Gina was well acquainted with the room and feeling a bit possessive of it. The room was a safe haven where she could slide into her assigned berth and stretch out, plug in headphones to listen to music through the sub's internal audio system. If she closed her eyes, she could forget the next bunk was a foot above her head, and the wall was just inches from her shoulder. The berth was the only personal space she had — storage under the bunk could fit a few clothes and small belongings — and a curtain could be closed to block out sights if not sounds.

Gina relaxed on the bunk and let her mind drift. The temperature stayed cool, and she was glad for the layers Bishop had suggested she wear. Sleep was getting easier to come by. She was exhausted with the flow of people, along with the volume of information she was trying to absorb. This experience was intense. The nervousness about being underwater was still a constant edge, but if she stayed busy, she could push it aside. Bishop had been right to insist she come. She could do this for five days of a sea trial. But she didn't understand how men could face doing a 90-day patrol.

Life aboard the boat had an interesting tempo. There was not an extra man aboard the submarine — they each had a full job to do, with each depending on the other, and they worked hard. She had absorbed that fact early on. It was a privilege to watch them efficiently and competently go about their work.

The meals were good, better than most restaurants. She was getting used to Bishop's questions when they shared a meal. He had her talking about Chicago, high school, Jeff, movies she liked, people she had worked with, things she wanted to do in her lifetime — anything but the sea trial they were here to conduct. It felt like he was deliberately avoiding any conversation that had a work tone to it. She appreciated that.

So far she was handling the stress of it all reasonably well. Her speech had frozen twice with Bishop. Once when she was trying to answer a question he posed about her mom, and once when he surprised her with a question about Jeff and Tiffany. She appreciated that Bishop handled it by simply settling back in his chair, his hands linked loosely across his knee as he waited, relaxed, for her to get past the freeze. He never asked about the speech problem. Bishop was simply good company. And he was doing his best to encourage things between her and Daniel.

Whenever Daniel came off watch, Bishop would within a few minutes excuse himself so Daniel could have her undivided attention. Gina was grateful and somewhat surprised by the effort Bishop was making to further the relationship. Bishop had concurred with Jeff that Daniel was a good man and was now going out of his way to be helpful in seeing that things had a chance to develop.

Knowing Jeff and Bishop both expected it to work out with Daniel felt like a bit of unexpected pressure — that if it didn't, it would surprise and disappoint them. She hadn't expected that when she asked for Jeff's help, but realized now that she should have. Of course, Jeff would expect it to work out. He'd chosen a good guy for her to meet, so why wouldn't it work out? The situation made her a bit uneasy, and she felt an odd burden that it needed to be a success or Jeff would be seen to have made the wrong choice for her.

"Quit borrowing trouble," she whispered to herself. She liked Daniel Field. He made her laugh. He was good company. The sea trial was giving her some extended time in his company to talk about anything that interested her, to watch him work. Getting to know him was not hard. What to do with what she was learning about him was the question, and how was she supposed to sort out all those impressions in such a short period of time?

The events of the last couple of weeks felt

like a compressed dating relationship. Since the dinner introduction, she had been to a concert with Daniel, boating with him, met several of his friends, and enjoyed two evenings of music. After one dinner, he'd picked up the guitar to play part of a set with the group onstage. She'd even joined him for some batting practice. Added to that, she had now spent a large chunk of the last three days talking with him. What she was learning about Daniel was gradually making a full picture.

Was he the one? When she'd met him initially, she'd hoped he might be. Was there anything she had seen so far that told her something different? She hoped never to have another breakup with a guy, and she'd rather not get so heart-bruised if this one was also not going to work out. Was there anything that suggested they were not going to be a good match? She was pondering that all-important question when sleep finally overtook her.

One of the things Gina liked most about Daniel was watching him work. He loved his job. He brought the same focus to it as he did to the music he was passionate about. She was learning a lot about sonar just by observing what he would glance at and set aside as not a concern and what he would spot on the screen and focus in on, revealing something interesting in the waters around them.

Gina watched him now as he leaned forward in his seat, one hand pressed against the headphones he was wearing to bring the sound that much closer to his ear as he dialed in the focus. He smiled.

"Got it." Daniel held out the headphones. "Gina, listen."

She pressed them against her ears. Her eyes shot to his, and she grinned. Whales were singing. "This is wonderful."

"One of the side benefits of patrolling around the oceans. These whales are far away, but it's a large group."

"I listen to the tapes of these encounters in the lab, but it's not the same as hearing it firsthand."

"It's beautiful. Hold on, let me give you another sound." He moved the cursor.

She grimaced. "It sounds like fingernails across a blackboard. What is that?"

Daniel laughed. "A fishing vessel with a poorly maintained engine."

"I see why you can tell ships apart without seeing them."

"They sound very different from each other." He moved the cursor to another spot on the screen.

"That's more like a deep bass, humming."

"Very good. It's a freighter out of Hong Kong."

"Give me another one."

Daniel chose another line in the waterfall display.

"It sounds like a rockslide."

"It is. An underwater one, about five miles from here. There have been repeated rock-slides over the last half hour."

"I can see why you like this job, Daniel. It's like a puzzle that you play by hearing rather than sight."

"The more time listening, the better my memory for the subtle differences. I could teach you some of this if you like — you've got a good ear."

They had been at sea five days now, the last of the sea trial tests were finished, and the sub was heading back toward Bangor. "Could you help me distinguish the *Ohio* from the *Connecticut*?"

Daniel nodded and shifted the display to a wider view. "You have to find them in the first place. Watch the middle screen. We're looking for an interruption in the waterfall that looks a bit like a fishhook."

Gina was enjoying herself, Mark thought,

listening to her laughter as he moved through the control center to join her in the sonar room. If she had requested to stay onshore, they would have been okay on the sea trial, but she would have missed the rich experience of the last five days. The last of the planned maneuvers were complete, and they were now nearing home, the sea trial finished.

Bishop tapped on the sonar room door, and she turned from her conversation with Daniel, smiled at him. Bishop loved her smile. "We're getting ready to surface, Gina."

"Oh, that's good news!"

He laughed at her relief. "Want to come to the control center and watch it?"

"I'm fine here. Thanks for asking. I'm learning how they tell ship traffic apart."

Bishop nodded, shared a smile with Daniel, and headed back to join the *Nebraska*'s captain.

Bishop tapped on the sonar room door again a few hours later. Gina slipped off the headphones.

"Come topside and see the ocean at night," he invited.

She hesitated.

"Trust me, Gina. I won't steer you wrong."

She set down the headphones and came to join him. "I'm not particularly brave, Mark," she said softly.

"You won't need to be brave, just careful. Borrow from my experience and simply do what I do. It's well worth the risk to see what it's like topside right now."

She nodded and came with him into the command-and-control center.

He held out an insulated jacket. "You'll find it helpful to wear this."

She slid it on.

"Start up and I'll come up behind you. The XO is topside and expecting you. He'll help you step off the ladder when you enter the sail."

She took a deep breath and started climbing the ladder. Bishop followed and stepped out beside her in the sail. It was like a balcony with a high, solid wall of the *Nebraska* hull on all sides of them, the lookout posts up yet another ladder to an even higher perch. The breeze was calm, the sky filled with stars, the water bright with reflections of the moon on gently rolling waves. She tucked her hands deep into the jacket pockets.

"That's Washington State ahead of us, and that's Canada on your left," Bishop said, pointing. A night view didn't get more exquisite than this as land rose up ahead, forests of trees, communities built down to the shoreline along inlets, the streetlights forming ribbons through the trees.

"It's truly beautiful, Mark."

"We don't often return home at night, but with three subs to transit, we'll use the dawn to our advantage. You can already see it beginning to brighten on the horizon."

She glanced around, seemed to be fascinated looking from the sail at the size of the *Nebraska*'s trailing curved hull. In the moonlight the huge circle hatches of the 24 missile tubes were only an impression in the otherwise smooth deck. She started to say something, and her words froze.

He felt her frustration, saw it in the way she grimaced and her hands tightened. "Hey, relax." He rested his arm across her shoulders, turned her slightly into his body away from the lookouts and the XO, and waited for the words to return.

"It never happens this frequently," she finally whispered. "I don't know what's changed."

"Don't worry about it. What were you going to say?"

"It's odd to know something this heavy floats."

Bishop chuckled. "It defies common

sense, doesn't it?"

He tapped the solid surface of the sail. "A boomer is one solid mass of metal."

She leaned her arms against the surface near the windshield and watched the water and the glistening moonlight and the approaching land for half an hour.

"I'd like to go below now, get some sleep," she eventually said. "When we reach the pier in about 14 hours, I want to be ready to hit the lab and find out what the *Ohio* was hearing while we were actively pinging."

At first, Bishop was surprised by her plan to immediately go to work, but then decided he wasn't surprised at all. Sleep wouldn't come while she wondered at the answer, so she might as well see what the data from the *Ohio* looked like. "Sounds like a good plan," he replied.

He turned on the red-light flashlight — the color helped protect night vision — to illuminate the hatch, and he lifted the grate for her. "The ladder treads will be a bit slick, so take your time. I'll go first and stay just below you."

He stepped down, waited for her to begin her descent, and carefully confirmed she had her footing on each rung. She stepped off the ladder inside the command-and-control center, where he helped her off with the jacket. "Like an escort to the stateroom?"

"I'm good. Thanks for showing me that, Mark."

"You're welcome. Sleep well, Gina."

"Good night."

Bishop watched her leave and then headed back topside. He nodded to the XO guiding the *Nebraska* home and took a spot at the back of the sail. The stars in the night sky were still bright even as the coming sunrise began to lighten the horizon. He let himself consider a thought he'd been holding at bay for the last week.

He'd made a mistake, he finally let himself acknowledge, telling Jeff no regarding dinner with Gina. She was young, but he thought now he could have looked past that. She was interesting. He enjoyed her smile and her laughter. And if he'd spent the last few weeks dating her instead of ceding that ground to Daniel, he might have been able to move beyond the surface questions by now to begin learning about her dreams and hopes, the core of who Gina was.

Bishop sighed, accepting reality. He might believe now he had made a mistake, but he couldn't undo how facts had changed. Gina seemed genuinely happy in Daniel's company. Jeff had chosen a good man, and Bishop agreed with the choice. Daniel had been telling her stories from prior patrols, making her laugh, talking about his family and hers, sharing history — everything a guy hoping to court her would be doing. Jeff had been right to introduce the two of them. They would make a good couple.

Bishop had planned to call Jessica, but he hadn't followed through. Jeff's description had simply been too accurate. Jessica was the kind of lady who would take dinner to someone who was sick, bake a cake for a friend, run errands to help a neighbor out. She would be a wonderful wife and mother one day, and life would be peaceful. But there weren't layers to her.

Bishop had thought a woman like Jessica was what he wanted, someone who would give him a peaceful life and a happy marriage. He found himself now wondering if what he really wanted, what he had really been waiting for, was something more complex. Gina defined that characteristic in every way he could measure it. Her age, her smarts, those thoughts which tangled her in knots, the relationship failures of her past, that tendency to get easily hurt. Setting out to have something with her would have been a careful adventure, and he'd let her slip through his fingers. Even encouraged it to happen, for Jeff to introduce her to Daniel, and done what he could to make sure she had the time during this trip to get that relationship on a solid footing.

Jesus, do you have any idea how I'm supposed to get myself out of this jam I've put myself into? he prayed, wondering if God would take pity on him. He'd finally met someone interesting, someone who had his attention, and he'd mishandled it before the possibility even got any traction.

10

Mark waited for the high-tech security pad to place the digits one through nine in a random order on the keypad, then searched for the digits he needed to enter the building security code. The door clicked, and he pulled it open. The entire Naval Undersea Warfare Center's new acoustical research lab was an SCIF building, protected against electronic eavesdropping from outside. He headed up the stairs, provided a palm print, and was granted access to the second-floor labs and offices.

Mark paused before he tapped on the open corner-office door. There was something very pleasant about watching a woman absorbed in her work. Gina had been here for the majority of the last seven days, and he didn't think it had registered with her yet that it was Saturday. Toombs had found her a permanent office, and the desk surfaces were cluttered with open books, printouts, Post-it notes. At the moment she was studying data flowing across the screen and watching the picture on the second screen shift — wave forms of the audio, he realized, the visual form of the data he was accustomed to seeing on a waterfall screen. Her algorithms were turning parts of the data stream orange and red and deep blue, and she hit the pause button to study the screen.

Her concentration broke as she realized someone was watching her, and she turned, her surprise followed by a welcoming smile. "Mark."

"How's it going?"

"This is the first configuration, the *Ohio* recordings," she said, and pointed to the screen and the flow of color in the sonar data. "It shows the ocean filled with geological noise. He's hearing the ping; he just thinks it's ocean noise."

She shifted the cursor and zoomed in on a section of the audio wave form. "Here's the ping. But the sonar algorithm isn't picking up anything unusual to classify this as something to analyze further. When I force the audio stream through the deeper analysis, the software says it's a rock falling — which it actually is, as that was the sound I used as my cross-sonar ping." She frowned slightly at the screen. "I'm not sure I could even write an algorithm that would identify this as something for further study or that could see it as something deeper than *just* a rockslide. It's possible I've created something I can't even deconstruct."

Bishop smiled. "It's good then, the data."

"Better than I expected by far." She changed the data stream and the colors shifted. "Here's the coastal water ping. A cross-sonar ping has limitations where you would expect, in the noisy environment near the coast. The range it works drops down significantly. In the open ocean you can get an additional 60 miles on average. As you get into the coastline and the noise picks up, the added range falls to just over 15 miles."

"That's still very significant for coastline work."

Gina nodded. "I think the Undersea Warfare Group will decide to deploy this capability in relatively quick fashion. The risks to cross-sonar are minimal compared to the visibility this offers. I think the returns are well worth the additional risks."

He leaned against the corner of her desk. "How long do you need to complete the review?"

"At the pace this is going, I'll be finished

by Monday."

"I'll let Rear Admiral Hardman know."

Bishop wasn't at all sure how to handle matters now with Gina. Given his own recently acknowledged interest in her, he was trying to find that elusive line between their genuine friendship and wanting to bring it to another level. He deliberately brought up the question he was curious about. "Are you going boating with Daniel this weekend?" He was aware Gina and Daniel had been out together several evenings in the last week.

Gina nodded. "Lunch on his boat tomorrow, followed by an afternoon on the water. We're fitting in what we can before he heads to Groton for five weeks at sub school."

Bishop would have straightened, but he forced himself not to move from his perch, to simply nod. "You'll miss him."

"He's nice company," she replied. He thought she sounded a bit cautious.

He raised one eyebrow. "What just passed through your mind?"

She shook her head. "Are you heading home?"

"I am. I just swung by to see if I could talk you into wrapping it up for the day. Jeff has called me twice to say you need to be badgered to get out of this office. I noticed he has given up on calling you."

She smiled. "Guilty. Give me the long side of 20 minutes and I'll be done with what I want to get finished for the first pass. The idea works. Everything from this point on is simply polish to answer the question of what specifically gives the algorithms trouble."

"I'll go let your security know you're finishing up so they can pull the server card for you when you're ready."

"I'd appreciate that, Mark."

Bishop got into his car, set his soda in the cup holder. Daniel Field was heading to Connecticut for five weeks. It was an unexpected opening. He thought about the situation as he watched Gina's security walk her to the sedan they were using to chauffer her around.

By the time Daniel left for Groton, Gina would have spent enough time with the man to have formed a solid impression. If she was looking at Daniel Field as the answer to her hopes and dreams, Mark would back off. But if there was a gap there, some maneuvering room, a soft opening, he had five weeks while Daniel was away to find out if there was something possible for him with Gina. If he did nothing, he would lose her for good — to Daniel Field or another man like him. He didn't want that to happen, but neither did he want to play with this woman's heart. She deserved better. But he'd like to find out if a future with her was an option.

Getting this woman to see him as more than a friend of her brother's would not be simple. She knew him as Jeff's friend, Melinda's husband, commander of the USS *Nevada*. He'd measure the success of the next few weeks by the amount of time he was able to spend with her. He needed to add to that list of how she saw him.

He wasn't going to come at her directly with an invitation to a movie and dinner. She no doubt would get flustered, come up with reasons to decline — she was seeing Daniel, she was living here only temporarily, she was getting over a broken relationship, there was too large of an age gap — whatever the reasons she would offer him as a polite way to say no, it would complicate things. He didn't plan to offer her that opening, not until she was at least comfortable with him.

It would be good for her morale to know that two men thought she was worth their time and attention. Nothing would help her recover from the bruised emotions Kevin had caused more than to realize she was liked by two guys. He didn't mind that idea at all. But he wasn't going to ask her to choose between himself and Daniel, because at the moment, she'd choose Daniel. Mark would work first on changing what she knew about him. Then he'd tell her he was seriously interested. It was a plan, one he could work with.

He followed the security car with Gina through the Bangor base and onto Highway 3 heading south. He'd decided to restart his social life, and he realized he'd already done so in a rather unexpected way.

Gina Gray. Gina B . . . No, he wouldn't go there, not yet.

He watched the security car turn off toward Jeff's condo, and he headed on toward his own home. The odds were slim that there was any hope for him, but he had worked on small hope before. Until there was an engagement ring on her finger, there was still a chance.

The ocean tank was full. Bishop eyed it with some well-deserved caution. His XO was 12 feet below him, leaning into the open hatch of the compartment butting up against the tank. "What have they built for us today, Kingman?" Bishop asked his XO.

"A torpedo room."

"This is going to be interesting. Who's up for this training session?"

"The weapons group, and level three and four flood-suppression teams."

The torpedo room mockup was part of a real sub, decommissioned, cut into sections and turned into full-size training compartments. They were going to face actual flooding today. A metal plate was holding back the ocean tank water. When people were in place for the drill, that metal plate would lift, a not-yet-announced problem with a hatch or a pipe or the hull would occur, and water would rush into the submarine compartment just as it would if the sub were out at sea. Only here, if the team learning how to combat the flooding got into trouble, the metal plate could be lowered in place and the water would recede.

Bishop had endured flooding in the missile bay when a missile tube failed to hold its seal, in the sonar dome when an accident had breached the hull, and in the command-and-control center when a ballast tank had failed. It had been a while since he'd fought flooding in the torpedo room.

The door to the adjoining teaching wing of the building opened. His XO met up with him on the observation level while more than 50 guys — a third of the gold crew —

entered the training facility, fresh from morning lectures on flood-control procedures.

"Gear up, gentlemen," the XO called. "Weapons team, first watch, you're with the captain. Flood teams three and four, you're with me." Kingman glanced back at Bishop. "Captain, permission for spectators to head to the bleacher seats?"

Bishop smiled. "Granted. Someone put personal video on this. I want to see how many times I get knocked off my feet this session." He took off his watch and emptied his pockets, wanting something salvageable at the end of the day. He was due for a refresher course in flood control and had written himself into the training exercise. He would be in the compartment on an unrelated matter when the trouble began.

The training personnel conducting the drill joined them, carrying fluorescent numbers to slap on the back of uniforms to make the video easier to analyze. Bishop joined the six men of the weapons team as they took up stations in the torpedo room.

The drill began as a normal load-and-fire procedure. The torpedo — real but with no charge inside — moved along the tracking rack, was loaded into the tube, the hatch sealed, the tube pressurized to fire, and the outer door opened. Without an ocean to speed into, this torpedo would be caught by a steel net inside the tank.

"Torpedo three, fire."

The torpedo man fired the MK48.

A real explosion shook the torpedo tube and echoed back into the torpedo room, vibrating through the hull. The tube hatch slammed back open, and water abruptly flooded into the sub compartment. The man nearest the hatch stumbled backward as the force of the water hit him. The man closest to the firing panel slammed a hand down on the flood alarm, setting off a piercing warning alarm throughout the ship. The nearest weapons man to the intercom grabbed the mike to send a flash message to Control. "Explosion, deck four. Torpedo tube three fatally damaged, hatch blown open, full tube flooding of the torpedo room under way."

The flood-suppression teams for levels three and four rushed down the ladder and the narrow passageway. Having to abandon the torpedo room to the incoming water, sealing the door, and welding it shut was the last step a boomer crew wanted to take, for it would leave the boat defenseless. The flood team entered the room, closed the hatch door behind them, and prepared to fight the water instead.

"We plug it," the flood officer ordered, shifting people to the most effective option possible to stop the water. The damaged hatch door was struck with sledgehammers until it broke free. The tube cap was unbolted from the first torpedo tube and hefted into place. Brute force got it tipped up while the water pressure did its best to shove the cap back. The torpedo loading arm provided leverage to force the circular metal cap against the open torpedo tube while the flood officer clamped a vice down from above. Men scrambled to wrap the tube tape into place — tightly woven rope designed to build a seal one wrap at a time to hold against the water pressure. Water, now at mid-thigh, slowed, then stopped flooding in. The finish man lit a torch to weld the patch in place. Men stood, heaving to get their breath back.

Bishop shook his head to toss wet hair and water out of his eyes. "Wallace, we've got to get more body weight on you. The water was tossing you around like a twig."

"Felt like it too, sir."

"Did we save the boat?" Bishop demanded of the training officer watching from above.

"First crew to do so."

Back slaps among wet men made the

battle with the torrent of water worth it.

"Open the drain," the training officer called. "Weapons team, second watch, you're up. Let's run variation two."

Bishop left the torpedo room for another view of the damage the charge had done to the missile tube. The training facility routinely set charges to take out pipes, valves, and casings, taking advantage of the decommissioned parts coming off the old diesel boats to bring realism to these training exercises. But this was the first time Bishop had felt a missile tube blow. He hoped he never experienced one in real life.

The hull had taken the blast with some compression dents, but had held. The outer door of the missile tube was in shreds, the inner core had held, but its form distended outward like a balloon filled with too much air. They were fortunate this was a salvageable failure. In order to teach flood officers how to make that final "abandon station" call, some tests were deliberately built as situations that could not be saved.

Bishop wiped water off his face. Three more drills to go. At least he was already wet.

"Mark."

He swung around toward the door of the

255

Squadron 17 ready room where he'd re-treated to do some paperwork. He'd changed into a dry uniform and was finish-ing towel-drying his hair. He'd had his feet knocked out from under him three times before the afternoon was over. And he had a good-sized bruise on his thigh from a wrench that had slipped during the last drill. "Hey, Gina."

He removed the towel from his head to get a better look at his guest. "What's wrong?" Tear traces wet her cheeks, and she wiped her hands hard against them. He dumped the towel and went to meet her. "What's happened?"

"I got designated a national security as-set," she said. "The security is going to be permanent, even after I leave Bangor."

Talk about bad timing for that news. He took her hand and pulled her through the building, pushed open the back door, and led her outside, heading by habit toward the gable-point picnic tables where they could have a conversation in private. "It's necessary," he said quietly as they walked.

She wiped her eyes again. "It's going to mess with my life forever. I'll be attending mothers' meetings with a security guy driv-ing me there, grocery shopping with some-one tagging along. Do you know a mom who's going to want to have tea with the lady who has security there to check who's at the door?"

Mark couldn't hide the smile. She'd gotten up quite a head of steam. "Mothers' meetings — you're thinking PTA meetings?"

"Whatever they're called," she muttered. "I stood out in college for my youth; now as an adult I get attention as the woman who can't go anywhere without security. People are going to think I'm some big-shot attorney, or a crime figure's wife, or just another pretentious rich person. I might as well stick a fork in having a new friendship of any substance." She looked over at him and stopped abruptly. "It's not funny."

"It's not remotely funny," Mark said soberly, trying to stop his smile. "But your word choices and where your thoughts run to — imagination isn't your problem." He sighed and wrapped his arm around her shoulders, tugged so she'd walk with him again. "Gina, you knew it had to be done. What's in your head is dangerous information, and that makes you a target."

"What I know will become dated. It might be new today, but it won't be a decade from now."

"And you'll figure something new out next

257

year, and the one after that. The Navy is rightfully worried about your safety. We don't need some country hijacking all that knowledge by snatching you one day. You're at risk not only for what you know today, but for what you'll figure out in the future."

"It's that — I get no choice in this . . . the security. It just happens. It's yet one more thing that just happens because I'm smart. I wish I were average. There are days I so wish I were average."

He stopped, turned her toward him, and hugged her. Eventually he felt her relax in his hold. "Pity party over?" he whispered.

She gave a broken laugh. "Yeah."

He set her back from him, tipped up her face. "I talked with Rear Admiral Hardman about getting you designated a national security asset. I'd rather have you alive and mad at me in 10 years than missing and nobody sure which country snatched you."

She was struggling with what to say, and he simply waited. Her life had just gotten more complicated, more restricted, and he was one of the causes. He'd take whatever she wanted to say as the consequence of his choice.

"You just *had* to protect me," she finally whispered.

"Something like that."

"You give me a headache, Mark."

"You'll forgive me." She had come to tell him about it — before or after she'd told Jeff? Daniel? He wondered at the order even as he tried to figure out something, anything, to make this less of a burden on her. "I can't sugarcoat this, Gina. It's going to be difficult for the rest of your life. But on the bright side, you might as well come up with something profoundly earthshaking now. It can't get much worse than this, no matter what you discover."

She laughed, and it sounded genuine.

"Come on, let's get something to eat. I don't mind if security is following you around." He resolutely turned her toward the parking lot.

Mark stopped to buy carryout Mexican and turned the car back to Bangor base. They'd have their meal at the SCIF building, where she spent much of her time, where they could have a conversation without concerns about who might overhear. They settled in an empty conference room.

"Eat something, Gina. Don't just push it around the plate."

"You can finish mine. My appetite is gone when I'm having a truly miserable day."

"You like the three guys who provide

259

security now. Is that going to change —
more people, a new routine? Have they
said?"

"Connolly told me it depends on where I
decide to go after Bangor. If I move back to
Chicago or head to Pasadena, the guys who
work with him will likely change. But Connolly is pretty sure he's with me for the next
year, possible two. He said a woman would
likely join the group, so it's a little less
intrusive when I'm out shopping or visiting
friends. It's still a three-person team rotating on 12-hour shifts."

"You can work with that."

"Like I said, I don't have a choice." She
tried to smile, sighed instead, and pushed
her plate over to him. "I've been through
the five sea trial tests. I'll be ready to present
the material in a couple of days. It's time to
hand this off."

He accepted the change of subject. "Then
let me talk you through what will happen
from here. You'll sit down with Rear Admiral
Hardman and Lieutenant Commander
Toombs, present the data to them. Jeff and
I will be there to handle any questions they
have regarding the sea trial. The admiral
will then formally report to the Secretary of
the Navy. He's been keeping the SecNav
apprised that this idea exists and that it was

looking promising.

"There will be a commanders' meeting here at Bangor next week. What you've discovered will be presented in an urgent meeting to the captains and the sonar chiefs of the ballistic missile submarine crews who are not out on patrol, and to as many of the captains and sonar chiefs from the fast-attacks as can make it here."

"It's going to be a big group?"

"Probably 50 guys, maybe a few more."

"I was thinking I would do a video for my presentation," she offered, "similar to what I did during my college days. Present the data of the sea trial, show the wave forms, narrate over the video what this idea is and how it operates. I might be able to handle some questions at the end of the session, but asking me to present it to this group is asking for more than I can handle. I could do an accompanying paper with the mathematics of it, the theory, so it could be handed off to the Undersea Warfare Group without needing a lot more explanation from me. The algorithms are pretty simple to follow."

"That will work, Gina. Whatever you are comfortable with will be fine." Bishop hesitated, then added, "Daniel can help you put that video together. He can even do part of the presentation for you if you'd like. He's good at conversing on the finer points of sonar operations."

"You think that would be possible?"

"I'll talk to the admiral. It would only take bumping Daniel's departure date for sub school back a couple days. I'm certain I can get it arranged."

"That would help a great deal, Mark, thanks."

Bishop already knew what it was like to be squeezed between a rock and a hard place. Organizing things for Daniel to help Gina prepare for the commanders' meeting was the right thing to do. But it also meant Daniel would be the one Gina was leaning on to get her through a very stressful day.

Bishop walked through the room where the meeting would be held tomorrow, confirmed the projection system was set up, that there were sufficient chairs for the 62 people now expected to be in attendance.

"I've got the final video."

Bishop looked over as Daniel entered the room. "Good. Put it in to play and let's check the sound from the back of the room. How many times did she redo the intro?"

"Nine. I thought the fourth take was fine, but she was worried she was looking slightly off-center to the camera."

"She's able to talk off the cuff for the rest of the video — what a cross-sonar ping is, how it operates. But the three minutes on who she is and what this meeting is about causes her enormous stress. I haven't yet figured that one out."

"It's the only time she was on camera," Daniel said.

"Okay. I should have recognized that one."

Daniel started the video. Because Bishop knew her pretty well by now, he recognized the nerves Gina was feeling during the opening introduction. Then the image changed to computer-generated displays of the audio recordings taken during the sea trial, and her voice-over sounded comfortable and confident. The presentation was concise, detailed, effective. They had both heard the main section of the video several times now, and Daniel turned it off after they were comfortable with the sound levels.

Bishop slipped on the lapel microphone he would be wearing and moved to the front of the room, checked sound levels with Daniel at the back. Rear Admiral Hardman would be in attendance, but the presentation on what tactical changes would be implemented had been passed to Bishop. He didn't have to ask if he was being prepared for that flag officer rank one day. Hardman was good at pushing his line officers into new and greater responsibilities.

The Secretary of the Navy would be issuing new operational directives for all submarines. A torpedo would now be kept hot in the launch tube, and torpedo countermeasures would become the full-time responsibility of the weapons officer's deputy chief. Other nations might not know yet how to do a ping that couldn't be heard, but the U.S. Navy would shift and practice tactics before it became an issue.

"Could I ask you a question, Commander?" Daniel asked as Bishop slipped off the microphone. "A personal one."

"Sure."

"Why did you arrange for me to be doing this, sir? Helping out Gina? Especially since you're interested in her yourself."

Bishop glanced over at Daniel. "Why do you say that?"

"The sea trials — and since then — Gina is with me, or she's with you. I don't think that's happening by accident. And I've noticed you're no longer wearing your wedding ring."

Bishop glanced down, flexed his fingers. "She's been designated a national security asset."

"She told me. But that has nothing to do with this, sir. She may not have noticed yet, but I have. So why give me a clear avenue with her?"

Bishop didn't try to dissuade Daniel from what he'd noticed. "She likes you, and I play fair. Whoever ends up with her is going to have a very good day. The other is going to be a gracious second. We understand each other, Daniel?"

"Absolutely. I'd wish you good luck, sir, but I like her too much to do so."

Bishop smiled. "Have to say the same." He weighed the reality, then asked the question first on his mind. "Anything going on with her you think I should know about?"

"She really wants to get out of Bangor, start working on something else," Daniel replied.

"No surprise there. Has she chosen between Maryland or California yet?"

"She hasn't said."

Bishop nodded. "She's going to be exhausted after the presentation tomorrow, and you're heading to Groton the next day. If you haven't already asked her about dinner, I'd ask her early."

"We've got plans," Daniel confirmed. "I realize I'm swiftly going to be at a tactical disadvantage. I'll be in Groton for five weeks."

"Be glad it's not a three-month patrol," Bishop replied.

Daniel nodded. "One of us is going to be a lucky man."

"I have a feeling it's going to be you, Daniel," Bishop said, trying to be objective. "She's dating you, and she's not the type to keep her options open simply to make comparisons. She'll make a decision when she's ready."

"I think we'll both know before the summer is over, sir."

Bishop thought Daniel was right. "You're ready to handle the sonar questions?" he asked.

"I think so, though her paper on the theory is stretching what I can follow. But given the group that will be hearing this idea for the first time tomorrow, their questions should stay in a ballpark I can answer."

"I read the paper and understood it was elegantly above my pay grade," Bishop mentioned. "I saw it work — that's the territory I need to know."

"Same here." Daniel hesitated. "Do you suppose she's ever going to stop discovering things?"

Bishop shook his head. "Comes with the

territory. From listening to Jeff, she seems to waffle between stressed out with a discovery and bored, and a new discovery seems like the easier of the two situations to deal with."

"I haven't seen 'bored' yet," Daniel said, "so I'll take Jeff's word for it."

Bishop shut off the lights and locked the room. He debated for a moment about the wisdom of letting the conversation drop, felt compelled to say one more thing. "Daniel — don't hold her back. If Gina chooses you, give her room to keep exploring, whatever you have to do career-wise."

"Already concluded that, sir. If she's got a flaw, it's the desire to have someone's approval. She's too willing to please. The wrong guy, and she'd turn off the smarts just to fit in as his wife. No way that's going to happen on my watch."

"Thanks for that."

Daniel smiled. "I see who she is, sir, same as you."

11

The commanders' meeting about Gina's creation of a cross-sonar ping was breaking up, and a group had gathered around her to informally ask more questions.

"What's next for you, Miss Gray?" an officer asked.

Bishop rested his hand against the small of her back, letting her know she wasn't facing the questions alone.

"Research on the sun — solar flares, coronal mass ejections. I've been studying the oceans for a decade, and it feels like it's time for a new challenge."

"Our loss, I'm thinking," the captain of the *Pennsylvania* replied.

The meeting had taken six hours with a short break for lunch. Bishop would give himself decent marks on the afternoon session, discussing the tactical implications, but he was relieved the day was done just the same.

Daniel Field joined them. "Ready to go, Gina?"

"Yes." She excused herself with a smile and gathered up her notebooks.

Bishop gave Daniel a nod, knowing he was planning to take Gina out to dinner. His own plans for the next few hours would include a casual version of the afternoon session, held on his back deck with some steaks on the grill. Commanders didn't have a chance to get together very often, and his evening was booked to catch up with his fellow officers.

Bishop stopped when Gina's hand settled on his arm. "Thanks for getting me past today, Mark."

He smiled and lightly covered her hand with his. "You did fine. Go enjoy the evening with Daniel."

Bishop was trying to be fair. He knew there was a powerful marker going to be laid down tonight on Daniel's side and didn't want to dwell on what it might be. That Daniel might propose wasn't outside the realm of possibility. Bishop would consider any state of affairs that didn't include an engagement ring on Gina's finger tomorrow as good news.

It had been a long night. Bishop settled

269

back in a chair at Jeff's kitchen table while his friend lifted bacon out of a skillet. "Word has it the fishing is good along the south bank below the bridge," Bishop mentioned. "Want to run out with me for a few hours?"

"I'm game," Jeff said.

Bishop heard footsteps on the stairs.

"I didn't know you were coming by," Gina said, hesitating in the doorway. She was dressed in jeans and a T-shirt, still barefoot.

Bishop checked out her left hand, relaxed, and gave her a comfortable smile. "I brought the bakery part of breakfast," he replied, nodding to the sack of fresh bagels he'd picked up an hour before. "Jeff and I are talking about going fishing. Want to come along?"

"I'm planning to take a day off — wander a bookstore, watch a movie, take a nap."

"Sounds like a good day," Bishop said. She pulled out a chair, and he slid the bag over to her. "Cream cheese packets are in the sack too."

She reached for one of the plastic-wrapped knives and retrieved cream cheese for her bagel. "Dare I ask about feedback on the presentation yesterday?"

"Solid. Lots of kudos for you. But you don't need another day talking about work. How about another question."

She laughed softly. "Tell me about the fish you're planning to catch."

"I'm hoping for a decent-size bass, but I'll settle for some crappies or catfish. It's more a trip to test out a couple of new lures. And I want to get enough sun that I'm glad for the sunscreen and the sunglasses."

He wasn't surprised at her decision to pass on fishing. It wasn't Gina's preferred way to spend a few hours. But it was just as well since he wanted a chance to ask Jeff some questions. What he wanted for this week was to feel out where she was with Daniel and put down some markers of his own with her before she left the Bangor area.

Bishop stepped into Jeff's living room. Gina muted the game show on television. "You're back early," she said. "Catch something for lunch?"

"The fish weren't biting, and Jeff got a call from Tiffany. He decided helping her move some furniture was a better use of his time. I'm heading back to my place, unless you would like to take a short trip? I'll take you to visit my favorite bookstore."

"Where is it?"

"Seattle."

She hesitated, then turned off the television. "I'd like that."

271

"I thought books might get your attention."

"It's the chance to wander and browse that I like the most."

He drove them to the ferry going across Puget Sound rather than drive down to the Tacoma Bridge. Once aboard, they climbed to the upper deck, and Bishop handed Gina a sandwich he'd had packed in his fishing cooler. She leaned against the rail and took a bite. He suspected she'd be tossing bread scraps to the birds if she wasn't hemmed in by dozens of other passengers.

"Melinda and I used to make this voyage a couple times a month," he mentioned, opening the wrapper on his own sandwich. "She'd go to wander the clothing shops, and I'd spend a few hours with a college buddy, climbing the rock wall at the Gate Ridge gym. She and I would meet up for lunch, then wander along the waterfront like tourists. Or some weekends we'd go the other direction, head to Olympic National Park and spend the day hiking together."

"You climb?"

"Talk about it, practice, but rarely actually go. If Melinda's schedule was free, I'd rather simply hike with her. We became bird watchers — or more accurately, animal watchers. She would count squirrels, give herself points for rabbits, raccoons, deer" — he smiled — "and complain if I was making too much noise, scaring the wildlife away."

"She liked the outdoors?"

"She learned to. At first she humored me and came along because she enjoyed the long conversations we would have. But she came to love the outdoors nearly as much as I do. The last years without her — I've climbed a few times, and done some serious hiking, but I've outgrown my inclination to see how difficult a terrain I can master. I've become more a fisherman."

"Did you blame God after Melinda died?"

He looked over at her, surprised. "Interesting question."

"I'm sorry. It's prying. I shouldn't have asked."

He rested his forearms against the railing, mirroring her stance. "It's all right. A car accident killed Melinda, not God."

"You weren't mad?"

"A deeper emotion than that, I think. I was devastated. Mostly that God had known it was coming, and that He hadn't warned me. I regretted how much time I'd wasted that last year doing less important things than being with Melinda."

He searched to find the right words.

"You've lost people important to you, Gina, so you know what that rip feels like in your life. What I wished for most of all was to have had more of the good before the crushing hard years came, before I was dealing with the grief. I was mad at God for that, that I hadn't been able to have just one more day, just one more memory, before it was over."

"Your memories are good ones."

"They are," he agreed. "I haven't idealized those years, just remembered the good and forgotten the hard. As I look back, they were on the whole very good years — almost a decade. Nothing since has been as enjoyable. There have been great experiences. Commanding the *Nevada* has been wonderful. But life overall has never been as good as those years I was married." He pulled himself out of the reflection to look over at her. "Why do you ask?"

"You seem . . . I don't know, you talk comfortably about Melinda, about your life, and seem content. I don't think I've ever had that. There are always pieces missing that seem to be overwhelming holes in my life."

"Contentment is a choice, I've discovered. You have to accept reality to have contentment, even if you wish that reality would change. You're single, Gina, and you don't want to be. You don't want to accept it."

"Maybe it is that."

Bishop smiled. "No one says you had to live life the easy way, Gina. God would rather you be at peace with circumstances, but it's not the end of the world to realize you're having to struggle. Maybe that's what gives you determination to keep trying to change your life."

"As long as it doesn't lead to a bad decision just for the sake of making a change."

He heard something in her words that had him turning to fully look at her. "What's going on with you and Daniel? Something in your voice keeps sounding slightly worried when you're talking about your life. Spill it. What's going on?"

It was a long time before she answered. "I would like to be the one who is a good wife for him. He's a wonderful guy. But I'm worried I'm not the right wife for him."

Her words once more surprised him. "Why not?"

"I don't like the water, for one thing, and that's where his relaxation and restoration comes from — surfing, water-skiing, boating. And his passion is music. He loves listening to it, playing his guitar, being around musicians and what they're creating. I can appreciate it, but I don't share it that way. He needs someone who shares at least one of those passions, either the water or the music. I'm not a good fit for Daniel, for what he needs." She looked over at him, questions in her gaze. "Not going to say it's not a concern?"

"I'm impressed that you realize it should be a concern," Bishop replied. He rested back against the railing, thinking over what she'd said.

Gina shifted so the wind would blow her hair back from her face rather than across it. "I'd love to think I could adapt and be comfortable in that world of musicians, be a good hostess as friends and family came to enjoy the beach and the boating. I want to be that person. But there is nothing in my history that says I am. Is the *wish* to be different on my part strong enough to adapt, to meld the differences?"

Bishop ignored her question for the moment to ask one of his own. "What are your must-not-haves?"

"He can't drink, smoke, be financially irresponsible, have a roving eye, or a history of letting people down."

He smiled at the concise list. She was pretty good at first principles.

"He's got the majority of my must-haves,"

she continued. "He loves God, is close to his family, has a kindness that runs deep. I can trust him. The problem isn't with Daniel. The shortcomings are with me. His hobbies, his recreation and entertainment, often happen on or in the water, surfing, boating, water-skiing. If that isn't on his must-have list — finding someone who shares his enjoyment of the water — it should be."

"Why don't you like the water?" he asked.

"It's powerful. It's relentless. It erodes the shorelines. It pounds rock into sand. It kills people when it's violent — storms and tsunamis and rogue waves. It takes your breath away and you drown."

"You're afraid of it."

"Basically," Gina replied with a nod.

Bishop tried to figure out what to say. He should have known if he opened the door, she'd take it, and it left him in a quandary. By the time this conversation was over, he was going to be helping Daniel with the answer. Yet it would be better for Gina if he gave her the nuanced answer she needed to hear rather than the simple one that might help him.

"In a good marriage, you have to share some interests in life," he began, "but not all of them. You work around the ones you don't have in common. Daniel's enjoyment of the water, and your caution of it, is a big one to work around, but it's possible. I think you could learn to share his appreciation of music — the compositions, the structure of the music, the way the instruments work in harmony. There are interesting pieces to explore that you'd enjoy. Shared interests are part of what makes a relationship work. If you're totally different in how you prefer to spend your leisure time, it's hard for a marriage to thrive. You're right to understand that."

He studied her face, trying to read her expression. "Daniel may not consider love for the water to be on his must-have list, Gina. He could be perfectly content with you coming down to the dock, helping him around the boat, and then waving from the shore as he takes off with friends to water-ski for a couple of hours while you relax on the beach with a book. It may be simply a wish-for on his part, not a requirement. Have you talked with him about it?"

"Not yet."

"You need to. There's always a tension between who you are versus who you want to be. It's one of the most powerful emotions driving people. But you can't build a good future on the hope you'll become something different once you're married. It doesn't work that way."

"If I end a relationship with a great guy simply because he loves the water and I don't, I'm probably going to regret it for the rest of my life."

Bishop understood her point. "There's no perfect fit, Gina. There's only 'good enough.' Figuring out where that love of water falls on the list is going to be a nuanced problem to sort out. But you're wise to realize it's there. Most people can't name the concerns before they get married and then wonder at the collision that comes after the ceremony. You need to get this right. Because a bad marriage is much worse than being single."

"It seems so trivial. He likes to boat, I don't."

Mark shook his head. "Misreading something that could reflect many hours a week of your lives is not a minor miss. If you both had a passion for the water, there would never be a tension about how you spend your free time. If you don't share it, there always will be. That wears on a marriage.

"The goal of dating is to figure out who you really are, who he really is, and think through where you fit together and where you don't. If you match up well, the marriage thrives. If you don't match up well, you end up with a struggle. You *can* make it work — two people being open and flexible can get around nearly any obstacle — but you both might have been better off not having to deal with those issues all the time. You can't ignore differences, no matter how wonderful the guy is. You can only decide if the marriage will work in spite of it."

Gina studied the approaching shoreline. "Not going to tell me I'm thinking too much?"

"No. Not on this." Bishop relaxed beside her, thinking back. "I got lucky with Melinda. I was totally green for what we needed to make a marriage work, but I was blessed with someone who both fit me well and who had the ability to adapt easily where there could be tension. Actually, I learned how to do that from her. She was a rare find. I'm not expecting that same serendipity if I marry again. It will be a good fit before I offer a ring."

He was surprised at the place Gina was in her relationship with Daniel. Her concerns seemed like ones she'd be thinking about after three or four months of dating, not in the first few weeks. She was watching for stress points, he thought, having come through three failed relationships, wanting to spot problems before she got her heart broke again.

"One last comment, Gina?"

She glanced at him, nodded.

"You could work it out with Daniel. There are guys who love to hunt whose wives never come along, and the marriage thrives. Guys who love to golf. Boating may create a big hole in your schedule, but it's still possible to have a peaceful, good, solid marriage. You simply both have to be comfortable with the way it will be after you marry, rather than get married holding expectations that end up not being met. Don't say no, if this is the only concern. Say maybe, and then talk it through in more depth."

Gina slowly nodded. "Thanks for that advice, Mark."

"Sure." He was trying to play fair to Daniel and to her, even if she didn't understand the dilemma he was in. He wanted her to be happy, and in a good marriage. If that turned out to be with Daniel, he would deal with it and be glad for her.

The ferry slowed on its way into the dock area. Bishop led Gina down to the lower level and his car, and they joined the slow procession roll-off from the ship and into the city. Bishop was comfortable with the silence. He hadn't expected such a revealing conversation. He was beginning to realize he'd underestimated her again. The personal matters were getting a great deal of thought and attention on her part. She got on well with Daniel, but she'd also been noting the details while getting to know him.

Bishop glanced over at Gina with a new topic. "Jeff mentioned that Thomas Keller at the Jet Propulsion Laboratory has offered you a position with the Sun Research Group."

"He has."

"When will you be leaving?"

"I haven't said yes to the offer yet, but it's an open invitation to come whenever I'd like to join them. They're undertaking a five-year project with the goal of modeling the sun's dynamics. I've still got the second sonar idea to look at — the data set you were able to get for me of an all-quiet boomer with a cross-sonar search to find it. It will probably take just a few days, maybe a week to look at the data and check out the idea. If I don't answer my question about it while I'm here, I'll wonder about it for months until I can come back to take a look at the information, so I might as well get it done before I go."

"Personally speaking, I'm glad you'll be around for a few more days." He kept his voice casual, but the comment was anything but.

"When does *Nevada* gold leave for its next patrol?" Gina asked.

"September first."

"Daniel and *Nebraska* blue are heading out to sea mid-November."

Bishop nodded. "They had a longer shore rotation than normal as the *Nebraska* needed to be dry-docked for maintenance. You'll have some time when he's back from sub school to see him before he leaves on patrol. But there's no getting around the fact submariners and our deployments can be hard on relationships."

"I'm figuring that out. How did you and Melinda handle the separations?"

"I've turned out to be somewhat of a letter writer."

"Really?"

"Most guys who deploy on boomers acquire the habit."

She didn't follow up on the comment, and he let the topic drop. He'd kept his letters to Melinda, and they were some of the most revealing ones he'd ever penned. She hadn't been able to read them until he was back from patrol, but she had loved the fact he wrote them for her. He'd learned to be a good husband in part by thinking about her while on patrol, mentally reviewing how their marriage was doing, and making some corrections where he needed to when he was back onshore.

When Bishop pulled into the bookstore parking lot, he touched Gina's arm before she could open her door. "Here's the plan. We've got three hours to scope out the shelves, and I'll buy the fiction you like. And if you hold your nonfiction to under 30 books, I'll carry them for you."

"You don't need to buy the fiction," she protested.

"My treat. It will please me, so be kind and say yes."

She smiled. "I never turn down books, Mark. Deal."

They went their separate ways for the first hour, then Bishop found her in the biography section and settled in to browse with her. She would scan chapter headings and then read three to five pages of the book before making a decision. Four biographies were added to her stack of books before she moved on to mathematics and the physical sciences.

"Why don't you find a table and chair, Mark? This is going to be a slow perusal. I see several I've not run across before."

"In a bit," he replied, resting an elbow comfortably on the next section of shelving. "Why do you enjoy these kinds of books?"

"I love listening to people. A book is someone taking time to develop a thought — create a hypothesis, present evidence, argue a point, draw a conclusion, make their case. Some do it primarily in mathematics, others in lecture format, while others present ideas and build reasons for their conclusion. Books are enjoyable hours of listening to experts on various subjects. I might not agree with everything, but that's a minor point to why I read what they've written. I like the fact they make me think." She added two more books to the stack he held for her.

"If you buy a dozen books, how many are useful to you?"

"Maybe one or two."

"I should have recommended a good library."

She smiled. "This way I get to donate to Goodwill some fascinating books other than popular fiction." She added another book to the pile in his arms. "I do have a bit of discipline to what I read and when. And I have a yearly book budget, which is exorbitant, but I stay within it."

"I'll find a table so you can read a few more pages from these and make sure they're firm choices."

She nodded. "Appreciate that."

Her buying spree ended at 24 volumes. He carried them for her to the checkout counter, watched her sign the credit card slip without a wince after hearing the total. "What's the most you've ever spent on books?" he asked, curious, as he paid for the novels he'd bought for himself and for her.

"I bought a retired professor's library once."

"I could see you doing that. What about your more routine book buys?"

"I've spent five hundred a time or two. Most visits are a few hundred." She glanced over. "You seem surprised."

"Not surprised. Just adjusting to your cost of doing business. Books are certainly cheaper than postgrad class tuition. The way you read, you could test out of most of the classes required for another degree."

"I have done that more than a few times. My parents agreed with your premise — books were cheaper and faster than college courses. They bought a lot of college textbooks for me. I've never changed that habit."

"How many advanced degrees do you have now?"

"Six. I'm still a registered student at three universities. I sit down occasionally and test out on classes, talk with an advisor, and put together a study plan and a research project to finish up another degree. I use them as milestones to judge when I've adequately understood a particular subject. The fact I'm a registered student means I can audit classes, stop by and discuss matters with a professor, pursue what interests me with less of a hassle than if I were merely a guest."

"When did you earn your first Ph.D.?" Mark asked.

"I was 21."

"Are you working on one now?"

Gina nodded. "Satellite dynamics. I've got a research project about the upper layers of the atmosphere, how it heats and expands, its interactions creating satellite drag. I'd like to get a working model of the upper atmosphere figured out. It hasn't been a priority. I pick it up when I've got a few days free, but I enjoy the challenge of it. I'm doing it in coordination with NOAA and NASA, using satellite data from instruments they have aloft, and ground-tracking station data on the precise satellite locations themselves."

"Sounds complex."

"Moderately so. It's mostly data intensive."

Bishop put her two bags of books into the back seat, held the passenger door for her. "I know this area well. We can afford an hour before we take the ferry back across the Sound. Want to enjoy a bit of being a tourist?"

"Sure."

He pulled a map out of the glove box, scanned it to confirm the exit he wanted.

"Where are we going?"

"Do you like surprises?"

"Not particularly."

He smiled. "We're going to the seashell museum."

She looked at him, trying to decide if he was serious. "You're not kidding."

"You can see sea lions whenever you like. Just come down to the Delta Pier when the sun warms the hull of a submarine and watch them sunbathe. And seals are a pretty common sight on a boat ride. Dolphins and the occasional whale can be found with a little effort. But intact seashells — that's a museum specialty."

The museum occupied what had once been a general store, the entrance fee was a dollar, the store shelves had been turned into displays, and the shells were accessible to pick up and study. They came in all sizes and conditions, most of them donated by collectors, who liked to come and enjoy the display, see their names on the cards alongside their shells.

Gina picked up a beautiful pink-toned spiral that had once found a home in the waters off Australia. "Just think of the creature that once lived in this shell and called it home."

"It's beautiful." Bishop wandered around with her, enjoying watching her interest in the minutest details.

"I've always found it fascinating that God made sea creatures' shells so interesting," she observed, "colorful, functional, and yet their bodies are ugly, mostly gray and slug-like. Shells don't decay like plants do, and most abandoned shells get taken over by another sea creature or eventually broken up on the rocks. Beaches made of crushed shells are some of the prettiest in the world. Oh" — she spotted a shell on a lower shelf — "this one has black bands inside, like a tiger shell." She carefully picked it up to turn it over. "See how the width of the bands widens the further out they are from the shell base and how the bands aren't evenly spaced? It looks like a number PI progression in both distances and width. This is so cool." She fingered the smooth, hard surface on the inside. "This one would be vibrant underwater. The stripes would pop as a rich luxurious gray." She carefully set the shell back on the shelf.

They wandered the museum for half an hour. Bishop bought her two shells from the gift shop, both her choices smaller than her fist. "I'll use them as paperweights," she told him as she tucked the purchases into her purse and followed him outside. "This was an odd stop, Mark. Interesting, but odd."

"The novelty of it intrigues me. And I was curious how you'd react," he said.

"What were you expecting?"

He smiled. "Not what you offered." He held the car door for her, then circled around to the driver's side, started the car, pulled out into traffic. "Go ahead and select a favorite book from the bags. I won't mind if you read on the trip home." She opened a sack and selected one. He glanced over. She'd pulled out a romance.

Ten minutes later, she set the book aside. "How was I *supposed* to act when presented with all those seashells?"

He glanced over, as much interested that she'd come back to the question as the fact she'd asked. "I think of it as my adaptability test," he answered. "If you never picked up a shell, never offered a comment, if you had tried to express knowledge you don't have — well, the shell museum is the definition of an unexpected place. There aren't people around you'd be trying to impress, but you're with me. So what do you do? Say you think it's childish? Try to show some polite interest? Have a genuine interest? I bring potential *Nevada* gold crewmen over here occasionally just to see how they react to the museum and to the idea it's where I brought them."

"Mark . . ." She started to say something, then laughed. "I'm not sure what that makes you."

"The captain. I use what's available to me. The smart ones simply ask some questions, figuring I'm going to test them on something. I like the guys who tell me it's an odd destination, guys who roll with it and show some interest, guys who ask if we're done after five minutes. Those are ones I can work with. Men who can't figure out how to handle themselves — what to say, who offer an odd joke, try out sophomoric humor — are the ones I'd rather not have on the *Nevada* gold crew. They're exhibiting a problem with adaptability."

"So the fact I was curious was a good thing?"

He shrugged. "It told me you can be

genuinely interested in seashells. Your going along with the destination was another reminder that you're willing to please. That makes life easy for those around you, but it can also make it difficult at times to figure out what you really like."

"I'm not sure I appreciate being the recipient of one of your 'tests.' "

He smiled. "Now that was the answer I was hoping for. Delivered with a bit of sting too."

"Warn me it's a test next time."

He looked over at her, realized she was embarrassed when he might have expected mad. "Gina, you were worried about Daniel and how you can make it work. I wanted to show you two things. You're more than willing to go along with someone else and what they suggest, and you handle it gracefully. But you have to be willing to say it doesn't interest you and be okay saying that too. Relationships are two layers of conversations. Adapting and also speaking your mind. Don't be so agreeable when you're dating that someone can't figure out who you really are and what you actually like."

She slowly nodded. "That's decent advice."

"I wonder if Daniel even knows how you feel about water. He'll have seen the hesitation, but have you given him the full picture? Will you get stressed if he's out surfing and a wave takes him under? If he's out boating and the weather turns bad? Don't be so agreeable that someone can't figure out the real you — that's one piece of advice. The second part is more subtle but just as important. Be adaptable, agreeable, willing to go along with someone, but don't color away the truth.

"You may find you can adapt and get comfortable boating with Daniel, navigating, handling the radio, being out on the water to watch a sunset — as long as he never approaches a redline. Those visceral 'If you do this, you don't love me because you're putting yourself in danger and disregarding how I feel' redlines. You've got one about water, if you're afraid of it. If you're going to panic and feel deep fear when he surfs a big wave, because he might get sucked under when he's knocked off the board, you have to tell him. You can't surprise him later with those kinds of details about who you are."

"He's supposed to change and no longer surf big waves because I feel a fear that he doesn't?"

"Love doesn't step across redlines. A relationship can't survive repeated breaches of those types of boundaries and remain healthy. You have to know where his lines are, and he has to know yours. And you both have to respect them. If I was genuinely worried about Melinda driving a long distance late at night, she would get a hotel room and make the second part of the trip the next day. Or if it's snowing with some ice, and she didn't want me on the highway, I'd spend the night on base. Those are minor redlines, but you don't dismiss what someone cares deeply about."

She sighed. "If I wasn't a nervous Nelly about water, this would be so much easier."

"How do you feel about the fact Daniel is a submariner? Honest answer, Gina."

"I can cope with it," she said after a moment. "It's not like I haven't felt that low-grade fear whenever I know my brother is out at sea. But statistically I know Jeff is safer in a submarine than he would be driving on the highway to and from the base. So I feel the fear, but I force it aside with logic. I've never asked Jeff not to be a submariner."

"You've worked hard, though, to make his job safer by improving sonar and the seabed navigational maps."

She nodded.

"That seems a reasonable reaction to the worry."

"It at least works for me."

She let the conversation drop, and he didn't try to follow up with another comment. She returned to the book she'd selected and read until they were back on the ferry heading across the Sound. When she joined him on the top deck to watch the sunset over the water, she dropped one of the shells he'd given her into his hand. "You'll need one, when you're going to tell me it's another test. Just give it back to me."

"Okay." He put the shell in his pocket, tried not to read into it anything more than she intended.

She brushed her hair back as the wind blew it across her face. "This was an ideal day, Bishop. I love bookstores. And I appreciate the conversation. Thank you. I needed the break."

"I know you did." He would have liked to intertwine his hand with hers, but instead he put his hands in his pockets. "I enjoyed myself too, Gina. You're good company. And a pretty good sport."

"I'm really not that adaptable."

He lifted one eyebrow.

"You just haven't hit anything I care that critically about yet."

"You're known to dig in your heels?"

"Jeff says I'm obstinate. I like to think I'm simply right."

He smiled and nodded. "Good to know."

12

Bishop skirted around those getting off work and headed up the stairs of the acoustical research building. He glanced in lab three, saw it was empty, and moved on down the hall to Gina's office. She looked totally absorbed in the data she was studying, and two Big Gulp cups were stationed near her elbow. She'd discarded her shoes. Bishop smiled as he tapped on the office door. She glanced over, and her frown of concentration at the screen eased as she offered him a brief smile back. "Hi, Mark."

That intensity had been there too often this last week. "Can I talk you into a coffee break?"

"If you make it a Diet Coke, sure." She slipped on her shoes, then closed down her work, and the screens went back to their spiraling log-in prompt. She opened the wall safe and placed her notebooks inside. "Were you down this way for a reason?"

"I came to find you."

It looked like she didn't know what to do with that statement, and she finally just nodded.

He led her downstairs and stopped at the vending machine to buy them each sodas. "It's a beautiful day. Let's take a walk." He held the back door for her so the suggestion wouldn't require a decision.

Outside, she paused and lifted her face toward the sun, her eyes closed. "Nice. It's been too many hours at the screen lately."

He gave her a moment to enjoy the outdoors, then opened his soda and she did the same. He nodded toward the path that followed the river to the picnic area. "What has you worried, Gina?" he asked as they fell into stride.

"What do you mean?"

"You're back at the terminals, working on the sonar data, putting in as many hours or more as you did when you first arrived in Bangor. You're working on your second sonar idea. And I'm beginning to know you . . . something has you worried."

They reached the picnic area, and she sat down on one of the picnic tables, pulled her knee up on the bench and draped an arm around it. "I thought it was a far-fetched idea and I wasn't expecting it to work. I just wanted to check the data to confirm it. I've realized I made a mistake. I'm having to write a lot of software to put the idea into more than just a conceptual form — to make it tangible — but the idea is turning out to be rather robust."

"Tell me."

She bit her lip.

He took a perch on the table beside her. "That bad, huh?"

"I wish there were times I could unfold my life differently. The security guys assigned to me are warranted, Mark."

The admission told him a lot. He reached over and put his hand atop hers. "Straight out, and as concise as you can explain it," he recommended.

"What if you could find a submarine, not by listening for the noise it makes but by listening for the silence created by its presence?"

She let him think about that statement for a moment before she continued. "The ocean is noisy. Every direction has a slightly different sound, depending on what is going on in that part of the sea. But no matter which way I turn to listen, there is ocean noise . . . unless something significant is in the way, blocking the sound." She paused again, and bit her lip.

"I listen for the silence where there should not be silence," she told him, "and I can tell something is there. Submarines are big, and they block the ocean sounds I should be hearing. With cross-sonar running, I can pinpoint where the sub is. It's the silence that gives the sub away. You only need cross-sonar running and a different way of listening."

Bishop felt something shift in his understanding of her. "It's another conceptually simple idea," he said softly, "but profoundly powerful." Her genius was being displayed by the very simplicity of her ideas. A submarine blocked ocean sounds she should be hearing. The ramifications of that simple idea were breathtaking. "Okay, Gina." The implications began to take shape and he absently squeezed her hand. "Okay."

"The range is massive, Mark. The *Connecticut* and the *Ohio,* running cross-sonar, were easily able to locate the all-quiet *Nebraska* when they were 100 miles away. They did it in every ocean noise condition. During the fourth test, the glacier ice, there was also something else in the data. I found the USS *Kentucky.* It was 213 miles away. It wasn't even in the sea trial plan; it simply happened to be on patrol the next grid over.

"And the kicker?" she added. "This works

best where other sonar techniques struggle and break down. The more noisy the environment, the better and faster it works."

Bishop absorbed that fact, shook his head in wonder. "This will solve the problem of how to conduct search operations inside the littoral zone — the roughly 50 miles from the continental shelf to the shore, where the water depth is less than 500 feet and the ocean ambient noise is so loud that conventional sonar struggles. The sound of the surf crashing against the shoreline, currents running fast in shallow waters, and boats of all types is too much noise for conventional sonar to overcome."

"This algorithm, listening for silence, loves that noisy environment," Gina confirmed. "The more diverse the noise is, the louder it is, the better this technique works."

"All it needs is cross-sonar to be running?"

"Yes. It takes at least four hydrophone sets a distance apart to isolate the noise that should be there and where the object blocking the sound is located."

He closed his eyes and tilted his face toward the sun, letting his mind see the pieces of what this was going to mean. "Could it work with cross-sonar running between two ships on the surface?"

"There has to be a noise source on the other side of the object you're trying to find. In shallow water, surface ships would have better success simply running cross-sonar with an active ping. But in deep water, this should work with some blind spots. Surface ships would see a submarine 30 miles away at a depth of a thousand feet, but they might miss a submarine that was near the surface 10 miles away."

"A battle group will be able to locate submarine threats approaching at much longer distances."

She nodded. Quiet stretched between them, and he didn't try to fill it.

"Sometimes, Mark, I'm so very tired of *thinking.* Sometimes I just want a break from all the ideas, a chance to be normal for a while."

He tightened his hand on hers. "I imagine you do. It will be okay, Gina."

She sighed. "I get to go through it all again, don't I? The presentation to Rear Admiral Hardman, the commanders' meeting, the hand-off to the Undersea Warfare Group."

He could hear the stress she was feeling as her voice faded. "Are you wanting to walk away from this right now? Let others step in and take what you've created and figure out the rest of it? Because they could, you know. You've got enough of it mapped out, it could be left right now in the hands of others."

"It would be a sloppy exit. I don't do sloppy, Mark. I have too much pride in my work and too much of myself invested. Thanks, but I'll get it done myself." She pushed a hand through her hair. "I'm tired. I need a break from this. I needed a break after I proved a cross-sonar ping worked. Instead I fell into a second idea that turns out to be larger, and the pressure I'm feeling is even heavier."

"Slow it down for the next month, Gina. Take the time you need putting this together. I'll help you get through. You've got my word on that."

She nodded. "Something I appreciate a great deal. I thought about not telling anyone this idea, but that would be putting my head in the sand. Would you tell Rear Admiral Hardman, but push it back timewise? I'll get the Navy what it needs; I'd just rather not be answering a lot of questions until I'm ready to make the presentation."

"I can do that." He thought through what was on his schedule for the next few weeks.

"How about Daniel — would he be able to help?"

She gave him a half smile. "I appreciate you finding reasons to put us together. Maybe the last few days to help with the presentation again. Right now it's simply studying the data and trying to get the algorithms refined. The idea works, but to be useful it also has to be fast. That takes finessing."

"Okay. What do you need from me today?"

"Let me go back to work for a couple more hours, then it would be nice if you'd take me home. I really don't want to have to ride with security right now. They remind me of how much I wish for the days before I had either one of these ideas."

"I can do that for you. Want to stop for dinner somewhere on the way?"

"Sure. Jeff's out with Tiffany tonight, and I'd rather not cook for one."

Bishop walked Gina to the door of Jeff's place. She idly spun the daffodil he'd picked for her when he stopped to get a copy of the *Kitsap Sun* to see what local restaurant coupons were being advertised. Dinner had been a quiet meal at an Italian place new to both of them.

"Good night, Gina. I hope you sleep well."

She nodded as she unlocked the door. "Thanks for dinner," she offered before stepping inside. He walked back to his car.

"Mark."

Bishop turned. Jeff had parked on the street since his car was in the driveway. "Hey, Jeff." It looked like Jeff's evening with Tiffany had ended early.

"Mind coming in for a minute?" Jeff asked, walking up the drive. "I need to talk with you."

"Sure." Mark followed Jeff inside. He heard the water shut off upstairs as Gina no doubt was getting ready to turn in.

"What's going on with you and Gina?" Jeff asked, slipping off his suit jacket. "I called her to check in and found out she was at dinner with you. That's three meals together — that I know of — recently. That's not like you, not if it's only work-related." They had walked into the kitchen, and Jeff pulled out a chair and tugged at his tie.

Bishop thought about it for a moment. "What if I told you I might regret saying no to your original suggestion that I ask her out?"

Jeff paused. "Does she know that?"

"I'm not asking her to make a decision between Daniel and me, Jeff. I'm simply

305

laying the groundwork so she knows she has options. Daniel will be back from Groton in a few weeks. Then we'll see what makes sense. She's rather busy at the moment."

Jeff frowned, and Bishop realized she hadn't told her brother yet. "She's made another sonar discovery," Mark said.

"No. She does not need this," Jeff protested, shaking his head. "Tell me it's small, just a little nugget."

"It's a whale," Bishop replied, shaking his own head with a rueful smile. "She's solved the littoral problem."

"How?"

"What if you could find a submarine, not by listening for the noise it makes, but by listening for the silence created by its presence?"

Jeff went still. "She figured out a way," he finally said, "to show when a sub is standing in front of a noise source?"

Bishop nodded. "And the noisier the environment, the better it works."

"Even I understand this one." Jeff rubbed his face with both hands. "What are we going to do with her?"

"Protect her," Bishop replied, going to the heart of the matter.

Jeff sighed. "What's the plan?"

"Tell Rear Admiral Hardman. I've got the

first half hour with him when he arrives back from D.C. Gina's already got all the data she needs to confirm that this works."

"That all-quiet with the cross-sonar search test we ran during the sea trial," Jeff said, guessing at the data source.

"Yes. She's working on the algorithms for what she calls a cross-sonar quiet search."

"It's going to totally change coastal water intelligence work," Jeff said. "Fast-attacks routinely move into the shallow waters to deploy or recover SEAL teams or tap into communication networks to gather intelligence. Stealth will be meaningless if our enemies learn how to do this. They'll see us coming just because we're there."

"Actually it's worse than that," Mark said. "Two surface boats running cross-sonar could do a quiet search and locate a boomer 30 miles away and a thousand feet below them."

"Do you ever wish she would stop having these sonar ideas?"

Bishop smiled. "I wish life could be so simple. We need to hear them, Jeff. But she would concur with you — she would like to never have a sonar idea again. She's really stressed out right now. She'd like everything Navy to go away for a while."

"She'll shift to working nights again if

necessary," Jeff predicted, "just to keep down the number of people asking her questions." He sighed and changed the subject. "If you're interested in her, are you planning to tell her? It seems to me silence isn't going to help you much."

"Eventually. Now's not the right time."

"So what changed your mind?"

Bishop paused, thought over his answer, for there was a line he wouldn't cross regarding Gina that extended even to her brother. "I like her smile." The answer was simple, but it summed up a lot of layers of who she was.

Jeff considered him. "I'd suggest you change 'eventually' to be more like *soon.* If you're serious, she needs to know."

"I'm serious," Bishop replied with a nod.

"She really likes Daniel," Jeff added quietly.

"I know she does. You chose a good man. It's going to play out however it does, Jeff. I'm determined she won't get hurt through this."

"I trust you, Bishop. I'd be steering you away if I didn't. Don't get me wrong. You were my first choice, but it's going to be weird having you date my sister."

Bishop tugged out his car keys. "I don't plan to say much about it with you, and I doubt she does either."

"I'll gladly stay hands-off unless I'm asked a question. The last thing I want to be doing is giving her more dating advice. I did that when she was 14, and she's remembered it," Jeff said ruefully.

Bishop laughed. "Good night, Jeff."

Commander Mark Bishop waited with the duty officer as the military jet touched down and taxied in toward a hangar. He moved to meet Rear Admiral Hardman when the jet stairway deployed. "Welcome back, sir."

"Good to see you, Bishop." Hardman handed his bags to the driver and motioned to Mark. "Ride with me."

He climbed into the back seat on the passenger side as the rear admiral settled behind the driver.

"We're secure here. What's the trouble?" Hardman asked.

"Not trouble exactly, sir, more like another surprise. Gina Gray's second idea is more powerful than the first. She's cracked the littoral problem — how to find a sub in the noisy environments close in to shore."

The admiral looked at Bishop for a while. "She's having an interesting summer, isn't she?" he said. "We've been hoping someone would get their arms around that problem.

What's her solution?"

"The ocean is noisy. A sub gives away its presence by blocking ocean sounds. She's listening for silence where there shouldn't be silence. The noisier the environment, the better this technique works."

"She's not giving us easy operational moves."

"No, sir. Two surface ships running cross-sonar can use this technique, so it's not limited to the sub fleet. It's going to improve battle group visibility considerably."

"Submarines used to be hard to find. Put together the range cross-sonar gives us, an active ping that can't be heard, and now this . . . she's turning the lights on in the ocean. She's done everything but take a photo."

"It sure feels that way, sir. We're going to have unmatched visibility underwater — at least until allies and enemies figure this out and can do it as well."

"When is she going to be ready to provide details on this latest idea?"

"I don't have that answer yet, sir. I know she's refining the algorithms at the moment."

"As soon as possible, Bishop. So if she needs anything, clear the path for her."

"Will do, sir."

"How are you managing juggling the *Nevada* and working with what she has going on?"

"I'm managing fine, sir. My XO is staying with me for another patrol, so we've been able to coordinate when I haven't been available."

"Good. I don't want to make the call to take you off either one, Bishop. But unfortunately for you, if they come into a hard collision, I would be asking you to give up the *Nevada*. Gina Gray appears to be working well with you, and I don't have to remind you that what she's working on is high priority."

"I would understand the decision, sir. I hope I never have reason to say it's become a concern, but I will inform you if it does. I won't shortchange either the *Nevada* or this new possibility."

"Good enough. Can you tell me one thing, Bishop? Is this the last of her sonar ideas for now?"

"I believe so, sir." Bishop hesitated, then added, "She thought this one wouldn't work. She then checked the data to confirm that and was surprised to discover just how robust and workable the idea is in practice."

Hardman smiled. "Good to know she surprises herself sometimes. The SecNav

311

watched her first presentation, got to the point in the video where she said her idea was to remove the man-made noise of the ping and send a recorded ocean sound instead. He stopped the video, turned to his deputy and asked why the Navy hadn't hired this woman back when she was in college and originally gave them cross-sonar. His deputy opened the background file on Gina Gray and told the SecNav she'd turned down a job offer, a fellowship, a block grant through the DoD, and a consultant role, but she would appreciate it if the Navy let her brother, Jeff Gray, interview for a position on the USS *Seawolf.*"

Bishop smiled. "Sounds like Gina."

"See if there's anything in particular she would like, Bishop. We'll accommodate her if we can. A paycheck for a few weeks of her time doesn't seem like adequate compensation, given the ground she's breaking for us."

"I'll ask, sir."

13

Gina heard the soft footfalls of Mark's tennis shoes along the hall by her office, then the familiar light tap on the door, sounds she had grown used to over the last week, as he joined her. He didn't smell of sweat or salt water or smoke from a fire drill, so it had been a rare day spent in the office rather than the training facility. A deep lavender rose slid into the vase beside her terminal, where the daffodil had finally wilted and been removed.

Mark leaned against the corner of her desk. "You need a break, Gina. I can almost see that headache."

"I still can't get the speed I want in the object-shape algorithm." She leaned back in her chair, rubbed at her neck. She turned toward him, raised an eyebrow at the civilian clothes. "Getting ready to play hooky?"

"PR people with a camera have been dictating my day. They're doing an update on one of the 'life in the military' brochures. Melinda roped me into the first one, and the Navy hasn't let me bow out of the assignment since." He turned his wrist so she could see the time. "Sunset means call it a day."

"I really wanted to get this particular algorithm figured out." She shifted the keyboard and saved her work, then pointed the mouse at a private data file. "You want to see something fascinating?" She'd been monitoring what was happening with the Sun Research Group. She replayed the solar flare which had occurred that morning. The image from the SOHO satellite feed was breathtaking. The solar flare coiled out from the sun's surface in a fiery loop, then burst into pieces.

"This is what you're going to work on next?" Mark asked, intrigued.

"Yes. What causes them, how they form, how they behave, what happens to that massive burst of heat and light and energy as they come apart."

"I can see why you're looking forward to it." He watched the replay of the solar flare, then looked over at her. "You need an evening away from sonar algorithms and work or *you're* going to burn out. Wrap it up and come with me, Gina. I'll find us a movie to go see, a late dinner afterwards."

She blinked in surprise, then looked away, at the rose, seeing it in a new light. "Mark, I'm dating Daniel," she said quietly.

"I know. I made a mistake when Jeff first suggested I ask you out. I bowed out and said no because of the age gap between us. I'm correcting that error in judgment. I can't think of someone I would enjoy spending an evening with more than you."

She wasn't sure what to say, and too much time passed in silence to be comfortable. Her embarrassment about what to do just kept growing.

Mark gently smiled. "Daniel and I both like you, Gina. Enjoy it. It's considered a good thing."

She shook her head, confused. "I can't break up with Daniel just so I can have dinner with you."

"I'm not asking you to do that. Call him, tell him I invited you out, see what he says, then say yes. I'm looking at a lady in desperate need of a night off. Trust me and come. A casual, come-as-you-are date. Starting 10 minutes after you let Daniel know." He picked up her cell phone and held it out to her.

"You're not going to accept no, are you?"

"I'd prefer a yes."

■ ■ ■ ■

She chose an action PG-13 movie so there would be fewer awkward scenes to sit through and, surprisingly, felt herself relax in the nearly empty theater. She loved the big-screen movie experience. She shared popcorn with Mark, reached for another handful as the movie previews started. "I don't understand why you want to spend an evening with me, Mark."

"We need to work on your self-esteem," Mark said. "I enjoy your company. I've been thinking about asking you out since the sea trial."

"I've never thought of you as . . . well, date potential," she said, feeling seriously uncertain about how to proceed. This was the guy she had always thought of as Jeff's friend, someone she knew she could trust, and now it was pivoting into something she wasn't sure how to define. "Tonight is a one-off break from work. It can't be more than that."

He shrugged. "I'll take what I can get, Gina. I put myself in this bind. I let Jeff's suggestion slip by me, opened the door to have him introducing you to Daniel. I'm not asking you to get me out of the mess I made for myself. I'll settle for the fact you're dating Daniel, and you're getting to know me while he's away."

"I already know you pretty well."

He glanced over, raised an eyebrow at that. "Do you?" He shook the bag of popcorn, and she reached for another handful. "You don't know me yet, Gina," he offered quietly.

She nodded, accepting the caution. "Daniel was more understanding about this evening than I would have been had the situation been reversed."

Mark smiled. "The thing about men, Gina, is that we're competitive. It's in the genes. Had he said he preferred that you say no, it would be an admission that he was worried that if you spent time with me, you would like me more than you do him. He had to say 'no problem' or it would have been a problem."

She ran that logic back and then laughed. "Guys' egos are odd."

"Seriously, I understand why you're dating Daniel. I hope I've let you know that I like him and I think he could be a good fit for you. I'm not trying to step on any of your decisions about him. I'm simply fighting a very tight calendar. If Daniel doesn't turn out to be your choice, I'd like to be at least a viable option before I have to disappear for 90 days on patrol. The *Nevada* returns in six weeks. I'll be coordinating the refit and then be away at sea. I don't have the luxury of waiting, Gina."

"That's what tonight is, a marker?"

"It's permission to get to know me."

She stared at him, surprised at the answer, then slowly nodded. Not as Jeff's friend, Melinda's husband, Commander of the USS *Nevada,* but the man, Mark Bishop. "Anything I want to know?"

He considered before he answered. "Within reason."

Her attention for the movie faltered as questions kept coming to mind. She wanted to know a lot of things. She wished she had a pad of paper and a pen. Even scrawling a few words in the dark on a napkin would be helpful to remember the questions. She finally reached for her purse and tugged out the university-offer letter — the envelope could be sacrificed. She searched for a pen.

Mark held out his pen.

"You're missing a good movie," he whispered.

"You can bring me to see it again," she whispered back and began writing reminder words on the envelope.

■ ■ ■ ■

Mark would give Gina points for focus. The envelope was crammed with writing across both sides. He took her hand as they left the movie theater. He might have only tonight before she marshaled her arguments not to see him while she was dating Daniel Field, and he wouldn't be able to fault her if that was the decision she reached. But knowing this might be the only casual evening he had with her for a while, he was determined to put some substance into it.

"Ask your questions. We're going to take a walk because it's a comfortable night and the restaurant I want us to try isn't far from here. I'll answer what I can."

She hesitated, looked at him twice, before she seemed to accept the open invitation with a cautious nod. "Why do you want to get married again?"

He glanced over, amazed at the opening question. "Interesting. Why I want to get married again . . . It's simple. I miss being a husband."

"That answer doesn't tell me much. Could you elaborate?"

"It actually tells you a lot."

He let her think about that rather than offer more.

"Why do you talk about Melinda so often?"

"She's my history, my point of reference for what marriage is like. You need to know some of my story with her to understand where I'm coming from."

"Why me?"

He hesitated, wondering what direction to take with his answer. He looked at her, smiled. "You're not boring. That is worth a great deal to me."

She bit her lip. The gesture reminded him again how young she seemed at times. He could guess at her likely rejoinder, the one which had just gone unsaid.

"Gina, I'm not making a play for your emotions tonight because I just tossed the idea of me being a date possibility at you. I won't unpack the emotions I feel about the matter until you've had some time to shift what you think about me. It wouldn't be playing fair."

She nodded. "I think I'm grateful for that."

He tightened his hand on hers. "I'm not going to kiss you good-night for the same reason. That has nothing to do with what I'd like, and everything to do with what I think is best for you."

"Okay." He felt her hand relax in his. She looked down at her envelope and bit her lip again. "You didn't have a family with Melinda. Was that by plan?"

"We would have liked to have a family, but we hadn't yet begun pursuing medical reasons for why Melinda wasn't getting pregnant." There was some remembered regret with that answer, that they had not had children even though he was glad a young child hadn't been faced with losing a mom. Gina seemed to recognize the emotions around this too, for she changed the subject.

"You like fishing, hiking, rock-climbing. What else do you like to do?"

"Watch baseball. Build stuff around the house. Read."

"I don't have a sense of what your time is like. I know you're at Bangor for long hours during the week."

"Some of that is the job, some of it is that I enjoy being around the guys. It's not a 40-hour-a-week job, but it's a manageable career. There is always something to do at Bangor, so I've fallen into the habit of being there rather than in an empty house."

She stopped asking questions. He gave her a few moments, then squeezed her hand. "What's wrong?"

"I'm interviewing you."

"That's a bad thing?"

She nodded.

He laughed. "Gina, one of the things you've got to get past is the idea there's a right way to begin a relationship and date. What's wrong with asking for information?"

She didn't reply.

"You want swept off your feet, dazzled, pursued," he guessed.

"Maybe some combination of that."

"Gina, I appreciate romance too. The sentimental cards and the special meals, the gifts and the feeling of being together, focused on each other. It's a good part of marriage, and I'm not going to be immodest and say I wasn't pretty good at the romantic gestures. Melinda had a special spot for a DQ Blizzard delivered to her office. She also loved flowers of all kinds, or small, inexpensive gifts wrapped in pretty paper with a bow. And I enjoyed giving them to her, for no reason other than to see her smile when I handed her the package.

"Given time, I'll find the simple things that have a tangible meaning for you. At first guess, your short list is probably time, and substance in a conversation. I'll figure out what matters to you, if you'll let me. But I'm asking you to please take seriously the fact that all I've got is six weeks before I'm tied up preparing to leave again. Ask your questions so we can get some of the surface stuff off the list early on." He glanced over. "You should have asked me by now if I smoke, since that's on your must-not list."

"Do you?"

"Nope, never have."

"Are you financially responsible?"

She had braved asking another of her requirements, and he smiled as he answered, "I'm a careful planner, and a bit on the thrifty side. You seem looser with money than I am. I'd guess you have an inclination to buy whatever you need, but I think you also keep your need list short."

"That's accurate."

"What else was on your list? Oh yes. I don't drink because I don't like the taste, rather than object to it on principle. Melinda would have said I'm a one-gal kind of guy. And I do my best not to let people down."

"Jeff says you're a person people lean on."

He nodded, accepting the description. "Some of that is the type of job I have. I've got a young crew. The commander is the voice of experience and reason and direction for everything sub-related, and that trust tends to expand so the crew also

323

includes career advice and family concerns."

They reached the restaurant and found it moderately busy. He asked for a table off to the side of the room, held Gina's chair for her. "I can tell you that the chicken and the seafood are both good choices here," he said as he sat down across from her.

She scanned the menu. "I'm comfortable with the scallops and a salad." She set aside the menu and reached for one of the hot rolls their server had brought. "Next note on the envelope — I was going to ask about your biggest disappointment in life, but I want to stop with the questions for a while. You can ask a few, if you like, or talk to me about the next few weeks."

"You're nervous."

"I never would have thought in terms of you and me. You've been a wonderful friend in every way, but I'm uncomfortable sitting here, Mark. I'm dating Daniel. I shouldn't be here."

He pulled out his phone and punched in a number. "Daniel, tell her again she has your permission to see a movie and have dinner with me. Yes, I'm aware of the time in Connecticut."

He handed over the phone.

"Hi, Daniel." She listened, shot Mark a surprised look, then smiled. "Thanks, Daniel. Go back to sleep."

Mark pocketed his phone. "Okay?"

"I've been told to order something really expensive for dinner and enjoy myself."

Mark chuckled. "Sounds like Daniel." He scanned the menu, chose shrimp and steak for himself, set the menu aside. "Okay, I'm too old for you?"

"I don't know how to answer that question. If you were 60 and I was 30, it would matter. So I know it's relevant, but I don't think your age — or mine — has come up during my three hours of thinking about this so far."

"You seem rather young to me at times, Gina. Bright certainly, but maybe a bit insecure? I don't think you have a lot of confidence around guys."

She simply nodded.

"Has it always been that way or has it gotten worse with Kevin being the latest blow?"

"My track record leaves me cautious."

He wondered what it was going to take to repair that damage. "Answer me one question, Gina. Why do *you* want to get married? Not the answer that sounds correct, but the one in your gut that might even embarrass you a bit to put into words."

She flushed, but finally answered him. "Since I was a little girl, I've always wanted to be married. I wanted someone to be my knight in shining armor to rescue me from trouble and love me. When you're 14 and at college, you dream a lot about being rescued."

He considered her words for a long moment, then nodded. "Melinda said she was 12 when she decided for sure she was getting married one day. She knew she would look fabulous in a wedding dress, and she wanted that album of photos with her looking her best to have for the rest of her life. The guy in the picture didn't even have an image yet. She just wanted the wedding dress."

Gina smiled. "You love that story."

"I do. It amused me when she told me, but I made a point of giving her that huge wedding album as my wedding gift to her. She used to look at it once or twice a year, delighted with the memories of that day. Childhood dreams can be powerful things, Gina. It's good to know they are there."

"Did you have one?"

"Starting at about age 10. Not about marriage directly. I just wanted her to *like* me. The *her* varied through the years with whatever crush I had going at the moment." He broke a roll in two. "It's still a powerful dream. I'll appreciate it a lot when you decide that you like me, Gina, as something more than a friend."

"You mean that?"

"I do. If you make that decision, it will matter to me a great deal."

14

Mark chose the indirect route to their destination to avoid a steep gradient in the hike.

"Do you consider this a date?" Gina asked.

He was surprised she would have to ask. "Sure," Mark said. "I'm planning to share my superduper spot to watch the fireworks. And the second folding chair I'm lugging up this hill for sure makes it a date."

"Because you forget to mention there would be 80 or so friends of yours coming along."

Mark laughed, looked at the crowd climbing to various elevations on the hillside, then back over at her. "Fourth of July spent with the gold crew is tradition. If I'd mentioned them, you might not have spent so much time getting ready for the evening, and I appreciate the results. You look very nice."

The gold-colored top she wore was the

perfect shade to go with the gold crew colors, and there were red, white, and blue shoelaces in her tennis shoes.

"Thank you. I tried my best."

"Did Jeff make sure you packed marshmallows?"

She patted the backpack strap on her shoulder. "Right before he took off for points unknown with Tiffany."

"He probably had a boat in mind, so they could watch the fireworks from the water and have some privacy."

Mark spotted the point he preferred, saw the XO had dropped the captain's colors at that location to save it for him. He picked up the gold flag and slid it into his pocket. "What we won't have tonight is privacy, as every member of gold crew is now trying to figure out who you are. Once they have a name, speculation will circle whether this is a date or if it's me doing a favor for Jeff." He opened the two folding chairs and settled hers on firm ground.

"The hike down this hill in the dark is going to be tricky," she noted.

Mark glanced over at her. She'd ignored his comment and changed the subject. Interesting. He scanned the crowd. "I would bet there are more than a hundred flashlights on this hillside right now. It's rather pretty when people begin to move down the hill. This spot has been the *Nevada* gold crew's gathering place on the Fourth for the last 20 years. The members of the crew change, but the Fourth of July assembly here continues on. The campfire by the pavilion will be lit soon after sunset, to be ready for marshmallow-toasting when the fireworks have finished."

"What did you bring us for supper?"

He unzipped his backpack. "Peanut butter and jelly sandwiches."

"What kind of jelly?"

"Strawberry."

"You were talking with Jeff."

"It didn't take that much sleuthing. You're a creature of habit, Gina. I rather like it." He handed her a sandwich, accepted the soda she put into his hand in return. "I'm glad you decided to come."

"I can't see the fireworks from Jeff's condo."

Mark smiled and settled back in his chair to eat his sandwich and drink his soda.

The calendar had given him a way to convince her to come out with him for a second date, and he would take any help from whatever direction it came. She wasn't comfortable seeing him while dating Daniel, and he admired that about her, though he chafed at the restrictions it created. Tonight the goal was to create a good impression, make a good memory, be sure she enjoyed her time with him, and do a final gut check that Gina really was the woman he wanted to pursue. When Daniel returned, this situation was only going to get more complex.

Mark Bishop spotted Daniel Field getting off the flight at the Seattle airport and moved to intercept him.

"Commander. I didn't expect you to be my ride, sir."

"A lot has been happening the last few weeks in Gina's world. I'm here to fill you in on the drive to Bangor. At least my perspective on it."

"Appreciate that. I think. I've got a duffel checked," Daniel said, and they headed toward baggage claim. "She's mentioned your two dates, sir. I'm gone five weeks and you complicate things with only two dates? I'm almost embarrassed to say how worried I was about being gone."

Mark just smiled. "You've got stiff competition, Daniel, even if it doesn't appear that way yet. But we'll set that aside for now, as it's sonar matters that are going to step on us both."

"She's figured out something else?"

"A submarine, sitting in front of a noise source, is visible."

Daniel winced. "A quiet sub, and she still turns on the lights?"

"That's the sentiment going around. When she's ready to present the idea, it's going to need another video, another commanders' meeting. You're being drafted to help out."

"Glad to do so, sir."

"Your first priority — she needs a break tonight, and you've been nominated. Interrupt her, take her some food, and make her laugh. She'll be glad to see you."

Daniel smiled. "That I can do."

"If there's something you can help her with, make the offer — the video, the paper, but don't push if she says she's got it covered."

"I'll go easy. How many hours has she been putting in?"

"She hasn't slept in that office yet, but she might as well have. I tugged her out for the two dates she mentioned. She wants this done and handed off. I think she's close to being finished. The algorithms are working. She just doesn't have the speed she's looking for yet, and keeps coming up with new ways to cut down the amount of processing to be done."

At the car, Mark handed over the working draft of the paper Gina had written. "Read while I drive."

Daniel read for 35 minutes. "She's off the scale with her ability to do sonar math. It looks like she just jotted these equations down on the page, drew some arrows, sketched a smiley face beside the proof it worked, and photocopied the pages. The pages on the idea and the theory behind it, the background — I can see her struggle to get that discussion smoothed out and concise. I may be able to help her polish that a bit more."

"She's been working on sonar for so long, the math is second nature to her," Mark concurred. "Whereas the document is more a pitch, as in 'Trust me, this idea works, and here's why it's viable.' "

Daniel nodded. "Drop me off at the acoustical lab rather than housing. I'd rather see Gina first before the stack of mail waiting for me."

Gina wasn't sure what made her look over her shoulder. The sound of footsteps, a shift of the door? "Daniel!" She spun around with delight, the headphone cord tangling around her chair's arm. "I thought your flight was coming in tomorrow."

"A standby seat came open," he replied, reaching over to recover the headphones. He punched the recording that had finished playing to start over, listened for a moment, and grinned.

"I like the recording you made for me," Gina said. "It helps me concentrate when I'm working."

"I'm glad. It's one of my better sessions on the guitar." He set aside the headphones. "I missed you, Gina. Five weeks was a long time."

"I missed you too." He looked better than her memory of him.

"Bishop said you've got another idea and video for us to work —"

"I do," she put in, "and I'd appreciate the help."

"He'll clear things so I can give whatever time you need." There wasn't a second chair in the office, so he disappeared for a minute and came back with one.

She reached over and pulled the headphone jack, turned on the speakers so they could both hear his music.

"I want to apologize for going out with Mark while you were in Groton, Daniel. I feel awful about that. The circumstances of that first invitation — if I'd had a few more

334

minutes to think about it, I would have figured out a way to decline. And the Fourth of July, I got into a bind. If I'd said no, Jeff would have insisted on staying home with me rather than going out with Tiffany."

"I'm not surprised Bishop asked you out. I've known for a while he was interested, Gina."

"You have."

"You didn't notice when he stopped wearing his wedding ring? Or notice how many times your paths were crossing?"

"I admit, I've been clueless."

Daniel laughed. "You called me. That was a nice gesture, and all I needed from you. I don't mind the contrast with Bishop. We're different guys."

She didn't know what to say. She did like Mark, even if she couldn't figure out what to do with his interest in her. "Well, I won't be seeing him again while you're here."

"Why don't you assume you'll have to play that by ear, based on what Bishop does? We're fine, Gina. I'll tell Bishop if he's stepping on my toes and ask him to back off. Mark and I understand each other. It's honestly not going to bother me if you two grab a meal occasionally or go for a walk. I know he's a good man who'll be in your life because of your brother no matter what happens this summer."

"All right, Daniel. Thanks."

He studied her, smiled. "During the flight back I decided it was probably an appropriate time in our relationship to lay my cards on the table. And since you've had some miserable conversations that start this way, I'm going to give you a better version of this speech right off the bat. Let me do that now."

He took a deep breath and looked intently at her. "Gina, it's my hope and intention that we end up somewhere permanent, if that's where this leads both of us. You and I are very well suited in many ways, and we've got some differences to work through. That's the value of time together before 'permanent' is on the table. There are things for both of us that are cautions, which need more time, but there's nothing that says I don't want to pursue this with all my heart. Is that clear enough for now?"

The conversation was pushing toward somewhere she did want to go, and she could feel herself blushing. "Yes."

"When it's time for you to make the decision on where you want to move for work — California, Maryland, back to Chicago, wherever — it will be time to decide about us, and whether a long-distance relationship makes sense. These kinds of decisions are good things, Gina, not something to worry over. I *would* like you to consider coming with me to Georgia for a few days after you finish up work here and this presentation. Come meet my family and see my home. Have a few days of a true vacation."

She had worried about Daniel feeling hurt, not being as interested in her when he returned, and instead he was moving rapidly, even beyond where she had thought they were. He *was* interested. Seriously interested since he was suggesting she meet his family. "I would like that, Daniel."

"I'm thinking maybe five days — a couple for travel, three days there. Enough time I can show you the sights and what I like best about Georgia, for you to get to know my family."

"What will you tell your family?"

"That I'm bringing home a good friend. I'll leave unsaid the fact I hope it becomes something permanent one day. They'll likely make that leap without the words." He smiled. "I've got a big family. If you like them, it may seal the deal in my favor."

"Family should be a factor," she said softly, still adjusting to the idea he'd just asked her to meet them.

He tilted his head and changed the subject. "Your tan is fading."

"I found I actually miss our Sunday afternoon outings on your boat," she replied, then hesitated, remembering Bishop's advice. "I do need to tell you one thing. You must have noticed I'm somewhat afraid of the water. It's going to scare me if you surf a big wave or go out boating during bad weather."

"I realized that, Gina. When a guy becomes a husband, he has a responsibility not to take as many chances as when he was single. It's called common sense. You'll depend on me not to get hurt or killed chasing an adrenaline rush. I'm not saying it will always be easy to adapt, but I'm willing to tone down what I do on the water. I can live with that."

"Is there something you've noticed about me I'll need to change?"

"You and I have different tempos as it relates to work. I can call the workday done, and when I walk away from the sub, I can relax, go be on the water or go play guitar with the guys. You find it difficult to relax. Your head is always at some level at work — the job is always with you."

She glanced at the desk full of notes and the terminal with multiple screens of code open. She'd been right here for most of the last five weeks. "I'm afraid you're right about that."

"It's the nature of what you do, Gina, that new concepts come at any time of day or night. You should be grabbing a pad of paper and pen when the ideas are there. I might be able to help you, though, when it comes to leaving the desk and stepping away from it all for a while, to find the value in rest and play."

"The last five weeks prove your premise. My life was more balanced when you were in Bangor than it was when you were in Connecticut. You're good for me, Daniel."

He started to say something, then must have thought better of it. He leaned back in his chair, crossed his hands on his knee. "I thought up a few jokes to tell you while I was in Groton. Want to hear them?"

"Sure."

"What color is red in the dark?"

"I don't know."

"I don't know either."

"That's awful." But she couldn't help but laugh.

Daniel smiled. "What time does the sun come up?"

She shook her head.

"Sunrise."

She laughed. "Awfully lame."

"They get worse. What times does a bear get up?" He waited a beat. "Whenever his wife wants him to."

She struggled to stop the laughter. "Please don't quit your day job. You must have had a lot of downtime out there."

Daniel smiled, then leaned forward and gently kissed her. "I'm glad I'm back."

"Wrapping up for the night?"

Gina turned, saw Mark walking down the hall toward her. "Yes. I just pulled the server. Connolly is securing it for me." She glanced back toward her office, noticed the light was off. Daniel had gone downstairs with the box of books she'd asked him to carry out for her. She fell into step beside Mark when he gestured to the stairs.

"Thanks for sending Daniel over. He's been a help."

Mark held out a bag of pretzels. "You're welcome. Did he make you laugh?"

"Yes," she said, smiling as she pulled out a pretzel.

"Good." They headed toward the entrance.

He really had stopped wearing his wedding ring. She had to be the most unobservant woman ever when it came to guys. Mark wasn't here by accident tonight; he'd come looking for her. She wasn't ready to deal with Mark and Daniel in the same evening. "I'll have this idea on video and ready to present in a few days."

"You had a breakthrough?"

"A lot of small things that finally yielded the processing speed I need." She'd pushed through work that should have taken five months in five weeks, and she was feeling it.

"Daniel is still here?"

"Yes. A friend dropped off his car. He's giving me a lift home."

"Anything I can do for you?"

"Would you proofread the document for me this weekend?"

"Sure. Are you okay, Gina?"

"What . . . why do you ask?"

"You look somewhat overwhelmed."

She didn't respond right away. "Yeah, I am." She was having to make decisions about what to focus on when she was done here, where to work next, what the future was with Daniel, what to tell Mark.

He stopped walking, held her gaze. "I'm not apologizing for my part in your feeling overwhelmed. But the fact that you are bothers me."

She half smiled. "I wouldn't know what to do with it if you did apologize," she admitted. "Daniel said you picked him up at the airport. Why are you being helpful against your own interests, Mark?"

"Maybe I'm simply thinking of yours first."

"Don't hurry me to make a decision."

He smiled. "It's not in my interest to do so — you'd choose Daniel. The *Nevada* is back in port in two weeks, and I'm soon going to be as overwhelmed with work as you've been. But I'm in the office tomorrow with no meetings on the schedule. Want to stop by?"

She should tell him no. Only four hours before, Daniel had leaned over and kissed her. "I'll see," she finally replied. She did like this man. She just didn't want to be involved with him until after she'd made a decision about Daniel. And she had no idea what that decision should be. She didn't even know what she wanted anymore.

"Quit worrying," Mark said.

She glanced over at him.

"I can see your thoughts running in circles."

Mark was beginning to understand her as well as Jeff did. She'd always wanted someone who could see the real Gina. Through the outer door's glass she could see Daniel loading her box of books in his trunk. "I need to go."

"You do." Mark held the door for her. "Good night, Gina."

"Good night, Mark."

Gina wasn't surprised to find Jeff waiting for her. He'd been remarkably quiet about what was going on with Daniel and Mark, but she knew her brother hadn't missed much. At least he hadn't turned on the porch light when she'd arrived home with Daniel to see her share a good-night kiss. She set the books Daniel had carried to the door for her by the stairs, then went and found a soda. She settled on the chair across from the couch, and Jeff muted the show he was watching. "I'm going to Georgia with Daniel to meet his family," she told him.

Jeff sat up straighter on the couch, leaned forward. "Okay."

She half smiled. "It's just a visit."

"Nothing is 'just a visit' when it involves family, Gina, you know that. You've decided you're serious about him."

"I might be. He's a wonderful guy."

"Bishop is interested too."

"I know."

Jeff studied her, then said, "I like Daniel — I'm the one who introduced you, you'll remember. That said, even if there's nothing wrong with him, he still might not be the right choice for you."

"You think Mark is a better option."

"You'll have to decide that, Gina. Daniel is a great guy, but I had Bishop at the top of my list for a reason. Stay in Bangor a while longer. Hang out with Bishop and get to know him. Give both men some time."

She thought for a long moment before answering. "The *Nevada* returns in two weeks. The one thing Mark doesn't have is time. I'm going to Georgia with Daniel. That's what's in front of me at the moment. I'm not going to figure out the answer to the rest of it tonight. Where to head next for work is also in play." She rubbed her forehead and the headache that was forming. She'd prayed for one good guy to be interested, and now she found herself struggling over what to do with two. At the moment, she had no idea.

"You're still thinking the Jet Propulsion Laboratory and Pasadena?"

"Yes. You'll be glad to get your space back so you don't have to think twice before you invite Tiffany over."

"I don't mind the company. The house has never been cleaner than it is now."

She offered a smile. "Thanks. You've never got up the nerve to ask me, but just for the record — I like Tiffany a lot."

"I think I love her," Jeff admitted with a self-conscious smile.

"You've been pretty focused on her ever since I've been here. I've been wondering what you're thinking, and I'm glad. I'd like you to get married before I do." She laughed at Jeff's expression. "Don't worry, I won't push."

"Appreciate that," Jeff said. "I got word the *Seawolf* is needed to backfill the USS *Jimmy Carter* on a visit to Guam," he mentioned. "I'll be away about 10 days. Unfortunately that may overlap with the commanders' meeting, depending on when you're ready to present your idea. I'm sorry about the timing."

"It fits the way this month has been going. Daniel will be there, and Mark. I should be okay. When do you leave?"

"Probably three days. I'll know more tomorrow."

"Let me know." She got to her feet. "I'm beat, so I'm going to head up. Good night, Jeff."

"G'night, Gina."

Her thoughts didn't settle as she turned in for the night. She lay staring up at the ceiling, thinking about the turn life had taken, the guys now in her life.

Daniel Field. A wonderful man of faith, but one whose world was very different from hers — music, boating, a full schedule of people and friends. Actually the kind of guy she'd hoped to meet. No fatal flaws, just lots of good qualities in different measures. It would be so easy to fall in love with Daniel. When he smiled at her, she felt good about herself and life. She loved being considered his girlfriend.

She didn't know if she was what he needed in a wife. She didn't want to disappoint him. She wasn't at ease with people like he was, and she'd never kept a full social schedule. If Daniel fell in love with her, he would be compromising to accommodate such things as her fear of the water. But should she allow him to make those compromises?

"Lord, what do you want? What's best for Daniel? What's best for me?" she whispered, wishing that God would answer her out loud so she could have an immediate and certain reply. God had been helping her figure out puzzles since she was a little girl, and He would get her through this personal one. But she missed the certainty that came with a scientific discovery. In contrast, relationships were fluid and never absolute, just degrees of being the right decision. She wished with Daniel everything had been positive with no hesitation points. But she was wise enough to see she wasn't a perfect fit for him — she was merely a good one. So did that mean he wasn't the perfect fit for her?

A good marriage was her dream, and unless she turned both Daniel and her off the road they were on, he was going to ask her to marry him. This relationship could very well go the distance. She closed her eyes, seeing the day coming when Daniel would ask the question, show her the ring. She felt a stirring of joy at the idea. But also some stirrings of uncertainty rather than peace. She so feared making a mistake.

If only Mark hadn't said anything. She'd been clueless about his interest until he'd spoken up. She would have continued to see Daniel, only thinking about how to make it work with him. Now she was trying to weigh a second possibility that didn't fit into any of her assumptions.

Mark Bishop. An older man, a genuine Christian, married before, a friend of her brother — not what she had been visualizing. But maybe what she needed? She'd promised herself to consider anyone who was interested. She did like him. That was the emotion and thought that kept coming back to the surface.

Mark showed up, and she felt safe. He was a leader in charge of a crew, a man others looked up to. He'd also be able to take charge of things for her if she let him, be that buffer she needed, longed for. He treated her with gentleness and care, and she appreciated that more than she could put into words.

She didn't know Mark well enough yet to know where she'd have to compromise, or him with her. She didn't see anything about Mark that worried her. He seemed to have a quieter personal life, more in sync with her own. She felt alive after a conversation with him. Even his prior marriage to Melinda was beginning to feel more like a positive rather than a negative. She did like him. Mark saw her, the real person, she thought, better than Daniel did. But he was older, maybe too likely to take total charge of her life, and the thought of being a commander's wife — his career was only going upward in rank. There would be expectations for the role his wife should take. She had no idea how to fulfill that place, and she'd hate to be a liability to him.

The idea of choosing between the two men ran contrary to her sensibilities. The choice would have to be independent decisions. And it was only fair that Daniel was the one who should have the first decision. She'd go to Georgia, hope it helped her resolve what she wanted.

She groaned, folded a pillow over and wrapped her arms around it. How was a woman supposed to handle this kind of situation? She'd been trying so hard to get the next relationship right, and she was at risk of having a double flameout.

She knew Mark's encroachment into Daniel's territory was out of character for him. It told her how very serious Mark was about her, or he wouldn't be conducting himself this way. He never would have spoken up while she was dating Daniel.

But what if she ended up deciding no with Daniel, didn't see Mark for a 90-day patrol, and Mark changed his mind during that time? Mark only had a couple of weeks relatively free before the *Nevada* returned. If she wanted to spend time with him, get to know anything else about him, this was the window, and it was closing fast. But she couldn't take it. She couldn't do that to Daniel.

Her summer had turned so very complicated. *Do the right thing.* That decision was the only thing she could settle on for how to proceed. She asked God once more to make clear what that right thing was. At least for the immediate days ahead.

With word having gotten out about the last meeting, 74 men now packed into the room for the sonar presentation. No one wished to miss this one. Even as Bishop watched it for the fourth time, he had to admire the video Gina had put together. There hadn't been any information sent out about what was coming, and he was seeing the discovery's impact through the officers' first reactions.

The large screen on the wall shifted to show the audio lab. Gina installed her cross-sonar upgrade on two existing sonar station terminals, one labeled the USS *Ohio* and the other the USS *Connecticut,* then turned on the sea trial raw audio recordings from around Glacier Bay. She started cross-sonar between the two terminals, pausing to make sure the video camera was in focus.

She typed in the command for a cross-sonar quiet search. The USS *Nebraska* appeared on the waterfall screens 60 miles away. Moments later, the group could see USS *Kentucky* on the screen more than 200 miles farther out.

Urgent, quiet conversations between sonarmen and captains began around the room.

Bishop pressed pause, rewound it, and replayed the demonstration. "To confirm the obvious, this new technique has some range."

"It's just software?"

"Yes. The audio was recorded in May of this year. Gina's processing it differently and is getting substantially more range."

He resumed the video, and the presentation shifted to a computer-driven animation Gina had created to model the idea. It showed ocean noise being heard in every direction, then a submarine appeared, and there was a quiet spot in the ocean as the submarine blocked the sound behind it.

There was a groan from the middle row. "The quieter the sub is, the easier it is for her to see it."

"Yes. A submarine is big and it blocks sound — that's the heart of her idea. A noisy environment makes a quiet sub stand out like neon."

The presentation ended with a model of how this would also work from two surface ships. Bishop shut off the video. "A document on the theory behind this idea is being passed out. I'm opening the floor to questions on the video and paper. The tactical conversations for how to deal with this we'll reserve for the afternoon session."

Gina slipped away from the presentation halfway through the Q&A. Bishop, moderating the session, saw her go, shot a look at Daniel to see if he had noticed. Daniel was already moving. It was 40 minutes before he returned. He wrote a note, folded it, and passed it forward with Bishop's name on it. Bishop opened the paper while listening to a question from the captain of the USS *Maine.*

Not a speech freeze. The remark about visibility risk.

Bishop nodded to Daniel. As soon as he practically could, he called the morning session of the meeting to a close and let the informal discussions ahead of the afternoon session begin.

Mark found Gina at the picnic tables, watching the small whitecaps forming on the water. He took a seat on the table beside her. "Hey, lady. Tell me what's wrong?" He could make a pretty good guess.

"They started talking about how to deal with the fact that U.S. subs could be seen at a distance, and it . . . it just . . ." She didn't try to finish the thought.

He dropped an arm around her shoulders,

hugged her, pretty sure she'd accept the gesture as intended, knowing she needed it. "You have done extraordinarily good things with what you've developed in your work life — the seafloor maps, cross-sonar — all good outcomes. And now cross-sonar with a ping, finding a sub by silence, both have good and dangerous qualities. Don't beat yourself up over it, Gina. That's going to be true of most discoveries along this line."

"I wanted submarines to be safer. I've now made them, in the long term, less safe when other nations realize this can be done. And I've ended up with security around me for the rest of my life." Her voice caught and she shook her head. "It's becoming a very bad work year."

"These techniques may be known only by the U.S. for decades. And regardless, knowing is a good thing, not bad. We'll figure this out. There are some tactically smart guys in that room. I'm one of them, if you don't mind my saying so. We'll use this capability to make the fleet safer. Trust me on that."

She didn't say anything. He gently turned her chin so he could see her face. "Okay?"

She gave a jerky nod as she blinked back tears.

The threatened tears were killing him.

"You did wonderfully on the video, Gina — the paper on the theory, the software algorithms. It's a clean hand-off, very professionally done. I'm proud of you. I know you don't feel this right now, but you did a really good job. This discovery is a very big, very *good* thing."

She looked away. "Do you need me at the afternoon session?"

"No. Daniel and I can handle it. I'm sorry Jeff's out at sea right now. You could use him by your side today."

Silence stretched between them for a moment.

"I'm going to Georgia with Daniel to meet his family this weekend."

"I heard."

"No comment?" She glanced over at him.

"It's the right thing to do."

She shook her head. "I can't figure you out at times, Mark."

He rested his hand over hers. "If I'm going to have a chance with you, the door will stay open, and there will be reasons you or Daniel — or both — choose that course. Go to Georgia. Give Daniel a solid chance. I'd rather win your heart knowing you're sure about it than leave opportunity for questions that could haunt you sometime in the future. I'll deal with what comes. Whatever it is."

"When I get back, I'll need to make some decisions on what work comes next."

"Then put aside thinking about any of the future issues until after you get back." He reluctantly glanced at his watch. "There's time for Daniel to run you home before the afternoon session. Let him. Everything you need to do to hand this all off to the Undersea Warfare Group is done. It works. All the software is there, all the data from the trial. It's not like they can't turn it on, use it, and understand it. You don't have to be here to explain more than you have."

"Okay." She slid off her perch on the table. "I'll go start packing for Georgia. You're a nice man, Mark. An awfully nice man."

"Gina?"

She turned.

"I think you know there's nothing casual about my interest. But if the right answer is no — to Daniel, and later even to me — let yourself trust your own judgment. You've not been the one to drop out of a relationship. You've hung on, afraid it might be the last guy who would ever be interested. Don't do that this time. Trust your own instincts, your own judgment. If neither one of us is the right answer, be wise and brave enough to say that."

She nodded slowly. "I think God gave you a wisdom gene."

"It's called being old," Mark replied dryly.

She laughed and turned, headed down the path. He didn't immediately follow. She had to be willing to leave the door open for him, and he needed that to be her decision, free and clear. It was the most risky move he'd ever taken, making sure any hold he had on her was as light as he could make it. But it was the right thing to do . . . for her sake and for his own.

15

She liked visiting Georgia with Daniel. Gina had worried her speech would freeze, worried Daniel's family would ask questions about their relationship she wasn't prepared to handle, worried the security that traveled with them would be too intrusive — all of that along with bracing for the possibility that Daniel would propose. It had been a lot of baggage to carry with her. But the final day in Georgia, Gina woke up without the pressure of any of it.

She was staying at his youngest sister's home in a guest room that was comfortable and spacious, much nicer than a hotel. Daniel wasn't going to propose today. He might very well have on his sister's porch last night, but he wouldn't ask hours before they boarded a flight back to Washington State. She was glad he hadn't, even as she was more certain than ever that if he did, she should seriously consider saying yes.

She loved his family. From his mom, Janine, to his uncle Solomon, to cousins so numerous she couldn't remember all their names. Daniel had brought her here with a clear purpose in mind. He had wanted to see how she interacted with his family, if his family liked her, and she was passing his unspoken test. She knew she was getting high marks. Even his mother had turned from gracious hostess to teasing mom with her. She'd seen Daniel relax as the days had passed.

Daniel would be waiting for her when she appeared for breakfast. She dressed with care and straightened up the guest room, repacked her luggage, then walked through the house to the kitchen. Daniel was turning pancakes. He grinned as she appeared. "Nice shirt."

She spun in a circle, modeling the shirt with the photo of his high school band on it, from a boxed collection found in the attic. She'd discovered all kinds of interesting stuff when his sisters began talking about Daniel and his youth. His sisters were the good kinds of friends to make — interesting, quick to laugh, and genuine. Gina picked up an orange from the bowl and absently peeled it while she watched Daniel fix breakfast.

Daniel slid a plate over with the first of the pancakes on it. "Go ahead and eat while they're hot. What would you like to do for our last morning?"

She sat down, segmented the orange, and offered him a slice. "How about another game of checkers with your dad? And I need a couple of recipes from your mom to take back with me."

"Easy enough. I'd also like us to fit in a walk — we'll ditch family for a few minutes. The flight is at 2:30, so we'll leave my parents' place about noon."

"Sounds like a plan," Gina agreed, cutting into the stack of pancakes.

"Your brother called this morning."

"Oh? What's going on?"

"I'm to tell you, when you're sitting down, that Bishop got injured during a flood drill and broke two fingers in his left hand."

She carefully put down her fork.

"A nub — new-to-the-boat sailor — misjudged a pipe repair, and Bishop stopped him from taking a blow to the head that would have put the kid down with a severe concussion. They were installing a casing pipe. Think inch-thick steel, four feet long — something not easy to stop once it's in motion."

"Command of the *Nevada* is Mark's

dream job," she said, trying to keep her voice steady. "Will this injury cause problems with his ability to take *Nevada* gold to sea the first of September?"

Daniel shook his head. "Beyond the fact he'll have to live with Tylenol in its strongest form, it shouldn't. Medical will clear him before then."

"What am I supposed to do when I see him? Say 'ouch' and never mention it again? What's the correct way to handle a submariner getting hurt?"

"With Bishop," Daniel laughed, "bake the guy some cupcakes and tell him 'good job.' He's not going to mind a couple of broken fingers compared to having to tell some 20-year-old's parents their son is in intensive care with a fractured skull."

"Okay. How many bones have you broken, Daniel?"

"Hmm, five." He rubbed his ribs as he turned the pancakes. "Can't say the last was one I'd like to repeat, but the rest were kid injuries from learning how bikes can flip, skateboards can crash, and stairs are not for jumping down from one landing to the next."

She smiled. "I'm relieved that's all, given the stories I heard from your sisters."

"I considered it my duty as the only son

to prove girls fragile and guys tough. They used to squeal at the worms and spiders I introduced them to, and let's not mention the snakes. Mom made me behave, but if I didn't push back a bit, my sisters would have had me dressed up in preppy clothes with the sleeves of a sweater dangling over my shoulders."

Gina laughed and pushed the pancake syrup toward him as he sat down with his own plate. "It's the stories that make the best memories."

"You've heard a few of them. It would take decades to tell all of them, the way my sisters embellish history."

"I like your family, Daniel."

"I'm glad. They liked you too. I never heard Solomon say so many words in one conversation before."

"I'd love it if you could snap a family photo for me before we leave, something I could have on my phone." She already had numerous photos of their Georgia stay on her phone, but none was a group photo.

"I can do that," Daniel agreed.

Bishop half listened to the instructions his XO was giving the sailors clustered around the table to his left while he scanned the TRIPER report. *Nevada* gold would have eight new sailors joining this patrol. Preparing men for what gold crew expected during a deployment began long before the boat pushed away from the pier.

Blue crew would bring the *Nevada* back into port next week. Gina was due back in town tonight. Bishop forced himself to ignore that second thought and focus on what he was reading. The TRIPER list of equipment scheduled to be pulled out and replaced with refurbished parts ran for pages. This 25-day refit — maintenance and resupply — was going to be unusually aggressive. He hoped *Nevada* blue reported in with no missile problems to sort out. It wouldn't take much to push the work schedule into missing their September 1st patrol date. It never looked good — for the crew or captain or onshore maintenance — when a boat had to shift a scheduled departure date back.

Water dripped from the ice pack balanced on his left hand, and he hissed his annoyance as the ice numbed his little finger. Having his two middle fingers taped together with a splint was bad enough. Having his little finger also ache added further insult to his discomfort.

Someone knocked on the door as he was tearing off a paper towel from a roll he'd stuck in a desk drawer.

"I thought you'd be halfway to Seattle by now," Bishop commented as Jeff took a seat across from him.

"I got their flight time wrong — they came in earlier. Should I give you the good news or bad?"

"Depends on your read of my mood."

"There wasn't a ring on Gina's left hand when she got off the plane."

Bishop felt an intense layer of relief. "The bad news?"

"I'd say my sister is falling in love. She looks very comfortable with Daniel and is starting to tease him. It's noticeable, the shift. Sorry, man."

"Yeah." Bishop pushed aside the report and tugged out more paper towels.

"You want to come get fussed over by Tiffany? We're meeting to share a pizza."

"No. Go away, friend."

Jeff tapped his fist on the desk. "Still no ring. Remember that."

It wasn't much comfort. Bishop carefully flexed his little finger. It just meant he'd get another few weeks of misery, followed by a patrol and news when he got home that Gina was engaged. Or married.

The front doorbell rang. Mark muted the

ball game and leveraged himself out of his favorite leather chair. When he opened the door, he wasn't that surprised at his visitor. He stood for a moment absorbing the fact that part of a week with a lot of sun had brought a few freckles out on her nose and turned her skin a rich tan. He pushed open the screen door. "Hello, Gina."

"Sorry about your hand."

It was throbbing in time with his heartbeat. "So am I."

She was carrying a cardboard box. "I'm supposed to give you these, but rather than hand them to you, I think I'll just put them in your kitchen." She headed through the house.

Bishop decided he might as well follow. "What did you bring me?"

"Cupcakes."

She lifted the lid, and he saw each cupcake iced with a letter. *Good Job, Mark.*

"Who ate cupcake 12 from my dozen?" he asked, curious.

"Trust you to notice. I sampled the one that didn't get a letter. They're good."

He took an *o* as it had the most icing. "You can have another one," he generously offered. He pulled out a chair and took a seat at the kitchen table, carefully peeling back the paper from the cupcake. "Did you stop by to tell me you're getting married?"

"You're in an interesting mood."

"I am."

She walked past him and ruffled his hair. The move so surprised him, he nearly dropped the cupcake.

She pulled milk out of his refrigerator, got a glass from a cupboard, raised it with a question in her eyes. When he shook his head, she poured milk for herself. "Daniel has a good family. I enjoyed getting to meet them." She settled into a seat across from him. "I hate to fly. Every time I go up I'm convinced the laws of aerodynamics don't make sense and we're going to fall out of the sky and go splat."

He smiled at her word choice, eyed her cautiously, and began eating his cupcake.

"What were you thinking when you grabbed that pipe?" she asked.

"I was reaching for the guy who was about to get hit by the pipe. The casing was supposed to hit the hull rather than the hull *and* me." He looked at his injured left hand. "Broke the bones above the first joint. It's going to be a long eight weeks wearing the brace, but they'll heal."

"I'm glad."

She reached for a cupcake, choosing the *k.* "Daniel offered to give me some time to think about things. He wants to propose if I would like him to do so. One of those agreements where he won't ask unless I want to say yes, so I don't have to turn him down."

Bishop nodded. "What are you thinking?"

"That I need to go work on something else. The solar flares. Satellite drift. I need to get away from Bangor for a while."

"Thomas Keller at the Jet Propulsion Lab is waiting on your call. You want me to escort you to Pasadena, get you settled in with a new research group?"

"I can work remotely with JPL while I get up to speed on the sun research being done. I don't have the energy left for new people and feeling out the dynamics of another research group right now."

"Chicago?"

"I think so. It's home. It's where I can cocoon for a while."

"Then let me get you there."

"That's why I came by. You said you were flying to Chicago on the seventh to see your brother Bryce and meet his wife, Charlotte. I'd like to travel with you, if you don't mind my white knuckles."

"I don't mind."

She studied his bandaged hand. "You aren't going to fuss at me when I carry my own luggage, are you?"

"I might let you carry part of mine," Bishop replied, considering his hand.

A comfortable silence settled over the kitchen. "Change your mind about some milk?" Gina offered.

"Sure."

She poured him a glass and refilled hers.

"You had a good time in Georgia?"

She pulled out her phone, opened the photos folder, and handed it to him. Mark slowly tabbed through. He stopped, shot her a surprised look. "He had you up on water skis?"

"For a full 20 seconds I was upright."

"What did you think?"

"Before or after my heart tried to jump out of my chest? I understand now why people would consider it a thrill. I let his sisters talk me into trying. Daniel tried to veto the idea. I should have listened to him, because I'll never do it again."

Mark moved through the rest of the photos. He stopped on one, closed his eyes for a brief moment, then handed the phone back. She'd been sitting with Daniel on a porch swing, the photo probably snapped by one of his sisters. Daniel had a coiled strand of her hair around his finger, was looking at her, and it was a lover's look. "He's a good man," Mark said, his voice sounding heavy in his own ears.

"Yes," Gina replied softly.

"You could do worse. A lot worse."

"I know." She looked over at him.

He wanted to add that she *could do better,* that she was looking at *better,* but he was no longer sure.

She pushed back her chair. "I'm leaving before I eat a third cupcake. Jeff said he could give us a lift to the airport."

Mark rose to walk with her to the front door. "It's a plan."

"Take care of yourself, Mark."

"I will," he promised. He watched her through the screen door as she walked to the car, where security was waiting, and turned away when she was gone. Whatever came, he was going to handle it with some grace. He owed them both that.

16

Gina's home in Chicago was a large two-story with a long front porch, situated in an older suburb of Chicago. Mark liked it on sight. Built in the 1920s, the house was painted white with blue shutters, had colorful hanging baskets of flowers on the porch, and it all set a welcoming tone as they walked up the sidewalk. A line of tall evergreen shrubbery provided privacy on both sides.

"A neighbor has the touch with the flowers and takes care of the house when I'm away," Gina said. "I can never get them to bloom as beautifully."

She unlocked the door and they stepped inside to the fragrance of lemon oil, ginger, and sugar cookies. The mail that hadn't been forwarded was neatly stacked on a side table in the hall. She set her one travel bag by the staircase, having shipped the rest of her things to arrive in a few days.

The hardwood floors gleamed. The ceilings were tall, the walls mostly white, the area rugs a mix of bold Southern colors. She favored solid wide-plank furniture in a light oak, and wingback chairs. Mark could see three built-in bookcases just from where he stood in the entryway.

She had 8×10 photos of interesting phenomena on various walls, intermixed with photos of her brother and parents. The Earth from space, a photo of the deep ocean currents, plankton blooms in the ocean, a mega-pod of dolphins numbering in the thousands, and photos of the sun — spectacular coiling solar flares, full eclipses. "I like your home," he decided.

She was standing where they had entered, letting him look around. She smiled at his remark. "Thanks. I've lived here since I was 14. My parents bought this place because it was near the university where I was going, but I would have chosen it for myself. Come on back to the kitchen. I don't know about you, but I'm parched. I was trying to avoid drinking much on the flight."

He paused in the sunroom off the kitchen, touched a finger to Saturn and it moved away on its trajectory around the sun. The other planets moved with the breeze created by the door opening. A few random gray chunks slid on strings cutting across the planets' orbits. "Asteroids?"

"And some comets." She pointed out the large oval loops that set their trajectories. "It helps me understand things if I can see them in motion."

The model was old, handmade. "When did you create this?"

"I was 10, maybe? When we moved into this house, Jeff helped me hang it in here. It still looks nice on a sunny day."

She pulled sodas out of the refrigerator. The counters were clear, the tables too. Either she was remarkably neat or she let a housekeeper put away any clutter.

"You let the house stand empty while you were in Boulder?" It didn't smell like a closed-up house.

She opened a cookie jar and found Oreos to go with the sodas. "I've been back here for a few days most months. I've got a friend who rents half the double garage and keeps the yard mowed and snow shoveled for me, and another who lives in New York and will stay here in the guest suite rather than rent a hotel room when she's in Chicago. My neighbor was the housekeeper for us back when my mother and I first lived here, and she still comes over to give me a few hours during a month for things like dusting and the flowers. Security in the house is good. This is home base. Neither Jeff nor I want to sell it. I figure one small-scale work project in Chicago a year is enough to pay for the overhead of keeping this place, and it's worth that."

"A good arrangement." Mark glanced around. "Still, let me walk through the house, confirm everything is secure before I leave."

"Sure. I'm going to go talk with Connolly about the security and hear what he wants to do now that we're here."

Mark did the walk-through, checking window locks and exterior doors, scanning for water leaks or moisture problems, quickly realizing the house was much larger than it appeared from the curb. Four levels, if he counted the finished attic, along with an unfinished basement, two formal offices, three bedrooms upstairs, a master suite with a bath on the main level.

She had space here, room for ideas to flourish. He passed framed schematics of airplane designs and a framed periodic table, paused at a round table to pick up one of several model rockets on display. The anatomy models and a cutaway motorcycle engine she had once mentioned sat neatly on shelves in the attic next to an array of papier-mâché models on different subjects. Books were tucked everywhere and seemed to span every subject, from practical ones on cooking to complex tomes on mathematics and biochemistry. Her collection of fiction swung toward sci-fi from the forties onward, and she favored fantasy in her movie collection. In a place of honor in the living room was a wall with submarine photos and her own submarine fleet on display.

Mark heard Gina rejoin him. "You're a collector."

"Of a sort."

"I saw a second electrical fuse box in the basement. Was that for the computer equipment? Your offices look configured for high-speed connections and graphics."

"The majority of the house was rewired about eight years ago. I can't replicate an audio lab or the multiple display configurations likely at JPL, but I can do just about any modeling I want to from here. I turned a closet into a server rack, so I've got good data storage options. The bottleneck used to be the link between this house and the university, but that was upgraded back when I was doing the original cross-sonar work for the Navy. I could work strictly from here if necessary, but I find the walls closing in on me after a few weeks. So I prefer a university or research group, even if I'm working primarily on my own task."

"JPL is lucky to have you next."

"I'm looking forward to thinking about the sun for a few months."

Security was with her at the house, so she'd be fine here. Mark noted the time and accepted reality. "It was a very early morning, and a long flight. I'll head out, Gina, let you get settled. I'll be in touch before my flight leaves tomorrow."

"Please say hi to your brother for me."

"I will." She walked with him to the front door, but he found he didn't want to say goodbye — it seemed too permanent a word. "I hope you find the next few weeks a restful break."

She hugged him, surprising him. "Thanks for bringing me home," she whispered.

He hugged her back. "Think of this as a vacation, but don't forget Bangor," he replied softly.

She stepped back, offered a full smile. "Impossible. Enjoy a day seeing your family. I'm going to call Jeff, tell him I've arrived safely."

The smile caught at his heart, and he gently ran a finger along the side of her face, seriously considering kissing her goodbye.

Instead he forced himself to step out with a comfortable smile. "See you later, Gina."

"You're a man with a lot on your mind."

Mark accepted the glass of iced tea his brother held out to him. "Thinking about a woman."

His brother smiled. "That would explain it," Bryce said as he sat down in a deck chair with his own glass.

Mark considered his brother — it had been a while since they were last together, but they had picked up where they'd left off with ease. His brother looked a lot more relaxed than Mark remembered. "You and Charlotte make an interesting couple. She's an extraordinary sketch artist."

"She is. You should see the art at the gallery. What's here at the house is just a hint of what she's created recently."

Charlotte had left the brothers to talk for a while around the outdoor table and catch up. It had been a nice lunch, and she had left a good impression. "I like her," Mark offered, knowing the words were unnecessary but wanting to offer them anyway.

His brother had waited a long time to marry, and Charlotte was different from the person Mark had expected — not the social butterfly he thought his brother would attract, but a woman who was quiet, careful, a bit reserved. Her affection for his brother was obvious. They were newlyweds, and it was on display in the ways they would share a thought with a glance, a touch, a private smile. Their relationship had all the hallmarks of a good, solid marriage, and Mark was relieved to see it.

"I knew you'd like Charlotte," Bryce replied easily. "What's her name, your lady?"

Mark smiled. "Gina Gray. Not my lady . . . yet. She's considerably younger than me. Eleven-plus years younger."

"Didn't expect that from you," Bryce said, interested.

"I didn't either. Jeff Gray, the commander of the *Seawolf*, has been a friend for years. Gina's his sister." Mark flexed his left hand, the broken fingers and splint making his other knuckles ache. "How did you know Charlotte was the one?" he asked.

"We didn't have that moment. I married her first, fell in love with her second," Bryce said. He waved the glass he held, dismissing the questions the remark created. "Circumstances made it necessary. Neither one of us regrets it."

"Pregnant?" Mark asked. He knew there wasn't a child around, but miscarriages happen.

"Nothing like that. Her grandfather's will was . . . interesting. It's how I met her, helping her settle the estate. I asked her to marry me, she thought about it for several months, said yes." Bryce leaned back in his chair, glanced with obvious affection toward the studio, where Charlotte was visible through the glass as she straightened up items around her drafting board. "For more reasons than I'll be able to tell you, it was a good decision, Mark, the right one for both of us. I hate to think what life would have been like had we not made the commitment to each other that we did. I love her because she's Charlotte. Because she trusts me. Needs me. And loves me back."

Mark felt his emotions settle at the brief facts and description of their relationship. Bryce was deeply in love with his wife, however they had gotten to this point. "I noticed the security around the place. It came with her?"

"Yes."

"Gina's been designated a national security asset, and she's chafing at the security that comes with it."

"You adapt because you have to. Are you going to be back in Chicago more often now?"

"Patrol is taking me to sea for 90 days.

After that, it depends on what happens. She may be engaged before I get back. My fault. I let the door open, and he's a good guy. I put the woman in a bind. She doesn't want to choose between us, and I've complicated her decision about Daniel."

"She knows your interest?"

"To some degree."

"You'd better change that, Mark. Three months is long enough for the whole world to change."

"I thought I might talk to Dad after dinner tonight, see what his advice might be."

"You'll find it useful. I did."

Mark tipped his head toward the house. The simple introductions today, the care being taken when Charlotte talked about her life and family, the simple fact there hadn't been a wedding where brothers were invited to stand as best men, plus Bryce's comment that he had married before he fell in love — it all added up to a conclusion in Mark's mind, and a question. "When are you planning to tell me who she is?" he asked quietly. There obviously was history there with Charlotte, and the security that came along with her.

"I'm not," Bryce replied. "But you'll make the connection one day. Dad knows, Mom. Or Charlotte might tell you."

Mark nodded. "Gina comes with her own complicated history. She's smart, Bryce. Genius-level smart, with some sonar work that is causing both turmoil and joy throughout the submarine fleet. Nothing will ever be simple with her."

Bryce smiled. "Face it, Mark, the Bishop brothers don't do easy. We never have."

Mark leaned his head back against the chair, smiled. "Have to agree with you there. Have you heard from Jim lately?"

"No. He's at least on the ground somewhere, now that the space shuttles have flown their last missions."

"His favorite toy got put into a box and taken away."

Bryce chuckled. "He must feel like that at times. Though why he thought riding to work on a rocket built by the lowest bidder was a safe career move, I'll never understand." The two men laughed together.

"We'll have to corner him at Mom's birthday party and see if we can talk some common sense into his future plans," Bryce suggested, then looked over at Mark, considering. "You should invite Gina to the birthday party. Charlotte and I would enjoy meeting her. Our parents would too."

"Maybe," Mark said.

He was coming to the conclusion he

needed to change tactics with Gina. How he had handled the summer might have been the best — and, really, the only — avenue open to him, but it wasn't going to work for the situation now. The calendar was pushing him out to sea. And Daniel was waiting for Gina to give him the go-ahead to propose.

Mark needed a plan that fit the current circumstances. She wouldn't love him yet; she was barely beyond thinking of him as a date. Bryce's surprising admission, learning to love Charlotte after the wedding, was shifting his own thinking. Mark wondered what his father would say tonight. He needed the family's advice. His parents had always been there when he leaned on them for wisdom, for counsel, for the certainty he'd be loved even if he got life wrong. Family was where he was going to lean tonight, and hope to get this sorted out in his own mind.

Mark finished the drink. Bryce got to his feet, motioned for the glass Mark held. "Refills coming up. What time are Mom and Dad expecting you?"

"Five."

"Charlotte's going to come out here with her sketchbook and capture your pretty face before you leave, so Mom can have another of her missing boys on the family wall."

Mark wanted to wince, but didn't. It sounded nearly as bad as having his picture taken. "Do I have to do anything?"

Bryce laughed. "Charlotte hates when people pose. Talk to her about Gina — that will put a smile on your face, and on hers."

Mark arrived five minutes early at his parents' home, with Charlotte's sketch, neatly framed for his mother, carefully held under his arm. It had taken Charlotte considerably longer to frame the sketch than to make the drawing. It was an extraordinary likeness, he had to admit. Mark hoped for the day he could get Charlotte and Gina in the same room and get a sketch of Gina.

The conversation with his parents flowed easily throughout dinner, catching up on his sisters and their kids, events of the last six months in his parents' lives, their questions about his crew and deployments. He shared what he could, appreciating their interest. It was good to be home. Mark had forgotten how much he enjoyed simply listening to his mom's laughter. After dinner, Mark settled on the back patio with his father for a more serious conversation.

He couldn't ask Gina to wait, to give him a chance, without offering a reason. Refit and a 90-day patrol was too long a time to leave things as they stood now. Mark looked over at his father and opened the conversation where his own thoughts had ended. "I'm considering asking a woman considerably younger than I am to marry me."

His dad leaned forward to set aside his coffee, but said nothing, simply nodded for Mark to continue.

"I've known Gina Gray for seven years, almost eight now. Her brother is a good friend of mine. Circumstances are . . . rushed, I guess. I'm going away on patrol for three months. If I don't say something, she could very well be engaged when I get back."

"She's seeing someone else?"

"It's . . . complicated."

"When has your life not been, son?"

Mark smiled at his dad's remark. "Worse than normal this time, Dad. Not her fault. I even approved when she was first introduced to this guy, then later I changed my mind and realized I was interested myself."

"At least you were smart enough to recognize it. Why Gina?"

"I love her smile. I love her laughter. I am in awe of the way she discovers simple but genius things." Mark thought about her, wishing he had the right words to explain.

"She wants a husband. I've been in that role. I could be a good one again. I want a wife. I want someone to share my life with — my faith, my house, my time, and my dreams. I want someone to be there when I come home, who wants to hear about my day. I want to hear about her day. And she'd be my first choice."

"Put the time pressure aside for the moment. If you were not going to sea for three months, if you were staying ashore, what would you want right now?"

"Time for her to get to know me."

"Not time for you to get to know her?"

"I know her, Dad. I know her life story, what she's like. What she's already accomplished leaves me in awe. There are more layers, sure, there is always more to learn — but I do know her. She doesn't have much self-confidence, and she has a tendency to over-think everything to death. She's too eager to please for her own good. But some of that is her youth, and a lot is the current situation. Everything else is the kind of mix I would love to have in a lady. Time with her is a joy. You'd like her, Dad. Mom would too."

"I'm sure we would. You're a good judge of people, Mark. And nothing I'm about to say should be considered a negative reflection on those two statements." His father leaned forward and linked his hands together between his knees. "I remember well when you sat at the kitchen table and told your mother and me you were going to ask Melinda to marry you. You were nervous and confident at the same time, and so eager to get those words said that very night — so she'd say yes and you could start planning the wedding — that you had to leave immediately to find her just as soon as you told us your plans. I know that was then and this is now, but I'm not hearing that eager joy in your voice, in your words. I'm hearing a man searching to find a solution to the fact his job is going to mean there's a separation coming. A man backing himself into a marriage proposal as the answer to that problem."

"Not because I'm reluctant, Dad. Because I'm scared down to my bones I'll get one chance with Gina, and it's coming too early. We've barely been on what you would consider a traditional date to this point. I haven't told her I love her."

"Do you?"

"Yes." Mark didn't hesitate to say it, thought about it, and added a nod. "It's a different emotion than with Melinda, but it's solid and deep. I wake up wondering what she's doing, and hope she's having a good day, and create reasons for our paths to cross. I'm emotionally invested in her in a way I haven't been with anyone since Melinda. I do love her, Dad."

"Whatever the two of you decide now, the separation is still coming, and she might change her mind. You might change yours."

"I won't change mine, and I understand 90 days will mean a lot of time for second thoughts. But if I say nothing, there's a good chance she'll get engaged to Daniel. Even if it means blundering badly, the risk if I say nothing is too great."

"Then ask." His dad placed a hand over his son's. "Mark, you'll have my blessing and that of your mother. You'll give your heart with those words, and we'll pray her answer is what's best for the both of you. Just be prepared to accept either response with grace. The situation you describe will be difficult for her. She's not going to want to hurt either of you. And she's going to have to hurt one of you."

Mark felt his heart hesitate a beat as his dad's words sank in. He was going to put Gina in a position to hurt either himself or Daniel, and the way she had felt rejection personally in the past, she would move heaven and earth not to do that to someone else. He sighed and shook his head. "You're right. But I still have to ask."

His father smiled. "You love her, son. I don't doubt that. And in a few years you'll be glad you asked her even if she tells you no. It's good to see you loving someone again. Your mother will be especially pleased."

"I need for Gina to say yes."

"Ask. Then give her some time before you expect an answer."

His flight was scheduled for two p.m. Mark Bishop walked up the front sidewalk to Gina's Chicago home shortly after ten a.m. Arms full, he leaned an elbow against the doorbell, heard footsteps on the hardwood floors. The door opened, and Gina stood in front of him — better rested, in a light-green T-shirt and jeans, white socks on her feet, with damp hair still curling around her face.

"Hi, Mark. What on earth — ?"

"These are for you," he said, shifting what he held. Two very wiggly kittens were trying to climb the cotton of his shirt. "You're not a cat person, and these are only on loan, but they will be good company for a couple of weeks. I would have brought you puppies, but they were impossible to catch."

She took the black furry kitten, then eased

the chocolate brown one into her other arm. She started laughing. "Where did you find them?"

"My sister's drowning in seven kittens and five puppies. She'll locate homes for all of them, but it's going to take a few weeks. These two are drinking milk and eating soft kitten chow, generally well behaved and hungry for attention. So I borrowed them for you."

She grinned. "What are their names?"

"Trouble and Double Trouble. They didn't want to stay in the box for the drive over here."

Gina laughed.

"Go on in with them, and I'll get their stuff from the car."

Mark returned to the vehicle, hauled out the large box that would serve as a bed for the kittens at night. Gina's smile and laughter had helped ease the worry he'd felt about this being a good idea or not. He didn't want to leave Chicago, leaving her alone, not after dropping the bombshell he had planned. He wanted something that she would find to be a comfort. Kittens would at least be a distraction when her churning thoughts wouldn't let her sleep.

He settled in the living room with Gina, playing with the kittens, watching them explore the room. Gina was stretched out on the rug, using a feather duster as a toy for them to chase. The kittens started climbing on her jeans, trying to balance themselves on her knees to look around.

"I would guess from seeing these two that you've now caught up with all your family?" Gina asked.

"I spent a few hours with Bryce and Charlotte, had dinner with my parents, stopped by both sisters this morning, and doubled up on breakfast. How have your last 24 hours been?"

"I unpacked the boxes Jeff sent from Boulder, did laundry, turned in early, slept late. I loved every minute of it. I was pouring a bowl of cereal for a late breakfast when you rang the bell."

"You look rested, for the first time in a long while."

"Give me a week of sleeping in and I'll start to look lazy." She scooped up a kitten. "These two are adorable."

"My sister's number is on the card, and she'll come pick them up without any questions being asked should this gift turn out to be not so adorable. Otherwise expect her to call and say she's found permanent homes for them sometime within the next month. The shelter passes on pregnant cats to her for a month or two of home care, so the kittens are born with safer birth weights. They have a better chance of being placed if they've been played with in the first months of their lives."

"I think I can manage these two for a couple of weeks. What made you think of bringing me them?"

"My young niece was carrying a kitten around in her pocket, wanting to know if she could take it to school for show and tell. It had become her new best friend and was going everywhere with her. If a kitten is good for a little girl, I figured two kittens would be good for a grown-up girl."

Gina smiled at his words, looked down at the two. "You're probably right."

Mark kept the conversation casual until shortly before he had to leave to make his flight. Gina was fixing tea for herself after making coffee for him. One kitten was playing with her sock foot. The other was now under the kitchen table, chasing a sunbeam that came and disappeared as the sun occasionally slipped behind a cloud.

"Gina, I need to ask you something."

"Sure." She turned toward him with a smile, setting aside the spoon for stirring sugar into her tea. His serious expression registered, and her smile hesitated.

"Please don't get engaged while I'm on patrol," he said. "Please give me a chance to show you why I would make a good husband for you."

"Husband . . ." she breathed, her eyes wide.

"I would like you to marry me, Gina."

She paled, and her fingers tightened on the mug. She very carefully nudged aside the kitten so she could steady her balance.

"Not something you expected to hear?"

"No," she whispered, looking very shaken.

"I would like very much to marry you. I want you as my wife. I love your smile. I love your mind. You've awakened feelings in me that I thought were long buried — tenderness and concern, protectiveness and passion, pride and joy. I watch for you to enter a room, and I can't stop my smile when I see you." He eased his arms around her as he spoke. "I love you, Gina. It would be my ideal future if I could wake up with you beside me for the rest of my life." He leaned his forehead against hers. "Love me back," he whispered. "I want to be your husband. I want you to be my wife."

"Mark, I —"

He didn't let her finish. "Would you think about it while I'm deployed and give us a chance to talk when I'm back from patrol?

Will you grant me time I don't deserve but desperately need?"

She wrapped her arms around him, still holding the mug, and rested her head against his chest. He finally felt her nod.

He ran his hands gently down her back. "Okay. Okay," he whispered again, taking a deep breath. "Thank you, Gina."

17

Disembarking from her flight, Gina had never been so glad to see Daniel as she was at this moment, catching sight of his face and seeing only concern. "Thanks for meeting me, Daniel."

"No problem. Glad to be of service," he replied as he took her carry-on bag and transferred it to his shoulder. "But whatever you're thinking of doing, you need to slow it down a bit."

"He asked me to marry him, out of the blue, and then he flew off across the country. He knows I'm dating you," she said, all the emotions of the long night tumbling out. The impact of it had been building ever since Mark had left for his own flight.

"I've got to admire the man," Daniel said. "He had the guts to ask you cold. It's not only a class act, it's impressive tactics." She began moving toward the airport's exit, but Daniel took her elbow and turned her aside to a row of seating away from the flow of passengers coming and going. "Gina, you owe him an answer, but not one made after a sleepless night and a flight across the country. It won't do either one of you any good if you tell him no while you're feeling like this. One look at your face and I know you didn't come to tell him yes." He led her to a seat and then took the one beside her.

"Daniel —"

He put a finger across her lips. "Listen. You were oblivious to the fact Bishop was interested in you. Now you've just gotten your eyes opened, seeing he's got real emotion behind his decision. You're so confused, you're just frustrated he put you in this position. So slow it down. I'm here to turn you around." She blinked at the firm statement and watched while he dug a travel pack of Kleenex out of his pocket. "You can't see him, Gina. Not now, not like this. You'll only end up regretting it. I won't let you make that kind of memory."

"I came to tell him no because I can't marry him," she whispered.

"You came to tell him that he panicked you. And you also wanted to see how much damage it did with me when I heard the news," Daniel corrected. "You haven't had time to think much beyond that. For the record, you and I are fine. I don't think you prompted this, that you were somehow leading both of us on. This has classic Bishop written all over it," he added, sounding reluctantly impressed.

"He asked me to wait for him to get back from patrol. That's months away, Daniel. And I was flustered enough in the moment that I agreed to it."

His hand wrapped around hers. "I'm going to be deployed too, Gina, and it's not like a few months' wait is going to disrupt what else might be. You aren't ready for me to propose — you and I both know that from Georgia. We still need some time, and this turn of events doesn't change that. All it does is change the order in which things are going to happen. Bishop deserves a considered answer from you, a thoughtful and prayerful one. The man asked you to marry him. I respect that. Even if he is stepping hard on my toes. I'll wait until you decide what you will do with his proposal before I'll consider making one of my own."

"I'm telling him no."

"I hope you do," Daniel said. "And I hope you leave the door open for me to make the next proposal. But I won't let you make a mistake by rushing an answer to Bishop that you haven't handled with the respect it deserves."

Gina slipped her hands out of his to wipe her eyes.

"Do you love him?" Daniel asked softly.

"I've been on all of two official dates with him, and the second barely constituted a date. I like the guy, Daniel, but he's miles ahead of me, proposing out of the blue like that." She pushed away more tears.

"Was it a good proposal?" Daniel asked, using a tissue to dry her cheeks.

She remembered the words and cried even harder. "It was beautiful."

Daniel wrapped her in a hug and rocked her. "Face it, kiddo, you've got two men who really, really like you."

She half laughed at his words. The tears finally eased even if the pressure in her chest didn't.

"You were always going to have to say no to one of us," Daniel pointed out. "You just assumed it would be Bishop. Now maybe it is Bishop, or maybe it's me. Trust us to be men about this, Gina, that we'll handle it with grace. It's not going to come back at you with more pain because you have to make a decision. We *know* you have to make a decision. And right now you owe Bishop an answer to his proposal that comes from your heart, not your panicked emotions. You can't do that without giving him the time he's asked for."

He gently lifted her chin and looked her in the eyes. "I'm not going anywhere, Gina. All that's changed is that the timing has shifted around, and now you need to consider Bishop first. That's not such a bad thing from my point of view. We're different guys, Gina. Take your time. There's no need for this to end with regrets.

"*Nevada* blew a missile tube and is back early. It touched the pier four hours ago. Bishop is three days away from hand-over and command of the boat. The man will have the world on his shoulders getting the *Nevada* ready to go back to sea by the first of the month. Even working 24/7, gold crew is going to have its hands full making that date. Do the wise thing here, Gina. Go back to Chicago and enjoy some rest, or work on something that isn't sonar-related. And wait. Let the decision about Bishop be made after he's back from patrol, after you've had more time with him."

She wiped her eyes again. "I can't believe you're saying that, Daniel. You're sure?"

"I know it sounds crazy, but I'm trying to act in your best interests. He asked you to marry him. That's not a simple statement, not from him, and it won't be from me. Though I still hope you choose me, you can't make this decision quickly. He's too good a man. I deeply respect him, and he deserves your full consideration. Otherwise I might always wonder, and maybe you would too."

He was calming her down and talking sense into her, and she forced herself to accept that, to take a deep breath and nod. He'd just cancelled her plans, and she was going to let him. "Thank you, Daniel."

"You can call me anytime. I'm still planning to send you music tapes and try out jokes and be in your life until I head to sea myself in mid-November. I might even hop on a red-eye to Chicago before I ship out. Nothing's changed with us, Gina. We're still in the days after Georgia. As difficult as this is to sort out, Bishop and I really are different sides of the same coin. You want to get married. One of us will likely be the guy. That's still the reality. Okay?"

She nodded.

He gently kissed her. "We're good. Now let's get you on a flight back to Chicago."

Bishop saw Daniel Field waiting on the pier side of the *Nevada* walkway. He pushed his notes into his pocket, left the *Nevada* deck, and headed across to meet him.

"Can the tube be repaired?" Daniel called.

"No. It took out the venting stack when it failed. Tube four is now the red-line item for the coming refit. If we're lucky the re-pressure coils are intact, but we won't know until the missile is out. Blue crew wants the last days before hand-over to solve what failed. I'd want to know the same. Irish is moving the boat to the explosive wharf within the hour to start getting some answers."

Bishop knew Daniel wasn't here for news about the *Nevada*. He would have heard by now, either from Jeff or from Gina herself. And whatever Daniel wanted to say, Bishop was braced to accept it. He was well aware of how this whole thing looked.

"Gina was here," Daniel told him, his voice lowered as the two drew closer together. "I convinced her to take the afternoon flight back to Chicago. You might want to have some flowers or something waiting for her when she gets home."

Bishop felt his heart stop. "She flew —"

"She was here to tell you no. And I don't want her no to you to be some spur-of-the-moment panic."

"Security was with her? She's okay getting home?"

"Yes. We had a long conversation. I got her calmed down before she left. She'll be fine. And she's not going to want you to know she was here. You pushed too hard, Mark. She had a night to think about it, and she panicked."

Bishop struggled to get his mind around the news. "Thank you, Daniel."

"I still want to be the one who wins the girl," Daniel said, "but I can play it fair." He met Bishop's gaze. "I find it interesting she called me to meet her at the airport, not Jeff."

"You matter to her. We both know that."

Daniel offered his hand. "No hard feelings, whatever comes?"

Bishop felt like he was getting a break he didn't deserve. He took the handshake. "Never let it be said we couldn't handle matters with some class and honor."

"I'll settle for not having fists thrown when she chooses me."

Bishop had to laugh in spite of the difficult subject.

"Kittens, Bishop?" Daniel shook his head. "You really are playing hardball, sir. She said she left them for a temporary 24 hours back with your sister. Gina likes your sister, by the way. The kittens are now named Pocket and Pages. I hope you like cats. I was a dog guy, so this is going to take some recalibration."

Bishop heard the warning and winced. "So was I."

Daniel laughed. "I'll pray you get through refit in one piece. I don't envy you the next three weeks. Or the 90-day patrol coming after that. If for some reason I don't see you again before *Nevada* departs, good sailing, Commander."

"Same to you and the *Nebraska,* Daniel."

Gina had been back at her Chicago home less than an hour, trying to settle the kittens and unpack her carry-on bag, when the doorbell rang and she reversed course to answer it. She opened the door to a deliveryman.

"Miss Gray?"

"Yes."

"These are for you." He carefully handed over a bouquet of roses and a gift-wrapped package.

"Thank you."

"I'd say someone likes you," he replied with a smile before turning back toward his van.

She carried the flowers into the dining room, gently set the vase on the table. A dozen roses in all different colors, beautifully displayed. She searched but found no card, leaving her to wonder if they were from Daniel or Mark. She opened the package. A book about kitten care, with an envelope on top. She opened the envelope and slipped out a page. It was the printout of an email from Mark.

Gina, I mentioned I was a letter writer. Technology has let me get this one to you in faster fashion than with a stamp.

I thought it might be easier for you to read these words than answer the phone and hear my voice for our first conversation after I shook up your life. I meant what I said. I would love to be your husband. I would love for you to be my wife.

Refit is going to be time-stressed. And unfortunately, phone reception within a sub is poor. Phone before five a.m. or after midnight and I'll probably be at the house and able to catch the call. I have no expectations that you'll call, no expectations you might come to Bangor before I depart, as I know you need time to think. I just wanted to say I'm ready to listen, and I look forward to the day I'm back with you. I already miss you, Gina.

God's honest truth, with all the emotion and decisions of the heart and mind and will these words mean, I love you. Give me a chance to show you I can be the husband you deserve and need.

Yours, Mark

She carefully folded the note and slid it back into the envelope. Her heart felt like it was breaking. She didn't love him. She had to tell him no. But the man was holding his heart out to her.

She wiped at tears. The last 24 hours felt like someone had picked her up and shaken everything she knew about herself. "I'm such a fool, God," she whispered. "Thank you for having Daniel intercept me and turn me around. He saved me from a very bad fumble in how I handled this."

She'd been ready to go over a cliff, and she knew God had used Daniel to stop her. She felt ashamed now, replaying mentally the words she'd rehearsed during the flight west. She had gone from being stunned he'd proposed to wishing Mark hadn't asked her, not when she was seeing Daniel, not when Mark was leaving for patrol, to being upset that he'd proposed. Her words would have carried the emotion of saying no, as well as the added edge of frustration that he'd put her in this position. It would have been wrong on so many levels to reply to his proposal in such an emotional state. And she would have never forgiven herself once she had calmed down and realized what she'd done.

The first marriage proposal she had ever received, from a man who meant the words *I love you,* and her heart didn't know what to feel. She curled up on the couch with the two kittens in her lap, and she let herself cry the tears still held in her heart.

18

Bangor was beautiful in the fall, the trees now in the process of casting aside richly colored leaves and preparing for winter. Gina felt a calm that hadn't been in her life for a long time. Bishop had been at sea for two months, and Daniel would depart on the *Nebraska* in two weeks.

Her flight had arrived early. She waited at the parking lot near Delta Pier, leaning against the side of her brother's car and drinking the coffee she'd brought from his place with her. She didn't want the coffee, but she needed something in her hands. She saw Daniel coming and straightened as he said a few words to the men with him, then broke away from the group to come over and join her.

"You had a good flight," Daniel said, dropping a kiss on her cheek.

"I did." She offered Daniel the coffee she had brought for him. It was her first time back in Bangor since her panicked flight months ago, and while she'd talked regularly with Daniel, this was the first time seeing him in person in many weeks. She'd missed him. The smile was still there and quick, but she could see changes too in the months since Jeff had introduced them. There was another year of life and maturity being etched into his face.

He was studying her with equal attention to detail. "You came to have 'the talk.' That solemn expression is a giveaway."

"Yes."

He reached for her hand. "Let's take a walk up to our favorite vista point."

As they walked, Gina said quietly, "I can't marry you, Daniel."

His hand around hers tightened, but he said nothing.

"I don't love you," she whispered, having to force out the words. "I want to. I wish I did. I've spent the last months praying I'd wake up one morning and realize with blinding clarity you're the one, that I love you. And instead it's been the certainty that I need to recognize the truth. It isn't going to be, Daniel. You and I are a good fit, but not the best one, not the one you need, not the one you deserve."

His silence continued. She risked a glance

at his face. "Mad at me?"

"No." He sounded resigned. He glanced over at her, offered a small smile. "It's been the best summer of my life. I can't be mad." His thumb traced the back of her hand, then he released it, and she felt the loss of contact like a rip into her heart.

"Is it Bishop?" he asked after a moment.

"No. That is . . . no, at least not yet." She bit her lip. "I so wanted to fall in love with you, Daniel. You're an absolutely wonderful man, and everything I hoped for in a husband. It's not you. It's me. I'm not the woman who is the right wife for you. I'm so sorry about this, about how long I let it go before I reached that conclusion."

"Don't be. You've made a decision, and that's a good thing. We handled the summer well, Gina. I can't say I'm not intensely disappointed, but I'll survive. I do appreciate you telling me before I left for patrol."

"I brought you a gift, a handmade 'joke a day' for your time at sea. It would mean a lot to me if you'd accept it."

"I will," he promised. "Don't be sad. I know you're worried about how things might unfold with Bishop, but there's no need for you to be. You reached a decision about me; you'll reach one with him. If it's no to both of us, you'll be okay, Gina. You will find the right one someday."

She was rejecting him, and he was comforting her. "Can I hug you without breaking your heart even more?" she whispered.

He turned her toward him, folded her into his arms. "I'll hug you," he said. He sighed. "I appreciate you making a decision about me on its own, not a you-chose-Bishop-over-me one. That helps at the margins."

"It was never a choice between you two. I promise you that, Daniel. Never a comparison."

"Thank you for that."

"I'm going to miss you," she whispered, her voice wavering as she eased away from the hug, accepting that this goodbye was coming by her hands.

Daniel shook his head. "I'm not going anywhere. We're friends, Gina. I want that from you. You aren't going to change your mind, as you took too much thought to make it. So I'm not going to linger around hoping to hear that you've reconsidered. But I will be around when you need a friend. I trust you. And you can trust me when you need an ear to listen, a shoulder to lean on."

"I don't deserve that."

"I do. It's a selfish request, Gina. I need to know you're okay in the years ahead. We stay friends — that's my price for accepting your no."

She solemnly nodded and took a deep breath, let it out, held out her hand. She'd kissed him for the last time, and those memories were now tucked away in her heart. "Friends."

They solemnly shook on it. Daniel turned her back the way they had come. He smiled. "Got a joke for you."

She groaned.

"A walrus went to see the dentist to complain about a toothache."

She let herself laugh as she listened to the joke, even as her heart broke under the weight of the first door she'd closed by her own hand. She hoped she hadn't just walked away from the best guy she would find in her lifetime. But it was the only decision that came along with peace. She wasn't the right lady for Daniel Field, to her deep regret.

Her phone beeped as they neared the parking lot. She pulled it from her pocket.

"Trouble?" Daniel asked.

"An alert from JPL. A solar flare happened eight minutes ago." She scanned through the numbers in the initial alert, the first flash readings the sun observatory satellites measured. "One of the largest on record. I'll be busy when I get back to Chicago."

"You like the work?"

Gina tried to be objective about it. Work had become a place to hide from her tangled personal life, and her emotions about it were complex. "It's something else to think about. I'm good at the work itself, the large data sets. I'm enjoying the process of it, the distraction. And at least I can't get myself in trouble with the sun like I can with sonar."

"Don't ever regret what you did for the Navy," Daniel assured her. "We've started using the new capabilities to good advantage. Boomers are now given cleared water to sail in, the area swept by fast-attacks running cross-sonar searches before we arrive. We will meet up now during patrol with one of the modified boomers carrying Tomahawks — either the *Ohio* or the *Michigan* — and take another deep look at the waters around our patrol box. The visibility is better, both in accuracy and distance. My job is much safer than it was. It's an invaluable improvement, Gina.

"When trouble eventually comes — and it inevitably will, for the world never stays at peace — submariners are going to stay alive because of what you gave us this year," Daniel added. "Boomers will have what they need to remain well clear of the trouble. And fast-attacks now have the ability to wade into that trouble in more effective ways.

"We've had several meetings working out new tactics. You should see some of the advantages you've given fast-attacks when it comes to operational decisions. The U.S. may not even be in the fight; we may simply be trying to keep two other nations' combatants separated. Fast-attacks are better equipped to do that job now."

"Thank you, Daniel. It helps to know you see it that way."

They walked in silence for a minute.

"Bishop is back in another month," Daniel said.

She nodded.

"He's going to have spent the 90 days wondering what you're thinking."

"I consider matters with Mark suspended, awaiting his arrival. I've been deliberately avoiding thinking too much about what I will say. But I'm going to be kind, Daniel. No quick emotional words this time. You were right about what he deserves."

"If you decide to tell him no as well, send him to me. We will commiserate together out on a boat somewhere with a couple of fishing rods and a bunch of sunscreen and memories of the wonderful girl that slipped through our fingers."

She offered a brief smile. "Thank you for being so kind about this."

"If I thought I had a chance of changing your decision, I'd be in the middle of a new pitch right now, Gina. I don't want to let you go." He looked away for a moment, and his voice sounded tight when he finished, "But I'm going to handle this well for my own sake as well as yours."

"You deserve a wonderful wife, Daniel."

"Someday that prayer gets answered for me," Daniel replied. "You'll find a husband too, Gina."

"Maybe. I don't have the courage to do this again. If the right answer with Mark is no, I'm going to take a break from that dream, at least for a while. It hurts too much, having to say no."

19

What felt like the longest patrol of his career was finally coming to an end. Bishop watched the sun dip into the western horizon, then lifted binoculars to scan Delta Pier as the *Nevada* drew near, hoping to catch a glimpse of Gina among those waiting. He heard, but ignored, a conversation above him by the lookouts as they did the same.

The crew knew the captain had a romantic interest, that this patrol had been spent hoping for a message from her. He'd added her name to his second sheet so she could send a family-o-gram or get updates about the boat from the ombudsman. There had been no word, and his crew knew that too.

Bishop didn't see Gina on the pier. He took a deep breath and forced himself to push aside the disappointment. His XO radioed the second tugboat approval to nudge the *Nevada*'s tail, and moments later the soft thud of contact echoed over the water. Bishop had spent the last 16 hours of the transit in the sail, there if Kingman needed assistance with the maneuvers, but the man had the job well in hand. The journey had been spent with little to do and too much time for Bishop to think about what might be waiting for him onshore. Or not . . .

Bangor Base was a big place, so Gina not being at the pier didn't mean she wasn't in the area. Jeff was at sea, but she could be staying at Jeff's place, could have left a message for him with the ombudsman, could be with the families in the squadron's ready room, or for that matter could have left a note on his own front door. But the early discouragement had found a foothold, and it ate away at the hope he'd held on to during the long three months.

He watched, alert for problems as the boat was nestled in against the dock and the mooring lines thrown across. He waited until the dock chief raised his hand, signaling he was satisfied with the position, and the tugboats had reversed, easing back from contact, before he relaxed. He slid off his sunglasses and turned to his XO. "You did a good job."

"Thank you, sir."

Kingman looked exhausted. The transit had absorbed every bit of his skill for those last 16 hours. But there was a quiet confidence in the reply that hadn't been there on their last patrol. Bishop was pleased to hear it. It was part of his job, training his men, then giving them the experience so they could learn the nuances of the sub when at sea.

Bishop could teach his XO how to direct the boat, train him and the crew through the drills on how to accomplish the boat's mission with excellence, show the officer how to lead the crew by being an example. Bishop could teach Kingman through conversations and history what it meant to be a captain, what boomers and fast-attacks had done over the years, why a captain made a certain decision during a crisis, and the outcome. The part Bishop was still searching for with Kingman was how to help him be prepared for the responsibility that came with the captain's chair. Knowing how to do each part of the captain's job was different than being ready to step into the role. All the unknowns and eventualities required another level of honed instincts, insight, and instant decisions.

Bishop knew the XO wanted that depth, was working hard and studying hard, was doing anything and everything his captain asked of him, was putting his heart and soul into *Nevada* gold — and he was close, but they weren't quite there yet. Bishop carried the burden of command, the responsibility for the lives of 155 men, the safekeeping of nuclear weapons, and the responsibility to fire them when ordered to do so by the commander in chief. A man had to be able to bear up, thinking clearly and confidently, under that pressure. It wasn't just competence a man needed to be the captain. The command of a ballistic missile submarine took personal courage. It was that intangible element that was still unknown, untested, with Kingman. Was he ready? Bishop would be doing the man no favors if he misjudged the answer to that question.

He'd personally been taught by good men, and he would get the job done with Kingman and get him ready for that first command of his own. Finishing that job would have to be the focus for the next patrol. This one was three days away from hand-over to *Nevada* blue, and what could be taught had been done.

"Your choice, XO, first overnight watch or second? I'll take the other."

"I'll take tonight's watch, sir."

Bishop smiled, having expected the answer. It was brutal on a tired, overworked body and mind to sleep at home for a night in comfort, then spend the next night back in a sub bunk.

Bishop moved from the sail back into the command-and-control center, glad to finally have the splint off his fingers so he could transit ladders without the extra care with every motion. He picked up the intercom. "*Nevada,* this is the captain. Welcome home. A good patrol under difficult circumstances. Thanks to your extra effort, we met every date and every mission objective. Families are gathering at the Squadron 17 ready room. Enlisted not assigned duty stations for the overnight watch are dismissed after the boat is secured. Report back to the boat at 0900 for hand-over preparation. All officers please report in now. Captain out."

He headed forward to the radio room to secure the authentication codes. He'd be able to get free of the *Nevada* in about six hours. If Gina was in the area, he would find her before the night was over.

Gina wasn't at the squadron's ready room, nor was she at Jeff's place. She wasn't waiting for him at his home. Mark felt the discouragement fill him as he unlocked his front door, let himself into the house. He went straight to the phone and played the messages on his second private number, given out to only his family and close friends. There was no message from Gina, and the recording space was not full.

"God, this simply hurts." He let the pain flow out in the quiet words. He looked at the time. By now it was after one a.m. in Chicago. He was home for only six hours before he was needed back at the *Nevada*. It was possible she was in Pasadena, working at the JPL facilities. He didn't let himself dwell on the fact she could have changed her mind and might now be engaged to Daniel. He'd track her down, find out, and he'd deal with what he found.

Getting home from patrol to deal with personal concerns was a reality every submariner faced, and it never got easier. The ombudsman had handed him the shore update summary with a quiet "Welcome home" but without her normal accompanying smile, and as he'd read it, he understood her sadness. Due to the requirements of the job, the Navy passed along no bad news to a crewman while a ballistic missile submarine was on patrol — it wasn't a place for a distracted or grieving man. So the bad news piled up.

Two of his men tonight had walked into

homes to find their wives had left and filed for divorce. Four girlfriends had called it quits. Two miscarriages, five babies born healthy, a wife arrested for drunk driving, a teenager in a serious car accident, two deaths of grandparents, a heart attack of a father. What he was dealing with was a hole in his life where he longed to have Gina Gray. As tough as this was, he knew he was in far better circumstances than some in his crew.

His attempt at convincing himself he wasn't doing so bad lasted about as long as it took to draw the next breath. The sorrow and disappointment was intense. Mark looked at the time and considered again calling Gina, but accepted reality. Tracking her down and finding out what he was facing was an endeavor for the morning, not the middle of the night.

The mail his neighbor had brought in during the patrol was piled on the dining room table. Mark skimmed through the envelopes, separating first class and everything else, so he had a sense of what was urgent. An envelope with Gina's return address stopped him, and his heart constricted. He held it a moment, sure this was not going to be good. He split it open and pulled out a note card.

If you can come to Chicago, I would like to have dinner with you and talk. Your Gina

His breathing started again. It wasn't much, but those last two words, *Your Gina,* gave him a sliver of hope. He looked at the date on the postmark. Two months into his patrol. That could be good or bad, depending on how her perspective might have altered in the month since she had posted this.

Come to Chicago and talk. She wasn't coming to Bangor, so she was still feeling cautious about being around the Navy. If it came down to it, he'd retire after his three years commanding the *Nevada,* his twenty years in the Navy, and move back to Chicago to be with Gina. Most of his family was there. He could adapt to being a civilian again and find something interesting to do.

He searched to find another letter from her, but there was nothing else. Hand-over to *Nevada* blue was in three days. He'd make travel arrangements for Chicago for the day after that. He would wait to call Gina and ask her to join him for dinner once he was in Chicago, so he could effectively address whatever she told him in reply. She was at least giving him an opportunity to make his case. Or was her decision already made? But would she tell him no over dinner?

He went to bed hanging on to that sliver of hope the note offered.

20

A dusting of snow covered the ground, but Chicago had yet to get its first December winter storm, and the evening was mild. Four months and eight days since refit and the 90-day patrol began. Gina had been the first thought when he woke up, the last before he slept. Mark parked in her driveway, retrieved his jacket on the passenger seat, picked up a single orchid. Gina was on the front porch in a light jacket, working on a potted plant set on a tall stand. She looked up and smiled, lifted a hand in welcome when he got out of the car, but otherwise she stayed focused on her task. She'd turned on the porch lights as the evening light was beginning to fade.

She might be engaged by now. She might be going to turn down his proposal, and this time Daniel wouldn't be there to run interference. Regardless of what was coming, Mark was going to treasure what he could of the evening in case it was his last with her.

Her smile and hello were a bit tentative. He would have given her a hug, but he responded in kind. He stayed at ground level and rested his arms across the stair railing, working to maintain a relaxed posture while she finished up rescuing the plant.

He loved her. It took no more than the sight of her and that smile for the emotions to turn his chest tight.

"I planned to be ready early, and instead I'm way behind schedule," she said.

"That's okay. I take it you weren't the one to knock over the plant?" Her front door was open, and there were two half-grown kitten faces and a puppy looking out through the glass of the storm door.

"The three chased each other into the sunroom where I had this plant. The cats dashed behind the pot, and the puppy got to taste dirt before his body stopped. I think the cats were smirking about that."

Mark smiled. "Poor little guy. What's his name?"

"Your niece named him Pongo, and I've found it has kind of stuck."

"Pocket, Pages, and Pongo. You've got a pattern going."

"I do." She pulled off her work gloves.

There wasn't a ring on her left hand. He felt some of the pressure in his chest ease. "How are you doing, Gina?" he asked.

"That's a rather long answer." She stored the potting soil, trowel, and extra pot in the closet at the end of the porch and picked up her rescued plant. "Come on in, Mark."

He followed her inside.

Mark picked up one of the half-grown kittens, watched the puppy with feet too big for his body tug at a tattered piece of fabric on which the other cat was lying. The cat flattened its ears and hissed, but didn't take a swipe as the puppy pushed its face into hers. Familiarity. They were playing together, of a sort.

Gina's home had lost the neatness seen during his last visit, and small changes had appeared: large, heavy pottery by the front door, a new coatrack, another bookshelf in the living room. From the look of things, she'd mostly been living on this main level. There was a sweater tossed over the couch arm, a stack of mail on the coffee table, Post-it notes beside the television remote, work papers and a writing board beside one of the wingback chairs. A laptop had been placed on the coffee table. She'd gone into the kitchen and found a tall vase for the orchid and risked placing it on that same coffee table, then retreated to get them both drinks.

Mark glanced up as Gina reentered the room carrying two glasses of iced tea. She'd left the room not just for the drinks, he thought, but to give herself a few more moments of space. Her words and smile might have been calm and welcoming, but it wasn't the full story. She hadn't been sleeping well. The dark circles under her eyes had the look of being weeks in the making.

This was a woman who was uncomfortable, and his silence was making her even less comfortable. But he didn't know what to say. He needed to get a read on what she was thinking before he could figure out what direction to go with his comments. She settled on the couch across from him. He sipped the iced tea she'd handed him and waited.

"Daniel and I talked a lot before he departed on patrol," she said quietly. "Before this evening continues, you need to know that he and I are no longer dating."

He hadn't expected that.

"I don't love him. I wish I did. I wanted to," she admitted. "I wanted desperately for that final piece of the equation to fall in place. I finally had to accept it wasn't going to happen."

"That had to be a very tough decision for you . . . for him."

"It was painful for both of us." She rested her arm along the back of the couch. "But deciding he isn't the one isn't the same as deciding you are."

"I accept that, Gina."

"I flew back to Bangor to tell you no, the day after you proposed. Daniel talked me out of it."

"I know that too. And now?"

She lifted one shoulder. "I'm not sure of anything about us. I'm trying my best to keep an open mind. I'm not trying to be difficult, Mark. I just don't know what to think, what to do."

"Gina, go back some months to before you came to Bangor. What were you praying for?"

"To find a husband."

"You've found one."

She shook her head slightly, rejecting his calm assurance.

"I accept your emotions are all over the place right now," he continued. "Answer me this. Would you be willing to spend some time with me, let us date seriously? Would you be willing to give us some time together

425

for you to get to know me better?"

She hesitated, then nodded. "Yes."

"I've got 28 days of leave. I'll be in Chicago for as much of it as you would like me to be. I packed so I'd be able to stay."

"I didn't expect that."

"I'm not telling you that to put pressure on you, Gina. Just that I think time together will be easier for you when it's on your own turf. I made a list while I was on patrol — things you and I could do together. You can choose as many items from that long list as you like for the next month. Or add some of your own."

He studied her face, wishing he better knew her expressions and could interpret what she might be thinking. "Talk to me. Just start somewhere and tell me what you're thinking about me, about us. Give me some sense of the ground you're standing on."

"I still lean toward saying no," she replied carefully, meeting his gaze. "I do admire you. You're a man who bears responsibility well. You're a leader and well respected. You had a good marriage. I trust you. I respect your advice. You're gentle with me — I think you see me and understand me better than most people. I enjoy our conversations very much. In many ways you fit me better than

Daniel. You have a quieter, more peaceful personal life.

"But the truth is, Mark, I'm too young for you. I'm chaos-writ-large at times. I'm emotionally needy. I'm unsure of myself. I'm not like Melinda. You need someone who has her life together. Mine keeps falling even further apart. There's the possibility of you becoming the top submarine guy in the Navy one day. You need someone with more social strengths, more people skills, to help with your career. I'd be a liability rather than a help. I don't bring much useful to the table as your wife."

He waited a moment to give her carefully thought-out statements some room. "Gina, I'd like you to see yourself through my eyes —"

"I don't want to spend my life feeling that gap I can never close," she put in, "between what you need and who I am."

He agreed with about half her statement. "Marriage is an interesting proposition, Gina," he finally said. "It's a relationship, a friendship, along with a rich, deep level of intimacy. It's a lot of things, dreaming together, planning a future together."

"I'd spend my life leaning against you, hoping you could get me out of whatever latest troubles I've gotten myself into."

"Your ideas and discoveries."

"Yes."

He smiled. "I was kind of looking forward to that part, Gina. I love how your mind works. I like responsibility — thrive on it. I could buffer some of what comes because of those discoveries, work out who should know what and when. Figure out the downsides and how to deal with them. We'd be a good team."

He pulled a folded sheet out of his shirt pocket. "I wrote you a letter while on patrol. I actually wrote you several, but this is the first and most important one. I'd like you to read it." He handed it to her. She hesitated a while before opening it. He knew the words, having thought about and read them over many times.

Gina, I once told you I would do my best not to steer you wrong. I'm still honoring that. I think you should get married because it's something you have dreamed about, looked forward to, since you were a young girl. I also honestly think I'm the right guy for you to marry.

I've been married before, and it was a good experience. I know this terrain. Now it's you I want in my life, you I want to build a new marriage with. I want to share breakfast with you, listen to what's got you fascinated, and find ways to make you laugh. I want to show you places I've been, introduce you to people I know. I want to make a home with you, and fill it with things we both enjoy. I'd like to spend the rest of my life loving you. I know you and I can sort it all out to have a good marriage, one we both find meets our deepest needs. Take a chance on me, Gina. You won't regret it. Be my wife.

> Yours, Beloved.
> Mark

She read it, read it again, and he simply waited. "It's a lovely letter," she whispered.

"I'm convinced you're the one for me, Gina, and I also believe I'm the one for you. I love you. Share your life with me. Let me share mine with you. Whatever is necessary to reach the point where you can make that decision, ask it, work it through with me."

She didn't answer him, just sat looking at the page. She finally wiped her eyes. "You're too far ahead of me, Mark. I can't think in terms of marrying you. Not yet. Even if you're right, the timing is wrong."

"Gina . . ." Mark hesitated. "Do you realize you're afraid to get married?" he asked gently. "Daniel would have been a good choice for you. I'm a good choice. When you find there are none of your must-not-haves and all of your must-haves, it's time to say yes. I love you. And I'm confident you'll love me well in return if you let yourself take the step. Say yes and marry me. Your doubts are real, but they won't survive first contact with reality."

She bit her lip. "Your certainty about this surprises me, Mark."

"I didn't ask you to marry three months ago because I somehow wanted to outdo Daniel. I asked because I love you, and I can see a very good future for us."

She said nothing, and he shifted the discussion slightly. "When my command of the *Nevada* ends, I'm not opposed to Chicago as our home base. I've got family here. I like the area. You don't have to consider returning permanently to Bangor. If you prefer to work in California, there are nice options for where to settle there. I'm not expecting you to give up who you are — the work, the continued pursuit of degrees and new subjects, the somewhat nomadic way you go from project to project. I just want you to share your life with me and let me share mine with you. I want to build something that is *us*."

He let the silence last more than a minute before he added, "I know this all sounds like a full-court press, even to me, but the reason I'm so certain about this is what I see in your face. You're afraid to seize your dream. Are you able to recognize that, Gina? The panic that came after my proposal, your decision to turn down Daniel — you want so much to be married, yet you fear failing and it's keeping you from accepting that this time a relationship will succeed.

"This is that moment, Gina." He leaned forward in his chair. "All you need to do is trust me, and reach for that dream. It's right here. A good marriage. Someone who loves you more than you can yet know. All you have to do is say yes." He watched the play of expressions across her face. "You will not be a disappointment to me. I see you clearly, I understand you. I'm not going to steer you wrong. I'm the guy."

"You don't know enough about me to say that, Mark."

He could hardly hear her words, her whisper was so faint. "I know enough that I can be the husband you need. You're the wife I want. I'm certain of that."

She got up from the couch, walked to the window, looked out at the night that had descended. He waited for her to make a comment, to give him a sense of what she was thinking. Instead she simply stood there, silent. She finally turned. "I need to tell you no, but it hurts too much to do that. Yet the longer this goes on the more hurt we're both going to feel later. Time isn't going to make things any easier."

"Why do you need to tell me no, Gina?" he asked quietly.

"I'm in trouble."

Her words made him blink, and tension coiled through his body. "Did something happen with Daniel — ?" He stopped as she immediately shook her head.

"No, no, nothing like that. Work trouble." Resigned acceptance passed over her face. "The kind that seems like a constant, recurring nightmare with me."

He could feel his emotions shifting as her tone registered with him, as he detected an underlay of fear he hadn't heard from her before. She'd changed the topic and driven them full speed into a brick wall. Of everything he had been braced to hear, this wasn't what he was expecting. "How much trouble?"

"So much trouble I'm actually considering marrying you before I tell you just so you'll feel *really* bad if you yell at me." She tried to come up with a chuckle at the end of that statement but couldn't pull it off. She wiped a hand across her eyes.

"Tell me," he said simply. "Just start somewhere, Gina. Wherever you like. I promise to listen."

"There's a photo on the dining room table. You should probably go look at it."

He held her gaze for a long moment, seeing so many layers of emotions in her — a lifetime of wishing she wasn't smart, wanting to be "normal," of pain that she couldn't avoid. He walked into the next room.

He turned over the large 24×36 glossy print on the dining room table. A simple picture, computer-generated, he was looking at a line drawing of the world's coastlines, the expanse of the oceans and landmasses in stark white. There were clusters of small objects near the coasts, a few objects in the deep oceans, accompanied by three numbers in small font beside them. A depth number, location numbers. He realized what he was seeing and his heart rate spiked.

He was looking at a photo of all the submarines in the world's oceans on — he found a date and time in the upper corner — the second of November, 8:17 p.m. He forced a deep breath, his heart pounding now. He'd just turned over a live explosive.

Gina came to stand beside him. She pointed out a few of the objects in the deep ocean waters in the photo. "These two are Russian Akulas. These two are British Astutes. This is an Australian Collins class. These are the eight boomers the U.S. had in the Pacific and Atlantic that day. These five are U.S. fast-attacks. Given the locations, these four are probably the diesel Kilos that China purchased from Russia. I can tell the submarines apart by their dimensions."

"Gina. How on earth — ?"

She didn't let him finish. "I want you to tell me it's okay to destroy this photo, to light a match and make it go away like it never existed."

"Gina . . ."

"It's an accident, Mark. That's all this discovery is, an accident no one else will repeat for a century or more. I want you to tell me it's okay to forget this ever happened, to erase it forever with a match, to be able to go on with my life."

He pulled out a chair at the table, nudged her into it. He hunkered down beside her to be at eye level, to be able to see her expressions. "You've got to talk through the building blocks that led to this before I can answer you. I promise you, we'll talk it through until you have an answer you can live with. But first I need some facts. When did you print this photo?"

"November 22nd, nine days ago. I did it here. I've got an architect's wide printer in the office upstairs."

"Who have you told?"

"You. Only you." She took a deep breath, let it out. "No one else can create that photo. The data no longer exists. I've destroyed or corrupted the original data files to prevent it from happening."

He felt some of his tension ease a fraction. "There's always a simple observation in your discoveries. Was there one that led to this?"

"Yes."

"Can you tell me about that?"

"I can show you," she said. She got up and went back to the living room, changed a remote setting so the TV displayed her laptop computer screen. She logged into the server deck and started a video playback.

"This is from the NOAA weather satellite EO-1," she said as he moved beside her to view the screen. "It orbits the earth every 21 minutes — one of many weather-related satellites NOAA has deployed. This particular video is from the infrared camera. The different colors are different temperatures.

The oceans are cooler here and warmer here," she said, pointing, "and rain is falling there. This data feeds into the weather models and helps meteorologists make their weather forecasts. This particular satellite has been in orbit about 10 years. There's nothing particularly unique about it. It's just a convenient one whose data I've used over the years to work on the satellite drag problem.

"There was a large solar flare on the 30th of October. I got an alert about it from the Jet Propulsion Lab in Pasadena. Beginning about 60 hours later, lasting four days, there were communication problems between satellites and their ground stations — these random sparkles you see in the video. A solar flare causes all kinds of changes in the earth's upper atmosphere as the high-energy particles in the solar wind hit the earth. Things like the brilliant northern lights that we see, but also more subtle things like satellites encountering additional drag as the atmosphere warms up and expands.

"I wrote an algorithm to clean up the video, remove the sparkles, so the data could process faster. Those of us who work with satellite instruments and large data files — it's not a large group, and most of us know each other, at least by email. Someone mentioned I had a cleanup algorithm that worked well. People dropped me emails, asking if I could run my cleanup algorithm on their data files too. Over the next week I cleaned up data from 32 satellites and 84 instruments, removing the sparkles thought to be transmission errors caused by the solar flare.

"I was surprised to find the sparkles appeared across every instrument — from the narrow-wave gamma ray and x-rays, the infrared, down to the very long-wave microwave and radio frequencies — every part of the electromagnetic spectrum had them being recorded." She paused and watched the video. "I finally got curious about the sparkles." She reached over and ran her finger lightly across the screen. "These random sparkles are not transmission errors. They're reflections from deep in the sea."

She didn't say anything more. She didn't need to.

Reflections. The underlying discovery was genius-level simple. He walked back to the dining room and looked again at the photo. "You mapped them to this?"

"With some rather elegant analysis, yes," she replied, joining him. "The solar flare's high-energy particles are reflecting off the submarine hulls, like a billiard ball bouncing off a rail. They scatter in all directions, and unlike visible light waves, water doesn't reabsorb them. Satellites circling the earth are at the right place and time to capture a portion of those bounced reflections. Once I figured out the satellites' orientation and the instrument angle, I time-synced the data sources and compressed back the motion video to the original shape and form of the object. I combined the various instruments' data and plotted the sparkles. And I saw every submarine in the oceans."

Every submarine, including the U.S. boomers that spent their patrols with standing orders to stay undetected. In the wrong hands, this photo would be devastating.

"We're going to eat something. What do you want delivered? Pizza? Chinese?" he asked abruptly.

"Chinese, if I have to choose between the two."

"What would you prefer?"

"Italian, maybe. Something with chicken."

"Have you slept much since this printed?"

"Not much," she admitted.

"Get comfortable on the couch, put your feet up, close your eyes, and catch a nap while we wait for the food. We'll talk after we eat."

She hesitated. He picked up one of the cats and handed it to her. "Is this Pocket or Pages?"

"Black is Pocket."

"Stretch out on the couch. I bet she's asleep before you are."

Mark walked over to the bookshelf, slit the plastic on a new three-pack of composition notebooks, took out the top one and pulled a pen from his pocket.

"You're welcome to use the laptop if that's a faster way to put your thoughts and questions in order," Gina offered, watching him.

"A notebook is easier to burn if necessary." He walked back to her, tipped up her chin, and kissed her. "We'll figure this out. Get that nap, Gina."

Gina was asleep. She'd finally told someone about the discovery, the photo, shared the stress of it, and her body was demanding rest. Mark knew what that stress felt like, could feel it still draining through his own system. *Lord, I don't know what to do here,* he said silently in a prayer that came from deep in his heart and his mind. The hull of a sub was unlike any other structure man designed in composition and form, and solar-flare energy reflected off of it — a simple discovery. Yet so breathtakingly complex in what it signified.

Gina, the genius. A term of affection, a term of endearment. Jeff said it, Mark thought it. But also in terms of fact. Gina noticed things. She simplified matters. She didn't see what she did as particularly a gift. Her discoveries *were* simple, most of them instantly understandable by others. She thought it was merely an oversight that someone else hadn't already done the same thing she thought to try. The simplicity in what she realized was what showed her genius. This photo was only round three of what life with her would be like. It would be a fascinating future, spending the next several decades with her.

This last discovery was an accident, but she'd had the skill to recognize that something more than transmission errors were occurring, had the skills to pursue the idea and take that data back to the underlying photo. Smart didn't adequately convey what it meant to say Gina had talent.

He loved her. And she needed him. This kind of discovery was something she shouldn't be asked to carry alone. She needed someone more than just her brother in her life. *Jesus, give me a heart able to see this woman clearly, one you love even more than I do. Help me see what she needs in this moment and in the days ahead.* He sat in a chair across from the couch, notebook on his knee, and watched her sleep.

She needed time, and that was the one thing this situation wasn't going to give him. She seemed to have lived her life at two speeds, the intellect and work and curiosity moving forward at such a speed that the personal side — the self-confidence, the relationships and friendships — were noticeable in how they'd lagged behind her work life. She needed time and confidence and friends, and someone to love her without limits. She'd thrive within that environment. He so wanted to be that person for her.

Mark didn't bother to wake Gina when the food arrived. He put her chicken Parmesan in the refrigerator to keep until she was ready to eat it, out of reach of the kittens. He started in on the lasagna he'd ordered for himself while he turned his attention to the problem she faced.

In his job he dealt with the more-than-theoretical reality of nuclear war. He had to balance hard concerns every time he took a sub out to sea. He knew how to make tough decisions, but factoring in the implications to Gina for this one was not simple. For a year now, Gina's sonar discoveries had grown progressively more revealing. She was at her limit. She desperately wanted to destroy this photo. Whatever decision was made now had to accommodate what Gina was feeling. Showing the Navy that photo would land a world of attention on her. That fact worried him.

She hadn't destroyed the photo before she had shared it with him. If he wondered if she trusted him, he had his answer. When her life was stressed beyond bearing, she had put it on his shoulders. He was glad for it. She hadn't told her brother about the photo yet — Jeff and the USS *Seawolf* had departed days before she printed this photo — and Mark was pretty sure he could convince her not to tell Jeff when he was back in port.

She'd just destabilized the strongest leg of the nuclear-deterrent triad: air, land, and sea. Land-based silos could be bombed, planes could be shot down or prevented from taking off. But ballistic-missile submarines at sea had to be found before they could be attacked, and she'd just taken a photo of every deployed boomer.

He leaned back in the chair, linked his hands behind his head. He was beginning to think she should burn the photo.

21

Gina slept three hours before she stirred. Mark looked over at her from his phone call and recognized this time the movement was more than a shift to change positions. "Thanks, Bryce, for the news that it's ready," he told his brother. "I'll plan to pick it up in the morning." He tucked away the phone and watched Gina open her eyes and groggily move aside both kittens from their perch on her chest.

"Are you hungry now or are you craving more sleep? You can turn in for the night — I'll lock up for you," he said quietly. He knew security was around the house, but he'd make the checks just the same.

Gina sat up and pushed her hair back from her face. "I'm hungry, and I'd rather talk."

He handed her the notebook with his notes. "I'll reheat your dinner."

He came back with a plate and saw the

notebook on the end table. She was playing with the puppy.

"Has Pongo been out?" she asked. "I fenced the backyard for him."

"Twice. He brought back a chewed-up work glove the second time."

"He acquired it when I made the mistake of leaving the pair within his reach. He thinks it's a game."

Mark set up a TV tray in front of her with the plate, silverware, napkin and glass, then took the puppy. "Enjoy."

She ate with an appetite he was pleased to see. "I'm sorry that Jeff, Daniel, and I were all unavailable when you printed the photo, Gina. That you had to make this discovery and realize its scope on your own."

"God heard about it," she said, and he heard sadness in her words. "I knew . . . early on I knew what was coming. Each pass through the data, every sparkle that resolved back to its originating point — I knew what it meant. Made me pretty sick the first 48 hours. But I've grown resigned to the reality. My life is forever going to be like this, Mark. Finding out stuff I don't want to know, that I don't want others to know. But I'm going to get wiser about what to do once it happens." She looked over at him. "I want to burn that photo," she said with conviction.

Mark thought it might be necessary. "You said no one else could create this particular photo. That the data no longer exists."

"I've checked a number of the satellite archives. My cleaned-up file was retained, not the original file with the sparkles. These are very large data files. You don't keep extra copies of them around without a reason.

"I corrupted my own copies of the instrument data. I ran an algorithm across the videos, intentionally removed some of the sparkles that were there, introduced new ones. The data will look normal to someone playing back the video image, but it can't be used to generate a photo."

She reached for the napkin. "The algorithms I used to build the photo have been isolated onto one of my data servers upstairs, and I physically pulled that card and have it stored in the safe. I can clear it with a powerful magnet and wipe it forever."

"Good to know. Those are crucial security steps."

Gina nodded. "I was thinking it might be possible to do a preemptive safeguard against someone else discovering this. If I can get my algorithm installed as part of the satellite receiver's software, the sparkles could automatically be removed from the video. Most of these satellites use a common down-leg protocol. Call it a transmission-error cleanup algorithm. Solar flares are going to keep happening in the future. The key point to intercept and mitigate this is at the receivers."

"I like the idea. It's a solid way to play defense." Mark reached for his notebook and jotted down the information. "I've got a short list of critical questions to ask, Gina. Let me ask them, then we'll come back to this."

"Sure."

"After a solar flare," he said, looking at the first page in his notes, "every submarine in the ocean is vulnerable to being seen from space for how long? Starting 60 hours after the flare and continuing for four days?"

"The peak visibility is early in that window, at about 72 hours. You might be able to start finding useful information 40 hours after a solar flare in the narrowest bandwidths. The reflections taper off with time into the longer radio wave-lengths and have dissipated after four days."

"How often do solar flares happen?"

"The sun has active cycles and dormant periods, lasting about 15 years. The sun is active right now. Solar flares in the upper right quadrant of the sun are those that affect the earth. High-energy bursts are hitting the earth once or twice a month right now."

He glanced again at his notes. "Have you read any scientific paper, heard anyone at a conference, or come across any reference in the literature that suggests anyone else has wondered correctly about even small pieces of this science?"

"Satellite technicians trying to get data sent and received cleanly have made numerous references to the problem of glitches in the data stream, and it's become accepted wisdom that the sparkles are transmission errors caused by a solar flare or other sun eruption. There are technical discussions on how sensitive to tune the receiver — you don't want to be requesting constant re-transmissions when it's actually a data problem. I've seen nothing else that overlaps any other part of this."

"You're still an outlier right now."

"Yes." She leaned her head back against the cushion of the couch. "You can't convince me someone else is going to stumble on to this, Mark, simply on the predicate that other people are smart too. For me it was pure chance, essentially an accident. You have to have access to multiple satellite data transmissions across a wide variety of instrument types and have collected data in the days after a significant solar flare. You have to guess that the transmission sparkles are actually reflections, then have the skill to reconstruct original shapes from motion video in data that gives you an occasional point or two to work with. The odds of this sequence of events coming together again . . . well, it would be easier to be hit by lightning twice."

Mark thought the odds were even longer than that, but he was looking at the exception, looking at someone who had actually figured it out. "Do you think there's a more streamlined way to get this image, now that you know it's possible to see into the oceans using solar flare reflections?"

"I've been thinking about it. The solar flare is a necessary requirement. Beyond that —" she paused a moment — "it's only guesswork, but the multiple instrument types are likely a necessary condition. You need to see across the energy spectrum to gather enough reflections. Sparkle data from 5 satellites wasn't effective, nor was 10. I needed 17 data sets to get the first glimmers that an actual object was there, 23 to see a shape, and all 32 to get the resolution necessary to distinguish one submarine type from another. Not to mention I had on average four days' worth of video from each instrument to work with. Some combination of that data volume is going to be a necessary factor — the number of satellites and the hours of video.

"The strength of the solar flare is also likely a key variable. The stronger the solar flare, the better the photo. This was the strongest one on record since observation satellites have been aloft. A single reflection off a submarine isn't useful data. I need a bunch of reflections off a hull in order to see a shape, compute its depth. There are tens of millions of high-energy particles thrown out during one of these solar flare bursts, but they still have to hit a very precise spot on earth and then have a satellite in the right location to record the reflection. Creating an image . . . again, it's long odds."

Hearing her lay out how many variables had to come together for her to make this discovery got his attention. That reality made their considerations about what to do even more layered.

"Hold on a minute." He got up and took her plate back to the kitchen, giving himself some time to reflect on an idea that had been slowly taking shape over the last hour. He returned and handed her the ice cream carton and a spoon. "Pass it over to me when you're done."

He sat down, made several more notes, put his idea aside to come back to at a later time, then resumed his original questions. "A photo of where the world's subs were positioned two weeks ago is interesting history, but a photo of where subs were at two hours ago is actionable. How fast can the satellite data be turned into a photo?"

"Throw several powerful computing clusters at this data, it could be fast. Maybe an hour or two?"

"Real time?"

"No. There's a threshold number of sparkles that have to be captured. The photo resolution goes from a faint smudge, to fuzzy, to solid mass, to detailed enough to tell if it's our sub or someone else's. The software could be optimized to focus on only one part of the ocean, then look for the early clues, that it's an object big enough to be a sub. A massive amount of computing power, a maximum number of satellite data sources landing on that key window of time about 72 hours after a solar flare — you might be able to get a fuzzy photo of subs in the northern half of the Pacific that is an hour old. That's probably best-case: a photo about an hour old."

An hour was actionable intelligence. And military history had taught him how important accurate, current information was to a situation. "Gina, I've got some thoughts beginning to jell. They range from destroying the photo to giving it to the Navy now, to a more finessed option of saying nothing about this capability until a situation warrants the risk — such as tensions rising, a war threatening to break out — and we judge the timing of revealing this capability against the risk that an enemy learns it can be done. I'll be back in the morning with more detailed thoughts. Leave everything as it is for now, Gina. Don't destroy the photo or the code. Give me that much as a promise."

She finally nodded. "I do want to burn it, Mark."

"That's factored into my thinking, and it's why I'm asking you not to do anything just yet."

"I'll leave things be for the night." She passed over the carton of ice cream. "Are you staying at a hotel?"

"My brother wouldn't hear of it. I'm staying with Bryce and Charlotte for the night. I'll give you their phone number in case for some reason you can't reach my cell." He spooned a corner of the ice cream carton, glanced at her. "Why did you decide to tell me about this discovery?"

"I wanted to burn the photo and not tell you, not tell anyone. Then I thought about you getting back from patrol and knew you would come to have a conversation —" she paused and let out a long breath — "and I'd look guilty, and you'd ask what was wrong, and I'd have to lie and try to convince you nothing was wrong. It just seemed easier in the end to simply show you the photo."

He smiled. "I appreciate that. Marry me, Gina. You need me. I want you as my wife. There are worse reasons to get married."

"There are better." She bit her lip. "I don't love you, Mark."

"Yet," he qualified. "You don't love me yet." He considered her, then dipped the spoon back in the carton. For her sake he was working hard not to show how much it hurt to hear her say that. But he also heard the underlying tone, and he understood more than she might like him to. He'd go hug the woman, but she wouldn't understand the emotional spectrum playing out inside him tonight.

"I'm going to guess you don't know what you feel right now," he finally said, "besides a layer of fear, a tangle of 'why is he interested in me?' and a wish you wouldn't have to make another important decision right now." He didn't wait for a response but headed to the kitchen to put away the ice cream. When he reentered the living room, he leaned over the sofa and kissed her. "Come say good-night, lock up behind me. I'll be back at nine a.m. sharp with some possibilities."

"You weren't kidding when you said you had some work to do."

Mark looked up to see Charlotte leaning against her kitchen doorway. He'd appropriated the table to work on a decision tree, factoring through different crisis situations and what a photo of the sea would do, both pro and con. The months at sea had beaten him up physically, but he could still drum up focused concentration when it was necessary. He glanced at the clock. It was three a.m. "I'm making progress," he said.

He tossed a couple of kitchen towels across the pages that were classified as Charlotte came into the room, wearing jeans, a sweatshirt, and a pair of faded blue socks. She made herself a cup of tea. "I find it fascinating that you went to the sea, your brother Jim went to space, and Bryce is content to stay on terra firma and be a businessman."

"He's got a good head for it," Mark replied with a smile as he took a long stretch. "And unlike Jim and me, he doesn't need a rush of adrenaline with his job."

She brought over the pan of brownies she'd baked earlier that day and took a seat at the table, sliced off a sliver for herself, passed him the pan and the knife.

"Couldn't sleep?" he asked.

"Sometimes it bothers me waking up to a guy in the room," she admitted softly, "even when it's my husband. You have questions about me. It's nice of you not to have asked them."

"My brother adores you, and you love him back. I figure the details matter, but not that much."

"I'm Ruth Bazoni."

He managed to stop the shock from showing on his face, but she smiled slightly, and he registered he had let the brownie drop.

"I'm sleeping with your brother, literally, or trying to, but I'm not very good at making it through the entire night yet. He's a patient man. We've managed to get to a very nice good-night kiss. Another five years, maybe we'll have progressed to second base."

"I'm sorry, Charlotte."

"So am I. It's three o'clock, so tonight was actually a good night. I keep a private bedroom suite upstairs with double locks inside the door as a security blanket, but I consider it a step backward when I need to retreat there. When the memories of the past mean I can't stay with Bryce, I tend to head to the studio to get some work done." She gave him a smile. "My career has been thriving lately. Anything you need before I go there tonight?"

"I'm good."

She got up from the table. "You're worried about your Gina."

"Yes."

"Patience is a good answer most of the time."

"For her own good, I'm going to have to rush her. She needs a buffer, some protection. That can't be done well without the leverage of being her husband."

Charlotte nodded. "Being a bit of a white knight runs in your family, I've discovered. I'll leave you to your work, Mark." She walked through the kitchen to the studio at the back of the house. Soft music soon drifted into the kitchen.

Ruth Bazoni. Twenty years ago, she'd been at the center of the most famous kidnapping case in Chicago history. Three ransoms, four years, before cops found her two abductors, shot them, and rescued her. And she'd married his brother Bryce. Mark considered that fact and slowly nodded. Bryce was the right man for her. None of the Bishop brothers ever did simple or easy. He smiled. If Gina found the courage to say yes, she'd find she fit in well with his family.

Gina offered to fix waffles for breakfast, and Mark wisely said yes to give her something to do, also mildly interested that she could cook. He sat at the center counter and watched her work. She stacked two waffles on a plate for him along with butter and syrup. She ate hers with melted butter and powdered sugar, cleaned up the kitchen, and finally stopped and leaned against the far counter. "Okay. I've eaten. Had my second cup of coffee. Give me the bad news."

He smiled, appreciating her matter-of-fact attitude, though he was sure it was not easy for her to maintain. "It's not all bad news, Gina." He picked up his coffee, needing the caffeine after a night with barely three hours of sleep. "As I see it, you have three good options, and a few other decent ones." He nodded to the stool beside him. "You might want to sit down for this."

She took the seat beside him as he cut into the last bites of his waffle. "Bottom line, the Navy needs the photo, Gina. You can't burn it," he said simply. "That wasn't my initial reaction, but that's where the possible outcomes have led me. For the foreseeable future, during the years the U.S. is the only one with this capability, it comes close to guaranteeing there will be peace on the high seas. We will know where everyone is — at least after sizable sun flares.

"In the longer term, the implications are that submarine warfare becomes similar to chess. Every piece on the board is seen, and how you move your pieces determines the victor. It would no longer be a battle fought in the dark. Seeing exactly where the other's boats are at — and the U.S. dominates with the number of assets we can deploy — it's poker where you can see the other guy's cards. That's a better game to play, a safer one, than information we're working with now. How long till somebody else figures this capability out is unknown, but I don't think it happens anytime soon. We're probably talking years if not decades before anyone else has the capability. The Navy needs the photo."

She listened without offering a comment. He slid back his plate and gave her a reassuring smile. "How that might happen is where you have options." He thought about the order to present those options.

"First option is, you do a video, write a paper, package your software algorithms — as you've done for your other discoveries — and hand it off without ever coming to Bangor. Stay in Chicago and continue with your JPL work. Step back from this. Let me deliver it for you. I'll make sure no questions or comments come your way, that is, if you want to take a hard break from all this."

He waited a moment, but she only nodded.

"Second option, you guide someone else into discovering the same thing you did, have someone else produce a photo. *How* we guide that person to figure it out — that might be more fantasy than reality, but we can work through it. This has advantages for you, chief among them being your peace of mind, as someone else will be credited with the discovery."

She nodded again, but didn't comment.

"Third option, return to Bangor with me," he continued, "show the Navy the photo, accept what you found, don't run from it, and let me help you. There's more for you to do. Getting the photo created in the shortest amount of time, working out the minimum solar flare strength and number of satellite data sources necessary to create the photo. And you're able to do that faster than someone else who would have to come up to speed on the details. Operationally it's also safer — limiting this capability and the details of how it's done to just you for now. I prefer this third option, as I think you need to stay involved — up to the point that everything's refined and ready to be passed on — but I'll understand if you prefer one of the other options."

"You really think a photo of every sub deployed around the globe makes U.S. submarines safer?" she asked.

"I do." He reached over for one of the oranges in the fruit bowl and peeled it with his knife, then looked at her. "There's warning time, Gina. When a solar flare happens, the U.S. will still have a couple of days to position its submarine fleet where it wants them to be before the lights turn on. Cross-sonar clears out safe zones for the boomers to move into. Fast-attacks move into precautionary positions. When the photo shows where our submarines are, where any enemy ships are, there will be no weak spots. We'll be ready. And as others move, we can move to counter them. Tactically a photo makes the U.S. fleet safer. And with the capability to know for certain where others are, we could begin to deploy and operate the fleet very differently than we do now."

She thought about it for a long moment. "And if I told you I still wanted to destroy the photo?"

"I'd have to think hard about what to do, Gina. I think I'd have to tell Rear Admiral Hardman what I saw and point the Navy in the right direction for the research. I'd do what I could to minimize how much attention came back to you, but I do think my pledge to the country, to the Navy, might make it necessary to inform Hardman that this concept is possible." He held out one of the orange slices to her. "We're going to disagree occasionally, Gina, on what is best to do with a discovery. That's one of the reasons these kinds of decisions are never simple. There are two perspectives, and both might be valid. I'd like to think you'll come to trust me on these difficult calls.

"But whatever your decision regarding this photo, it doesn't change the bigger picture. I want you to marry me. I'd like you to marry me before we show this photo to the Navy. I'd have more influence as your husband to control what may unfold, to push back for you."

She didn't say anything, her eyes directed toward the window. He let the silence linger, finished the orange, and waited.

Gina finally looked over at him. "It's not going to be possible to steer someone else into making this discovery. It's a nice 'what if,' but there are too many pieces to sort through and put together. I'll have to be the one to show the Navy the photo. But even if I agree to do that, there's no reason to view that decision and getting married as linked."

"Gina, I want to be your husband. And getting married now could be a good buffer for you. You could say 'See my husband about that' when the questions start coming. I can tell the Navy to go through me on any concerns, that I have the authority to speak for you. You'll find life is a lot easier — maybe even happier — if you marry me before this goes any further."

He waited a moment and smiled. "I'm going to make one last pitch, okay? My best one. Then I'll let this topic drop, I promise." He waited for her to glance up. "I know the package may not be ideal. I'm older, I've been married before. But the 'content,' those characteristics you're looking for, are what you want. We share a deep faith in God, a strong work ethic, a sense of ambition, alongside a personal life that is quiet

461

and, for the most part, peaceful. We have a willingness to be open with each other — a verbal intimacy, if you will — a desire to listen and share what we're thinking and feeling.

"I love your smile. I love the way you light up when someone compliments you and offers approval for what you've done. I love the fact you're smart, that you haven't pulled back from what God created you to be. I enjoy your company, Gina. That might sound simplistic, but it sums up a lot of good qualities. You don't nitpick, you don't complain, you try to adapt to situations. You and I would have a good life together."

She bit her lip, and he reached over, gently brushed a thumb across her mouth. "I'm a good risk, Gina. Take a leap and make the decision that your future is with me. Trust me, trust the fact I love you. I'm not asking you to have everything sorted out and not have any doubts. I don't need that from you. What I need, what I think *you* need, is a yes."

He watched her face as he pulled a small box out of his pocket, opened it, and removed a ring. He took her hand, gently placed the ring in her palm, closed her fingers around it. "Please say yes, Gina. I had it made for you. I think you'll like it."

She opened her hand to look at the ring. He'd commissioned it before he left for patrol. It was a beautiful ring, he thought. Gold, with rose diamonds set around an oval-cut white diamond, the ring had been made at his brother's jewelry store with input on the design from Charlotte.

"How long do I have to think about this?" Gina whispered.

"Ask anything you like, but when your questions run out, make the decision," he counseled gently. "I'm thinking the end of the week. Tell me then what you want to do about the photo, and what you want to do about the proposal. More time than that isn't likely to make this any easier, for you or for me."

She finally nodded, staring at the ring nestled in her palm. "Okay."

He leaned over and kissed her. "Please say yes, Gina." He considered it a good sign that she didn't give him back the ring. She slid it onto her right hand ring finger for safekeeping.

"I can see why you enjoy working here," Mark said, following Gina down the steps of the university library. The campus was a peaceful place to visit, even with December classes now heading to finals and students in a hurry filling the walkways. The snow overnight had coated the grounds and it clung to trees, making the scene into a clean vista. He shifted the two books he carried for her and reached for her gloved hand.

"I've spent a good portion of the last 15 years wandering this place, talking to people, listening, learning," she replied.

Gina was relaxed for the first time in the last three days, Mark thought. He thought she had made a decision, but he didn't push to hear what it was. She'd suggested a walk this morning, and he'd been glad to oblige. She'd tell him her decision about the photo and about his marriage proposal when she was ready. He could give her another few days — not much more than that, but for today he could wait.

"Have you ever thought about teaching?" he asked. "Seminars, one-week concentrated classes, something on a topic you love?"

"And if I had a speech freeze?"

"It hasn't been a problem lately."

"It's a mystery when and why it happens, but I still try to avoid situations where it's going to be an embarrassment to me and others if it occurred. Besides, teaching isn't my thing."

"I've got a lot of questions, Gina, that I've never asked and would like to about your speech. Let me give them to you, and you can decide if there are some you might be okay with answering, or not." She shrugged, but nodded, so he asked what would help him to know. "Do you feel it start? Do you have any warning? What are you thinking during those moments when you can't talk? What does it feel like as the words return?"

She smiled briefly at the scope of the questions. "I have a thought I want to express and find I can't. I think my jaw begins to lock up, the muscles around my throat begin to feel stiff, and the words shut off. They get tangled up, and then it feels like everything that goes into talking is simply frozen. It's deeply frustrating."

"Scary?"

"When it lasts a while. I'm actually more alert and aware than normal when it's happening. Speech is a no-thought-needed kind of action, much like breathing. When it stops working, and I'm mentally trying to remember how to speak, to intentionally move to make sounds, it's nearly impossible to get my body to cooperate. I feel a sense of adrenaline and panic, frustration, a lot of embarrassment."

"Is there anything you would prefer I do if it happens?"

"You handle it well, Mark. You relax and

wait. That's what I need to do as well, relax and wait for the problem to clear itself. But I find that very difficult. I feel like I should be able to fix what's wrong, but I don't know how, particularly when I don't know what just went wrong."

"What's the longest it's ever lasted?"

"About 17 minutes. I was 15 at the time. Even Jeff was beginning to cry when I got so emotional about it. The panic was probably why it lasted so long. If there is a trigger, I think it's being put on the spot to say something, having others waiting on me to answer. I need some time to organize what I want to say, then say it clearly, and when I get to feeling rushed —" she waited a moment, then finished — "it's like my words trip over each other and stop. The only word I can find to describe it is *freeze*."

He tightened his hand on hers. "I'm so sorry it happens."

"So am I. Being in college at 14 didn't help matters, though I've never had a doctor directly come out and tell me that was one of the reasons this developed."

She pointed to the building up ahead. "I wouldn't mind seeing if Professor Glass is in town. He teaches chemistry. His subspecialty is high-energy particles, and I find his personal library very useful."

"Sure."

If she decided to stay in Chicago, she'd be returning to this campus as part of her routine. She was known here, and he watched as people came over to say hello, to ask her questions, and fill her in on details about research topics that quickly went into depths he couldn't follow. She had a place here and belonged. She would need that if her answer was to stay in Chicago, and he was glad to see it for himself. He would prefer she be in Bangor with him, with Jeff, but at least Chicago was an option that would be familiar ground to her.

Part of the equation he was quietly sorting out was how to give her the best future possible. What was needed in their lives was what was best for them both. He wouldn't mind teaching military history if the best for him was to retire from the Navy. Part-time professor, spend some hours working with Bryce, find a business they could dig into and build together. Maybe locate a leadership forum where he could serve as a speaker. Being a civilian would be a workable transition for him.

"What are you thinking about?" Gina asked.

"Life."

"You were smiling."

He squeezed her hand. "Life is good. Tell me about Professor Glass. You had him for a class?"

"Four classes, when I was 15 to 17. And he let me spend a summer semester as his grad student when I was 18. I love chemistry, how atoms build objects, and how atoms themselves are built. Chemistry has some of the best mathematics of all the sciences. All of it is interesting — there are no boring parts."

Mark laughed. "I saw some of your molecule models at the house. I could tell you liked building them."

"Colored balls and straws — chemistry construction sets were my version of kids' building blocks. The objects that got built actually meant something, and that's what always fascinated me. I could shape the molecules that made up wood, then imagine my model shrinking down in size to be one small spot on the tabletop. From chemistry I learned a love of microscopes, and then the opposite direction — telescopes. Things get very small and very large. I love that about creation. It's never just about the obvious you see. Everything is made up of more parts."

"Tell me more about your summer as a

grad student," he said, slowing their pace down a bit. "What did you work on?" Mark found it fascinating how Gina changed when she talked about science. Her voice grew more animated, and she relaxed further. She might be young, not comfortable on more general topics, but she had a solid confidence about her work. She needed that confidence on personal matters too, and he wanted to be part of helping her find that.

"You're smiling again," Gina said. "Come on, give. What are you thinking about?"

They had reached the top of the stairs into the building. He reached over and opened the entry door for her, saw the hall was empty on the other side, and took the opportunity to lean over and kiss her. "I love you," he replied. "I was thinking about that, and the fact you have a face I never tire of looking at. I also like listening to you talk about your science."

She didn't know how to respond. His hand on the small of her back directed her inside. "Thank you," she finally whispered.

He smiled. "Say yes. You won't regret it." He saw a directory for the building on the facing wall. "Which floor do we need?"

She glanced around, blinked. "Two."

"That I can get you this flustered should tell you something, Gina." He chuckled, and her blush deepened as she headed up the stairs. He caught up and slipped his hand around hers again. "Sorry."

"I didn't mind. Only stop doing that."

He laughed again but did his best to talk only about the school as they continued the tour.

Gina followed the puppy through the snow as she walked beside Mark, the moonlight reflecting on the piles of white pushing back the darkness.

She had said no to Daniel Field because she thought it was the best decision for him. She had wanted to fall in love with Daniel, and she finally had to accept it wasn't going to happen.

Saying no to Mark Bishop as well . . . she didn't want to take that step. She didn't want to say no. But she wasn't ready to say yes either. She glanced over at him, walking beside her with his hands in his pockets, a calm, relaxed certainty about him. He'd handle whatever she decided, about the photo, about his proposal. He had a steadiness she envied.

She liked him. A lot. She trusted him. But *love*? That was the crux of the problem. She didn't love him. Maybe he was right, and it was a matter of timing. She didn't love him *yet.* Maybe she *could* love him. Or maybe it was going to be months of time with him, and she'd reach the same conclusion she had with Daniel. Wanting to love him, wishing she could, but never reaching that point.

She'd never imagined a man like Mark as her husband. She was still struggling to get her mind around the possibility. The few times he'd kissed her, she'd wanted to lean in against him and just let him fold her in his arms and hold her. She'd once thought that if she let him, he was the kind of guy who would take charge of her life, take the decisions and the weight of it for her. He'd protect her. The idea had great appeal tonight. And yet she couldn't embrace it. He was a good man. He was convinced they could have a good marriage. But he was so far ahead of where she was in her thoughts and emotions.

She could avoid the conversation for another day, but it would only delay and not change what she needed to say. She was turning down good guys and it was breaking her heart. "I've made some decisions, Mark."

He reached over and took her hand. "I know."

She heard the quiet steadiness in his words, but felt his tension in the hand that gripped hers. She was oddly comforted by that fact. "You're moving too fast for me," she whispered. "I hear the words *I love you,* and I know you mean them. It breaks my heart that I can't say the same in reply. I don't love you, at least not yet, Mark. You're too far ahead of me. I can't accept your marriage proposal right now."

He stopped walking, and she saw him close his eyes. Then his hand holding hers tightened. "You're not saying an absolute no."

"I want us to see each other until you have to go back on patrol in May. I need more time. I'll give you my answer before you deploy."

He turned and folded her into a hug, let his chin rest against her hair. He didn't say anything for a long time. "You've got a boyfriend and a steady date from now until May," he finally replied. "Just promise me you'll give me as much of your time as you can over these next months. Don't run scared, and don't over-think it. Don't walk away from something good because it seems like too much of a risk."

She nodded because the words weren't there to reply. She wanted to cry, because she was breaking this man's heart. He knew she was stalling and tipping toward telling him no.

He nudged up her chin and gently kissed her. "I promise I'll do my best to play fair. You can trust me, Gina, with your heart *and* your future. Give us a chance. A good chance."

"Can I keep wearing your ring?"

"I'd like it a great deal if you would." He eased back a step, visibly forced himself to relax. "Come on, you're cold, and the puppy is going to bury himself in a pile of snow." He put his arm around her and turned them back toward the house, holding her close against the cold.

They arrived at the house, stepped out of boots and pulled off coats, while the puppy shook himself, then raced into the living room. Mark led her into the kitchen. "I don't know about you, but snow burrows the cold right into my bones." He pulled out a stool for her, got mugs down, poured some of the remaining coffee for himself, made hot chocolate for her. The temperature had been cold enough to numb fingers, and she appreciated the warmth of holding the mug. She caught his gaze when he smiled at her, this man who wanted to be her husband. She felt the warmth of that smile and offered one of her own, still tentative but genuine.

"Will you agree to show the photo to the Navy?" he asked quietly.

"Yes." She drank the hot chocolate, grateful to have it to occupy her attention. "And given that — tell me the plan. What happens next?"

If she felt nervous, he seemed calm, as if he'd already absorbed her decision about marriage and adjusted his plans. "We'll fly to Bangor, show Rear Admiral Hardman the photo. He'll have some questions."

"An understatement," she offered under her breath.

Mark heard her and smiled. "What I'll need is for you to write a paper, maybe create a video, similar to the last two presentations. Hardman will take the photo and paper to the SecNav. Then the goal will be to refine the process to generate the photo in the shortest amount of time possible. You'll need access to the various satellite data feeds, with computing power at your disposal, and, at the right time, we'll identify the people skilled enough to take this over — that's going to be my priority." He set aside his coffee. "You should come back to Bangor, Gina," he suggested. "Jeff is at sea. You can stay at his place, and your pets can stay with me."

"I was thinking I could stay in Chicago," she said, "write the paper here, create the video to explain what this is, then transition to Bangor to work on the algorithms and the processing speed."

He thought about it and nodded. "That works too. You and I could go out to Bangor for a two-day trip, show the Navy the photo, then come back here for a few weeks — spend Christmas and New Year's in Chicago. I'm sure my sister would be willing to take care of the pets while we're gone. We could drive back to Bangor in early January, take the animals with us then. I'm going to predict that in about six months you'll have your work finished and handed off to a skilled group of people able to create the photo. Then you'll only be needed if something unusual occurs."

She thought a moment, then nodded. "When my job winds down, yours will just be getting started — what to do with the information contained in a photo when it prints."

"The Tactical Command Center is going to take the brunt of that impact, and I think it's likely Hardman assigns me to that working group while I'm onshore," Mark agreed. "I won't minimize how much this is going to change the Navy. Combined with the prior two discoveries, the photo will mean a radical rethinking of how submarines deploy. My workload will be both intense and heavy for at least the next year, and in the middle of that I'll be heading back to sea on patrol in May for 90 days. That's going to make its own set of pressures for us."

She blinked, realizing he still was talking about the future on the assumption she would say yes. She couldn't help her smile, oddly grateful he was still willing to be sure of her decision. She needed one of them to be that confident. She wanted to be loved, she wanted what he offered. She just hadn't reached the point she could say "I love you" to him, and accept what he so willingly offered. One of them needed to hold on to the faith that this would have a happy ending.

Mark took the empty mug out of her hands and got up to pour her the last of the coffee. "You're still cold, so drink that, please." He slid the sugar bowl over, then leaned back against the counter.

She stirred sugar into her mug, glanced up at Mark. For the first time in months, at least for the moment there were no more immediate decisions to make.

"We'll be okay, you and I," he said.

"Promise me that?"

He nodded. "I love you, Gina. I got to the final destination before you, that's all. I'll wait. You're going to arrive there too — I have faith in that fact."

He took the last swallow of his coffee. "I didn't say this earlier, because it wasn't appropriate to bring further pressures into your decision, but I want to mention something I see."

She straightened on the stool, giving him her full attention. "Okay . . ."

"You've been turning on the lights in the ocean this entire year. This photo is simply the latest in a series of discoveries. A cross-sonar ping can actively search out a sub. Listening for the silence created by a sub's presence can locate a sub at great distances. Now, for a brief few days after a solar flare, the oceans yield an extraordinary photo showing us the locations and types of all the submarines out there. I don't think your discoveries this year have been random accidents.

"I don't think it is chance that you had a deep familiarity with the oceans, were handed such a wide array of satellite data after a solar flare, were curious about the sparkles, and had the intelligence and technical skills to figure this out. I think God put you at this place and time for a reason. There may be a purpose for why these discoveries have come now."

She was startled at the idea he was suggesting. His tone was serious; this wasn't a casual thought, but something he'd been pondering for a while.

"If there ever was a reason God might change what we know about sonar and visibility at sea," Mark continued, "it would be when nations are heading toward a collision. China and Japan are edging toward war. North and South Korea are an incident away from conflict. Russia and Iran once again are the center of new global tensions. Maybe with the right knowledge, the U.S. can influence what comes to pass. Maybe God just turned on the lights so we can see what's coming. And He used you to do it."

"You believe that?" she whispered.

Mark nodded. "There's a statement in Hebrews that talks about Jesus, now at the right hand of God, sustaining everything by the power of His command. He is in charge. He's building His kingdom with the church. Governments are in His hands, to rise or fall as God decrees. I don't think it's happenstance you've spent this year shining a spotlight deep into the ocean. I don't think God wastes our time or our talents when we follow Him. I believe He knows these discoveries are going to be necessary in the days ahead. And He equipped you to find them."

"Do you have any idea the pressure that makes me feel if you're right?"

"I didn't mention it to cause that, Gina, and there's no need for it to feel like pressure. Do what you were made to do — continue to discover things, be curious. You don't have to figure out how everything fits into the big picture. That's God's territory. He'll put together the pieces where He wants them to be. But I'm intrigued that what's unfolding right now might be something we'll look back on decades from now and see as the moment when God rearranged scientific capabilities for His own purposes."

"It's an interesting idea," she finally replied.

"It's fine to be skeptical of the idea," Mark said. "Just consider a year from now if I wasn't on to something with the thought."

22

Commander Mark Bishop followed the duty officer into Rear Admiral Hardman's office. "Thank you for fitting me in on such short notice, sir."

"No problem, Bishop," Hardman said, in the midst of filling a briefcase open on his desk. "You don't say 'urgent' unless it's warranted." The admiral glanced at the map tube Mark carried but didn't comment. Instead he said, "I hear congratulations are in order."

"Thank you, sir, but premature. I'm dating Gina Gray and hoping for a yes to a marriage proposal."

"You'd be a fortunate man."

"Agreed, sir."

"And she'd be a fortunate woman." Hardman didn't wait for a response. He finished loading his briefcase, locked it, and handed it off to his duty officer. "Set that by my suitcase for the flight. I'll be there shortly."

"Yes, sir."

The admiral waited until the duty officer had closed the door. "You've interrupted the beginning of a month of R and R," he mentioned. "Should I be sitting down for this?"

Bishop smiled at the half-humorous words. "We've got an issue, sir, the makings of a new discovery . . . and some inherent problems it presents." He slid the photo from the tube, unrolled it across the desk. He'd penned notations alongside the objects' locations and depths, adding as well the sub names Gina had given him.

Hardman's eyes swept across the photo, then went back again to study the various objects for a few moments before looking up at Bishop. "Gina?" he asked. At Bishop's nod, he said, "Come with me."

Mark rolled up the photo and slid it back into the tube. The admiral led the way out of the office, bypassed the elevator, and took the stairs down three levels to the subbasement. Hardman used his palm print and punched in the security code, nodded to the armed security officers on duty, and then proceeded into the Tactical Command Center.

The room's lights were dimmed to half strength. Theater seats stretched along the east wall for those watching events unfold. Large screens shared data feeds and tracking maps of the worlds' oceans, coordinating with Kings Bay and the Pentagon on the facing walls. The three-location Tactical Command integrated all known information about subs at sea — the U.S. fleet along with those of allies and enemies — and coordinated plans with Strategic Command and the Battle Surface Groups. This was the place where everything related to operational matters for the American submarine fleet came together, and all tasking orders for the fleet anywhere in the world originated here. This also was where sea rescue headquartered should a sub get in trouble.

Captain John Strong, in command of the TCC, came to meet them. "Sir." He had commanded the USS *Ohio* for three years, moved on to command a sub squadron, and now ran Tactical Command at Bangor. When it came to men with operational experience, Bishop felt like he was standing with two of the nation's best officers.

"You know Commander Mark Bishop," Hardman said. "I need to see everything we knew about the world's oceans on November 2nd, 20:17 hours."

Strong was a professional with too many years behind him to do more than lift an eyebrow. "Yes, sir." He spun around. "Lieutenant Stacks. Please give me November 2nd, 20:17, on the boards."

The three men watched the giant screens on the wall scroll back through the stored files and stop at the requested date and time. There were dozens of submarines mapped to areas with varying degrees of certainty. Four blue grids marked boomer patrol boxes for those on hard-alert that evening. A red square with a widening red-dashed circle marked a Russian Akula that with time could have moved from its last contact into a range of ocean waters. Green trails showed the tracks of two British subs being picked up on a seafloor hydrophone line south of Iceland. Several submarines were black-flagged — known to be at sea, away from their home port, but with no data on their present locations.

Rear Admiral Hardman looked over. "Let's see it again, Bishop."

Bishop laid out the photo on a nearby table, and the three men huddled around it, made silent comparisons. Gina was not only spot-on with the locations, every submarine unresolved on the board was represented on her photo, signifying both location and depth.

"I'd like to have more of these, sir," Strong

483

said while studying the image. "It would be a whole lot easier to do my job. That's as beautiful an image as I have ever seen, even while it makes my heart land up in my throat."

"Strong, hand off to your lieutenant. I need you for the next hour."

"Yes, sir."

As Strong moved away to do so, Hardman picked up a phone and told his duty officer to reschedule his flight. He then led the way to the adjoining conference room, turned on lights, and pulled out the first chair. "Bishop, your lady is having quite a year."

"She moved to studying the sun to get away from working on sonar, only to tumble into this. It's deep-ocean reflections off hulls after a powerful solar flare."

Hardman half laughed. "You have to love the woman." He tipped back in the chair and sighed. "All right, talk to me."

Captain Strong joined them, and Bishop laid out the details in as orderly a fashion as he could. Gina had begged off being here for this conversation, and Mark felt the responsibility to handle this for her and do it well.

"What does she need?"

"She needs to be copied in on a lot of satellite data — in real time, if possible —

during the weeks after a solar flare occurs. Computing power. A place to work. She thinks processing time can fall to an hour for a preliminary photo. It's not going to be in real time, but it's going to be pretty close and useful."

Hardman and Strong looked at each other, smiled at the understatement.

"I suggest we give her an office here," Strong said. "We're going to want to see the photo as it develops, and, ideally, the data never leaves the TCC. We're the sink for security purposes."

"Makes sense," Hardman agreed. "Find her space just off the floor, even if you have to credential her out of the Pentagon to make it happen."

"Yes, sir," Strong replied.

"For the satellite data, Bishop, see what existing hubs at NOAA and NASA can give us, pick up a mirror of the data with them through a research department at DARPA. What they don't have, let's figure out how to get without having the Navy's fingerprints on the final destination. You've got the list to work from?"

"Yes, sir," Bishop said, making notes for himself. "She'd like to see 32 satellites in total, but she doesn't know about the military ones sniffing for nuclear- and chemical-weapons tests. She might find those instruments helpful as well since some of the data is recording over the oceans."

"Approved. For computing power, it makes sense to hit the clusters if she can disperse the processing — so tap NSA, DARPA, DoD, and NASA. Once there are a few photos developed and there's a sense of the capacity needed, we'll dedicate or shift computing resources as necessary."

Bishop said, "I'm proposing she put together the paper and video at her home in Chicago, sir, while we set up for her here. She's been trying to move away from Navy work, and I need to give her the assurance she will have some distance from it eventually. I'm thinking six months into next year, once processing time has been optimized, she's able to hand off this capability to others."

"Agreed in principle. We want her next game-changing idea. We don't need her spending time managing the concepts she's already discovered. Talk to the Undersea Warfare Group and figure out what names make sense to consider for the technical talent. Strong needs to sign off on them, as they'll be working here and reporting to him once the hand-off is made."

"Will do, sir."

"How soon on the paper?"

"The week before Christmas, hopefully. It depends on the next solar flare. The idea is to develop a second photo as proof this is repeatable, even if it takes several days to gather the data she needs and process it."

"Agreed." Hardman lightly tapped his fingers on the table. "The photo gives us actionable intelligence on how everyone is configuring their forces." He looked at Strong. "Give me a print of our display for this same date and time. I'm taking both ours and Gina's for a sit-down with the Sec-Nav tonight. I have a feeling tomorrow morning I'll be showing them to the president."

Strong rose from his chair. "I'll get it printed for you now, sir."

Hardman turned back to Bishop. "Is Gina up for a meeting with the SecNav?"

"She's going to push back hard on the idea if I ask it of her. I'd prefer not to ask."

Hardman nodded. "The *Nevada* goes to sea in May?"

"Yes. I'd like to still be in command, sir," Bishop added.

"You will be, Mark. I'm merely wondering who we slot to be her buffer when you're gone. The *Seawolf* is going to be busy this year with both the *Jimmy Carter* and the

Connecticut in dry dock. I doubt Jeff Gray will be ashore much beyond brief supply stops."

"Daniel Field, sonarman with the *Nebraska.* She trusts him."

Hardman made a note. "When the *Nebraska* is back in port, I'll want a conversation with him. Tell me this, Bishop. Is there any way we can get her on the government payroll for more than an idea or two? If she gives us motion video of the oceans next" — Hardman shook his head even as he smiled — "she's changing this job. Mine and a whole lot of others, and more than any other individual I know. You do realize, don't you, that she's got a gold override flag on her file? Meaning she can work on any research project, covering any topic, associated with any government funding grant, and it's given automatic approval. Her hiring would even trigger additional research funds for the project. She's got *carte blanche* — she just doesn't use it."

"She likes to drift, sir, rather than do any particular thing for very long. She's worked on sonar and topology because it makes Jeff safer, on the sun because it's an interesting data set. Beyond that it seems to be whatever comes along that's interesting. She doesn't like to be bored. She's got some model rockets on a table at her Chicago home with exhaust forms I've never seen before. One day I'd be interested to see what she's thinking about them."

"For security's sake, I'd like to see her on this base, with an office here, exploring any subject she wants. We can drop a secure connection to any university in the world if that's what it takes to keep her in one place."

"I'm beginning to think long term about something similar, sir. It's useful to know there are those options."

Hardman glanced at his watch. "I'm going to be in the air within the hour. Will you be around to take a call tonight if the Sec-Nav wants a word?"

"Yes, sir."

Hardman smiled. "Tell her thanks, Bishop. The Navy appreciates this."

"She wanted to burn the photo," Bishop mentioned, knowing that keeping Hardman in the loop on the details was one of the best assets he could give Gina.

Hardman blew out a long breath. "Scary thought, but I would have been tempted to think the same in her place." Hardman got to his feet. "Keep me in the loop, Bishop. Anything you need with getting her set up and comfortable here, I'll clear the way for you."

"I appreciate that, sir."

They had been back in Chicago for 10 days. Mark was staying at a hotel nearby and would often walk over to Gina's home in the morning, spend most of the day with her. He had missed this part of being in a relationship: the lazy walks together holding hands, talking about nothing more important than what they should have for dinner or which movie to watch that evening. She had finished writing the paper, laying out the science behind the photo, and was planning to start work on the video later that afternoon. By unspoken agreement, they were both avoiding any topic related to marriage. They were simply spending time together. He loved walking with her, letting the conversation wander across topics.

Her phone chimed, and Mark paused while she slipped off her glove and pulled the phone from her pocket to look at the text message.

"Promising?" he asked.

"JPL," she confirmed. "A solar flare happened six minutes ago." She scrolled through the numbers. "Moderate strength, but it's edging toward center quadrant, so this will be a glancing hit to the earth. It should be able to generate a photo, but the resolution of sub to class type will be soft."

"A good step toward finding out where the limits are," Mark said.

"First data is 60 hours away."

He looked at his watch, calculating. "We can do a lot in the intervening hours. What catches your fancy? A museum, art gallery, shopping mall, bookstore?"

"Do you have to ask?"

"I don't mind carrying your books, precious," he replied with a smile.

"I like that word," she whispered, glancing over at him. "You've used it a few times. Is that your favorite choice of endearment?"

"I never used it with Melinda," he assured her, understanding what lay behind the question. "I simply look at you and that's the word that comes to mind." He took her hand. "Have one for me yet?"

She wordlessly shook her head.

"You can practice if you like, try out various ones."

She looked at him with a shy smile. "Maybe."

Over Gina's shoulder, Mark watched the photo develop. He was looking at the future of submarine operations — being able to see where everyone was positioned. The data was six days old. He'd told Gina to focus not on the speed of developing this photo but simply the steps necessary to generate it, so he could watch the whole process. That had been fine in theory, observing what she did, but after his first contact with the multitasking involved, he'd settled for a general awareness of the process. His arm across her shoulders, he looked at the screen and hugged her. "Nice job, precious."

"Thanks. Resolution will improve as it processes. But that's the picture of the world for December 23rd, 14:10 hours." The subs were becoming distinct forms. "When it finishes processing, I'll be able to classify most of them by type and give exact locations and depths. The flare triggered more data than I expected."

He nuzzled her hair. "You smell good."

"Quit getting distracted." But she smiled and nudged his chin with her head. "You'll give this photo to the Navy as well?"

"I will."

"This means we head to Bangor."

"After New Year's Day. I want a bit more time without gold crew able to find me. Can I watch the video this afternoon?" He'd been watching sections of it as she created the computer-generated illustrations, but she hadn't shown him the opening yet.

She'd done at least five recordings that he was aware of, probably snuck in a sixth after he left her last night. She was nervous, and he'd like to help get her past that.

"I'll show it to you after dinner. I'm going to tweak a few things."

"After dinner," he agreed.

She turned in her chair to face him. "When we get to Bangor, when I turn my focus on getting the speed of processing the photo refined, I'm going to get lost in the work, Mark, and you'll need to let me. I promised you my time, and I meant that. But I can feel the wall of work to be done, and I don't want to disappoint you over the next few months with how completely absorbed I am in this job."

He understood her concern, but he wasn't worried. "I've watched you the last couple of weeks, watched your thoughts disappear into a problem you were trying to solve. I've got no illusions the job ahead of you is going to be easy or quick. To get that photo to process within an hour, you're going to have to do some of the most brilliant work of your career. We'll figure out the balance, Gina. That's a promise. There will be time for us *and* for the work." He tipped her face up to his and smiled. "You're talking to a boomer captain. I understand the pressures of work. I also know how critical this project is."

"Thank you, Mark."

"For what?"

"Seeing me."

He didn't entirely understand what was driving her remark, but he understood the emotion in her voice. "I don't feel like you're choosing between work and me when you spend time solving a problem, Gina. It's not a competition between work and a relationship. You're doing what needs done. I approve, if you need to hear that put in words."

"When Kevin . . ." She bit her lip and didn't finish. He waited, but she didn't say anything further.

"Gina, I think you give work your best effort when you're dealing with a problem. When you're with someone, you also try to give that person your best. Maybe you've not been as comfortable with people and relationships as you are with science, but it's not for lack of getting your priorities right. I'm a smart guy — if I need an hour of your time on a busy day, I will tell you so. I won't leave you guessing. We can fit a good relationship into the tempo of things. I'll prove that to you over the next few months. Just watch and see."

She finally nodded. He read in her face the doubt she felt, and wondered at the history she still didn't talk about. At least this concern he was sure he could fix, showing her over the next few months *how* it was all going to work out. Their responsibilities were big in both their lives, but a relationship could still thrive in the midst of that.

By mid-February, Mark Bishop knew the routine of the Tactical Command Center as well as he did the functioning of his own gold crew on the *Nevada.* He could, at a glance, recognize when men were back in the room, back on duty, and when it was not their shift. This was one of those nights. The TCC was busy and on alert, though conversations remained low-key and the lighting subdued.

China was undertaking a major fleet exercise, and a significant number of its 62 subs were at sea. Japan had countered by deploying a number of its surface ships and most of its 20-strong submarine fleet to observe.

A solar flare of moderate intensity had erupted 70 hours ago, giving them a well-timed look at the world. Gina had the processing time down to under four hours now. For a test of a photo, this was as authentic as it would get in peacetime conditions.

Mark watched the photo develop. The stretch of waters from Taiwan to North Korea had always been a volatile part of the world, and China's military exercise only made it more so. There was a great deal of activity in the East China Sea and the Sea of Japan. It was South Korea and its 14 subs that were the wild card in the deck. They had always made port calls in Japan, but four were now all the way south watching China's military exercise. It was a recipe for trouble and risked an incident that could spiral into something much bigger.

Farther out in the Pacific, the number of subs dwindled to a handful. Given the overlay they could map from other information, two of those developing smudges in the photo concerned him.

Mark pointed at the screen, with Strong looking on. "These are going to resolve into the *Alabama* and the *Maine.*" He marked the two U.S. subs. "This we know is the Brits' *Triumph.* But these two over here, at least one is likely to be the Chinese Kilo that put to sea last week, the one we lost track of. I'd recommend we get the boomers out of the way."

"Agreed." Strong wrote down the coordinates and passed the note to the lieutenant handling communications. "Send informational EAMs to the *Alabama* and the *Maine,* 'Possible Kilo within a hundred miles of the following locations.' "

The officer nodded and turned to code the messages.

Strong, studying the photo, said, "I'm not sure how this kind of time-delayed photo will play out during a war setting, but for simply keeping two opposing forces apart, it's ideal."

"We can guarantee our boomers clear, safe seas," Bishop agreed, deeply appreciating the security this photo gave them. "Our tabletop gaming of scenarios keeps pointing to the confirmation factor as the most valuable part of these photos. The TCC is plotting locations and movements of submarines worldwide, and now there's a way to check the work and know if the assumptions on the board about sub type and place are accurate. Those we have lost track of are suddenly back on the board — the photo fills in the question marks. That certainty fades away as time elapses between solar flares, but it all shoots back to high confidence when another picture arrives. Coming every 10 to 14 days isn't as ideal as every few days, but it's a workable number."

Strong nodded. "The smaller-footprint submarine operations — sonar, the addition of a cross-sonar ping, listening for silence — give our boats a good analysis of what's around them, and they can see the near contacts of more immediate concern. It's on the big picture where this solar flare photo matters."

"I think so, sir. If a nation is preparing to go to war, if a threat is more than rhetoric, we'll see indications of it in the deployments. Knowing one boat location is useful, but knowing every boat location — that's deep-level intel."

"A year from now we'll have collected the pattern of deployments for every nation, be able to map routes they like to use, know patrol days at sea — basically read their playbook. It's going to be a fun year, Bishop."

Mark saw Gina, looking relaxed, coming their way with a bag of pretzels in her hand. She'd be around the TCC monitoring the photo processing, but her work was basically done once the photo began to appear.

"A nice job, Gina," Captain Strong said.

"Thanks, Captain."

She held out the pretzel bag to Mark and then Strong, offering to share.

"Want to slip away for some dinner?"

Mark asked her.

"In another few hours maybe," she replied, studying the developing photo. "I'm thinking the development time might be directly tied to the solar flare strength. The hotter the flare, the more reflections, the faster the photo processes. It seems like common sense, but I need to run the math to be sure. Should take me about an hour. It's either the solar flare strength or it's the orientation to earth. Maybe a coil that pops right toward us provides more reflections than a hot flare that's at an angle to earth. It would be nice to predict how long this processing would need to run before we can get enough resolution to put a class-type name to a sub."

"Go tug at the idea. I'll be around."

She nodded and disappeared toward her office on the north side of the TCC.

"She's getting more comfortable here," Strong noted.

"She is," Bishop said, watching her enter the office and slide shut its glass door.

"Officially she's here working on the integration of the new seabed topology maps. That introduction works most of the time, but occasionally someone will narrow his eyes, and you can tell he's realized that her classified badge is several levels higher than topology maps would warrant. Sometimes they'll ask 'Cross-sonar?' — trying to confirm a hunch — but only a couple have asked her directly about the latest cross-sonar upgrades. The number in the know on this photo remains less than 20. It's confined to the TCC's chain of command. Gina still has some privacy."

"That's good to know." Bishop felt his phone vibrate and glanced at the message. "*Nevada* gold final fit reps are in," he said.

"Good crew?"

"Looking to be my strongest yet," Bishop replied, pleased. *Nevada* blue would be touching the pier in six weeks. Three days later, *Nevada* gold would have "their boat" back. He understood the crews' proprietary feelings about it, and he was ready to take over command. He glanced toward Gina's office, could see her already focused on the computer screen. "I'll be back in a couple of hours, sir."

"I'll call if something changes," Strong told him.

"Appreciate that."

Bishop gave her two and a half hours, then returned to Gina's office, saw she was still writing in a composition book. A bag of M&Ms lay open on the desk. He took a handful and settled into the extra chair. When he'd been setting up the space for her, he'd made sure there was an extra chair, bought her a couple of colorful paperweights, added a dozen fiction paperbacks to the shelves for when she needed to fill time while data crunched, and removed the clock so she wouldn't keep thinking about how she was working late.

He couldn't fix the fact she worked just off the TCC in a basement without windows, but he'd done what he could to brighten her office with photos and posters, fresh flowers on the desk, music of her choice. He'd tucked a small refrigerator into the corner and kept it filled with apples, oranges, cold drinks, and water bottles. Three large flat-screen monitors dominated the desk space.

The screen showed the emerging photo, and every smudge was now a tightly defined form. Getting the final level of resolution to tell a British sub from a Russian one would be another hour, he thought.

She finally stopped writing and looked over at him. He asked, "So what's the verdict on a solar flare?"

She swiveled her chair toward his, stretched her arms to relieve the tension in her shoulders. "A loop shooting toward earth is much more important than the amount of energy being released. A small pop at us is better than a wallop that glances by."

He nodded. "Sounds like common sense to me."

"Still nice to know now it's true. I'm going to lower the threshold for assuming a solar flare has useful data. We might actually be able to get a smudged version of a photo every seven days or so — not enough reflections to be able to identify one sub from another, but enough to say one is there."

"That would still be very valuable and useable data."

She nodded and found her shoes under the desk. "Are you ready for dinner? I'll need to come back."

"I'll bring you back," Mark said. "I'm thinking Chinese. I'd like some won tons. How about you?"

"Works for me."

He was still trying to decide what would be best for Valentine's Day. She hadn't dropped any hints, and he wondered if she was even aware it was two days away. He was leaning toward a few dozen roses and a concert he had heard was good, but he might be misjudging that part. He wished

Daniel was onshore so he could get a recommendation on the music. Valentine's Day was up there on the same level as her birthday — days a guy needed to handle with care, and some elegance. He glanced at the ring on her right hand. He wasn't going to propose again on Valentine's Day, it was too soon, but he'd like that ring on her other hand.

Gina split open her fortune cookie as they walked out of the restaurant. Evenings were still cool enough to need a warm jacket when they walked at night, and she pushed the plastic wrapper into one of the jacket's pockets. "Daniel gets back with the *Nebraska* next month."

"I'm aware," Mark replied, interested that she had brought it up.

"Tell me you're going to be okay if we invite him over for steaks on the grill."

"He'll decline."

"We should still ask."

Mark nodded. "I've got nothing but goodwill toward Daniel. We'll invite him to dinner, and when he thinks up an excuse, just mention you're going to invite him again. A long patrol, coming back to find you're dating me — it's going to sting even as he adjusts to the reality. Give him a month or two, Gina. He'll handle the news as graciously as he did your decision. Just for the record, I'm fine with him being around, whether I'm there or you're on your own. I trust the man. I trust you."

"That helps, Mark. He's a friend." She was quiet for a minute. "I want to show him the photo."

"I already told Hardman we should bring Daniel in on what's going on with the photo. If he's willing to take on the role, I'd like him to be your buffer when Jeff and I are at sea."

"That would be very helpful. Do you want me to mention it?"

"I'll talk to him," Mark said. "I'd suggest leaving it be for a while, let Daniel choose the time and place to re-engage. He will when he's ready."

"I'm hoping that's the case. It was hard, this last year, trying to be fair to both of you."

"I know." He felt her look his way.

"I did make the right choice — just in case you're wondering — to say no to him," she said. "But it still hurts like crazy that I had to disappoint him."

He reached over and lifted her hand, kissed the back of it. "Daniel will be fine. Just give him some time before you expect too much, Gina."

Gina sat in Mark's living room, idly thumbing through a magazine while the kittens tumbled over her feet. Dating Mark was so different from what she had expected. Given how certain he was that things were going to work out, how sure he was that she would eventually return his love, she had assumed he would continue to press his case. He hadn't. His proposal was never far from her mind, but he didn't mention it. They went out to dinners and to movies, took long walks, did the more ordinary things together — grocery shopping and errands and projects around his house. She spent her off-hours with him. He'd had her building bookshelves with him the prior weekend, the puppy and kittens scampering across the boards he'd cut to fit the space. He was showing her his life, inviting her into it, and she appreciated that more than she could put into words.

Most mornings he would pick her up at Jeff's and drive her to work at Bangor, meet up with her for lunch or an early dinner. She had come to count on his hugs, the way he would smile when he first saw her. He said "I love you" often, and the nonverbal ways he showed her that truth meant as much as the words themselves. He reached for her hand whenever he could. And after an evening together, he would take her to Jeff's, kiss her good-night on the front steps, not follow her inside. Mark was playing fair.

For Valentine's Day he had brought her two dozen roses of all colors and arranged a limo so they could travel north into Canada and see the sights around Vancouver. They had talked for hours during the drive up and back, about nothing in particular, but it had been the best date she could remember.

Trying to return the favor, she'd taken the afternoon off and fixed Mark dinner at his house — pork chops with dressing and an apple pie — and since he'd demolished two chops, she concluded the meal had been a hit. Mark had pushed her out of the kitchen; he would do the cleanup since she'd fixed the excellent dinner.

She set aside the magazine and picked up the oversized sack she'd brought in. She knew Mark's house well enough now that when she needed a pair of scissors to remove the tag from a new dog pillow for Pongo, she pulled open the first drawer of the side table in the living room.

She pulled out the pillow and placed it in the nook by the front door. Pongo had pulled one of Mark's socks from the hamper upstairs and triumphantly brought it down to play with. Gina rescued the sock and took it into the laundry room. The dog followed, and she picked up Pongo and hugged him.

She would have tossed in a load of laundry for Mark, but it felt like that would cross too far over the line of being a wife. She put Pongo down and did open the dryer, tugging out and folding the towels they'd used after giving the puppy a bath.

She didn't feel comfortable keeping the animals at Jeff's place without asking her brother first. She'd offered to get an apartment where she could have the animals, only to have Mark point out that regardless of whether she said yes or no to his proposal, he was going to be gone for 90 days beginning in May, and he'd rather have the pets around the house and someone coming by to feed them than have the house sitting empty during his deployment. While she was at Bangor, he would keep her pets.

If they did one day marry, the man would be easy to take care of, she thought, for he was neat in ways she hadn't expected. His home was lived in but orderly, and it always felt calm being here. The pressures of his job, of hers, didn't get to invade this space. She liked being here.

She could hear Mark in the kitchen, loading the dishwasher. He'd take her home soon, back to Jeff's, kiss her good-night at the door, and whisper "I love you." She knew him. And what he had hoped for, prayed for, was happening. She could feel herself falling in love with him. She didn't dare examine the emotion too much, frightened it would disintegrate if she analyzed it further. But she was aware it was there. And it felt really good, if rather tentative. She had felt it growing over the last few weeks.

She joined Mark in the kitchen as he picked up the metal pan at the end of the counter. He'd made Rice Krispie bars earlier in the week. "Last one. Want to split it with me?"

"Sure."

She opened a drawer and pulled out a knife. He shook his head, held it out for her to take two bites, and then ate the rest. "Love these things," he said as he licked the sticky marshmallow off his fingers. "Want to go by Gary's tonight for a game of pool with him and his wife before I take you back to Jeff's?"

"I'd like that."

He looked over at her a second time, catching her tone. "What?"

"I really enjoy dating you, Mark."

He leaned over and kissed her. "Just figuring that out?" he teased.

She laughed. "Want me to make a batch of peanut-butter cookies tomorrow? We need more desserts."

"Sounds good to me." He glanced around. "The kitchen is good enough. Let's go play some pool." He reached for his keys on the counter, and they walked out to the car. "You didn't say much about your day over dinner," he noted as he opened the car door for her.

She shrugged. "Not much to say. I worked on speeding up the shape-detection algorithm this morning, then came over and puttered around to fix dinner."

He settled in the driver's seat and backed out of the drive. "Having problems with the work?"

"I'll figure it out eventually." She slipped her hand in his so she could divert the conversation.

Jeff's place seemed very quiet. Gina missed her brother. She wished he was around to talk with on a night like this. She curled up on his couch and tucked a throw around her bare feet, nursing a mug of hot chocolate. She thought about picking up a book. She wasn't tired, even though it was late. She was still remembering the feelings that came with Mark's hug good-night.

Love had crept in while she wasn't looking. She did love him. The realization had come into her life so gently she couldn't pinpoint when she first knew. *"He's the one, isn't he, Jesus?"* she whispered. There was such a deep peace with the recognition of that fact that it overwhelmed everything else she felt. She was in love with Mark Bishop.

She turned the ring on her right hand. The man was going to be so ecstatic when she told him yes. She felt treasured, cared for, just being with him. Add the words *I love you* to what she could say to him, and the coming months were going to be a joy for both of them. She smiled to herself, thinking about the next few days, how they might unfold. A personal dream from back when she was a teenager was now becoming a reality.

She sipped the chocolate. She would need to tell Daniel soon, before he found out from someone else. She owed him that much.

Gina knocked and then walked into Mark's home the next morning, carrying his Saturday paper. "I picked up bagels as promised," she called.

"Blueberry?" he called back from the

kitchen.

"I remembered." She found Mark at the kitchen sink, rinsing out the kittens' bowls, then pouring fresh milk. It was so much like him, taking care of the details without being asked. She set the sack she carried on the kitchen table and went over to wrap her arms around his waist from behind. She rested her cheek against his back and whispered, "I love you."

She felt his body go absolutely still. She'd had no plans to tell him this way, this soon — the words just came out, her heart so full they had to be said. His hands settled across hers, and he slowly, carefully, turned around, not letting her step back from the embrace. She was startled to see there were tears in his eyes. "You mean that?" he asked, his voice husky.

"I love you, Mark Bishop, and I would really like to marry you."

The joy that filled his face took her breath away. His hug enveloped her. "Thank you," he whispered, choking up. "When?"

"Soon is good," she whispered, thinking about how fast May was going to be here. He would be gone on patrol for three months.

Mark rested his forehead against hers, and she felt him relax against her. The last weeks

511

hadn't been easy on him, she knew. He sighed, tipped up her chin and kissed her. "I love you, precious." He lifted her hand, slid the ring from her right hand, and gently put it where it belonged on her left. "It looks good there."

"I love the ring."

He kissed the back of her hand.

She smiled at the gesture. "Thank you for asking me, Mark. It was a beautiful proposal, and I'm grateful for it, and the ring. I really am honored that you asked."

He rested his arms across her shoulders. "The honor is mine. Don't get embarrassed and formal on me now." She caught his gaze, and he smiled at her, this man who would soon be her husband. "I leave for patrol in May. If we get married soon . . ." He stopped and studied her. "What are you thinking?"

She knew where her heart was. "I'm not sure what you'll think of this idea, but I was wondering if maybe . . . would you be okay with two weddings? A private ceremony as soon as possible, and a larger church wedding after your patrol — when Jeff's back onshore and all your family can attend — and maybe have it in Chicago?" She'd thought it all through the night before, and she didn't want to wait. A quiet marriage ceremony to begin their life together held a lot of appeal for her. She saw the surprise on his face.

He gently ran a hand along her arm as he thought about it. "You're worried about your words locking up on you."

She reluctantly nodded. "If I've said the vows in a private ceremony, the marriage will already be legal, so if there are problems when we have the bigger wedding with everyone there and watching, I can mouth the words and everyone will think I'm simply speaking too softly for them to hear."

He traced her cheek with the back of his hand, and she leaned into the warmth of the touch. "That makes sense, Gina. A private wedding here, and soon. Knowing my mom, my sisters, they will be overjoyed to help with a church wedding in Chicago and take over as much or as little of that coordination and planning as we like."

"We'll talk it over with them. A date in August might make sense."

He held her gaze for a long moment, then nodded. "Okay, my precious." His voice held so much emotion, Gina felt her own tears fill her eyes.

Mark Bishop was going to be her husband. She could feel the emotions overwhelming her, the impact of all it meant for her to say yes, to wear his ring, the forever-different life ahead of her. Ahead of him. He must have sensed it because his arms gripped her in a tighter hug, and she could feel his chin resting on her head. "We're going to have a good life, Gina."

She nodded against his chest. "I know."

He tipped her chin up again and smiled. His kiss held a promise that was gentle and soft and even kind, which also hinted at the passion that was waiting for her. "I love you. When the doubts come, remember that. You have nothing to worry about," he promised.

She wiped a tear away even as she smiled. "I know. A good life."

He nudged her toward the kitchen table, pulled out a chair for her. "Do you have a preference on where you would like to go for a honeymoon? Hawaii sound good? If we get married within a week, I can still find us a few days someplace and arrange leave before the *Nevada* is back in port."

The honeymoon that followed the wedding . . . She could feel her face growing warm as thoughts of its intimacy filled her heart — part of why she looked forward to being married, being a wife. But to his question, she hesitated, and finally admitted, "There are going to be enough transitions happening. I'm fine with home — either here or Chicago — and no one knowing where we are. We could have a more traditional honeymoon after the formal wedding."

"Sounds like a plan. But you're allowed to change your mind if you decide you'd like to head off somewhere."

"Okay."

He brushed a strand of her hair back from her face. "If this Bangor house feels too much like Melinda's space for you, we'll buy another place when I get back from patrol. I'm going to be flexible about that, Gina. I won't mind moving, if that's what you prefer."

"We'll talk about it another time. I like your home." She settled her hands on either side of his face. "You're sure, Mark?"

He grinned. "I'm marrying you tomorrow, Gina, if I can arrange it that quickly. I'm sure."

It took him two days. The courthouse, third floor, was not the most romantic place to seal a promise, but Mark would rather have the words than the setting. He gently kissed his intended bride. "You look beautiful."

Gina blushed. "You've told me that twice today already."

"And plan to tell you again," he said.

She'd chosen a floral dress, and he'd arranged a bouquet of petite roses to match. He was in full-dress uniform. They'd agreed to mention the news to his friends only after it was official, so they didn't have a best man and maid of honor for this first ceremony. He could tell she was nervous. "I'm planning to hold your hand through the ceremony, so if you need to pause for a moment, just squeeze my hand and take whatever time you need. It's not going to bother me. Or anybody else."

She nodded. He held open the door to the judge's chamber. "After you, soon-to-be Mrs. Bishop."

She laughed. "You're enjoying this."

"I like getting married," Mark agreed. He loved her smile.

"Me too."

23

"Commander Bishop."

Mark turned to see the duty officer for Rear Admiral Hardman heading across the parking lot from the TCC building, carrying a flat box. Mark had just left a meeting with the admiral.

"It's true, sir, you're married?"

"Yes."

"Gold crew —"

"Doesn't know yet. It was a private ceremony. Her brother is away at sea. We'll have the formal wedding when he can be part of it."

"That explains it. Hardman asked me to pick this up for you. He thought your wife would enjoy seeing it."

Bishop opened the box. The Navy wedding cross. It was a tradition among submarine captains to have their wedding date inscribed on the back. It hung in the chapel on base, beside a flag signed by every man who had taken command of a U.S. submarine in the last 20 years. "Tell him thank you. I'll get it engraved and bring it back to the chapel."

"Sir, I think gold crew knows. Your paperwork went to personnel this afternoon. If you were intending to keep the news a secret —"

"No, it's not a secret. Simply a scheduling matter for who we told and when. I hadn't expected the paperwork to be so efficient." Bishop pulled out his keys. "I appreciate the heads up. And given it, I'd best head back to the house."

The duty officer laughed. "Yes, sir."

Gina was waiting for him at the front door, his text having requested that she set aside the unpacking she was doing and meet him when she heard him arrive. He closed the front door with his foot and kissed her before gently setting her back and pushing her hair away from her face so he could better see her. "Gold crew got the word I'm married. We're about to be serenaded."

Her eyes grew wide. "How many?"

"At a guess, about 140, counting spouses. I spotted the cars assembling at the grocery store two blocks east of here. You might want to start some coffee," he said. "Tradition has it the groom gets tossed into the nearest body of water — and it would have to be March."

"You're serious."

He smiled. "Don't worry. They'll toss me into a hot shower after the river. Unfortunately I don't have time to change, which means my dress blues are about to get soaked."

"What do they do to the wife?"

He laughed. "You get presents. Typically candy bars or bags of M&Ms, sometimes fancier chocolates like truffles and chocolate-covered cherries. It's considered good luck to give something sweet." He heard sleigh bells in the distance. Gold crew would arrive carrying dozens of the bells to make a nice racket as they approached.

"Our ombudsman, Amy Delheart, will be the one to knock on the door and offer the first gift," he told her swiftly. "She'll stay with you and make introductions to the crewmen and their wives. I'm sorry about this. I thought I'd have another day before they could get things together."

Gina wasn't ready yet, he thought, to take on the commander's wife role, with gold crew wives looking to her for friendship, advice, and help with Navy concerns. He'd known he would have to finesse things, lean on his ombudsman to help her out. He'd planned on introducing his wife but in a smaller setting.

Yet Gina didn't look worried. "I'm getting candy. I don't mind my side of the surprise," she said.

"Amy won't leave your side. If you have any speech difficulties, she'll be right there and send someone to find me. She's aware it's a concern."

"Okay." She tugged his head down to kiss him. "Commander Bishop, who is getting me a photo of you being tossed in the water?"

"You're enjoying this," he said with some surprise.

"Absolutely," she said with a smile.

"That photo's going to be plastered on the gold crew bulletin board by morning."

"You're embarrassed."

"I'm going to look like an idiot."

The sound of the bells grew loud, and then the doorbell rang behind them. Mark held her coat for her, buttoned it. "Remember that coffee."

"I will." Gina moved to open the door.

"Mrs. Commander Mark Bishop?" Amy asked, a twinkle in her eye, holding out a foil-covered chocolate bar with a bow on top.

Gina grinned. "Yes, I am."

"I'm Amy Delheart, your ombudsman, and on behalf of *Nevada* gold, we would like to welcome you to the family."

"I'm pleased to join it." She stepped out to take the gift.

A song broke out toward the back of the crowd, a raucous one about sailors going to sea. Mark wrapped his arms around his wife's waist from behind and stood with her as *Nevada* gold came forward to be introduced. Amy neatly set their gifts, one by one, onto trays brought for that purpose.

"Hey, Commander. Congratulations."

Mark's smile couldn't be contained. "Kingman."

He was aware the 15 officers of *Nevada* gold were slowly encircling him.

Gina's hands covered his, and he felt her slide his wedding ring off, move it to her hand for safekeeping. Moments later, Mark laughed and didn't fight it as he was hoisted off his feet and carried toward the river amid the chaos and more laughter. Certain things a groom accepted with some grace, and getting dunked after his wedding was a long and respected tradition.

"What do I put in the family-o-gram to Jeff?"

Mark rubbed still-damp hair with a towel and leaned over Gina's shoulder to look at the form. He'd taken a second shower after the gold crew and families left since the chill was still in his bones. The form was short. Personal transmissions to a sub while at sea were limited. "You don't have to send one now. You can wait for a port call when you can send a longer email or phone him."

"I'd rather tell him now, before he hears it from someone else."

Mark turned over an envelope and wrote down a message for her. "Send this."

Jeff, I married Mark Bishop. Be nice to him when you get to shore. Gina.

She smiled. "Maybe. I was thinking more like this." She turned a scrap of paper, so he could read her draft.

Jeff, I married Mark Bishop. Don't say it was your idea. Gina.

He laughed. "Nice." He took her pen and draft and marked out a few words. He handed it back. "Send that."

Jeff, I married Mark Bishop. Gina

"Short and sweet," she remarked. "Very sweet, actually."

Mark kissed her. "He'll call, first chance he gets. Can I have my wedding ring back?"

She slid it off her finger and back on his left hand. "You like wearing a ring."

522

"Absolutely." He spread his fingers to look at it, then dropped his damp towel across her shoulders. "You handled *Nevada* gold just right. They liked you."

"I like them too."

"Give yourself time to fit into the role of a commander's wife. You'll be at my side for the commander's barbecue after the May patrol, and that will be the right time to take on hostess and commander's wife duties." He rested his hands on her shoulders and gently squeezed. "And don't borrow trouble thinking ahead, worried there's a lot of work to do for one of those events. Most of the details are simply a repeat of what we did the year before. Preparations are basically a shopping list and a credit card, a few calls to arrange extra tables and chairs, and some serious praying that it doesn't rain."

She smiled. "Okay. I can do that."

He ruffled her hair. Honeymooning at home wasn't such a bad idea after all. A couple of weeks when they could sleep in would do the start of their marriage a world of good. Her hand slid into his, and she stood and tugged him toward the kitchen. He decided she'd become pretty comfortable with him in the last few days. "Dinner, then we turn in," she suggested over her shoulder.

A month from now, that endearing blush would require more than a stray thought about their nights together, but he loved it all the same. He rested an arm comfortably across her shoulders. "How about I fix spaghetti while you box your candy gifts and put them in the freezer? It's going to take a year to eat that much candy."

"True. But it's a nice tradition, especially if you appreciate chocolate like I do."

He opened a cupboard and got out plastic storage containers for the candy. Gina sat down to box up the gifts. He dug out a box of spaghetti and a jar of sauce.

"Mark?"

"Hmm?"

"Would you mind if I use Melinda's things?"

Startled, he glanced over at her. He thought he'd done a good job of clearing away Melinda's things from the cupboards, closets, and counters. "What do you mean?"

Gina pointed at the colored glass bottles, then at the figurine saltshakers. "She collected nice items. And I found some things of hers upstairs in the bathroom — hair dryer and curler, bath soaps. Are you going to feel weird if I use what's around?"

He wanted to wince at the question he'd been trying hard to prevent, the collision of past and present. It wasn't fair to Gina. But he hadn't neutralized the house nearly as much as he thought he had. "It's not going to bother you?"

She lifted a shoulder. "I'm aware I'm borrowing Melinda's things, but I don't want to buy duplicates just to avoid what she chose or once touched."

"I don't mind," he said quietly.

"You haven't mentioned her name much lately. Has that been deliberate?"

He hesitated. "Yes." He stopped the dinner preparations to give Gina his full attention. "When I do mention Melinda, talk about her or about my first marriage, I'm not doing it to draw comparisons between now and then, Gina. I just want you to have a sense of my own memories, a sense of how history has shaped me. I'm willing to change and adapt. I want to learn all over again how to be a good husband to you, just as I learned with Melinda. I'm sorry I didn't think of the smaller things that would still show this house had once been Melinda's place. I don't want you to feel uncomfortable in your own home."

"Our home," she replied softly. "You were married to her, Mark, and made a good marriage. You built a beautiful home with her. And if you're asking if I want to change every quilt in the place, every photo on the wall, every knickknack just because Melinda might have been the one to pick it out, the answer is no. I've been getting comfortable here, even before we were married. I'll keep what I like, and maybe pack away what I would rather replace. I'll make this my home. For now, I'm simply trying to read where you are in the transition from wife one to wife two."

He took two steps to the table and leaned down to kiss her. "Loved wife one. Adore, love, and treasure wife two. All right?"

She kissed him back. "Yes."

"It'll be easier if we find a new place when I get back from patrol," Mark promised, thinking it needed to be a priority.

She shook her head. "Melinda had very good taste. I kind of like not having to buy every throw rug, seasonal place mat, front door wreath and Christmas decorations all over again. Give me until you're back from the May patrol before I have to make a decision on the house. If I need us to change houses, leave this one and its contents behind, I'll let you know."

"Any hesitation, we sell what's here and move, precious. Whatever it is, from the furniture down to the kitchen towels. It's fine with me."

She smiled. "I'll tell you." She pointed to the last items on the tray. "Which do you want me to leave out for dessert — truffle or dipped caramel?"

"Caramel."

She opened the freezer and stored four totes and several plastic bags of chocolate bar gifts, then opened the refrigerator. "Join me for a salad?"

"Sure."

She lifted out the ingredients, and he pointed toward a cabinet where she'd find the cutting board. They companionably fixed dinner together. "I don't mind being wife number two," she told him as he handed her a plate of spaghetti. He nearly bobbled the dish. His gaze caught hers.

She leaned over and kissed his cheek. "You're worried about it. Actually, I find it rather nice that you already have a sense of how to treat a wife and handle living together without me having to point out the little things that matter to a woman."

"You're not like her, Gina, even though in some ways you are. You both expect a bathroom sink clean of whiskers, for me to reach the tall things for you without having to be asked, for the coffee to be made so you can see through it."

She smiled at the last point. "Someday I'd

like you to tell me all the similarities and the differences," she said softly. "I'm curious." She was curious about a lot of things, but that was a land mine of a question. "I would find it helpful, Mark."

"Ask me again in a few weeks if you're still curious." He'd find a way to dodge the question by then. He held her chair, then fixed his own plate and joined her. He loved being married to Gina. It was never boring.

"What just caused that smile?" she asked.

He looked over at his wife. "You."

Mark propped his head on his hand. Gina was hibernating in the blanket layers, a woman who liked to be cozy. He idly turned strands of her hair around his finger. She was beginning to wake up, but he'd discovered she was slow about it. The journey was fascinating to watch. Melinda had always been early to rise, alert from the beginning, often up before he was. Gina was the opposite. He loved these moments in the morning, watching her wake up.

She sleepily blinked, finally focused on him.

"Good morning," he said softly.

She glanced toward the window. The blinds were closed, but a single ray of sunlight reached almost to the picture frame. "Still early yet," she replied, sounding pleased about that. She tucked her hand near her chin, offered a sleepy smile, and closed her eyes again. "My feet are cold."

He nudged her feet into the warmth of the blanket near his. "You lost your socks again."

"Hmm."

"You are an absolutely wonderful wife."

His words brought her eyes open, startled. "What?"

"I'm serious. I'm just wondering if you have any appreciation of how good a wife you are."

"Thank you," she whispered, looking bewildered, and beginning to blush.

"I was thinking back to life before we were married, and what a typical morning for me was like. It didn't have moments like this, where I could look at your lovely face and share a smile." He settled his arm around her. "The evenings lacked the laughter of getting tangled up while trying to pass in the hallway, playing backgammon, having someone to do a late night raid of the refrigerator with — hanging-out time. Not to mention the joy of having you beside me for the night. You're a very good wife, Gina. You love me well."

"I do. I *like* you well too."

He laughed softly, delighted with the new-found self-confidence that was appearing, and kissed her. "Pancakes for breakfast?"

"Sure."

He'd heard Pong bark when the news-paper got delivered. He'd have a dog and two half-grown cats checking out what he was fixing his family for breakfast. He'd have to drop a pancake or two and feed them his mistakes. These were the days he was storing up as memories for when he would be deployed. He hadn't realized how much he'd missed being a husband till he was one again. "Breakfast will be ready in half an hour."

Mark picked up his coffee along with books from the side table and moved toward the patio door. "Want to join me this morning?"

"I'll be out shortly," Gina replied, picking up the last wedge of her orange. She admired the fact her husband was disciplined about his time with God. It was a constant part of his morning routine, tended to come after breakfast and before he began the rush of his day. On good-weather days he'd sit out on the back deck; on rainy days he'd spread out his Bible and books on the kitchen table. She'd given him privacy the first few times, but he'd convinced her he meant it when he said it was fine for her to join him.

She took the notebook she used for her own prayer time out with her and curled up in a chair near her husband with her Bible, dipping into the Psalms, and then Paul's letters in the New Testament. She wrote out her prayer, then revised it and wrote it again. It took time to get her thoughts in order. When she was finished, she read it silently and signed her name to it, dating the page. She didn't take lightly what she prayed. She wanted to know if God had listened, what He said in reply, what the results to her prayers might be. She idly looked back through the last few months and felt a moment of frustration that not many had been answered with a yes. Twenty years of trying to understand prayer, and she found it was still a mystery what God would respond to with a yes and when He would be silent.

She glanced up and realized her husband had completed his devotions, was quietly watching her while he finished his coffee. He had closed his Bible and notebook, put his pen away.

"You like to pray," she commented.

"I do."

"Are you good at it?"

531

He cocked an eyebrow at her question. "If you're asking are my prayers answered, mostly they are," he replied comfortably. "But I think I'm probably more cautious than you are on what I want to risk asking." He smiled. "God no doubt likes your approach better. Your heart's on your sleeve when you pray and you lean forward into life. From the few you've shown me, you have big dreams and hopes in your prayers. I'm more cautious, and I basically pray God's words back to Him."

"How do you mean?"

"Take a verse like the one in Hebrews, 'Do not neglect to do good and to share what you have, for such sacrifices are pleasing to God.' I ask the same thing of God as He asks of me. We need two thousand dollars to fund the commander's barbecue when the *Nevada* gets back after this May patrol. I'm not sure where it's going to come from this year, since there are more demands on our income than usual and this isn't the kind of thing I'm comfortable spending our savings on. We need some extra income from somewhere to cover it.

"So the prayer is simple: *God, do not neglect to do good and to share what you have, for such sacrifices are pleasing to you.* God has control of the money to meet this need. I'm trusting He will come through by the time the patrol is wrapping up. If God doesn't, if He stays silent or says no, it will hurt, but I'll deal with that if it happens. The answer is His choice.

"It's a relationship, Gina, and a friendship. On the whole, I know God is good to me, even when I can't grasp why He chooses to answer one prayer with a yes and another with silence or a no. But if I don't ask much" — Mark shrugged — "it's a problem I struggle with, how much I want to ask and risk in prayer when I might only get silence in reply. I often think age has made me too cautious with God. Or life has."

"Is some of that a holdover from when Melinda died?"

He considered her question, then nodded. "More than I probably realize. I talked a lot with God during the years after I lost her, but for a time I stopped praying for specific needs. Any no, any disappointment, was simply too much to risk. Life simply hurt. It's gotten better with the passing years. God is kind, and He heals a heart and has answered nearly everything I've asked in the recent years, which has made it easier for me to hear the occasional silence. But some of that caution is still there."

"What were you praying for today?"

"The upcoming patrol. It's going to be hard on you, the fact I'm gone. And it's going to be hard on me, missing you and knowing you're back here alone."

"It's your dream, Mark, to command the *Nevada*. I can't wish that wasn't in your schedule, even though it's hard to think about you being gone all that time. But I want you to go, enjoy every minute of it with *Nevada* gold, do an excellent job, store up memories, and then come home and spend your R and R with me."

He smiled. "A well-crafted answer. You're making the transition to being a commander's wife."

She thought about it and nodded, surprised to realize how comfortable she was with the idea. "I am. And a commander goes to sea. I'll be fine, Mark. I know you'll do an excellent job and keep the *Nevada* safe, and while you're gone . . . well, I'll find a way to fill my days. I'll read more. Maybe go back to Chicago for a couple of weeks. Spend some time at the office just surfing around through subjects — and hopefully not find anything particularly surprising. Security is going to be around everywhere I go, so you won't need to worry about me locking my keys in the car or having a flat tire on a poorly lit road. Someone will always have a phone I can use."

"I'm glad they're around."

"Sometimes I forget they are, until I look back and see who's in the rearview mirror. Or I go through a door on base and hear someone walk in behind me, and realize it's the security for the new shift. It still catches me off guard."

"I sleep better knowing the security's there, Gina — there to watch out for you."

She nodded, accepting that. "I'll miss you, Mark."

"I'll miss you too, precious." He smiled at her. "Will you write me letters? I know they can't be mailed, but you could leave them for me on the bedside table. That way I can know how your days were going as they happened."

"I could do that."

Her husband nodded, pleased. "I'll look forward to reading them when I get back."

The *Nevada* refit was half done, and for once Mark had gotten home while it was still daylight. He took the glass of iced tea Gina offered with a grateful thanks. He'd swapped his sweat-stained shirt for a clean T-shirt, but otherwise hadn't changed, so his hug was brief. He needed a shower. "Any more groceries to bring in?"

"This is the last sack. You got the mail in?"

"On the desk," he confirmed.

He went to find the local news. When he sat down on the couch, his eyes closed of their own accord. Tired didn't begin to cover what refit did to his body. He heard Gina follow him into the living room a few minutes later.

There was a bow-tied box on her side of the couch, another on the floor. She opened it, laughed, and set it on the floor beside the second box. "What's this?" She held up a few of the magazines for him to see.

"You like to read. I bought you a few more things to read."

"The Economist? Chemistry Today? Science Digest?"

"Ever read them?"

"Not recently."

He'd bought her five years' worth of back issues off eBay. "Enjoy."

He felt her hand slide into his, and he smiled, wrapped an arm around her waist and pulled her over beside him. "I'm going to nap, you're going to read, and tonight we can snuggle." He rested his forehead against hers, sighed, considered stretching out on the couch to sleep right here, but a shower and a bed would suit his aching body better. He was heading there just as soon as he caught the local news and the weather update for tomorrow. He had gone up or down a ladder more than 40 times today — and that was after he'd started counting.

He felt her fingers stroke lightly across the bruise on his wrist. "Another accident?"

"A case of peaches," he said, shaking his head. "I joined the supply line, got distracted, missed a hand-off."

"What distracted you?"

"Someone asked if my wife was going to 'send off' the boat when we leave."

"What's that involve?"

"Traditionally? Or what I might let you do?"

She laughed. "Seriously, I should do something as the commander's wife. How about a joke a day you could read over the intercom?"

That got him to briefly open his eyes and lazily stroke her arm. "You don't tell very funny jokes."

"Okay, then a riddle a day, a puzzle or brainteaser."

"Better. I was thinking along the lines of 90 cute dog and cat photos, and I'd stick a new one on the captain's board every morning."

"That's pretty lame."

"Better than you showing up in a bikini and kissing the boat goodbye."

She laughed and leaned up to kiss him. "I'll think of something."

"Yeah. Turn up the volume on the news, would you?"

He felt a cat's paw on his shoulder and braced for the claws to find traction, but the animal landed lightly on his lap and head-butted against his chest, looking for attention. He obliged. He was coming to like cats — not as much as the dog, but they were mostly okay.

"I'm going to go walk Pongo for a bit. Chicken strips over rice for dinner in 30 minutes?"

It sounded wonderful. "I love you."

A hand patted his chest. "I love you too." He opened his eyes in time to see his wife disappear into the kitchen. He felt moisture in his eyes and blinked, felt a second cat bat a paw at his hair, and reached up to the back of the couch to haul the other animal down.

Lovable, fascinating wife. Good marriage. He was too tired to more than appreciate the fact that life had taken a very good turn.

The weatherman was forecasting rain, so tomorrow he would be climbing wet ladders. The *Nevada* needed grease, lubricants, oil, hydraulic fluid, filters, hose fittings, couplings, joints, pipes. Mechanicals were the focus tomorrow, and parts needed to be restocked. He'd be in the middle of it. A small thing, but when the captain showed up for the grunt work, sailors gave him the benefit of the doubt when he asked for the second mile at sea.

He'd have to make sure Gina didn't do something too corny or too memorable for the send-off. He'd be comfortable with a goodbye kiss at home and her not coming to the dock to see the boat off. He would have to emotionally disengage for 90 days, and the break was going to be a very hard moment — for the both of them.

Gina would inevitably change in little ways while he was gone. The young cats would fill out into full-grown cats. Even Pongo would have developed past the tendency to stumble over his own feet. *Survive refit, get the patrol over with, and get back home.* The days he had lived for the joy of command and patrol were slamming into the reality that he would really like to be home with his wife for the next three months rather than be at sea.

He was still mulling over that shift in his priorities and half dozing when Gina returned, Pongo racing into the room in front of her. The dog was determined to get onto the ottoman before the cats claimed it. Mark smiled at the ambition in the puppy. The cats left his lap to contest the matter. "What were those last three words you said to me?" he asked his wife.

"Love you too."

"Make it the last four words."

"I love you too."

"Last ten?"

She chuckled and, with one hand resting on the back of the couch and the other on his shoulder, leaned down to kiss him. "Dinner is about ready."

He let her pull him to his feet, slid his arms around her waist. "It's nice to hear the words. You say them beautifully." He rested his forehead against hers. "I'd like a real honeymoon after our big wedding. Hawaii maybe, or New York."

"Montana."

He grinned. "Where did that come from?"

"I've never been, and there's no water. I have to share you with the sea right now. I'm finding I lean toward being landlocked for the honeymoon."

"I'm inclined to accommodate you if you're serious."

"I've never ridden a horse."

He laughed. "Now the *real* purpose begins

to appear."

"You'd look good wearing a cowboy hat."

He kissed her. "I'll ask around for recommendations on Montana."

She kissed him back. "I'm so glad I married you, Mark," she whispered.

"So am I."

The world felt right just then, with no pieces missing. Mark hugged his wife and wondered if this would be the highlight of the year. They were facing their first deployment and separation. If he was lucky, the marriage would be able to absorb the absence and re-stitch itself back together without too much disturbance when he returned. But he had too much experience, both in his own history and with his crew, not to realize a marriage couldn't absorb this kind of separation without some price being paid. He hoped and prayed Gina was confident enough in the two of them to absorb the doubts and insecurities that would inevitably come. He rested his chin against her hair. "Promise me something, Gina."

"What?"

"Don't allow the age gap to bother you while I'm on patrol. Don't let yourself go back to thinking 'I'm too young for him.' "

She leaned back, puzzled. "Have I been

suggesting it's a concern?"

"Confidence is a fragile thing. You have it now, and I don't want you to lose it. You're the wife I need. The wife I want. I don't expect you to be able to handle everything that comes up while I'm gone. Check in with Amy Delheart. Jeff when he's around. Or Daniel. Don't let some idea of what a commander's wife is supposed to be to stop you from asking for help.

"You'll have the wives and girlfriends of gold crew calling you, wanting advice about the patrol, the Navy, their relationships, the separation. I want you to feel okay about handing those calls off to Delheart. I want you living the life that fits who you are — days at the TCC, working with the JPL group, traveling back to Chicago if it's useful — not getting derailed being the commander's wife, wondering what you signed up for and how you're supposed to help someone who thinks you have all the answers when you're practically the same age as they are."

She smiled and patted his chest with the flat of her hand. "I'm going to surprise you with how well I manage this patrol. I like being Mrs. Commander Mark Bishop."

"I don't want you to stop liking it, or liking me," he mentioned.

She grinned. "As if. Let's have this conversation again when you get back from patrol, Mark. You don't have anything to worry about."

"I'll worry anyway. It's what husbands do."

"Well, I'll try not to worry about you, no matter what. I have every confidence in *Nevada* gold, and in you."

"I'll be home safe and sound in 90 days," he said, determined to make those words come true. He leaned down to seal that promise with another kiss. "You can trust me on that."

"I do. Now go have your shower, then come eat."

24

Gina's send-off for the *Nevada* were caramels she and the wives of the gold crew had made, individually wrapped with a ribbon and note attached for every sailor, each package containing a dozen pieces. Bishop popped his first caramel in his mouth as he scanned the open ocean waters, leaning on the rail high above the sub. Bright blue sky, a clear horizon ahead of him, two Coast Guard cutters on escort, the smell of the ocean and the salt spray, the sun beating down on him — it all made him feel energized and alive.

"It's time," he said to his executive officer.

His second-in-command nodded. "It's going to be a good patrol, sir."

Bishop took one last glance at the coast behind them. They were leaving a lot of loved ones behind. He'd bring this boat back safe and sound. He looked over at his friend, smiled. "XO, clear the deck."

Kingman grinned, nodded. "Clear the deck, aye, sir." The XO looked up higher into the sail. "Lookouts, below."

Bishop stepped over to the hatch and headed down the ladder to command-and-control. He slid his sunglasses into the red case by the captain's chair, knowing if the world cooperated it would be three months before he wore them again. The windshield was hauled down from the sail, along with the communications gear, and the men on lookout descended. The crew around the center was eager — he could feel it throughout the room — the good tension of being back on a boat at sea, no more refit maintenance, resupply and upkeep. Now it was time to do what they were trained to do: go sailing.

"Sonar, control. Report all near contacts."

"Control, sonar. Surface contacts only. Two Coast Guard cutters, three personal craft, nearest vessel 200 feet off the port side."

"Very well."

He picked up the phone and called engineering for a report, then phoned the missile bay. Satisfied with their updates, Bishop turned to Kingman. "XO, make our depth 85 feet."

"Make our depth 85 feet, aye, Captain."

Kingman turned. "Lieutenant Olson, report on all hatches."

"I have a green board, sir. All hatches are secure."

The XO picked up the intercom and set it to 1MC. "Dive, dive, dive." He reached over and flipped the dive alarm switch, the distinct warble sounding throughout the boat. "Dive, dive, dive." He turned to scan the ballast board. "Helm, make our depth 85 feet."

The helmsman opened the valves. The ballast tanks filled with a *whoosh.* Above them, water washed across the hull and deck.

The XO checked with officers around the room. "Captain, the boat is tight."

"Very well. Come to heading 270, make our depth 300 feet."

The XO confirmed the order, turned to the helmsman and planesman to execute it.

Bishop reached for his notebook and his plan for the first day at sea.

"Steady on heading 270, depth 300 feet, sir," Kingman reported minutes later.

"Very well. XO, let's find out how the refit did. Angles and dangles at the bottom of the hour."

Kingman smiled and confirmed the command. He reached for the intercom. "*Ne-*

vada, this is the XO. Prepare for angles and dangles."

Gina watched a blip on the TCC ocean map move another dot to the west. She could pretend to work with the best of them when it suited her, and it suited her to be sitting at her desk facing into the Tactical Command Center with her feet propped up on the credenza drawer, a pad of paper in her lap. She was occasionally jotting herself a note because the idea she'd had during the night refused to shut off, but she was mainly watching the ocean board.

Daniel came in, slid an orchid into the vase on her desk. "From your husband. He wanted a fresh flower always on your desk while he's on patrol."

"A wonderful choice. I miss him, Daniel."

"I can tell. You've been practically haunting this place."

Bishop had been gone 19 days. Even Jeff's return on the *Seawolf* hadn't filled much of the hole she felt. She was glad Daniel was around. The initial awkwardness had passed, their friendship was intact, as solid as it had been when they were dating. She liked the fact she didn't have to plan out her words with him when she had a thought. "*Nevada* gold drew the north box for this patrol, didn't they?"

"Russia, China, North Korea — the top of the list doesn't change. Bishop will soon be in the middle of the Pacific with no one around him, if that helps."

"It does." There was a blue square on the Pacific map, marking off the north boomer patrol box. Somewhere in those hundreds of miles of water, the *Nevada* gold crew and her husband would take station. The area had been swept by two fast-attacks running cross-sonar. The area was clear. He would be as safe as was possible on a nuclear submarine hundreds of feet below the surface of the sea.

"What are you working on?" Daniel asked.

She glanced at her notes. "I'd like to be able to predict solar flares, at least the large ones."

"Think you can?"

She shrugged. "JPL has some interesting theories on what triggers them, and I've got a few ideas of my own, so maybe. I think it's magnetics in the core of the sun, rather than a building pressure like with a volcano here on earth, that causes the burst to flare out."

"Interesting." Daniel settled into the guest chair. "Jeff is looking for you."

"I got his call. I'm meeting him for dinner. You want to come with us? He wants to bring Tiffany."

"A replay of old times," he commented. "Jeff and the *Seawolf* are back to sea in 48 hours?"

She nodded again. "Resupply is about finished. They'll be making for Japan. Looking at that map, it makes sense. China and Japan are still skirmishing over those islands and the gas fields in the East China Sea. I just wish Jeff wasn't a fast-attack. They're likely to have him sit between the two sides like a referee saying 'Cool it, boys.' "

Daniel smiled. "Comes with the job," he said. "What time are you meeting Jeff?"

"Quarter to six."

"I'll come along," Daniel agreed.

Gina said good-night to the security officer who had escorted her home and stepped into the quiet house. Pongo made a dash from the kitchen to meet her, and she knelt to greet him. She missed Mark, more than she had prepared herself for. The nights were the worst. She'd lived alone for years, but it took only months with a husband for her to change so profoundly she struggled to be content on her own anymore. As had become a habit, she curled up on the couch in the living room, pulled out stationery and pen, and wrote him a letter.

Dear Mark,

I still haven't settled on an easy endearment for you like Precious, which you've given to me. I wish I did, so these letters would feel more personal. I'm missing you something fierce.

I went out to dinner with Jeff and Tiffany and Daniel tonight. A last gathering before Jeff heads back to sea. Daniel did his best to get me to laugh, and he's been faithfully bringing the fresh flowers you asked him to provide for my office. I'm still curious how you got him to accept that assignment, but he's mum about that last conversation the two of you had before you deployed. As nice as the evening was, I felt a huge hole that you weren't there with me. I kept turning to my left, expecting to see you beside me.

I don't have a particular reason to be writing tonight. You're going to get a stack of letters which say very little of substance. But I wanted to put on paper the fact I love you, I miss you, and I pray for you to safely come back home.

I found your glove-box note for me today. I was looking for the tire pressure gauge for Jeff to use when I saw the note with my name clipped to the registration and insurance cards. I read it and then put the note back in its place, so it will be there if it's needed. You love me very well. Thank you, my husband.

With much love, your
precious,
Gina

She folded the page and slipped it into an envelope, dated it. She would put the letter in the nightstand with the others for when he returned.

Her husband had surprised her with the numerous notes he had left for her around the house and office. She'd found the first one in her purse when she went to get grocery money at the ATM. Found the second one when she opened her Bible. Another had been taped to the top of the ice cream carton. The one she had found in the car this afternoon had been both loving and thoughtful, her husband planning ahead.

Gina,
If you just got a speeding ticket, know I'm praying it was a minor few miles over the limit and that you won't kick

yourself too much for the error. Money to cover a ticket is in my sock drawer if you need it.

Love, Mark

She had married a man who did his best to think through what might happen and be there for her even if he couldn't be there in person — it was the kind of man he was. And she loved him for it.

The cats and dog followed her to the kitchen, accustomed to her late-night stop by the freezer for a piece of chocolate, hoping she'd open the refrigerator and find a leftover to share. She picked up the puppy and hugged him. She noticed for the first time the second dog tag on his collar, turned it to read the words etched on both sides.

First dog of *Nevada* gold. Reward for return to Bangor submarine base.

"You're special, Pongo. Do you realize that?" She gave the dog another hug and set him back down. Mark was taking care of his entire family.

The first six weeks passed so slowly that by mid-June, Gina felt like she had aged a year merely from boredom. She was working too many hours just to keep her mind off the fact Mark wasn't around, wasn't there when she went to bed at night, wasn't there when she woke up. The dog had been in mourning since about week two, and now even the cats were beginning to look distressed.

She arrived at the TCC, showed her security badge at the door, and slipped quietly inside, knowing from the text Daniel had sent that the room would be busy tonight. She spotted him in the theater seats and took one beside him. "What's happening on the other side of the Pacific? Things still tense with the Chinese?"

"South Korea and Japan signed a mutual defense treaty to cover their territorial waters rather than accept U.S. assurances under our current treaties with them. The pact has got China very annoyed. There've been some naval movements around the two islands with contested ownership, as well as activity near the ocean-floor gas fields."

Daniel pointed to the map showing an enlargement of the waters between Taiwan and Japan. "That's Jeff and the *Seawolf* on station, hovering over the submerged seamounts south of Japan. He's been there about 30 hours, sitting in the midst of a buffer area that's shown up between the two sides."

"Is this posturing, or intent on the part of China's military?" Gina asked, keeping her voice low.

"Hard to tell." Daniel looked at his watch. "We're at 58 hours after the solar flare."

"It turned out to be a weak burst. First reflections might show up in the narrow wavelengths in a couple of hours, but the best we can hope for is the beginnings of a fuzzy picture in about 12 hours."

Captain Strong, pacing the room as he monitored the screens, paused to join the conversation. "That will still be helpful, Gina. I need to know how many subs China deployed, Japan, what South Korea is doing. How the boats are deployed tells me a lot about the difference between rhetoric simply for political purposes and true military intent."

"I hope it does help, sir."

"I'll take whatever I can get. What are the odds of another solar flare this month?"

"Reasonable, sir. A series of weak flares often indicate a stronger one is building."

Gina looked at the ocean maps. "Any change with North Korea, sir?"

"They've moved long-range missiles to the launch area on the East Coast, but they haven't fueled them yet. So far it's just been the usual rhetoric — Armageddon-level destruction of the South Korean capital, Seoul, a fire from above raining down on Japan — nothing particularly new about the bellicose threats. But with China annoyed, there may be less restraint applied to keep North Korea from overstepping a redline."

"Do you anticipate trouble?"

Strong smiled. "The only thing this job anticipates is trouble." He took the message traffic the duty officer brought over, scanned it, then glanced back at her. "Let me know if there's anything you need, Gina. I can use that photo."

"I will, sir."

He headed over to the communications desk.

"Do you think this escalates, Daniel?"

Her friend shrugged. "China and Japan have been heading toward a collision for over a decade, but I doubt either side particularly wants a confrontation right now. The question is, what does that mutual defense agreement trigger? South Korea joining up with Japan in defending the islands in dispute? I personally think the moral claim, the legal claim, of ownership is with Japan, but China obviously disagrees. Settling that dispute via the military is a bad outcome the U.S. would like to avoid."

"Hence the *Seawolf* sitting there like a referee to watch both sides."

"Yes. Your brother is good at his job. He can handle the assignment. And the *Ohio* and the *Michigan* are near enough for support without it appearing like we are deliberately trying to get involved in this shoving contest."

She knew Jeff and the *Seawolf* were well trained and prepared, but she still felt apprehensive when she looked at what was going on in the waters around them. The world didn't feel peaceful tonight, even though no one was shooting.

Gina looked at the large blue box farther out in the Pacific, which she suspected defined the area her husband had drawn for this strategic patrol. The *Nevada* was on her own in deep waters, for now safe — if anything that carried 24 Trident missiles and a nuclear reactor aboard could be considered safe. She wanted the men in her life back onshore without incident. A photo would help that at the margins. "I'm going to go get set up for processing that photo."

"Like some help?"

"I'd rather you keep an eye on the board and come find me if anything major changes."

Daniel nodded. "I can do that."

Bishop scanned the latest news bulletin. "XO, make our depth 250 feet. I want to hear commercial radio out of Japan."

"Make our depth 250 feet, aye, Captain."

Their patrol box was designed to keep the *Nevada* a safe distance from any adversary while also allowing minimum flight time for the missiles to reach the most likely targets. This patrol, their area was splitting the difference between defending Japan and South Korea. The tone of the news bulletins had changed over the last five days, and things were growing more tense topside.

Bishop could feel the sweat sliding down his back, even though the boat was kept at a cool 68 degrees. He stopped by the navigation table to check their position before moving forward to the sonar room. "Where's the *Seawolf*?"

"Here, sir." The contact was faint, visible only because they were at the southwest tip of their patrol sweep. Tactical Command was keeping a fast-attack between the two sides. It was a gutsy move if it worked, and horrifying to consider if it didn't.

"He's stationary?"

"The most I'm hearing is an occasional turn. He's holding station."

Bishop stepped back to command-and-control. "Conn, bring us to bearing 020."

"Bearing 020, aye, Captain."

They would lose the *Seawolf* as they headed to the other end of their patrol box, but it couldn't be helped. They normally ran solo while on a strategic deterrent patrol. But on this deployment he hoped to see one of the missile submarines converted to carry Tomahawks — either the USS *Ohio* or the USS *Michigan* — patrolling the Pacific nearby so he could link up and use cross-sonar to gain a deeper look at the waters around the *Nevada.* Tense times in the news meant militaries got more aggressive. He wouldn't put it past China to have a number of subs out searching for a U.S. boomer on Pacific patrol just for a show of presence, to remind them that China considered this half of the ocean theirs. Bishop wished he had one of Gina's photos on the screen in front of him right now so he could see everything going on.

They were due to move up to hard-alert status in 48 hours, taking over from the USS *Henry M. Jackson* as the lead boomer for the northern watch. He looked at his watch, walked over to the drill instructor. "Show me the last missile test times," he said. The boat felt ready, drills had been running smoothly, but he'd run another one if they could still improve execution times.

Gina counted 38 submarines in the waters stretching from South Korea down to Taiwan. Rear Admiral Hardman stood beside her, watching the photo develop. "An incredible sight, Gina, and very useful."

"Thank you, sir. Another four hours, I may have enough resolution to tell you sub type, and from that, nation of origin. It was a weak flare, and it's taking some time to get enough reflections." She'd been babysitting the data streams since the day before, watching the reflections slowly accumulate.

"China, Japan, South Korea — you don't want them playing in the same sandbox when one of them is mad. Find me when you have the detailed data. It's the South Korean subs that have me most concerned. They're farther south than they normally travel."

"I will, sir."

"Captain Strong, has the *Michigan* reached the patrol box yet?" Hardman asked.

"Twenty minutes, sir."

"Send an informational EAM to the *Nevada* and let her know that *Michigan*'s coming. I want them to link up and start a cross-sonar quiet search focused on the waters south of Japan just as soon as it's feasible. Find me that South Korea sub that should be docked in Japan and isn't."

"Yes, sir."

"Control, sonar. New contact bearing 078. It's the USS *Michigan,* sir."

"Very well," Bishop replied. He moved to scan the navigation table. "Conn, come to heading 090, make our depth 400 feet."

The order was repeated and executed. They had the towed array deployed. They could run a parallel track about 15 miles apart, cross-link sonar, and get their first good look at what was out there to their west. If they were fortunate, the range would give them visibility as far as the *Seawolf.*

"Sonar, control. Cross-link sonar with the *Michigan* as soon as we are in range, then run a cross-sonar ping focused on the last known position of the *Seawolf.*"

"Control, sonar. Cross-sonar on the first opportunity, then ping, aye, Captain."

The *Michigan* was a ballistic missile submarine of the same class as the *Nevada,* but the *Michigan* had been converted to carry Tomahawk missiles rather than Trident II D-5s. If a land war broke out, the *Michigan* would bring conventionally armed missiles to the fight. A submarine could fire the first missiles of an engagement without warning, while an air force bomber could be seen leaving base or be picked up on radar. The early shots tended to go to submarines. The *Michigan* had been in battle several times over the years. If a skirmish started, they would need to be prepared to disengage and separate quickly since the fired missile would give away the submarine location. But for now, the *Michigan* was welcome company.

Bishop watched on the navigation table as the distance closed between the two subs.

"Control, sonar. I have a cross-sonar link with the *Michigan,* sir. Beginning cross-sonar with an active ping now."

"Very well. Report all new contacts." Bishop deliberately made himself relax. The sweep would give him a very good sense if the *Nevada* was still sailing in clear waters or if they had unwelcome company.

"Control, sonar. Clear waters, sir, out 200 miles. We have reacquired the USS *Seawolf,* same location. Reading six distinct contacts in his vicinity, surface and submerged. Working to identify now, sir."

"Very well."

Jeff's *Seawolf* had been holding station over the seamounts south of Japan for the last several days. He could hide in and among the seamounts, rise toward the surface and show the boat on radar, be a quietly watchful presence to keep both sides honest. One side couldn't fire a shot and then claim self-defense with the *Seawolf* recording what occurred, able to prove who started the fight. It was a kind of brute-force diplomacy, the presence of the U.S. fast-attack keeping the peace. Bishop quietly said a prayer for his friend and new brother-in-law, then turned his attention back to the *Michigan.*

"Sonar, control. Start a cross-sonar quiet search. I'm curious if we can pick up anything north of Japan. In particular, what's South Korea doing?"

"Control, sonar. Starting a quiet search, aye, Captain."

"Torpedo in the water! Distant. Bearing 247 degrees."

Bishop hurried forward to the sonar room.

"Someone just took a shot at the *Seawolf.*" Sonar Chief Penn flipped a switch and put the audio on speaker. The sound of small explosions rippled through the sonar room. "Canisters, sir. Trying to confuse the guidance lock." More pops on the audio. "Emergency blow. He's heading topside in a hurry . . . he's clearing it. Sounds are separating."

"Who fired?"

"Not clear, sir."

Bishop walked farther forward to the radio shack, where all the printers had come active. "Traffic, sir. Lots of it. Tactical Command is ordering the *Seawolf* to *not* fire back."

Jeff was having a rough night. Bishop scanned the messages coming across, then stepped back into the sonar room. "Where is he, Penn?"

His sonar chief had overlaid the navigational topology map and now tapped the screen. "Here, sir. And maneuvering deep at a fast angle."

A smart tactical move to head down among the seamounts to give himself cover while National Command sorted out what had happened. Smart and would be very dangerous without precise seamount data and detailed navigational maps. Gina's early work mapping the ocean floor was saving lives tonight. Jeff could afford to wait and not fire back while the situation got sorted out.

"I think it was the *Son Won-il* that fired."

"South Korea?"

"Yes, sir."

"Radio, let me hear a commercial band out of South Korea."

He didn't speak the language, but he didn't need to. The station wasn't playing music, the words were urgent, stressed, and news was breaking.

The reasons a South Korean submarine captain would fire — would have permission to fire — made a very short list. A missile volley on the DMZ, North Korea launching a long-range missile with a warhead that hit something, a naval skirmish with a sunk vessel. The fact a South Korean captain had mistakenly fired on a U.S. submarine would raise massive consternation across the militaries of both nations. It spoke to the confusion going on at sea, the high tension level.

"Any change to the *Michigan* — course or speed?"

"No change, sir. She's starboard side pacing us, distance 14 miles."

Being able to run cross-sonar was what was giving the *Nevada* the visibility to see the *Seawolf,* so he'd prefer to stay paired up for now and have firsthand knowledge of what was happening. But they'd need to separate fast if orders flowed in. "Keep a tight eye on her."

"Yes, sir."

Bishop strode back to command-and-control. "XO, make our depth 500 feet."

There was nothing he could do on the USS *Nevada* but listen and sort out events as they happened. He couldn't move to help out the *Seawolf,* even if he would personally like to, not given this boat and her mission. But he could, and would, keep this boat safe.

He reached for the phone. "Weapons, load torpedoes, tubes one and two," Bishop directed. "Set range to magnetic search, 10 miles."

Gina heard the alarm even before the elevator doors opened, found Daniel waiting on the other side. Daniel grabbed her hand and rushed her through the Tactical Command Center doors as red lights began to flash. "What?" Gina asked. "What's going on?"

"Lockdown. Head to your office so we're out of the way and don't get tossed out of here."

She saw the ocean boards rapidly shifting to zoom in on the Ryukyu Ridge and Okinawa Trough in the East China Sea. "Tell me what's happened."

Daniel didn't stop to look — or let her look — until they were in her office. He turned to stand in the doorway and scan the boards out in the main area. "Someone took a shot at the *Seawolf.*"

Her response froze in her throat.

Daniel looked back when she made no comment and calmly stepped over to rest a hand on her shoulder. "Jeff's busy at the moment, but still very much alive." Daniel turned back to study the boards and added, "He just put the *Seawolf* 1,300 feet down into a canyon. That would be one intense roller coaster of a ride."

She couldn't get the words out to ask who had fired. *Please, Jesus, my brother is in danger. You've got to help him.* Every bit of emotion in her that she couldn't voice went into that silent request.

"I'm seeing Pentagon flash traffic warnings to South Korea and Japan," Daniel continued, reading the boards. "And lots of EAM traffic for the *Seawolf* not to fire back. This may be a friendly-fire incident, Gina."

She still didn't feel she could breathe correctly, but she managed to get two words out: "He's safe?"

Daniel's hand on her shoulder tightened. "As safe as you can be when your boss tells you not to fire back. He'll be fine, Gina. He's in a very defensible position, and it looks like they're sending the *Ohio* in as a backstop."

Rear Admiral Hardman moved across her line of vision, phone to his ear.

"Why lockdown?"

"Protocol, whenever there's hostile fire."

"Thanks for getting us inside," Gina said.

"Sure thing."

She could have been on the other side of the doors and not learned any of this until the patrol was over, if then. She wondered how many skirmishes like this Jeff had been in and never mentioned to her, how many Bishop had seen. "How long before it's certain it was friendly fire?" she managed to say to Daniel.

"I'd get comfortable. I think we're here for the next 12 hours, minimum, before they know enough to take TCC off lockdown."

"Sir, the *Seawolf* is staying where it was shot at?" Gina asked Rear Admiral Hardman, determined to keep her voice and questions calm, relieved she was able to ask the question of the man who would know. The world had returned to some semblance of normal in the last four hours, but the TCC was still sucking in massive amounts of intel on what had happened — if someone in South Korea had given the order for the *Son Won-il* to fire.

"We move the *Seawolf* out of the way even temporarily, we're going to have a Chinese sub moving into that square of the ocean," Hardman told her. "It's going to be a case of possession is nine-tenths of the law. We won't be able to move him out again. If China parks a sub there, Japan — or for that matter, South Korea — will try to dislodge him. We can't afford to let that happen. The *Seawolf* has to stay put. Right now we're the ref holding on to the football while the two sides argue with each other over who gets possession."

"And if it happens again? If someone fires on him again?"

"A mistake is one thing, but firing a second time — National Command doesn't consider that to be a mistake. Trust your brother, Gina. Commander Gray, the *Seawolf* and her crew, are *very* good at their job. We'll be exerting maximum pressure overnight to get this situation resolved before it escalates further."

She nodded. "I appreciate you allowing me to stay in the TCC."

Hardman smiled briefly. "I need you on the inside in the hopes we get another solar flare. I need a photo of which subs just put to sea, who got ordered back toward home waters. A picture would clarify a lot of questions right now. What people are saying is often not the same as what they're doing."

"Yes, sir. I hope we do get another solar flare."

She looked at the ocean map. The prayer came with the same intensity as before. She desperately wanted to help her brother and help keep her husband safe. *Please, Jesus, we need a flare. For my sake. For Jeff's. For Mark's too. A nice strong solar flare and, preferably, right now. Please, help me. Help us all.*

"How many games of tic-tac-toe does this make?"

"Just because you're losing," Daniel quipped, drawing another board for a new game, ignoring the question. They were sitting in the back row of the theater seats. The lockdown still hadn't lifted, but the situation appeared to have stabilized. Gina was beginning to feel hungry and wondered what would be sent in for dinner. They were now monitoring television channels for any word the incident had become public. So far, all was quiet.

Her phone signaled an incoming text. She pulled it out, surprised the message was allowed through. Outgoing calls on cell phones were being blocked. "Good news, it's JPL. There's been another solar flare." She rapidly read through the numbers. "A hot one, Daniel. And looping straight toward the earth."

"That sounds good."

She nodded. "Very good. In 60 hours this energy hits the earth's oceans and we'll get a very clear look at what's going on." At least now she'd be able to do something that might help, rather than just sit here and watch. *Thank you, Jesus, for this answer.*

Daniel set the alarm on his watch and got to his feet. "I'll give Admiral Hardman and Captain Strong a heads up."

CNN cut into their broadcast with breaking news, and Daniel paused, then sat down again. The picture changed to a live image of a missile streaking away from the North Korea coast. The image jumped around the screen, then steadied as the camera lens focused in.

"Ooh boy, this ain't good," Daniel breathed as the missile climbed.

The TCC was tied into the Pentagon video feeds. Displays shifted to show the Pentagon tracking. They watched as software computed the missile trajectory, and moments later two interceptor missiles fired from Guam. One slammed into the tail of the North Korean missile over Japan's territorial waters, the detonation sending shock waves across the screen.

"That wasn't just the intercept missile," Gina whispered, stunned at the force of the blast.

"No, that North Korean missile had a warhead aboard," Daniel said quietly, watching the video unfold. "That's the first time North Korea has put an explosives payload on one of those missiles."

"The second missile on the launcher?"

"I don't think anyone's going to let them fire it and find out what it's carrying."

Gina watched Rear Admiral Hardman pick up the phone. She didn't want a front seat to history, but she realized she had one tonight as events unfolded and orders and counterorders flowed out. She rested her chin against her hands on the seat in front of her and hoped her heart rate would slow down.

Jeff had spent a career training to be in the middle of trouble. Mark would enter this fight only if the world spun deep into chaos. And she wouldn't have been able to pick who she was most worried about at the moment. Her brother and her husband both needed to come home safely. "How many nuclear warheads does North Korea have?" she asked.

"Too many for tonight," Daniel replied, pushing to his feet. "They supposedly don't have them miniaturized enough to put on a missile payload, but I don't know who in Japan will want to trust the accuracy of that intelligence-community guess. I'll tell Hardman and Strong a hot flare is coming. They'll want that picture — need that picture, Gina. Subs are often the first movers in a fight. If Japan acts, we'll see them putting to sea."

"I've got a knot in my stomach that says 60 hours from now is going to be too late to be useful."

Daniel squeezed her shoulder. "We'll take what we can get."

She nodded as she watched the video replay. It was going to be a long night.

25

"Sonar, control. Report all contacts," Bishop requested as the time moved to the bottom of the hour.

"Control, sonar. Two surface vessels 50 miles out, bearing 039, USS *Michigan,* starboard side pacing us, distance 12 miles. Cross-sonar shows heavy activity to the west. The USS *Seawolf* is in and out of radar at bearing 260 — appears to be moving among the seamounts. Three distant contacts identified as Japanese Oyashio class submarines along bearing 210. Two distant contacts identified as Chinese Yuan class submarines along bearing 193. Numerous surface contacts along —"

An alarm interrupted the report, and the EAM box began to flash amber. They heard Emergency Action Message traffic for every boomer at sea, not just the *Nevada*. Bishop watched the flashing light on the box mounted at eye level near the periscope and waited for the radio room's call.

"EAM traffic for the *Nevada,* sir, requiring authentication."

The XO immediately reached for the intercom. "Alert one. Alert one."

Bishop snapped an order while heading toward the radio room. "XO, separate us from the *Michigan,* all speed. Make your heading 140."

"Heading 140, all speed, aye, Captain."

There were 15 officers aboard the boat, 5 of them currently on watch. The first two officers to reach the radio shack would begin decoding the encrypted message while the others moved to backfill roles.

The navigation officer and the weapons chief headed through the radio room connecting door to the adjoining operations control room. The captain often slept in the small room off the radio room during wartime so that messages could be passed to him as they arrived. For now, the bunk was a place to spread out top-secret code books. The radio room operators had some of the highest security clearances on the boat.

Bishop opened the room's safe, then used the commander's key to open the gray box.

"Captain, the authentication number is 24593," the weapons chief reported.

"I concur, sir, the number is 24593," the navigation officer repeated.

Bishop pulled the foil-wrapped package number matching 24593. Kingman joined him, and Bishop handed it to him. Kingman tore it open and pulled out the card. Bishop watched as his XO and the weapons chief worked through the long sequence of numbers and letters.

"We have an authentic message from Strategic Command," Kingman reported briskly.

"I concur, sir," the weapons chief said.

"Very well. Decrypt the message." EAMs arrived with the message scrambled into four-letter block groups.

The XO flipped through the orange-covered top-secret binder to the corresponding four-letter code leading the first message text block and entered *Nevada*'s decryption key. The message descrambled on the screen, and the printer behind them activated.

Bishop read the orders, pulled the print-out, and checked the authentication code against the card as a final verification. Bishop had hoped to never read this message without a three-peat of the word DRILL beginning and ending the message.

"We are in agreement it is an authentic

message, decoded correctly?" Bishop asked once all four officers had reviewed the text and the authentication card match. The boat didn't act on an EAM action order unless four officers aboard — the captain and the XO, plus the two working on the message — concurred on the decrypted message contents and authenticity.

"I concur, sir," each man in turn said.

"Weapons, enable the missile system."

"Enable the missile system, aye, sir," the officer replied. The weapons chief headed down a level to the missile control room where he alone had the safe combination and within it the key to enable the *Nevada*'s missile system.

Bishop looked over at his XO, then at his officers. "I want care, gentleman, nothing rushed, with an eye to every detail. Take your stations."

Bishop returned to command-and-control, reached for the intercom and turned the setting to 1MC. "*Nevada,* this is the captain. We have authenticated EAM traffic. Prepare to launch. This is not a drill."

The light on the commander's panel turned green, showing the missile system aboard the USS *Nevada* was now engaged.

"Weapons, load the launch package, Nevada Echo Charlie 792 on missiles 9 and 16."

The weapons officer read back the launch package code, confirming the order.

"Reading launch package Nevada Echo Charlie 792 on missiles 9 and 16," the XO confirmed from his station as the guidance systems on the missiles began feeding back flight information.

"Very well."

While classified above Top Secret, the launch packages did have a method to them. Echo Charlie was North Korea. The North Korean capital, Pyongyang, the nuclear reactor at Yongbyon, the weapons facility at Kanggyesi, underground nuclear storage and development labs — which of these locations would be hit, from one of them to all, would be determined by the fire order when it came.

Bishop's hands felt cold. If EAM traffic came in with the safe combination for the missile trigger, he would feel the full weight of this command.

They were only two EAM messages away from a missile launch, a captain's message signaling the U.S. National Command had moved to DEFCON 1, a war footing, and a fire order from the president.

That fire order would come in four parts.

A numbered listing of which locations in the launch package to strike, the time window for the *Nevada* to launch the missiles — coordination necessary so that the warheads didn't explode while U.S. Air Force bombers were within the target range — along with the combination for the safe aboard the *Nevada* holding the firing trigger, and a final authentication code direct from the president.

After the arrival of the fire order message, it would take the *Nevada* roughly 12 minutes to be ready to put missiles in the air. They would authenticate the message, come to launch depth, set launch pressure on missiles 9 and 16, and then fire the missiles within the specified launch time window. It would be the longest dozen minutes of Bishop's life.

"Sonar, control. Where's the *Michigan*?"

"Control, sonar. Separating rapidly, bearing 310, 32 miles."

Bishop looked to his second-in-command, read the contained tension he too was feeling. His question about how Kingman would handle command was going to be resolved by the end of this patrol. He trusted Kingman to be his second tonight, helping double-check every detail and order. "XO, make a visual inspection of the missile system to confirm our control board readings," he ordered.

"Yes, sir." His XO moved into the heart of the sub.

"Radio, control. Who else received directed EAM traffic in the last 20 minutes?" The messages might be encrypted, but the destinations told him a great deal.

"*Michigan, Ohio, Kentucky, Henry Jackson,* and the *Seawolf,* sir."

"Very well." That list told him the *Michigan* would also likely be sitting with missiles hot right now, prepared to fire. If a fire order came, he hoped it would be for conventionally armed Tomahawks rather than Trident II D-5s. He wanted to know what had just happened in the world to trigger this. Strategic Command would inform him soon.

He waited. And he hoped this order was only a precaution.

A warble alarm sounded in the command-and-control center. The EAM's amber light began to flash.

"Informational EAM, sir, for the *Nevada,* captain's eyes only."

"Very well." Bishop went to the radio room and accepted the printed message, stepped into the operations room, found the four-letter code block and the *Nevada*'s decryption key, entered it into the system along with his captain's code. The printer came to life behind him. He tore off the message and took it with him into the command-and-control center, reading as he went.

North Korea fired a missile, which hit in the Sea of Japan. Attempt to intercept the missile by U.S. only partially successful. Explosive warhead aboard. Believed at this time to be conventional. North Korea has second missile at launch site fueled. Launch deemed likely, but may not be imminent.

Bishop now had the reason for the launch-package order. Had that explosive payload been nuclear, the U.S. would already be laying down ordnance across the launch site and all nuclear facilities in North Korea, and the U.S. president would be in the Situation Room, deciding if a nuclear strike was required to take out North Korea's underground nuclear storage facilities believed to house its developed warheads. If their commander in chief gave the order, the *Nevada* was going to be on the receiving end of a fire order EAM. If it stayed with a conventional response, *Michigan* would get the fire order for her Tomahawks.

What Japan did in retaliation, what China might choose to do to influence North Korea . . . the situation was both volatile and unpredictable. Japan could hit North Korea back herself, or Japan could prevail on the U.S. to respond on her behalf. But the one thing Bishop knew about nations moving toward war, this wasn't going to unfold based on some rational plan, but as a series of provocations and responses based on the information at hand, whether complete or not.

Bishop passed the EAM message to his XO. Kingman read it, then quietly asked, "Do you still think the torpedo fired at the *Seawolf* was an accident?"

"I think it's China trying to provoke the other side into firing first. They rattled a South Korean submarine captain into making a mistake by firing on a U.S. sub. Now they're using North Korea to stir the pot and get a response from Japan."

"China wants the islands and the gas field as their price for exerting influence on North Korea not to fire another missile."

"That would be my read of it," Bishop replied. "It's going to be an interesting few days while that missile sits on a North

Korea launcher, fueled and ready to fly. Our intercept missile didn't score a direct hit on the first one. That's going to rattle the nerves even more."

"Does Japan back down? Concede the islands under dispute?"

"There are a lot of islands that are basically two rocks and a seal sunning itself," Bishop said. "Japan can't afford to set a precedent by surrendering on this dispute, but neither does it want to lose men and treasure defending rocks in the ocean. It's the gas field that is the real territorial fight, and it extends into international waters. They both want to develop the field. The U.S. has a hard call to make: fire a Tomahawk and take out the North Korea missile at its launch site, and by doing so enter the conflict, or continue to try to monitor and influence what unfolds, try to keep the two sides from a collision without directly stepping in."

"We can hold ready for launch for days. The crew is solid."

Bishop nodded his agreement. "That second missile is North Korea's leverage and their threat — what payload is on it, what it might hit. I think they're going to use it for maximum advantage. The odds are good they wait a day or two. They'll want the public outcry from the first missile to sink in first. They fire number two when they perceive it's to their advantage."

Bishop picked up the phone. "Sonar, control. Report all contacts."

"Control, sonar. Clear waters within our own sonar range. Surface ship traffic is now off scope to the east, the USS *Michigan* off scope to our north."

"Very well."

He considered where he needed the boat for the next two watches. He looked at the navigation map. "Navigation, put us in a diamond pattern for the next 12 hours, 3 hours per leg, squared off to the patrol box center."

"Yes, sir." The navigation chief traced in the plan and ran a vector. "Recommend *Nevada* turn to bearing 210 degrees."

"Conn, make your bearing 210 degrees, depth 600 feet."

The conn officer repeated the order and passed it on to the helmsman and planesman.

The problem with a boat waiting with her missile system engaged and a launch package loaded was the adrenaline every sailor aboard felt. Managing his crew was going to be as critical as managing the boat. Bishop picked up the intercom. "*Nevada,* this is the captain. If you are not on watch, find a bunk and get some sleep. That's an order."

He placed his hand on the shoulder of the man watching over the *Nevada*'s internal systems. "Lieutenant, set all audio channels to my personal playlist for the next hour."

The man smiled, the first seen in the command-and-control center in the last hour. "Yes, sir."

Bishop turned to his second-in-command. "Kingman, you're now off duty. I need you to get some sleep. You'll have the deck after me."

"Yes, sir."

Bishop picked up the phone. "Weapons, tell your two deputies to find their bunks."

"Yes, sir."

Time wore heavy on the *Nevada* when patrolling with missiles ready to fire.

"Lieutenant Olson. A question for you," Bishop said.

"Yes, sir."

"What does a Trident D-5 missile weigh?"

"One hundred thirty thousand pounds, sir."

"How do we keep the *Nevada* level once a missile fires?"

"Missile-compensation tanks, sir. They fill

with seawater to compensate for the lost weight."

"Good answer."

The force of the launch would push the boat down, but then the boat would abruptly bounce up one hundred thirty thousand pounds lighter. Seawater filling the empty tube would help with that weight differential, but they would still be thousands of pounds lighter in the immediate moments after launch.

The XO entered the command-and-control center. Bishop thought he might have slept a few hours of the six he'd been off duty. "The world hasn't changed," Bishop said by way of an update, and handed to the XO a thick stack of informational messages to read. Strategic Command had been using the time to backfill in everything that had occurred with the *Seawolf* and China's fleet, making sure all its commanders were fully informed. Buried in the general section on communication issues was the reference to a solar flare occurring and intermittent static expected on the comm radio bands. It was a nicely slid-in reference for those who knew what else it meant. Bishop glanced at the time in the note and then his watch; 42 hours from now there would be a photo, and he could think of nothing he would like more to see.

The reference to the solar flare also told him his wife was likely in the TCC right now. The *Seawolf* had been shot at with a torpedo, North Korea was firing loaded missiles, and he was getting launch preparation orders. His hope that Gina would have a calm 90 days was now a distant memory. He hoped Gina wasn't dealing with this alone, that Daniel was still ashore and able to help, but he knew there might have been a rushed deployment ordered when the trouble started that put the *Nebraska* to sea. He couldn't let himself think about what this might be doing to Gina . . . or how she would handle the next deployment when it came.

"I'm current, sir," Kingman said, reaching the end of the updates.

Bishop nodded as he accepted them back. "XO, would you like the deck?"

"Yes, sir." Kingman checked with every officer in command-and-control, picked up the phone and called engineering, then checked with sonar. "I am ready to relieve you, sir."

Bishop knew the pressure he was putting on his XO's shoulders with this decision, but he thought Kingman was ready for it. "Every 15 minutes, call sonar and ask for a full sweep, the radio room to ask about all new radio traffic of any priority, check with navigation for our position in the patrol box, ask engineering for a review of all pressure readings. Make sure the boat isn't going to ram into a seamount or otherwise miss a routine concern. Normal submarine operational warnings can get missed when one threat becomes the crew's entire focus."

"Yes, sir."

Bishop moved from the captain's chair. "The XO now has the deck," he broadcast to the boat. He turned to Kingman. "I'm going to sleep for four hours. Err on the side of waking me with news or changes in the waters around the *Nevada.*"

"Will do, Captain."

The phone woke him, and he was alert in an instant. "Bishop here."

"EAM traffic, sir, captain's eyes only."

"Very well." He pushed his feet into tennis shoes and ran a hand through his hair, headed out of his stateroom. Sailors made room for him in the passageway and on the ladder. Bishop could feel their tension as the crew members watched him climb up to the command-and-control center. He scanned the room as he walked through, nodded his approval to the XO at what he saw, then made his way to the radio room.

Bishop accepted the printout, moved into the small operations control room, and picked up the orange binder on the bunk. He flipped pages to the four-letter code leading the message text block and traced down the page to *Nevada*'s decryption key. He entered it and his captain's code into the system. The printer came to life. Bishop tore off the first page and read while the rest printed. He closed his eyes, breathed a prayer, and went to the command-and-control center to rejoin his XO when he had the full message.

"Bad news?" Kingman asked.

"China is missing a sub," Bishop said quietly.

Kingman winced. Bishop handed him the full message. It didn't say someone had fired at the Chinese submarine and hit it, but the Chinese surface-fleet movements showed the assumption they had made.

"Who do you guess made the error? South Korea? Japan?" Kingman asked.

"At this point it's not going to matter."

Kingman reread the message. "Do you think it's really been lost at sea? Or is it playing possum on purpose to give China another reason to escalate?"

"You can tell from the wording that Strategic Command is wondering the same thing," Bishop replied.

"Let's hope they get the *Seawolf* out of there."

Bishop nodded. The front line of this skirmish was coming right at the *Seawolf.* China was mounting an aggressive search to find its missing boat.

"The captain has the deck," he announced, taking authority back from the XO. He moved with Kingman over to the navigation table. "We know China's military is running on high alert. They've lost two diesel submarines in the past to accidents. It's possible, given the circumstances, they had a catastrophic failure aboard the boat. A torpedo accident, an engine overheated and got away from them. But knowing the *Seawolf* had been fired upon, China is going to proceed under the assumption it was hostile fire."

Bishop looked at the topology to their southwest. "The coordinates put the last known location of the Chinese submarine here" — he tapped the map — "south of the seamounts in the East China Sea. That's a tough area to search. Sonar has to be able to look down into the terrain to see what's in the canyons and valleys. It's going to take days to search a reasonable-sized area.

China will be probing there, but they'll be wondering who else is below them that might have fired on their sub."

Bishop shifted his attention to the waters around the *Nevada.* "As tense as this is likely to get, I think we're okay with our current patrol box." He thought about it and made a decision. "XO, ask the chief of the boat to join me. I'm going to put senior enlisted and senior officers on the missile deck for the duration. Then walk the boat, pass on the news as we know it, check in with the department chiefs. Make sure sailors know this is not going to be a quick step down in alert. Reinforce the order to get some sleep when off watch."

"Yes, sir." Kingman headed out of command-and-control and deeper into the boat.

Every navy in the world dealt with the possibility of a submarine going down. There were rescue plans and protocols to deal with all possible accidents at sea, including agreements between nations to help each other. But if this loss of a sub was the result of hostile fire . . . Nothing in the EAM suggested the *Seawolf* had reported hearing an explosion or a torpedo, but it was likely the fast-attack was still at depth for its own safety, preventing them from sending a message back to Command.

Bishop ran a hand across the back of his neck. What they needed right now was time for the *Seawolf* to report in with whatever it had picked up. They needed that solar flare photo to tell them where that Chinese submarine was. Bishop just hoped the situation didn't escalate further before they had the means to get answers. Solving this was going to take the coordination of a lot of people doing their jobs, some wise leadership in various militaries counseling patience, and waiting rather than taking action. But he didn't trust that to happen tonight.

26

"How long till we have a photo?" Daniel asked.

Gina didn't bother to look again at the clock. She'd been glancing at it every five minutes. "Six hours and forty minutes." It had been a hot solar flare, and she anticipated having enough reflections to generate a detailed photo shortly after the energy burst hit the earth. But that moment was still hours away. In the meantime, she was trying to figure out another way around the problem. "There's been no sign of debris?"

"No," Daniel replied, scanning the boards again, reading the latest updates. "No sign of an oil slick, floating salvage, or discolored water."

An ocean map lined with search grids showed just where China was deploying its assets, both air and sea. The U.S. rescue group was dispatching boats from Hawaii to offer their assistance once the submarine was located. Somebody just had to find it. Gina was doing her best to ignore the news headlines and the flurry of exchanges and accusations flying back and forth between China, Japan, and South Korea. Only one thing would bring clarity to this situation, and that was the location of the missing sub.

"Daniel, what causes a sub to disappear?" It wasn't the first time she had asked the question, but it was a useful exercise. Daniel settled into the guest chair to think it through with her again.

"A catastrophic accident aboard the boat, it ends up on the seabed floor. It gets shot at, the hull breaches, it ends up on the seabed floor. It goes deep beyond the reach of low-frequency radio waves, doesn't hear attempts to contact it, doesn't come up to report in — most boats go to those depths only when the boat has structurally cracked, is taking on water, and has lost ballast tanks."

Gina nodded at the grim list. "Anything that might cause a sub to disappear that would *not* be a catastrophic problem?"

"It could be deliberately ignoring attempts to find it. It could be sitting on the ocean floor on the continental shelf — around 400 feet — basically saying 'find me if you can.' Or it could have deliberately sailed at speed out of the area, trying to stay beyond where others would think to look for it, be ignoring radio traffic from its own navy, for reasons we can only guess at."

"Which would make this part of a plan to create conditions for a war, so we'll skip those possibilities too. What else?"

Daniel thought about it, finally shook his head. "China uses a 30-minute 'we're alive' transponder fail-safe, Gina. Someone aboard the boat has to literally turn a key every half hour and reset the timer to keep that equipment from going off. If no one resets the timer within 30 minutes, the transponder turns on and begins to send a ping. It's macabre, but China wants to know where its boat is so it can retrieve a hundred-million-dollar submarine, even if the crew aboard is asphyxiated from smoke and dies during a fire.

"If the crew's alive and are turning the key, and they aren't deliberately trying to hide, then maybe —" Daniel paused, struggled to come up with a realistic option — "maybe it's a case where they can't send a message out even though they want to. A fire could do it, but a fire would have sent the sub to the surface to vent smoke, and they would have been seen by now, if nothing else by a satellite scanning the area."

Daniel leaned back in the chair, ran both hands through his hair. "I don't know, Gina. The more you think about it, this is a destroyed sub, either by accident or hostile act. We're submariners, we stay silent in the ocean, but that's different from not being in contact with our own National Command. They were noticed as missing because they failed to report in when expected to do so. They're in trouble. It's the only thing that fits."

She looked at the ocean map. "The sub might not be where China thinks it is. A lot of assumptions have been made to determine where to search."

"That's very possible," Daniel agreed.

Gina set aside her notebook, considered the activity going on in the TCC, trying to find a distraction so she could let her mind run for a few minutes on tangents, see if an idea might jell. She turned toward Daniel. "What if it was a collision, two subs hitting each other? A South Korean sub tried to follow the Chinese sub too closely, and the submarines collided? That last photo showed 38 submarines in these waters, running around at speed, while at the same time trying to listen so they wouldn't hit something."

"South Korea, Japan, both insist all their

submarines are accounted for, that they didn't fire on this Chinese sub or otherwise engage it."

"Would they admit it if they were responsible?" Gina asked.

"After this amount of time, we'd know if they were searching for a damaged submarine of their own or had a damaged sub coming into port. They couldn't hide that level of activity."

Gina thought about that, reluctantly nodded. "Okay, I buy that."

She looked out at the TCC ocean map, saw it shift to the topology overlay where the *Seawolf* remained on station. "What if the sub ran into something, but something that wasn't another sub?"

Daniel shot her a look. "You're thinking of the USS *San Francisco*?"

Gina nodded. "That collision with a seamount turned the front of the boat into a smashed can, took out everything in the sonar dome and radio room. What's to say the Chinese sub didn't try to mimic what the *Seawolf* is doing, go lurk among the seamounts, only to run into one of them? China doesn't have as accurate of topology maps as we do. I should know, the U.S. classified the accuracy of my work to keep it out of the public domain, and it's doubtful

China has had time to steal that data and get it deployed on their boats. It would have been difficult for China to tightly map that area from its own survey ships without causing an international incident." She looked again at the screen.

"A Chinese sub," she thought aloud, "trying to get into the disputed area and show China's presence, heads into that group of seamounts thinking she can do what the *Seawolf* is doing. It doesn't take much to get a 300-foot boat that can't do tight turns into a jam and hit something. We've had boomers hit a buoy on the Hood Canal, and that's with the boat on the surface, guys watching with binoculars, and clear visibility. Submarines are not graceful when they're around objects, and those seamounts are towering hundreds of feet from the seabed floor. China may have a sub that hit one of them in the disputed area. Now that I think about it, I'm getting incredibly nervous about what Jeff is doing. A ten-second mistake, begin a turn late or with a bit too much speed, and the U.S. is also searching for the *Seawolf* on the ocean floor."

Daniel leaned forward in his chair. "Your theory is plausible. It's even likely. I buy the premise China's sub hit something, and if you're right about what happened, that search grid China is running should eventually find the boat. They're working toward that area around the *Seawolf.* It might take days, though. It will be difficult to find the boat on sonar if it's gone down in one of the canyons. To see it, the search vessel would have to be directly above it."

"We need to shorten the time it's going to take. We don't have days. If the sub ran into something, like a seamount, that makes this an accident. A tragedy, but an accident. They didn't have good enough topology maps." She thought about that for a moment, then turned around and spun the dial on her office safe. "Can you get me an outside phone line? Outside of the Navy?"

"Maybe. Lockdowns in the TCC are tricky. Who do you need to call?"

"I need to talk with Kevin Taggert."

"Taggert. Former boyfriend Taggert? You're sure?"

"Yes."

Daniel got to his feet. "Give me a minute."

Gina hung up the phone, still typing.

"What are you bringing across?" Daniel asked.

"Data from the Jason satellite for the last few days. And that visual data set on the second terminal is the current magnetic map of the earth."

Daniel studied the rotating orange and red ball. "It looks likes a deformed, half-dehydrated orange."

She smiled briefly. "It does. Everyone thinks the earth is this perfect ball of dirt with a hot molten rock core, when it's really a magnetized bunch of hot rocks flowing around under pressure. How much iron is in the ground, how deep the ocean is at a particular point, all affects the magnetic map of the earth."

She brought up the topology map for the Taiwan-to-Japan section of the Pacific on the third screen. She'd created these high-resolution maps, but their details still caught her breath with their beauty. They were a combination of the earth's magnetic field data with the Jason survey data.

"What are you thinking?" Daniel asked.

"If the missing submarine hit something, and hit it hard, it wasn't just the sub that got damaged. It would put a crater in a sea-mount, cause an underwater avalanche, and somewhere there should be a footprint of the collision. I'm going to build the seabed topology map as it existed last week and as it exists today. And hope we find a collision site and an answer."

"Interesting. How long will this take?"

The data mirror locked in. "Data is across. Alert Captain Strong I'm dispersing into the computer cluster a large-scale data problem, and I'm about to absorb a lot of computing power. I'm recreating the seabed maps for the East China Sea before and after this sub disappeared. I'll have those two photos in a couple of hours if this doesn't hiccup on me."

Daniel was out of the room before her sentence was finished.

"Admiral Hardman . . . we have an answer." Gina got the words out around a throat that was tightening, her speech starting to lock up, slightly out of breath after having run from the printer room with the photo of what they'd spotted on the screen.

"What am I looking at?"

Daniel stepped in to help her, spreading the large photos out on the nearest desk. "Something ran into seamount M6SN8 and hit it with such force it cracked off the spire and put a new cavity in the east side of the mountain. These are the before and after photos a week apart. This wasn't a geological, naturally occurring event. Something slammed into it. Sir, you need to ask the Chinese if their navigational maps show a seamount at this location. They probably didn't know it was there. We've had a repeat of the USS *San Francisco,* sir. Their sub hit it with speed, not realizing it was there."

"Where's the boat?"

"That's the good news, sir. We don't see the sub on the seabed floor in this area. We should see at least part of the hull in these photos if the impact led to its immediate implosion. So we assume for now the sub is still afloat. Afloat but badly damaged. From the collision impact, I'm guessing she's got very little of her front dome left, sir — sonar and radio are probably gone. And she's got ballast-tank problems, as the sub hasn't been able to surface for a satellite to spot her. The sub's probably trying to make it back home, but who knows if the crew can figure out which way is west right now. They may be traveling the wrong direction. If the impact site is right here, and she's been traveling at half speed at best, the sub is somewhere in this circle. The boat isn't going to be quiet, sir. We just need to get ears into the right area to hear it."

"China is searching in the wrong area," Hardman said, studying the two photos.

"Yes, sir."

Hardman turned to Captain Strong. "Send tasking orders to the *Seawolf.* Put it at this collision site and start a spiral search outward. It's the nearest boat we've got in the area."

"Yes, sir."

Gina felt relief, both that their discovery was being accepted as a workable theory, and that the *Seawolf* was being ordered out of her current position. "Sir," she began tentatively, "I know the topology map accuracy is classified. But if you send the Chinese the before and after seamount photos, maybe it gets them to calm down and see this as a possible accident while the search is under way."

"If we can't find the sub within the next several hours, we'll consider it. They know we can do a topology map of the ocean floor from space, but we'd rather not give away just how good these maps are." Hardman checked the time. "Where are we at for the solar flare photo?"

Daniel consulted the timer on his watch. "Two hours ten minutes, sir."

"That photo is going to be our best answer to this crisis. Let's hope the boat is afloat and the next photo can show us where it is."

The images were barely smudges, it was so early in the data collection. The algorithms showed a dot or two where a submarine might be. Gina had the stretch of ocean from Taiwan to South Korea spread across the three screens, zooming in to check out the smudges.

"Look at all those possible subs. I'm at 64," Daniel offered, leaning close to the nearest monitor as he finished his count. "There's hardly anybody left in port."

Gina watched a dot on the photo disappear. "Another half hour and the ones which aren't submarines will be scrubbed out. But at this point, all real subs should now be showing, so we can start overlaying what the TCC knows against this. We'll eliminate those we can identify."

Daniel pointed to the middle screen. "From the previous data we know these four subs are Japanese, these two are South Korean."

Gina dropped a blue circle around them.

"I think we can eliminate any points that China had a surface boat pass over during its search." She dropped yellow circles around them. "That takes most of these out of the equation. What else can we eliminate?"

Daniel pointed. "Anything to the east of this island can't be our missing sub, as the distance from the collision site is too great."

She dropped gray circles around them, then had an idea. "Daniel, see if you can get someone in the TCC to give us a real-time radio-wave-transmission map. We don't care what the content is, just that there's radio traffic originating from a location. Our sub isn't sending traffic, so any smudge sending out radio traffic is one we can eliminate."

"Great idea. Let me see what the guys can get us." Once more Daniel pushed back his chair and headed into the TCC proper.

The photo resolution was improving, turning smudges into more defined forms. Gina rolled her shoulders and neck to fight the tightness from her sitting so long. A third had been identified from TCC data, radio traffic had eliminated another third, and the distance from the possible collision site ruled out several more. The *Seawolf* was now named and circled in black.

She set blinking red boxes around four images.

Daniel turned to look at her. "You think?"

Gina nodded. "Get Hardman."

"This has to be the sub, sir," Daniel told Rear Admiral Hardman, pointing at the screen. "The other candidates imply a speed of travel from the collision site that, while theoretically possible, isn't practical for a damaged boat." Others were crowded into Gina Bishop's office to look at the marked-up photo.

"Captain Strong?"

"I concur, sir. If that's the missing China sub, she's quite a distance east of the collision site, and heading into the middle of the Pacific — meaning she's lost. But their premise of a collision fits the topology data. The sub's been found, sir."

Hardman nodded. "Flash orders to the *Seawolf* of a sub in distress, with these coordinates. Confirm and render assistance."

"Yes, sir."

"Follow it with a message to the *Nevada* to turn east and come within cross-sonar range of the *Michigan* again. Let's see what cross-sonar can pick up at these coordinates."

Strong hesitated. "Both are holding launch-hot missiles, sir."

"It can't be helped. If we've located China's boat, only to find it as she's sinking, I need the sonar recordings of what is happening before she drops to the ocean floor. If we can't give the Chinese back their boat with her crew alive, we'll need to be able to prove to their satisfaction we know where the wreckage went down. I can't give them the photo, which is why I need the cross-sonar recordings. But do warn our crews not to bump into each other."

Strong smiled. "Yes, sir."

Commander Mark Bishop leaned against the door and watched as Sonar Chief Larry Penn worked the hydrophone acoustics in order to get the best overlay.

Penn flipped a switch, putting the audio on the speakers. "That's got to be it, Bishop. The diesel plant is running, but those are damaged screws. And I'm hearing waffle bubbles. They don't have a smooth hull."

"Sounds a bit like a meat grinder stuck and trying to break free," Bishop decided after listening for a minute. "It's far east of the collision site, and well outside where China is searching."

"A weird place to be," Penn agreed. "Depth is fluctuating rapidly, presently about 300 feet and struggling to rise. This has to be the missing Chinese sub. I wonder how Command found it to give us these coordinates."

Bishop didn't reply to the idly asked question. Enough time had passed since the solar flare that he knew Tactical Command would have had a photo to work from. "Where's the *Michigan?*"

"Pacing 14 miles off our starboard side, sir," Sonarman Tulley answered.

"Keep a close eye on him. I want to hear any change in speed or direction."

"Yes, sir."

"The *Seawolf?*"

The sonarman monitoring the narrow-band console leaned forward and checked a line in the waterfall. "Ten miles northwest of the crippled boat now, sir, and slowing."

Bishop walked toward the radio room. He was hoping for an EAM that would let him step the missiles back a level from launch and remove the flight guidance package. He was hoping, but knew it wasn't likely to arrive soon. The nations involved had to move toward peace, a careful step-by-step process that took diplomatic time and attention.

If this was China's missing sub — and he thought it was — how the boat had been damaged was still an open question. North Korea still had a missile on the launch pad, fueled and ready to fly, with an unknown payload aboard. The world hadn't gotten safer yet; the situation had simply become a bit clearer.

Bishop quietly thanked God for the ability to get that photo. Clarity right now might be the one thing keeping the world from plunging into another war.

The Pentagon had a drone on station above the recovery site. Gina watched the video from the back row of the theater seats. Relief, joy, worry, fear — the emotions had all passed through her mind in the last few hours. At the moment she just wanted to close her eyes and for someone to say this was over.

China had three ships and a sub on the surface rendering assistance to the damaged sub. Crewmen were leaving the sub five at a time now, transported by small craft across to one of the surface ships. The USS *Seawolf* had been on the surface for a time, visible in the drone video feed, but had now slipped back into the sea.

The air cradle the *Seawolf* had deployed floated like a bright yellow bladder on either side of the damaged sub, replacing the buoyancy of the destroyed ballast tanks and holding the submarine on the surface. The *Seawolf* had shot the cradle out of a torpedo tube, then pumped in air from her own air locks to partially inflate it. It had given time for the sea-rescue ships to arrive on station and get more permanent ballast tanks in place. Thankfully the ocean was calm today;

otherwise holding the damaged sub at the surface would have been all but impossible.

"It's a wonder that boat wasn't destroyed at the time of the collision," Daniel said, holding out a sandwich he'd picked up for her.

"It looks like the collision tore a gash down the left side of the hull and crumpled the front," Gina said. "Any word on the crew?"

"Initial word is six seriously injured, three missing and presumed dead, out of a crew of 87."

She winced. "Families are going to be suffering tonight."

"They could have all been lost. That crew did an incredible job saving their boat. I admire what I see."

She unwrapped the sandwich, looked at Daniel. "We've proven this was an accident, a collision with a seamount, but the rest of the situation hasn't changed much. It just reverted back to where the world was before China's sub went missing. China and Japan are still in a territorial dispute over islands and a seabed gas field. North Korea still has a missile on the launcher, armed with an unknown payload."

Daniel nodded. "This incident and our response bought us some goodwill," he added. "One of the engineers aboard is the grandson of the Chinese premier. Our military found the sub, our guys helped coordinate the rescue. It means the U.S. saved some lives. China will feel honor-bound to listen to what our military has to say on the other matters of concern. That's a win-win all the way around. Maybe it's enough goodwill that China will help temper what North Korea is doing, send China's own fleet back to port, and let diplomats continue to negotiate over the disputed lands. This flare-up of trouble gets quieted back down. That's a good outcome. Nothing gets solved in the immediate term, but we get peace for another day. We were able to use cross-sonar, the topology maps, and your photo to unravel this mystery without giving the Chinese any indication we had those capabilities — another excellent outcome."

"I hope you're right." Gina ate another bite of the sandwich. "It was nice to realize the topology maps could be used this way. I wouldn't have thought of before-and-after maps to see a collision until the particulars of this event suggested it. And the solar flare photo worked, even if it was still a pretty fuzzy image."

"It told us right where to look. It was

wonderful. You said it was a hot solar flare. What are the odds we have another flare in the next week or two?"

"Maybe five percent. There won't be another one of size for another three weeks is my guess."

"You'll be able to get some sleep then. They're talking about lifting the lockdown in a couple of hours. Would you rather stay around here, or would you like me to see about getting you home?"

Gina looked at the ocean board. "Any word on where the *Seawolf* is heading next?"

"My guess, the *Seawolf* will move to provide fast-attack security for the *Nevada* and *Michigan.*"

That made sense to her. Something had to be done about the North Korea missile on the launch pad. But if she waited for the world to get more peaceful, she would never leave the building. Her husband and her brother were good at their jobs; they would handle whatever came. And she was going to trust them. "I'm ready to go home now."

"We are in agreement this EAM message is properly authenticated and decoded?" Bishop asked, looking around the assembled officers.

"I concur, sir," each officer said in turn.

Bishop turned to his weapons chief. "Bring the missile system back to quiet status."

"Yes, sir."

The weapons officer headed down a level to the missile control room. North Korea had removed its second missile from the launch pad. This particular crisis was coming to a close. "Thank you, gentlemen. Return to your stations."

Bishop went back to command-and-control, reached for the intercom and turned the setting to 1MC. "*Nevada,* this is the captain. We have authenticated EAM traffic. Stand down from launch."

He saw the palpable relief among those on duty and knew the feeling was now rippling through the boat.

The light on the commander's panel turned off, showing the missile system aboard the USS *Nevada* now disengaged. Ten days with the *Nevada* at launch status had ended without a missile being fired.

"Petty Officer Hill, how many days remain in this patrol?"

The officer reached into his pocket and pulled out a scorecard. "Days remaining . . . 26, sir."

"Circle today, if you would."

They would be coming off hard-alert in another two days — the USS *Louisiana* would take their place — and they would no longer be required to stay within the patrol box, only be near enough to return to it in a few hours should they be called back to hard-alert status. Bishop studied the charts on the navigation table. He was looking for an area in the northern half of the Pacific where it was unlikely they would meet someone else. There was normally a pod or two of whales traveling along the deep ocean current toward Alaska this time of year. "Conn, bring us to heading 030, make our depth 700 feet."

"Bearing 030, depth 700 feet, aye, Captain."

He'd go find those whales and follow them around for a while. The boat was facing a packed 26 days getting caught up on the maintenance deferred while the missile system was enabled. The normal halfway celebration with skits and jokes and videos from home, the surf-and-turf meal of lobster and steak, had been set aside by events. Off hard-alert now, he'd find something to give the crew some laughter and much-needed stress relief.

Nevada gold families would have seen the missile launch and the damaged sub on the news. Would they have anticipated the rest of it? The orders their husbands had received? When they reached shore, the crew would never talk about the fact they had enabled the missile system and prepared to fire — what happened on the boat stayed on the boat. But they would take the urgency, the weight of this patrol, home with them just the same.

Bishop pulled a photo out of his pocket, glanced at it, and slipped it back into the pocket over his heart. His wife knew. She would have been in the TCC and seen most, if not all, of what had occurred — enough to know the danger to her brother and to himself. He wondered what shape his wife and his marriage was going to be in when he got back to shore.

His XO stepped into the command-and-control center. "We've got a problem, sir."

"What is it?"

Kingman took his hand from behind his back and held up a full-sized lobster. "The cook says it doesn't fit in the pot."

Laughter rippled through the room.

Bishop smiled. Apparently the culinary crew had decided on a celebration for tonight. Bishop could see some obstacles with it, but nothing they couldn't work around. "I'll take that one broiled, butter on the side. Surf and turf at seven bells. We'll rotate one-hour watches. Ask Nicholas not to burn my steak this time."

"Yes, sir," Kingman said with a grin, then spun on his heel and left with the lobster. The culinary crew brought one live lobster aboard for the halfway night feast so they could fashion a center display and offer it to the captain. The rest of the lobster for the crew was in the freezer. Lobster and steak — it would serve a good purpose and give the crew a nice break.

Bishop felt himself relax. His crew was fine, his boat in good shape. The world was heading back toward peaceful. Twenty-six days from now he'd no longer be carrying the enormous responsibility of the *Nevada* and her mission. He'd end this patrol with a few more gray hairs, tired to the bone, but he'd get the boat home safely. *Nevada* gold could handle the rest of the patrol with the same skill they had displayed over the last several weeks. He settled into the captain's chair. And he said a prayer for his crew and their safety.

27

Bishop had long ago memorized the checklist a ballistic missile submarine executed once it nudged the pier. He scanned power settings on the command-and-control consoles, watched engineering reconfigure the boat to take power from shore in preparation for shutdown of the nuclear reactor. The officer manning the sequence had it well in hand. Bishop waited until the handoff was ready for the pier crew to physically connect the cables. "You did a solid job during this patrol, Olson," he said.

"Thank you, sir."

"Family waiting for you?"

"At the Squadron 17 ready room, sir. You?"

Bishop found the photo in his pocket that the ombudsman had handed him, along with her shore summary, and turned the photo to show the sailor. "My wife is at the vet with a sick puppy." Pongo had grown so much in three months he looked ungainly. Gina's note of welcome, along with the news, was scrawled on the back of the photo. It also had a border of X's and O's and a nicely drawn smiley face. Mark was taking it as good indication she'd meet him with a welcoming smile when they finally both got free.

The fact Gina was electing to take the dog to the vet rather than be on the pier to meet him — struggling to hide her emotions about what had almost happened — didn't escape his notice. He had the distinct impression her absence was deliberate. Gina was keeping arrival day low-key, trying to say with her actions that this was just a normal part of life and what a commander's wife did. She waved him off on patrol, said "hello" and "welcome home" when he got back. It wasn't what Mark had been expecting, but it had its interesting merits. She knew his focus had to be on the boat for the first few hours pier-side.

The photo told him she was okay — *that* was the important news. There wasn't anything in the ombudsman's shore summary about his wife having fallen and broken a leg or something of that nature. He'd scanned it for her name as soon as he was handed the document. His wife would find her way to him eventually.

Bishop pulled the note pad from his pocket and jotted down another three items to remember on his hand-over report. *Nevada* blue was going to be given a boat that showed the stress of this patrol. Missiles 9 and 16 were going to have to be lifted out and put on the test bench to confirm their guidance systems had properly cleared. Bishop was considering making the move to the Explosives Handling Wharf tomorrow evening to deal with those missiles before hand-over. But it might be better to leave it for *Nevada* blue to oversee, as the loading of new missiles without incident would be high on their own concerns list.

"Sir, your wife is topside."

Mark swiftly turned, nodded his thanks to his sonar chief, reached for his sunglasses, and hurried up the ladder into the sail. Gina Bishop had crossed the walkway and was standing on the steel deck of the *Nevada,* talking with his chief engineer and the *Nevada*'s ombudsman. Mark smiled when he looked down from the sail and saw her, then leaned his arms against the metal warmed by the sun. "Hi there, precious."

She looked up, smiled, lifted her hand. "Hey, sailor, welcome home."

"How's our dog?"

"No longer enamored with the flowers I planted by the back porch," she called up to him. "He ate a few, and the insecticide I used made him sick. At least the vet thinks that was the culprit."

"That would do it." He moved over to the ladder and left the sail for the deck.

She came to meet him and leaned against his chest in an embrace that turned into more than just a welcome home. It became a sanctuary for them both. "I'm so glad you're home, Mark," she whispered.

He smoothed a hand across her back. "Glad to be here." He waited to see if she wanted to say anything else, and when she didn't, he dropped a kiss on her hair and circled her shoulders with an arm. "How much new science did you have to invent to get us out of that jam?" he asked softly.

"I may have reapplied a bit of it," she answered with a small smile. "You had a busy patrol."

"I think you probably saw the worst of it," he reassured. "The *Seawolf* got home safely?"

"Docked last week," she said. "Jeff is getting married. He proposed to Tiffany about an hour after he stepped off the boat."

Bishop grinned. "Good for him."

"Going to be a few more hours before you

can get away?"

"About four."

"I'm thinking a fruit salad and omelet, hot shower and back rub, whenever you manage to cross the threshold of home. I'll tell you the rest of the news then."

"You've got yourself a deal and a date."

She held out car keys and a cell phone. "Security will give me a lift home. Call if you aren't going to make it before midnight." There was just the edge of a tremor in her hand as he accepted the keys, and he shot her a more careful look. Joy, not stress, but she was fighting not to shed tears, determined to make this casual for the sake of the crew. No scenes by the captain's wife, even though her emotions were running high.

He leaned down and kissed her. "Thank you for marrying me, Gina," he whispered.

Her full smile about stopped his heart, and she added to the emotion when she lifted her hand, rested it against his chest over his heart, and lightly patted him twice. "You look pretty good to me, sailor. Come home when you can."

Bishop laughed and pocketed the keys as she walked back across the gangway to the pier. His wife was learning to flirt.

■ ■ ■ ■

Mark walked through the door to his home shortly after nine p.m. At first the dog growled at him, but then he recognized Mark and floppily jumped and bumped his hand. Both cats stalked into the hall to see what the fuss was about and took a perch on the stairs to consider him.

The hall light turned on near the kitchen. "Your welcome-home committee needs more practice. I didn't hear the car."

He smiled and dropped his bag by the door. "They'll remember me after a few days." He joined her and folded her in his arms, content to simply hold her for a long while, relearning the smell of her shampoo and her habit of burrowing her hands against his chest between them. She let him take all her weight. She belonged here in his arms. Life felt good again. "Hi."

She leaned back and pulled his head down to kiss him lightly. "Let me get you fed."

She'd changed during the last three months, and he was beginning to notice a number of the ways. Definitely lost some weight — she'd felt thin in that hug. Her smile was more confident. And something else . . . "You changed your hair."

She laughed as she stepped into the kitchen. "Blame the wives of *Nevada* gold. We had this get-together at the beauty shop, a 'before the guys get home' party. It was a riot, but I nearly got turned into a redhead. I managed to get a hair color a shade lighter, plus highlights to go with a trim."

He gratefully accepted the glass of iced tea she held out. "Your husband likes it."

"Good, because the only option is to watch it grow out."

Melinda's colored bottles on display had been joined by pottery, the counter had acquired three cookbooks, a cake plate with glass dome had donuts under its lid, the kitchen table had been covered with a red-and-white-checkered cloth, and irises clustered in a tall vase.

Gina cracked eggs for an omelet. "Bacon, ham, mushrooms, and cheese sound okay?"

"Wonderful. Powdered eggs just don't cut it after a while." He got a spoon out of the drawer, retrieved the already made fruit salad from the top shelf of the refrigerator, found a smaller bowl, and pulled out a chair at the table. Fresh fruit had disappeared from the *Nevada* a few days before the eggs, and he'd been craving a good peach. To his delight he found a layer of peach slices in the fruit salad. "Anything else you ladies did together?"

"We had baking days, garage sales, kid-fun trips. There are a lot of casseroles shoved into freezers, so time doesn't have to be spent cooking meals, scrapbooks on what happened during the patrol, and a few houses with new paint jobs inside. We wives stayed busy."

Bishop laughed at the way she said it. Gina had settled in with the group, that much was clear. As the captain's wife she would have been invited to everything. Opportunities to make friends among the gold crew must have been abundant. "No major accidents or problems?"

"A snake in the yard I could have done without. I fell asleep one day and burned a pan of brownies, set off the smoke detector. And there are too many sounds in this house at night I'm not accustomed to yet, so security walked the place a few times when I was uncomfortable. I lost a cat on three different occasions — eventually figured out they were sleeping in an odd spot and ignoring me."

Bishop looked down at the cats now stalking the dog's tail. Pongo had crashed on his shoe to anchor Bishop from moving anywhere. "Cats will be cats," he offered. "I see bells on their collars — those are new."

"They've figured out how to move slowly enough so the bells don't ring."

Bishop grinned. "Of course."

She turned the eggs and added items to the omelet. "Jeff is off on R and R somewhere, but he promised he'll make Chicago on the 20th for our wedding celebration. Your mom and I have the invitations ready to go in the mail tomorrow if the date still works for you."

Bishop smiled. "It does."

"Good, because I already ordered the cake for that date."

She folded over the omelet and slid it onto a plate, brought it over to the table for him. She took a seat next to his.

"How's Daniel?" Mark asked.

"Good." She rested her chin on her palm. "He was invaluable at the TCC. He headed out with the *Nebraska* five days ago. I made him a dozen music playlists to take with him — our credit card kind of whimpered," she admitted. When he only chuckled, she went on, "I promised I'd keep an eye on the new saltwater aquarium he's added to his place."

Mark nodded and reached for a napkin.

"He pulled me into the TCC just before lockdown closed the doors, so we had a front-row seat to everything that happened. It was helpful to have him as a sounding board while it was unfolding."

"That's one of the reasons I wanted him with you."

"It helped, Mark, hearing his perspective. We figured out what happened with China's sub by creating new topology maps for the East China Sea before and after the sub went missing. We spotted the seamount it hit. From there, it was simply a matter of figuring out where the crippled sub was, and a photo helped with that."

"Your science did its job."

"A very good job," she agreed. "By the way, Daniel has recently met an ocean biologist. She's finishing a Ph.D. thesis on porpoise vocalizations, and the Navy has a lot of audio recordings that fit what she needs." Gina smiled. "I just might have introduced them."

Bishop leaned over and kissed her. "You might have, indeed. Does she like the sea?"

"Grew up in Hawaii, surfing for an hour before school most mornings. Her father runs a deep-sea fishing charter."

"Nicely done." He finished half the omelet. "What else did you do while I was away?"

"Missed you. Wrote you a bunch of letters. Thought about how much I'm going to enjoy Montana for a honeymoon."

"Three days to hand-over, and then it's a big wedding and a long honeymoon," he promised.

She reached over and ruffled his hair. "You need a haircut before then. I like it, but it's so not the normal you."

Bishop caught her hand and kissed the inside of her palm. "I lost a crew challenge at the halfway-night party and conceded not to see the crew barber until we were back onshore."

"Going to tell me the challenge?"

"Never."

She laughed. "The guys would have needed some levity by the end of the patrol."

"We got through it." He finished the meal and pushed back his plate. "I've missed your face, Gina, and your smile." He brushed her hair back. "I should have taken more pictures with me than I did. I nearly wore out the ones I had."

"I'll remember that for the next patrol. I kept finding your notes for weeks after you left. They were really nice, Mark."

"I hoped they would bring a smile."

"They did. Oh, hold on. I found something of yours." She left the kitchen and returned a moment later with a book in her hand, setting it beside him on the table.

It was a book of poetry, one he recognized.

He picked it up slowly, and it opened to a page his first wife had often stopped at. A note fluttered out. Mark picked it up. It was addressed to Melinda.

"Did you read it?"

"Yes. I was too curious not to," she admitted, sitting again beside him.

He nodded and opened the folded page.

Melinda, my love,

I know you read this book most often when you're sad. I wish I was there to dry your tears and hug you tonight and tell you I love you. Read page 92 and think of me.

Yours forever, Mark

"I remember writing this," he said quietly, then looked over at Gina.

She rested her chin on her hand as she nodded. "I'm thinking you'll leave me a note like that one, expecting me to find it one day. And for whatever reason it will remain for another decade or two where you placed it, so that someone in a future generation finds it and reads the words my husband wrote for me. They'll wonder about the love affair between Mark and Gina. You and Melinda had that for nine years — a good marriage and love affair.

Now it's our turn to build a chapter of that love story together. I get mushy just thinking about it," she said softly.

"You kept my notes?"

"I think it's good to have a relationship immortalized in words."

Mark thought of the notes and glanced back at her. "Including the one I left under my pillow?"

She smiled. "Yes, I found it the first night — when I slept on your side of the bed, missing you more than I can say. It would be incomplete without that one." She got to her feet, held out her hand. "A shower, a back rub, some sleep. What time does *Nevada* need you back?"

"Seven a.m."

"I'll nudge you that way at six."

He interlaced his fingers with hers, surprised how easily the first night was fitting them back together. "Are we really okay, Gina?" he asked, concerned he was seeing a determined all-is-well appearance rather than the layers below it.

"Yes. I love you. I know you love me. I'm not wasting tonight on what might have happened or what might have gone wrong. I've got a future with you, one I want very much. The rest is details."

He relaxed. She'd meant it. "We'll talk

about those details another day," he assured her as they walked upstairs together.

"We will. There's a honey-do list for you on your nightstand in case you get to feeling like I managed just fine without you. And a wish list of movies I want to see, and books I'd like you to buy me." She bit her lip. "Actually I bought most of the books and called them a gift from you, so maybe you should give me back that list to update once more."

He laughed. He switched who was in the lead and led her into the bedroom, saw the shoe box full of letters on the bedside table. "Do I start from the front or the back?"

"Oldest ones are in front."

He stepped out of his shoes, not letting go of his hold on her hand. She stepped out of hers, and the dog pounced on a sandal. "The pets fight over who gets to sleep in the dog bed downstairs. Most of the time the cats claim it first, and Pongo plops down by the front door so he can bark when the newspaper gets delivered at five o'clock."

"An interesting wake-up time for you." He turned on lights in the bathroom. "You repainted in here."

"Pongo attacked the shower curtain, and the new one didn't work with the walls, so I decided painting was easier than returning the shower curtain and selecting a new one."

"Works for me." He glanced at the mirror and accepted reality. He needed a shave or his wife was going to have whisker burns in the morning. He let go of her hand, but she merely created a space on the bathroom counter and perched there to watch him. "I'm going to cut my neck the way you're studying me," he mentioned.

"I missed this routine," Gina replied, smiling. "I had all these ideas for your first night back, and they didn't include watching you shave and talking about where the pets sleep."

"What did you have in mind?"

"I thought I'd kiss you senseless and then go from there."

Mark grinned. "I might let you do that. I'm glad you waited to get married, Gina. You could have settled down with some Ph.D. candidate back when you were 20, and then where would I be tonight?"

"Not as happy," she said.

"Your self-confidence is improving."

"I like being married. I like being married to you."

He leaned over and kissed her, transferring a good bit of shaving cream to her chin in the process.

She laughed and wiped it away, sliding off

her perch on the counter. "*Nevada* gold wives also went shopping together. Shall I show you what I bought for tonight with you in mind?"

"Not while I'm shaving," he replied with a laugh. He reached for a square of toilet paper to stop the bleeding from the nick on his jaw. "I lived through a tough patrol. I might not survive my wife flirting with me tonight."

She wrapped her arms around him and rested her head against his back. "I love you, Mark. I'm awfully glad you're back."

Mark set aside the razor and wiped a towel across his face, turned around and picked her up. "I adore you, precious," he said, finding he was so full of emotion at the moment, the words came out in a whisper. "Did you ever regret marrying me while I was gone?"

She shook her head. "Nope, not a single millisecond of time. You?"

"Never. I spent the patrol thinking about how soon I'd be home again." He rested his forehead against hers. He loved this woman. "Mrs. Bishop."

"Hmm?"

"Change of plans."

"Does it involve me having to find my shoes? Because I think Pongo just stole one of my sandals and took it downstairs."

Mark laughed. "It involves my bag I left downstairs, and a stack of letters I wrote you. I want you to start reading them while I get this shave finished and take a shower. Then I'll let you kiss me senseless."

"We need ice cream if we're reading letters."

"Works for me."

She reluctantly stepped away. "I'll hurry."

He smiled. "Start with the first letter and read them in order. There are only 10, but I added to each one over a few days, so they're long."

It was after midnight when Gina finally set the alarm for six so her husband could be back at the *Nevada* on schedule. As captain, it was important that he set a good example of being on time. In three days, though, he'd be on R and R, and she wouldn't have to give him up to the Navy in the mornings.

"I just realized you're ticklish," she said with a chuckle, letting her fingers slide back to that spot.

He groaned even as he laughed and caught her hands. "Go to sleep, Gina. I'm fried here. I'm getting too old for a young wife."

"I'd say you're about perfect." She kissed his chin. "Nice shave. But you missed a spot." She giggled as he rubbed her cheek with it. "Do you think we're going to be an old married couple one day?"

"How old?" he asked, his voice already heavy with sleep.

"Ninety, and a hundred."

"Sure. I'm in great shape. And we'll work on getting you to the gym occasionally."

"Hey."

He grinned and then kissed her. "Go to sleep, precious."

She closed her eyes because he needed the rest, and while she liked to tease him, part of being his wife was taking care of him. She could have lost him, could have lost Jeff, to what was heading toward a war. She was going to take care of her guys. The rest of life could revolve around that priority.

"What are you smiling about?" he asked. She opened her eyes to see him resting on his pillow, studying her face.

"Life is good," she replied.

"Hmm. It is."

"Good night, Mark."

She said it softly, deliberately, and after a quiet few seconds his arms tightened around her in a hug. "You're kind to me, precious. I love that."

She interlaced her hand with his, smiled,

and let them both drift to sleep. She had what she most wanted — a good husband. And she loved being a wife. Life was good. And he was safely home from the sea.

ABOUT THE AUTHOR

Dee Henderson is the author of numerous novels, including *Unspoken, Jennifer: An O'Malley Love Story, Full Disclosure,* and the acclaimed O'MALLEY series. Her books have won or been nominated for several prestigious industry awards, such as the RITA Award, the Christy Award, and the ECPA Gold Medallion. Dee is a lifelong resident of Illinois.

Learn more at DeeHenderson.com or facebook.com/DeeHendersonBooks.

The employees of Thorndike Press hope you have enjoyed this Large Print book. All our Thorndike, Wheeler, and Kennebec Large Print titles are designed for easy reading, and all our books are made to last. Other Thorndike Press Large Print books are available at your library, through selected bookstores, or directly from us.

For information about titles, please call:
   (800) 223-1244

or visit our Web site at:
   http://gale.cengage.com/thorndike

To share your comments, please write:
   Publisher
   Thorndike Press
   10 Water St., Suite 310
   Waterville, ME 04901